INHERITING FATE

CHRISTINE McFARLAND

SILENT  PRESS

Published by Silent K Press

Cover design: Damonza
Developmental Editor: Theodora Bryant

First Edition

Printed in the United States of America.
ISBN-13: 978-1-7334530-0-4

For Mom and Dad.
I wish you were here.

PROLOGUE

Idaho State Penitentiary
Boise, Idaho
August 21, 1894

The rattle of keys against the cast iron lock of the cell door made Carrington Chambers flinch. His heart hammered against the wall of his chest, making it difficult to breathe. But he didn't get up. He remained flat on his back on the wooden berth, eyes squeezed tight beneath the arm draped across his forehead.

"Get up, Chambers!" demanded the prison guard. Heavy steel hinges screamed in protest as the cell door swung open. The sound echoed along the stone corridor like the keen of a banshee heralding death.

How fitting.

Carrington rubbed sweaty palms down the sides of his legs. The calluses that had once protected his hands no longer scratched against the cotton fabric of his uniform.

Two years behind bars had softened him.

"Get up, I said." Multiple sets of boots scuffed against the stone floor. There were three guards. Always three, just for him. One of the jailers carried shackles, his movement signaled by the jingle and clunk of the irons as he advanced into the eight-by-thirteen space.

Carrington counted silently to ten in time with the staccato thump of his heart. The moment had arrived. He expelled a long, shuddering rush of air from his lungs and lurched to his feet.

The suddenness of his rising from the berth startled the guard with the shackles. The man went bug-eyed and jerked back. Realizing the others had seen his response, he collected himself, but his face twisted with anger.

"Hands out!" he snarled, the pitch of his voice a bit higher than before.

The other two guards withdrew solid wood batons from their waist belts. Carrington hunched his shoulders and turned to the side just as one guard's arm arced down. The blow of the weapon fell against the broad, flat space of his upper back and shoulder. He grunted but didn't react otherwise.

"Go ahead, try to run. It'll give me a reason to split your skull wide open," said the baton-wielding man as he lifted the weapon again. Before it connected with his back a second time, the guard holding the shackles stepped in front of him.

"You idiot. He ain't goin' nowhere. Besides, Sheriff Anders and the folks over in Caldwell won't like you doin' the job they been waitin' a long time for." He wrenched open the shackles and held them up.

Habit had Carrington lifting his arms high enough so the irons could be clamped about his wrists. The backs of his hands, once a healthy brown from being out in the sun all day, had faded to a pasty hue.

When the guard knelt to lock the fetters about his ankles, the acrid odor of stale tobacco smoke wafted up off the

2

man's clothing. Carrington's nostrils pinched in distaste as the smell collided with the ripe scent of his own unwashed body.

His legs shook, but pride wouldn't allow him to falter in his final walk. Stiffening his spine, he thrust his chin and chest out. With as much dignity as a condemned man could muster, he shuffled from the cell, chains jingling with each step—his death knell.

He'd been residing in the New Cell House of the penitentiary these last two years. Ironically, he had been part of the slave labor made to quarry the stone used in its construction during his previous incarceration, back when it was still the Territorial Prison.

The first tier of the New Cell House caged the worst sort of convicts—mostly vicious men who did unspeakable things to other human beings, landing them on death row. As Carrington passed each small steel-barred cell, the other inmates cheered. The raucous sound of loud voices and tin cups banging against the bars reverberated in his ears.

Near the end of the long corridor the words of one of the condemned rose above the din, loud enough for him to hear: "God be with you, boy."

Constrained by the chains, it was a slow walk across the building's main floor. Carrington stumbled at the doorway leading to the courtyard as he stepped out into the dawn's morning light. The guard who'd been assigned to keep one hand on him at all times tightened the grip at his elbow. The other two guards flanked his sides. A wall of intimidation.

Sweat beaded across Carrington's forehead as they marched him toward a black, wooden wagon with bars for windows on all sides. This was his transport to Caldwell, his hometown.

He wouldn't die at the prison, as he'd expected. Sheriff Anders, the man who'd arrested him two years earlier, demanded that his execution take place in Caldwell, so the town's people could watch him hang. Had the prison's general agent, kin to Anders, not agreed to his request, Carrington would have been the first prisoner executed in the recently named Idaho State Penitentiary. It gave him only a little solace knowing he wouldn't be forever remembered as *that* man.

His journey home was nearly a full-day's ride away. He wondered what was worse: being marched straight to his death or being left alone with his memories and regrets. Those wonderings were interrupted, however, when hours later, upon his arrival in Caldwell, the guards dragged him from the wagon. As it rumbled away, he saw that half the town's residents, all dressed in their Sunday best, were waiting at the street's end beneath the railroad's water tower. They fidgeted in the heat cast by the afternoon sun. At sight of him, the buzz of their casual conversations turned to loud, ugly slurs.

The guard beside him pressed a hand between Carrington's shoulder blades, nudging him toward the wood structure on the other side of the hostile crowd.

Many familiar and unfamiliar faces were among the blur of people he passed along the route. There were railroad workers and homesteaders, some he'd known since the early days when he and his Pa had first homesteaded here. There was the baker, the druggist from Isham's Drug Store, and the barkeep of the Sagebrush Saloon. He didn't immediately locate the town's more prominent residents, like the Strahorns and Steunenbergs, but he knew they'd be present.

Then he saw one of them. Off to the far left of the throng of people, the glass eye of a camera lens peered straight at him. Hunched behind the box and tripod was Albert "A.K." Steunenberg, newspaperman and owner of *The Caldwell Tribune*, there to capture his last—and only—image.

Steunenberg swiped an arm across his brow. Nervous? Perhaps, considering he had a front row seat to an execution. The first in years. To his left stood the Gilgan sisters, owners of the town's millinery and hairdresser shops. They were great supporters of the *Tribune*.

"Die!" one heckler hollered.

"Killer!" yelled another.

"Die-die-die," the mob began to chant, their fists pounding against the sky with each word.

Someone hurled a rock into the air, and it hit Carrington on the back of the head. His vision blurred at impact and he tripped on the first step to the gallows. Righting himself, he forged on, though his feet felt like they'd been dredged in thick sludge. The chains at his ankles rattled like musical notes amid the chaos around him. By the time he crested the platform, his shirtfront was damp from the sweat trickling down his neck.

There was barely time to comprehend his surroundings from above the crowd before he was shoved into place beneath the hangman's noose.

His eyes raked over the many faces of hate-filled onlookers, in search of at least one friendly one among them. Panic threatened to engulf him, and then . . . there, he saw them.

Blake Hanson and Suzanne Thomas stood at the edge of the throng. They were the closest thing he had to friends. Their expressions were blank, all emotions masked.

The invisible vise around Carrington's chest squeezed tighter. Fighting for control, he focused his attention on Blake and Suzanne. Suzanne's lips moved, saying words

Carrington couldn't hear. He frowned, his head listing to one side, like a dog hearing its master's voice.

A heavy rope slid over his scalp. The scratchy weave scraped a path along the sides of his face before settling about his neck. He jerked back, pulling away from the threat.

Blake tipped his chin down in a brief nod, while Suzanne's lips curved up slightly at the corners.

"Any last words?" Sheriff Anders' raspy voice cracked with the strain of speaking loud enough to be heard over the inflamed crowd. Anders leaned in close to him and muttered something against his ear. However, with the growing chaos below him and his increased anxiety, the words were indistinct—just a buzzing in his ears. Flecks of spittle hit his cheek and he reared back, slamming his head against Anders' face in his effort to pull away. Anders shoved back at him, causing his neck to strain against the rope.

What could Carrington say now that would change what was about to happen? He'd already spent two futile years trying to prove his innocence.

His mother-in-law stood in the front row, sobbing loudly, her face pressed tight against his father-in-law's shoulder. Carrington willed his wife's mother to look up, but her husband pulled her close and turned her, so her back was to him. The robust woman's shoulders shook with each wracking sob.

The primal instinct to fight swept over Carrington and he twisted and struggled against the noose. "This is a mistake!" he bellowed. "You want vengeance, but it's against the wrong person! I'm innocent!"

Gasps and slurs erupted from the crowd.

His father-in-law stepped forward, pulling away from his distraught wife. "No!" He poked the air belligerently with a bony forefinger. "You stole our Annie from us. May God *not* have mercy on your black soul!"

The murmurs of the agitated mass of people rose in volume again as their anger grew with each passing minute.

Carrington's rebuttal stuck in his throat when a dark shroud descended over his head. He thrashed about but couldn't shake it off. The crowd hushed as the words of the town preacher, Reverend Boone, who stood nearby, grew louder. Carrington hadn't been aware of the holy man's presence.

"For I am the Lord your God who takes hold of your right hand and says to you, do not fear; I will help you—"

"Carrington Chambers," Sheriff Anders interrupted, stealing from him his last rites. "You have been convicted of the murder of your wife, Elizabeth Anne Chambers. God bless her soul."

The sound of a woman's choked cry floated through the air. Like an invisible, ominous haze, it drifted beneath the folds of Carrington's dark world.

This was it. His whole life replayed in his mind. He saw his house, his barn, and the crops growing in the fields beyond. He remembered Annie; the woman he'd hoped to spend all his days with and raise a family with—before her untimely death.

"For that crime," the sheriff continued, "you have been sentenced to death."

A pall of silence fell over the crowd.

Carrington gulped for air as his heart skipped several beats. The sound of boots scraping on wood indicated the men around him had moved back, away from him.

His mind again filled with memories of his home. He was walking up the front steps to his house to greet Annie.

But the visage that presented itself behind his eyelids wasn't his wife.

Leaning against the railing of his front porch was someone else. Someone taller and with hair the color of warm, dark honey flowing about her shoulders on a gentle breeze.

"Wait!" he cried out, as the floor beneath him fell away with a loud crack.

ONE

Caldwell, Idaho
Present Day

Cassie McAllister wedged the cell phone between her ear and shoulder, and then glanced at her watch. The gold hour and minute hands both reached toward the twelve.

"I'll be fine," she said with more bite than intended to Andrew Gillespie, her friend and former psychologist, on the other end of the line.

"Does the general contractor have the security guy scheduled? And did the electricians get everything finished?" Andrew grilled.

"Yep. The security company should be here"—she turned the watch face up again—"any minute now. The electrician isn't done yet, but will be back soon, or so I was told." There was no point boring Andrew with the details about how the general contractor himself would be delayed a couple weeks. That would only make him worry and corroborate his belief that she had moved into a rundown shack in a small hick town—both of which he'd declared unfit for human occupation.

Through the plate-glass window in the living room of her new home, Cassie looked out over the dirt yard that doubled as the driveway. Beyond the expanse of dusty brown soil stood an ancient barn in desperate need of a new coat of paint. At least Cassie *hoped* that was all it needed.

Andrew's voice droned on in her ear. "Mmhm," she murmured, as a powdery dust devil swirled through the yard.

"I'm worried about you," he whined, his voice smooth, delicate—so Andrew.

"I'll be fine." Cassie pressed her forehead against the warm glass. "This is what my shrink suggested. Right, Doc? It's been almost seven years, Andrew. I'm just not as good as I think I should be." In the window's reflection, she watched the fingers of her right-hand flutter about her neck. With her index finger, she traced the thickened line of skin that ran from the hollow of her throat up to a spot below her left ear.

"You can't just move across the country alone. What about your fam—" Andrew didn't finish the word, but to Cassie the slip was like a hot dagger across a raw nerve.

"What about me? Your friend?" he rushed on.

"I'm certain you'll be fine without me. Besides, I'm only two states away." In a defeated whisper, she added, "I just can't do it anymore. If I don't find a way to get past this, get better, I'm just going to . . . to die. At least that's how it feels." She scrubbed the heel of her hand across her forehead. "And the voices are back."

As her former psychologist, Andrew had heard every ugly, angry, painful detail about her traumas and losses. And her fears. Now, he was merely her best friend and confidante, yet at times, she'd slip and speak aloud her problems before thinking through the ramifications.

"Voices? There's more than one now?" Andrew's concern raced through the airwaves.

"No. I meant voice. The same one as before." The voice, a woman's, was but a whisper, slightly higher in pitch than Andrew's. It always said only one thing: *"Save her."* After the initial shock of it resounding so clearly in her mind, Cassie had begun to believe it was speaking *to* her.

"Why didn't you tell me?"

"Because telling you means it's real. And I don't want to admit that I'm hearing a voice in my head." She'd first heard the voice a little more than a year ago, the day her parents died in a car accident. The voice had scared the hell out of her, and she'd immediately called Andrew. He'd reassured her, saying it was likely just a panic response to her recent loss, and that it would soon go away. Which it did. Until the day she'd learned about this house and her status as its new owner.

An attorney contacted her a few weeks after the accident to inform her that the property was part of a trust. Apparently, under the terms of the trust, as the first-born female offspring of Chandra McAllister, Cassie's mother, the property automatically transferred to Cassie upon her mother's death.

When she'd visited the house for the first time, she was surprised at its condition. It was old, but in relatively decent shape. Along with the deed she'd been given, with her name on it, the lawyer also had receipts and various documents reflecting improvements made to the property over the years. Some slips dated as far back as the nineteen-twenties. And though numerous renters had come and gone, the house never sold, which was quite surprising.

The bigger shock was that Cassie had never known of its existence. Not once while growing up had her parents visited Idaho, nor did they mention the house to her. Yet she'd seen her mother's name and her own name on the paperwork.

And now she'd never know why.

Her fingers walked across the scar on her throat again. Regardless of Andrew's reassurances, the voice manifesting after the loss of her parents was the spark that ignited her current actions. In a desperate moment, she'd concluded that her only hope of ever resuming a normal life, or something that resembled normal, would require a drastic change. So, she moved to Idaho. Into this house. Her inheritance. She was determined to fix it up, one board at a time, and fix herself in the process.

"I think you should come back and have tests run," Andrew said, interrupting Cassie's musing.

She turned away from the window and walked across the living room to the front door. Giving it a sharp tug, it opened. When she pushed on the screen door, the coil attached to the top gave off a disturbing screech. She moved the door back and forth, grimacing at the noisy, rusty spiral of wire. Her initial thought was to find a can of WD-40, but leaving it alone meant she'd always hear if someone was entering the house. She released her grip and let the door snap shut.

"Jesus, Andrew." She pinched the bridge of her nose, holding at bay the headache that threatened. "I think I know what's best for me. This is best right now. This place." She moved to the end of the covered porch that ran the length of the house, noticing as she went, the cracked boards and chipped paint of the weathered exterior. Pivoting about, she paced back to the other end of the porch, stopping near a wooden swing that drooped unevenly from a rusty chain.

"Refurbishing this place is going to be my therapy. Did you know the original part of the house is over a hundred years old? It started out as just a box, really. A homesteader's cabin, I think, is what they called it. It's practically on the Oregon Trail," she prattled on, excited by the extraordinary and fascinating details she'd learned so far about her new home's past.

An exasperated sigh reached Cassie's ear, and she grinned victoriously. Andrew's interest in history was very limited, regardless of its significance. She used that little fact to redirect his assessment of her current circumstances, but appeased him by saying, "I'm going to give it a year. I'll decide then what to do next, if things don't improve."

Things *had* to change, because if they didn't, she feared she'd be lost forever.

"Fine. I'd better not get any crazy calls from some new shrink, as you like to call us, saying you attempted to hurt yourself or . . . something worse. For that matter, I better not hear from anyone about you at all, especially another doctor."

Andrew teased, but Cassie knew his concerns over her mental state were genuine. She'd suffered more than one severe trauma in her life, and it stood to reason there was indeed the possibility she'd had some of those darker moments. But in truth, she'd never wanted to give up on life. In fact, she'd been fighting *for* it all along, hence the move to Idaho.

Forcing herself to be comfortable alone and independent of others again was worth the risk she'd currently undertaken. Especially now that the voice was back. She needed to exorcise her demons and moving to Idaho alone was how she'd accomplish it.

"Lucky for you I'm no longer your patient. I just need you to be my supportive friend," she said too cheerily, hoping to convey a confidence she wasn't sure she felt.

Their conversation wound down and ended minutes later with Cassie's promise to check in at least once a week. A light breeze kicked up. She breathed in a deep, cleansing lungful of air, allowing the soothing aroma of warm sage and fresh mint from a nearby field to wash through her.

"This is going to be my sanctuary." She eyed the porch swing longingly. That would be project number one.

TWO

Thirty minutes later, Cassie climbed down from the ladder, after having securely reattached the swing, and surveyed her handiwork. A memory of her dad's stern lecture on the proper use of tools flitted through her brain. She smiled at the happy reminder of life before her world had tilted sideways. Before she could drop the screwdriver back into the yellow box near her feet, a sound interrupted the quiet. It was a vehicle rumbling down her driveway. Gripping the handle of the screwdriver tight in her fist, she nervously awaited whoever was entering her domain.

A cargo van with Phelps Security displayed in bold, royal blue letters across the back panel braked slowly to a stop. A cloud of dust rolled over the van, partially obscuring the vehicle's occupant from view. Cassie offered a small wave as the driver opened the door.

"Afternoon, ma'am." A young man, probably in his late twenties, approached and stopped near the bottom of the porch steps. "You scheduled to have a security system installed?"

Cassie's tension ebbed slightly. "Yes. Do you, um, have an ID?" The kid turned and pointed at the van's bold lettering. Cassie shrugged, unwilling to accept that as sufficient identification.

The young man's forehead creased, and he scratched at his ear. "Sure. Be right back." He trotted over to his vehicle, retrieved a badge, then handed it to Cassie where she met him halfway down the porch steps.

Satisfied that Brian Atwood matched the photo on the plastic ID card issued by Phelps Security, she forced herself to relax.

He's just a kid, not an axe-murderer, McAllister, she thought. "Thank you, Brian. Come in, and I'll show you around."

They wandered through the house, room by room, with Brian noting the location of each window and exterior door. He asked if she'd considered adding security cameras. She had considered them, but her decision to forgo the extra protection was based purely on her need to break free of the chains that bound her. Fear was a strong chain, but her determination to be like most normal people was stronger. She hoped.

With the preliminary walk-through complete, she told Brian to call out if he needed anything and set about her own tasks.

She was in the middle of the living room, surrounded by mounds of boxes and crumpled newspapers—feeling very much like a kid on Christmas morning—when another vehicle pulled into the driveway. It was the electrician, as indicated once again, by a logo.

Wading through the sea of debris at her feet, she was near the front door when something in her peripheral vision drew her attention. She paused at the base of the stairs that led up to the second floor, the part of the house added back in nineteen twenty-eight, along with indoor plumbing. The landing above was dark, as it should be, since the electrician had yet to finish work in that area. A shiver raced down her back, but she shrugged it away.

Still holding an antique vase that Andrew had given her as a housewarming gift, she greeted the man standing on the other side of the screen door. He wore a blue ball cap high on his forehead. Across the top of his lip was a thick, black mustache, wide enough to cover the oversized space between his upper lip and the base of his nose. When he smiled, his top lip disappeared beneath a broom of whiskers.

"Hi. I'm the electrician your GC has working on the house," he announced.

Cassie tried not to gawk but failed as the man's visible bottom lip moved while his upper mustache-lip remained in place, much like a ventriloquist's doll.

She blinked hard to break her stare. "Uh, the GC?"

"Your general contractor? I've been working on the wires in the house? Got more to do to get the job finished up?" Each sentence sounded more a question than a statement. The tip of his tongue poked out and moved over one corner of his mustache, pulling some of the bristly hairs between his lips.

Cassie stifled a cringe when he began to nibble on the wiry strands. Forcing a smile, she requested identification. Even if the general contractor had hired him, she still needed to take her own precautions before inviting him into her home.

As old and pieced together as the house was, all the wiring needed updated. Considering the scope of work required prior to her moving in, the GC had arranged with Cassie to start that aspect of the job much earlier than the rest. The electrician, whom she'd not met until now, had already completed most of his work in the previous weeks. He still had a bit more to finish.

With introductions out of the way, she allowed Randy Price to go about his business, while she returned to hers.

The rest of the day flew by.

It was late in the afternoon when Brian interrupted her in the living room where she was rearranging furniture.

"Excuse me, ma'am?"

Cassie raised her head, exposing her neck. Brian's eyes flicked down then back up. He forced a smile, but the resulting expression had him looking a bit constipated. Cassie crossed an arm about her waist, rested the elbow of her other arm on her wrist, and curved her hand over her throat. It was a pose struck without conscious thought.

Brian shoved his hands in his pockets. "I've done all I can here, for now. The electrician says it'll probably be a day or so before he gets juice through the whole house. So, I'll have to come back."

The pit of Cassie's stomach fell.

"Have you put new locks on the doors?" She crooked an arm atop her head, fingers clutching at her hair. Hesitantly, she moved across the wood floor.

"Yes, ma'am," Brian replied with a sharp nod.

"And did you secure each window as you finished up?"

"I sure did."

At the bottom of the stairs leading up, she lowered her arm and began drumming her fingers against her thigh. Swiveling her head toward the kitchen—the other room that was part of the original layout of the house—she stared into the lit space, allowing several seconds to pass in silence. Then slowly, she began to nod.

"Okay," she finally decided.

Brian, who'd been pivoting on his heels in a circle following her movement around the room, grinned.

"Awesome! I'll touch base with the electrician and come back the minute he says he's done. Don't you worry, hardly anything bad ever happens around here." He extended one hand out. A set of shiny keys dangled from his fingers. "These are yours." They clinked as they fell into Cassie's upturned palm.

These four little pieces of metal were all that most normal people used to obtain safety and security in their home. Not everyone had advanced alarm systems, yet they managed to do fine. She swallowed past the dry lump in her throat.

"Thank you," she said in a voice barely above a whisper.

Brian nodded before turning to leave. Cassie followed him outside, the keys clutched tight in her fist. She waited on the porch, arms curled tight against her waist as he climbed into his van and drove off.

"It's okay," she reassured herself. *I hope.*

The screen door behind her screeched. "Well, I managed—"

Cassie spun around, arms raised in a fighter's stance. "Fuck!"

Randy froze, startled equally as much as Cassie.

"Son of a bitch! Don't sneak up on me like that!" she snapped.

The electrician held both hands up, palms out. "Whoa. Sorry, lady."

A few awkward seconds passed before she finally released her stance. One hand lifted and splayed around the column of her neck. The pulse beneath her thumb pounded wildly. "No, I'm sorry. I'm just jumpy in the new place. That's all. Brian said you wouldn't be able to finish up today?"

When Randy replied, he did so as if he were talking to a frightened child. He explained how he'd replaced most of the wiring upstairs and was close to finishing, but unfortunately couldn't get power on in that part of the house just yet.

"It's an old place with a lot of old wires," he offered in defense, before reassuring her that he'd return bright and early the following day. "The breakers are shut off to the second floor, so there's no risk of electricity running up there. Just don't go flip any switches on the panel." His tongue peeked out and caressed the corner of his mustache.

After thanking Randy for his work, she watched as he gathered his things and left. Cassie was now all alone.

Securing the deadbolt on the door, she decided it was time to relax, or try to, and adjust to being by herself in her new home. At night.

Following a quick change into an old t-shirt with a faded picture of Shania Twain on the front, paired with North Face shorts that somewhat resembled gym shorts from the eighties, she cozied up on her couch. The scent of new leather surrounded her. It was strong but homey.

She'd left one light on in the kitchen and switched on another located on an end table beside the couch. The golden glow of the lamp was just enough for her to read by. Sipping Merlot from a plastic cup, she flipped through the pages of a *People* magazine draped across her lap. Slowly, she began to unwind.

Unfortunately, old houses settle, and her nerves, already on high alert, settled with it much like a person learning to drive a stick shift—lurching forward, stalling, and then easing along smoothly until the next shifting of gears.

When she heard a soft thud somewhere near the kitchen, her fingers curled tight around the Rawlings baseball bat lying across her lap beneath the magazine. Jumping up from the couch, she advanced toward the sound, instead of moving away from it.

Just like those stupid people in horror movies did. Real smart, McAllister.

Determined to address her fears and not run from them, which is exactly what she wanted to do, she tiptoed into the kitchen. There was nothing suspicious there.

On her way back to the living room, she stopped at the front door and touched the already-turned knob of the shiny new deadbolt . . . for the fourth time that night.

With a long, tension-filled sigh, she resumed her position on the couch and reread the same article she'd been struggling through moments before. Just as the muscles in her neck began to loosen, she heard the distinctive creak of a floorboard. Her head whipped around toward the top of the stairs.

"Oh, for shit's sake, McAllister. If it's not a voice in your head, it's your imagination creating sounds. Get a grip." She winced, hoping she didn't jinx herself, as it had been nearly a full day since she'd last heard the voice.

Propping the bat against the side of the couch, within arm's reach, she eased back into the cushions and continued her perusal of the tabloid. Soon, the coziness of the house around her grew more familiar. She even relaxed to the point of sleepiness. With the help of the wine, she drifted toward slumber, curled up in a semi-ball, her head snuggled into a fluffy pillow.

Hours later, in the depth of the night, Cassie's eyes fluttered open and then closed again. When she forced them back open, she zeroed in on the corner near the fireplace. Did something move?

Her hand inched along the edge of the cushion toward the bat. She curled her fingers around the handle as she rolled up and off the couch. Still caught in the haze of deep sleep, she advanced toward the corner. Once near the fireplace, she used the bat to poke along the length of the wall, her unease fading with each solid thump of wood against plaster.

Satisfied that it was only her imagination gone awry, she returned to her temporary bed and let the night pull her under.

Just as her brain began the fade to black, Cassie sensed more than felt the particles of air around her thicken and swirl, causing ripples of goosebumps to gather on her skin. She tried to ignore it, until she heard the rich, tenor sound of a man's voice floating on the invisible molecules surrounding her.

"I found you."

Cassie bolted upright.

Shit.

THREE

No amount of coffee could ease the pounding in Cassie's head the following morning. Her fingers moved in rhythmic circles over her temples. She hadn't slept more than two hours. After hearing the voice.

The new voice. A man's voice.

"Why is this happening to me?" Her efforts to soothe the throbbing in her brain were proving pointless. She'd had some wine last night, but not much, so maybe there was a remote possibility the alcohol caused her to hear things. Unlike the woman's voice, which felt as if it was speaking *to* her from far away, this new sound was more . . . there, close by. However, a well-lit and thorough search of the room had proved otherwise.

She considered calling Andrew, but quickly quashed the idea. It would only be ammunition for him in his efforts to get her to move back home. Or to visit a psychiatrist. The idea of having to advance care to a real shrink, and not just Andrew's care as a psychologist, terrified her.

So, there she sat, mentally listing the positives that proved she was getting better on her own. She'd survived the night alone, and the woman's voice hadn't returned. The other little issue she'd deal with later, if it happened again.

This was the new and improved Cassie's way of handling scary things—deal with them head-on.

It was early still, only a quarter after five and the coolest, least stifling, part of the day in this semi-arid desert land. Cassie poured another cup of coffee in preparation of a long day of unpacking. However, watching the sunrise as dawn broke was too inviting to miss.

Armed with a cup of brew, she adjourned to the top step of the front porch. The cool morning air was ripe with the heady scent of sweet mint and rich soil. She breathed in deeply several times, filling her nostrils with the fresh, clean smell.

Dawn and dusk were her favorite moments of the day— eerie yet beautiful, those spaces of time when darkness transitioned to a quiet purple black. It was as if all the sounds in the world silenced, and things beyond normal human perception were free to move about to enjoy earth's beauty. She didn't claim to be a believer in ghosts, goblins, or other such spirits, but if they did exist, this is when they'd choose to roam.

After a quick search of Caldwell's local history, Cassie had learned there was certainly the potential for things from the beyond to linger about. The Oregon Trail ran through an area only a few miles from where she now sat. The town of Caldwell itself had come into existence with the arrival of the Short Line Railroad. Those two historic events alone brought strife and death in their reach for modernization.

The vast openness, warm climate, and rich soil in the area, along with the Homesteaders Act of 1862, created other opportunities for men as well, harsh times notwithstanding.

Many people died during those early days fighting for freedom and a place to call home. Most didn't get a second chance at life like Cassie had been given. Because of that, she appreciated these wondrous instances of beauty even more.

Her own fears quieted while sitting on that porch, right before the sun peeked over the horizon to chase away the shadows of the night.

Then it was over, and it was time for work to begin.

In the upstairs hallway, while lugging a box intended for the spare bedroom, Cassie faltered mid-stride. Hanging from the ceiling, a few feet away, were retractable overhead steps. She hadn't given any consideration to there being an attic in the house, but here was the access to that hidden space. The fine hairs on the back of her neck prickled to attention.

She eased the box to the floor, then inched the remainder of the way down the hall, stopping at the base of the hanging stairs. Brian, or possibly Randy, must have gone up there, she reasoned.

Suddenly, like a siren blaring within her head, a voice, the woman's voice, sounded.

"Save her."

Cassie clamped her hands over her ears. "Stop it! Why are you doing this? Leave me alone!"

She'd heard of people who'd suffered traumatic events and claimed to hear voices. Like in that movie, *Sybil*. But what she understood about that woman was different from her own experience. What was happening to Cassie wasn't an overtaking of her personality. It was just a voice telling her something, talking to her. Then it would be silent for indeterminate amounts of time. Why was it happening now? The attack had taken place years ago.

Growling with frustration, she chose to ignore the possibility that she had multiple personalities manifesting— even if there were now two of them.

Her new way of dealing with stressful matters had her climbing the steps to the attic before she could think why she shouldn't. Alert and ready to bolt if the need arose, she eased her head through the opening in the ceiling, peeked in, then quickly ducked back down. In that brief glimpse, all she saw was a window and a sliver of light in the far corner of the room—no bodies and no intruders.

Reinforced with a new sense of courage after not having been whacked over the head already, she stepped up and through the opening. With both feet still on the topmost step of the ladder, she turned in a half circle one direction then back the other way.

"Okay, McAllister. Nothing here but—" Her whispered words faded away as she squinted toward the light. There was a small door built into the wall off to her left. It was open just enough that Cassie could see the edge of something within. Bracing both palms on the floor, she bent forward to get a better angle. "Is that a trunk?" Before she could allow her imagination to fill the trunk with a corpse, she pulled herself the rest of the way up and through the opening.

The air in the attic was stifling. Before investigating what was behind the wall, she went straight to the window on the opposite side of the room and tried to push it open, but it wouldn't budge.

"Oh, for shit's sake! Open, you stupid thing," she grunted as she shoved at it again.

With her shoulder wedged beneath the lock mechanism of the window, she leaned into it, straining with the effort. Creaking groans of dry wood separating from half-century old paint punctuated the effort. Encouraged, she tried harder, and felt the frame inch up, scraping in protest along the wood slide. Upon achieving the halfway point, she slumped against the warm glass with a triumphant sigh.

A light breeze danced in and caressed her skin, touching on every drop of sweat seeping from her pores. A thin fog of dust particles shifted in the once still air. They danced about like tiny fireflies in the beam of light streaming through the window before disappearing to settle elsewhere about the room.

She pushed away from the wall and stepped lightly across the aged wood floor to the lit doorway. It wasn't until that moment that she questioned how it was possible there was a light shining in the room at all. According to Randy, the electricity hadn't been switched on yet to the upstairs part of the house. Assuming there was a rational explanation for it, like backwards wiring or something of the sort, she approached the door.

Carefully, she nudged the knob-less panel open, and bent to peer into the cubby. The angled ceiling formed the small space into a triangle barely large enough to fit the steamer trunk nestled inside. Cassie lowered to her knees and crawled in far enough to grip the worn edges of the trunk, before backing it out of its hiding place. With minimal effort, she dragged it across the attic, scraping a path through the unblemished accumulation of dust that carpeted the bare deck.

An icy foreboding crept up her spine. Clearly, neither Brian nor Randy had been up here. She forced that unsettling thought away.

The floorboards creaked beneath her as she plopped down cross-legged in front of the trunk. Blowing at the layer of dust covering the lid, she watched the haze swirl back and around on the faint breeze.

"C R H," she whispered as she traced a finger over dingy, yellow letters painted across the lid. One of the leather handle straps had worn through. The other remained intact;

it was dry and fragile. A thin layer of flimsy paper, dried and crackling like the shed of a snake's skin, adorned the luggage. When she touched it, it flaked away like the ashes of a cigarette. There were two tarnished brass latches affixed to the front of the trunk. She tugged on them until they released, then slowly lifted the lid, careful not to disturb more of the delicate paper.

What would she find inside? A mother's keepsakes of her child's life? A bride's wedding gown preserved for all time? A family's heirlooms? She smiled at her own romantic imaginings.

The trunk had to be very old, an antique possibly, with some value; she'd research it later. Maybe it belonged to a previous tenant. She made a mental note to search through the list of former tenants' names she thought might be somewhere in the papers she'd gotten from the attorney. Maybe she'd find initials matching C R H.

A trickle of sweat slid down her temple, and she swiped at it with her shoulder. Breathless with anticipation at the treasures she hoped to find, she peeked inside the trunk.

A balloon of pent-up air burst from her lungs, and she sagged with disappointment. There was no yellowed wedding gown. No hand-sewn quilt. No sepia-toned tintypes of an expressionless family preserved for all time. Instead, she found nothing more than a few old newspapers yellowed with the passing of time, and a book, its edges stained and frayed.

Lifting the contents out, Cassie set the book off to the side then splayed the papers in front of her. There were four. She thumbed through all eight pages of the April 22, 1890, issue of *The Caldwell Tribune*.

Intrigued by the prospect of more local history, she propped back against the wall beneath the window, and draped the pages over her bent knees. She had to draw her legs closer to read the typed print, as it was very small, much smaller than the typefaces used in modern papers. So many words packed into the oversized pages. The headlines were in the same-sized font but all capital letters. Five columns, each three inches wide, crammed full of black words.

On the first page, she found an obituary nestled between a note from a traveling commentator and a sale on parasols. Subsequent pages revealed news articles from various news agencies across the country, including *The Washington Post.* There were advertisements for shoes, livery supplies, hair-growing serums, as well as a cure for piles.

Curious what piles were, and what remedy was offered, Cassie spent a moment reading that one. Apparently, it was a common ailment since there was yet another advertisement below it that also guaranteed relief. Turning back to the front page, she peered closer, searching for something about Caldwell. Maybe she'd find out if anyone had died from piles. She chuckled at her twisted imagination.

Near the bottom of the third column, beneath the title of COURT NEWS – CRIMINAL, she read the first part of a notice that caught her interest.

> On Thursday of this week, Mr. Carrington Chambers was brought before the Honorable Judge Rayner on the charge of drunk and disorderly. He was charged $5 and costs.

Aside from politics and a review of a traveling professor's seven-day trek on the road, this was the first article about a local.

"This could be interesting." Cassie's finger tracked beneath the words, making it easier to follow the tiny print.

> Mr. Chambers spent the night in the cooler

following his arrest, even though he had sufficient funds to pay the fine. Sheriff Anders urged the judge to add a night in the jailhouse to his sentence, considering this was the fourth public drunk arrest for Chambers since his release from the Territorial Prison eighteen months past for the offense of murder.

A strong breeze wafted through the window, lifting the ends of Cassie's hair and fluttering the edges of the pages on her lap. She blinked hard and scrubbed the heels of her hands over her eyes when the words on the paper swirled, shifting in and out of focus.

"Must be the heat," she said, fanning her face with one hand. When she peered down again at the newspaper, she frowned. Did it seem . . . less yellow? The ink darker? *Seriously, McAllister?*

On the air, she imagined she caught a whiff of the sharp tang of ink. Then, a sudden dizziness swept over her, and she shook her head to dispel it.

"Save her," the woman's voice demanded in her ears.

The sound frightened Cassie more than ever before, mainly because of what followed. A thick bank of fog seeped from the walls near the still-lit cubby across the room. The murky substance slithered toward her. She kicked at it and tried to scoot away, but to no avail. It washed over her body, enveloping her, closing off the world around her while holding her captive in its opaque warmth.

It lasted a second, and then the fog shrank back into its hiding place, pulling her along in its wake.

FOUR

Cassie didn't feel right.

Her head throbbed and she had a god-awful taste in her mouth. She licked dry lips and groaned. *What just happened?* Had she hit her head on something? She stretched her mouth wide to ease some of the tension in her jaw, then pressed her hands to her face.

And froze.

Against her palms was the distinct scratchiness of wiry stubble along her chin and jaw. *What the—?*

"Get outta my jail, Chambers!"

A man's loud bark reverberated in Cassie's ears.

Another man groaned, the sound coming from as much inside her head as around her. She tried to find the source, but it was dark. Then there was a flicker of light—there!—then gone, then back again. Each laser beam of brightness felt like firebolts to her brain. Just as the light flickered again, in a most indescribable way her sense of awareness was forced back into a quiet corner as another consciousness came forward.

It was a man's consciousness.

Cassie was inexplicably aware of the person—the man. She couldn't see him, but she knew his thoughts. When he moved, she felt the flex and give of his muscles beneath her skin, the tightening of his pectorals and abdomen, all as if it was her own body moving. She knew, too, the headache she experienced was a hangover. His hangover. She even felt the recognizable twinge of discomfort when he scratched at his crotch. He had to pee.

Oh, my god! What is happening? Confusion quickly gave way to fear. She shrank back even further into the dark space around her as the owner of the body she felt she'd somehow transferred into began to wake up.

***

Daggers of light pierced Carrington's orbits, shooting straight into his brain. Wincing, he stumbled to his feet and shuffled from the cell, ignoring Sheriff Anders as he exited the jailhouse. Beneath the awning of the small wood building, he stretched tall and wide, groaning with unadulterated pleasure as his muscles creaked to life. Settling his Stetson on his head, he trudged off down the middle of the dirt-packed road that was Seventh Avenue, Caldwell, in the Territory of Idaho. It was early in the morning and the town hadn't yet bloomed with the hustle and bustle of life.

He missed the old days, before the Short Line Railroad came through, bringing people—lots of people. In the span of those seven years he'd been away in prison, the place had gone from a vast area with only a few settlers scattered about to a beehive of businesses, houses, structures, and those who occupied them.

Gone were most of the railroad workers he'd heard had been strategic to the town's boom. In their place came politicians and visionaries, like Robert E. Strahorn and the Steunenberg brothers, Frank and Albert. The Mormons arrived, too, as did men seeking a prosperous life, whether through farming the rich soil hidden beneath the sagebrush and shrub or running a business the town certainly needed.

They were mostly uncivilized people attempting to build a civilized town, expecting law and order, and not the wildness common in pop-up communities like these. Sheriff Anders was one of the more unscrupulous characters who made a pretense of being an upstanding citizen. He'd made it his mission to extricate Carrington, an ex-convict, from his town.

Two men engaged in a heated debate in front of the mercantile stopped their bickering as Carrington passed by. He ignored them and any other bystanders who happened to be about to observe his progress along the street.

The Herr Clothing Store, barbershop, and several other businesses along the row of storefronts were still closed tight to visitors. However, the boardwalk connecting the structures was swept clean, ready for another day of traffic. A narrow alley divided that first stretch of establishments from a newly erected hotel, the town's second. The fire of eighteen eighty-eight, two years back, took out many of the old buildings on Front Street. But no sooner did one disappear, another popped up in its place.

Near the intersection of Seventh Avenue and Front Street, the road ended in a T before a large water tower. Beneath the massive wood bladder, a black-bellied train belched a steady, deep *whoosh whoosh* as it waited for its next journey down the track. Beside the tower was a shabby structure—the train depot. It was a serviceable building where passengers could wait out of the elements. Carrington angled off in the opposite direction of the depot, along Front Street, moving past the Pacific Hotel toward the livery. There, he'd find his horse.

Far down the way behind him, he heard Anders yell out, "They shoulda thrown away the key when they had you locked up in that prison."

Carrington considered hollering back, but his splitting head wouldn't tolerate the percussion of his own voice reverberating against his eardrums. Instead, he brought his hand up level with his ear and lifted his middle finger.

A woman bustling down the steps of the nearby hotel, two young children in tow and one in her arms, hissed her disgust. "Children! Stay close to me." She thrust her nose high in the air and puffed out her chest like a turkey in rut as the foursome scurried past. "God will punish the wicked. Come along now, we must hurry and catch up with Father at the train."

The children sniggered as they hid behind the tent of their mother's plain dress. Tiny whispers of "murderer" floated across the air. Carrington tipped his hat at the woman, ignoring the haughty glare he received in return.

At thirty years of age, he should be fulfilling his dreams and shaping out a future for himself, something his father would have expected and been proud of. That dream had begun to fade. He doubted any woman would agree to marry him and raise a family with him, considering his past.

Upon entering the stables, he located his mare in the second stall. "Hey, Lady," he crooned. A soft snort greeted him. Before retrieving his saddle, which he'd located on the ground in the nearby corner, he slipped into the adjoining stall to relieve his bladder. With that out of the way, he bent to collect his saddle, noticing, as he did, that dust had settled on his boots, layering atop suspicious debris spattered over their surface. He tried, and failed, to recall the source of the splatter as he hoisted the saddle over the horse's broad back. After cinching tight the leather straps, he mounted up.

Exiting the stables astride Lady, he veered off in the opposite direction from home. He needed a dunk in the pond and a day's worth of sleep, but another need demanded his attention first.

The town was slowly coming to life. Those few shopkeepers who were out stopped their sweeping or window-washing to gawk at him. Carrington nodded at the barkeep smoking outside his establishment, the place where he'd squandered his money and hours the previous night. The squatty man, in his green satin vest and black trousers, rebuffed him. Probably due to something Carrington had done the night before—the act that landed him in jail.

He continued his trek along the road past the lumberyard and smithy. No matter how polite he was to others, very few exchanged a greeting. It didn't matter that he'd been a resident of the growing little community longer than most thereabouts. His father had homesteaded one hundred-sixty acres outside town before there even was a town. Nor did it matter that he contributed to the town's success by selling his crops at the local mercantile. His status as a reputable citizen was forever altered as a result of those seven years locked away in the Territorial Prison.

Turning down Tenth Avenue, he made his way past the homes lining the lanes on this side of town and drew to a halt when he reached the local boardinghouse. Dismounting, he looped the reins over a post and peered up at the three-story structure before him.

Five gabled windows along the top floor glinted the color of warm yellow as the morning's light hit them. The next level down were five more framed windows, draperies all shut tight against the early sun. The occupants within were wasting away precious daylight hours in slumber, though he supposed he was wasting the day, too.

He entered the boardinghouse through a door at the back of the building. The hard soles of his boots thudded loudly against wood as he made his way up the stairs. At the second-floor landing, a momentary sense of precaution made him pause. Upon finding no other occupants about, he continued along to the third door down the hallway.

With his reputation as a murderer, getting caught sneaking into a boardinghouse at unacceptable hours of the day wouldn't be overlooked, even though he was there to visit a friend who was a paying resident. The sheriff would use any excuse he could to toss him back inside a cell.

At his intended destination, Carrington stopped and braced one arm against the door jamb. He was about to knock when the door opened wide. Long, pale fingers clamped around his shirt front and yanked him forward into the room. This wasn't the first time he'd been greeted at the door before he'd had the chance to make his presence known.

"What are you doing here?" Suzanne Thomas demanded in a loud whisper. She pushed him aside and quickly shut the door, then pressed her ear against its surface. Wavy hair, a rich mahogany color, hung in heavy locks down her back. The ends skimmed the top of her buttocks which were nearly visible beneath the sheer fabric of her dressing gown.

One corner of Carrington's mouth quirked up, and a low, two-beat sound—part hum, part laugh—emanated from his throat. "I'm here for you, sweetheart."

She spun around to face him, a strained expression marring her pretty face. "I saw you coming."

Suzanne had a uniquely high-pitched voice that under normal circumstances Carrington found intriguing. Today, however, the sound grated over his dehydrated brain. His head drooped forward and he pressed two fingers against the spot between his brows. He noticed, once again, the spatter on his boots and wondered at it as he rubbed the top of one against the back of his leg.

Not wanting to explain himself, he deliberated over his next words. Suzanne had something he needed, something he knew she would offer, if she wasn't angry with him. He went to the window and pushed aside the curtain to view the street below. There was still no one about.

"Take off your clothes. Please."

Behind him, he heard her sharp, indrawn breath. "You can't just come sneaking into my room, Carrington, and demand I take off my clothes. If anyone saw you ride up, I'd be ruined!" She paced a few steps back and forth across the small apartment, her fingers clenched into fists against her waist. "Oh, dear, you're so thoughtless. You shouldn't be here." She stopped a few feet from him, arms crossed, one bare foot tapping silently against the wool carpet on the floor.

He set his hat on the back of the chair before a small table near the window where Suzanne had been having her morning tea. A *Ladies' Home Journal* lay open to an advertisement for new women's undergarments. He absently flipped through the pages.

Shame warred with his need.

"Nobody saw me come in. Now, could you pretend you're happy to see me? Come here." He was at her mercy, because he knew all too well that Suzanne would do only what Suzanne wanted to do. But she enjoyed their encounters too, so he knew he had a chance, regardless of the risk she worried over.

A mix of sympathy and suspicion washed over her face while she mentally battled her own desires. After a brief hesitation, she glided toward him, her gown floating around her like gossamer silk in the wind.

"Oh, Carrington, darling, of course I'm happy you're here." Her pale arms slipped around his waist. "I wasn't quite ready for you is all. Forgive me?" Raising up on her toes, she pressed her lips against his. When she leaned away, the smile she gave him was wide enough to show the nearly imperceptible imperfection in the top row of her teeth.

Their lips met again, hers parting beneath his. Carrington's hands roamed over the swell of her hips, in pursuit of the curved mounds of her backside. She squirmed against him, purring like a cat basking in the sun. The slight pressure of his arms had her now-pliant body pulled snug against his, causing his body to tighten with anticipation.

"I forgive you," he murmured as he nuzzled a sensitive spot below her ear. The reminiscent smell of yesterday's floral perfume greeted him. "I won't take much of your time."

By all accounts Suzanne was not one of the town's whores, at least not by trade. She was merely a young widow who'd become very knowledgeable in the fine art of lovemaking during her short marriage to a railroad man. That relationship ended soon after the tracks came through town when her husband was caught philandering with another worker's wife. Suzanne's husband was later found about a half mile from his home with a bullet in his skull. Suzanne, married at the age of seventeen, was a widow by nineteen.

In the years since, she'd heartily embraced her life as a widow and took a liking to Carrington, even when others warned her away. He was surprised she'd taken him to her bed and was admittedly shocked by some of the things they did together, even if they were pleasurable.

Her widowed status provided other freedoms as well, those that extended beyond the bedroom. Her father, a newspaper printing press operator at *The Caldwell Tribune*, allowed her to help in the print shop. It didn't take long before she was writing segments on her own and publishing them, whenever Arthur or Frank Steunenberg permitted. To date, she'd been given leave to submit articles about local events only. Coverage of politics fell to the brothers.

Carrington pressed hot, urgent kisses over her neck and shoulders. "You know what I want."

"But I'm expecting the Gilgan sisters this morning," she offered in a breathy voice. The Gilgans were prominent ladies in the community who'd taken Suzanne under their wing. They were part of the reason she was so strong and confident, especially for a young woman alone.

She gave him better access to her throat. "When are you going to marry me, Carrington? Haven't we danced around the subject long enough?"

Carrington frowned. The topic of marriage was brought up every time he saw Suzanne these days. But that hadn't always been the case. It was his own fault, he knew.

He'd mistakenly told her the story about how his father, right near the end of the gold rush, had struck gold up at Grimes Creek. However, nobody ever saw the treasure. Not even Carrington. It was rumored that his Pa built their house right on top of the fortune, in a place only he knew of and could access.

It was since that telling that Suzanne's interest in marriage to Carrington took hold. She might be an independent widow but becoming a rich wife by virtue of access to her husband's assets was too appealing an opportunity to pass up. Gaining entry to his home meant she could search to her heart's delight for the hidden gold.

But Suzanne was not the woman Carrington wanted to share his gold or his life with. He knew her motives were driven by greed. She didn't love him, and though he cared for her in his own way, he didn't love her either.

He sighed heavily against her skin. "I had a rough night, sweetheart." The admission slipped past his lips, which he instantly regretted.

She stiffened in his arms, her warm eagerness snuffed like a candle. "You were tossed in jail again, weren't you?" Her expression shifted from sultry and eager to one of reproach.

Carrington rolled his shoulders back, easing the tension there. He wasn't in a mood to discuss his failings or to pick out a china pattern.

His fingers squeezed a little tighter than necessary on the swell of her buttocks. She shuddered with a mix of pleasure and pain, desire winning out over censure. He sank back onto the chair before the window, then tugged at the bow near her throat. Her gown parted, and he eased the edges over her shoulders to expose her lush breasts.

"Carrington." Suzanne gave up all pretense of resistance as she angled into the space between his legs.

Dusky, peaked nipples bounced subtly before his face; he gently scraped his teeth over one. His hand sought purchase around her squeezable bosom, unable to wholly encompass the mass. With his free hand, he captured the hem of her dressing gown and pushed the wispy cloth up to her waist.

Suzanne growled her frustration before whisking the nightgown up and over her head. As she tossed it carelessly to the floor, she lowered to her knees. Eager fingers reached for Carrington's belt, making quick work of the buttons of his blue denim waist overalls. Her face was tense with hot arousal and she gasped with unrestrained pleasure before her lips closed around him.

Carrington heard the muffled rumble of voices and the snort of a horse outside the window. He peeked out. There was a glimmer of life forming along the streets now. He needed to hurry this up if he hoped to slip out of the boardinghouse unnoticed.

The pressure of Suzanne's mouth pulling on him drew his attention back into the room. He pushed her away and stood, drawing her up with him, then bent her over the small wood tabletop.

"Carrington," she purred, "someone might see us." Angled over the table, her face was inches from the window where the curtains were now opened wide to the outside world. She feigned concern but readily spread her legs and wiggled her hips at him.

He nudged her feet farther apart and eased into her welcoming body, stifling a grunt as she tightened around him. She was ready for him, but today he sought his own pleasure. It wasn't a kind thing to do, he knew. He'd make it up to her another time. He just needed this from her now, to help mask the loneliness, if only for a little while.

She began to rock against him, her cries growing more distinct. Maybe he wouldn't need to return so soon after all. Pulling her upright so her back was flush with his front, he silenced her by pressing his hand over her mouth. It wouldn't do either of them any good to wake the neighbors. Minutes later, she began to tremble with her release, bringing him along with her. He withdrew from her warmth, finishing off onto her gown lying at his feet.

***

Cassie's head snapped back, bonking against the wall. She gulped for air and rubbed at the bruised spot before jumping to her feet.

"Nononono." Her head shifted side-to-side in adamant denial. Fists clenched at her sides, she stared in shocked disbelief at the discarded paper lying in a heap where she'd flung it away from her.

"What. The. Hell. Was that?"

It was just a dream. It had to be a dream, she reassured herself. A dream that left her trembling with the aftershocks of a very apparent orgasm.

Her skin was flushed, and she could still feel the wild rush of adrenaline and surge of hormones that brought on that man, that Carrington person's, raging hard-on. The shame and sadness she sensed from him as he took what Suzanne offered washed over Cassie; it was overwhelming. Her legs wobbled beneath her.

"Holy crap! Is *that* what a guy feels every time he gets turned on?" She squeezed her thighs together as the fluttery pulsing in the region of her pelvis slowly ebbed.

She poked a toe at the yellowed newspaper. Reaching down, she pinched the smallest amount of one corner with two fingers and flipped back to the first page.

Five sentences.

There were only five sentences in the article reporting on a man named Carrington Chambers who'd essentially spent a night in the drunk tank. There were no specific details beyond that. No mention of a Suzanne Thomas.

How could she even know the name Suzanne Thomas? Yet with great specificity, she recalled the warmth of the woman's skin and the give of her body where Carrington's hands—Cassie's hands—had squeezed and caressed.

She sniffed the air, not daring to believe there was a whiff of whisky and sweat on it. She imagined there might be a hint of some flowery perfume as well, one reminiscent of the powder her grandmother used to keep in the bathroom when Cassie was a little girl. Chasing on the still air behind those odors was something musky and slightly seductive.

These were the smells of Carrington and Suzanne. And sex.

Cassie backed toward the attic's entrance, away from the paper like it was a feral dog.

She laced her fingers atop her head. "What would your therapist say, McAllister? He'd say you're—"

A car door slammed. She glanced at her watch.

"Shit!"

Racing over and grabbing the journal and papers up off the floor, she held them at arm's length and returned them to the trunk. After closing the lid, she bolted from the attic.

FIVE

"Three weeks? That's seriously the best you can do?"
Cassie had been trying for the last five minutes to convince
the general contractor's assistant that she needed the GC to
start work sooner than three weeks from now. So far, she
wasn't successful. She held the phone out at arm's length,
not caring to hear the woman's vague promise to relay
Cassie's concerns to the company's owner—the problem
himself.

"Fine," she said through gritted teeth. "If there's *any*
way you can persuade him, I'd appreciate it." Beyond
frustrated, she ended the call and threw her cellular on the
couch.

Not only was the main remodel going to be delayed, but
Randy, who'd left thirty minutes earlier, said he'd need at
least another day, too. Noting her distress at this
announcement, he'd heartily promised, again, to return
bright and early the next morning. Which meant she'd have
to spend another night in the house without the assurance of
safety her own Fort Knox provided.

She briefly considered getting a room in town for the
night but talked herself out of it. What good would it do?
From experience, she knew the voice would find her, at least
the one anyway, no matter where she was.

She slouched down onto the couch, legs out straight, heels planted on the floor, and her head tipped back against an oversized cushion. The meditative tick-tock of the pendulum in the grandfather clock helped calm her.

"You can do this, McAllister."

The previous night had turned out uneventful, except for the shadow near the fireplace and the voice she thought she'd heard. It must have been a dream, and fortunately, not one of her typical nightmares. Those consisted mostly of Jimmy Lancaster, her ex-husband. But he was locked up in a prison cell far away from Idaho.

If she dared call what she thought she'd seen a nightmare, because she didn't know what else to call it, at least it didn't seem threatening. She knew that feeling all too well.

That's because it wasn't real, you loon.

The ostensibly self-assuring statement didn't reassure her. But a quick glance at the corner near the fireplace revealed no shadowy visage. It was just a plain, empty space. She had nothing to worry about.

Until her thoughts returned to the attic. The place where she'd had her first . . . what? Out-of-body experience? Possession? Delusion? The lurid scene between Carrington and Suzanne niggled at the forefront of her mind.

The young woman had dabbed perfume just behind her ear. Cassie knew this because when Carrington nuzzled that area, the scent was stronger there. It excited him.

There was no way to explain how she knew that Carrington's body temperature inched up a notch when Suzanne's mouth engulfed his lower anatomy. Nor could she know that all his muscles seized, almost painfully so, for a split second when her tongue swirled across the most sensitive part of him. She couldn't know that Carrington had rough calluses on his palms that starkly contrasted with the smooth hardness of his cock. And, she really couldn't feel the way it swelled seconds before—

Cassie jerked upright and then leaned forward, pressing her elbows against her knees. Groaning, she dropped her face into her palms.

"Andrew might have you locked up if you even try to describe this to him," she mumbled into her hands. "There's only one logical answer." A fissure of panic opened in her gut. "What if this Carrington person is my alter ego?"

Over the clock's ticking, Cassie heard a sound near the top of the stairs. Upon inspection, she found nothing there and sat pensive, waiting, as the house eased again into a bloated silence.

She slumped forward, arms dangling against her thighs, head between her knees. Her traitorous mind drifted back to the attic and the lovers.

Like she was caught in a magnetic tractor beam, she rose to her feet. After avoiding the call of the trunk for most of the day, she was determined to prove that none of what she imagined that happened was real. With false courage guiding her, she plodded back upstairs.

Beneath the attic opening once again, she paced the hallway. Three steps one way. Turn. Three steps back.

"Come on, McAllister. What would your therapist say?"

Before she could chicken out, she rushed up the ladder into the attic. She faltered to a stop when she saw the light was off in the cubby where she'd found the trunk. It had been on when she left the room earlier that day, she was certain. She hadn't turned it off.

"It's an old light. It probably just died. Yes. That must be the case," she reasoned. "What other explanation could there be?" With a wary backward glance at the dark corner, she slowly approached the trunk.

A minute passed as she hovered over it. With immense trepidation, she gripped the edge of the lid. On a count of two, she flung it open and jumped back, no longer concerned about its fragility. Craning her neck, she peered inside, then dropped back on her heels when nothing lunged out at her.

Reaching into the trunk, and without touching even one tiny corner of the yellowed newspapers, she removed the five-by-eight sized journal. Nothing out of the ordinary occurred with the first touch, so she braced against the wall and tilted the book toward the sunlight streaming in through the window. Slowly, she lifted the front cover.

"Diaryofanniechambers," she read, fast, and waited for . . . she didn't know what.

Nothing happened, so she skimmed over the words again. The name McDonald, written before Chambers, had a line through it, and a heart circled the latter name. Cassie surmised this Annie person at some point had married Carrington.

"What happened to Suzanne?" The image of sweaty bodies molded together tugged at her concentration.

She thumbed through the diary, skimming past several pages of entries filled with elegant cursive letters. One page had been dog-eared, but she skipped over it and flipped back to the first entry.

July 26, 1890.

She noted the entry date was three months after the date referenced in the newspaper article she'd read earlier.

The one that didn't have Suzanne's name in it.

Since nothing had happened yet—no out-of-body experience or other such nonsense—Cassie decided to read on.

I met two men at the fair today. Carrington Chambers and Blake Hanson.

Air stirred around her. She ran her fingers across the top of her head, pushing strands of hair that escaped her ponytail off and away from her face.

The music had just started when I saw Blake walk around the dance floor, headed straight toward me.

She gave a quick glance around the room, making certain she was still in the attic, which she was, thankfully.

He was watching me.

Her vision blurred and she shook her head.

My heart was beating so hard, I thought someone might hear it.

The room around her began to tilt, and her heart started to race.

Before he reached me, I felt a tap at my shoulder. When I turned around there was the other man, Carrington. He has the most intriguing color of eyes. They're gray, like dark smoke.

There was no warning fog this time, just a swift blackness, like someone turned out the lights in Cassie's head.

***

The lights switched back on.

She was milling about near the edge of a platform, weaving her way through a throng of people. The air was filled with women's laughter and men's booming voices. The scrape of a violin tuning up sounded from somewhere close by. People were in a very festive mood.

Children darted through the crowd, squealing with delight while the adults mingled about, talking and laughing, enjoying the relaxed atmosphere. The smells and sounds were classic of any fair Cassie had ever attended. Wafting on the air was the scent of meat cooking, sweet dough frying, and summer. What was the occasion? she wondered.

If she believed what she guessed had just happened, according to the journal entry, it was July, summer. That explained the oppressive heat.

She tugged at the close neckline of her outfit, fingering the lace that scratched against her throat. The blouse she wore was white cotton and long-sleeved. The skirt, the color of milk chocolate, was probably the most modest article of clothing Cassie had ever worn; its length brushed against the ground. She lifted the hem a few inches and poked one foot out. A cotton petticoat hugged her leg, and beneath that were cotton stockings. On her foot was a black, chunky-heeled boot that laced up the front. She let the hem of the skirt fall back into place. As she raised a hand to touch the hat atop her head, she stilled.

"Ho-ly shit!" she exclaimed as the full impact of her circumstance hit her. Her hands—or rather the hands before her—weren't her long fingers with the pink nail polish she'd applied a couple days ago, nor was her skin tanned to a nice warm brown. These hands were petite and pale.

They had to be the girl's hands. Annie's.

"Holy shit," Cassie said again, a bit louder this time.

Two women nearby spun about, the tulip-shape of their dresses flaring, their hats wobbling, and their expressions most becoming of goldfish.

Stunned and still in a bit of shock at the unbelievable possibility of what was happening to her, Cassie smothered a nervous laugh with the palm of her hand. It seemed that her more colorful vocabulary was not commonplace here. Especially coming from a young lady.

"Elizabeth Anne!" Cassie whirled around. By way of Annie's thoughts, she knew the man issuing the stern address was the girl's father.

"Yes, Daddy?"

Daddy was older, with deep wrinkles about his forehead and around his mouth. Green eyes flashed behind silver-wired spectacles. Cassie noted that his attire wasn't as fancy as that of some of the other gentlemen nearby. This man had on a white shirt, no tie or ascot, and a serviceable jacket that hung loose about his entire upper body as if he'd shrunk inside it. His trousers were a dull gray, also much too large for his frail frame.

Cassie lurked behind Annie's subconscious, fully aware of her, yet also strangely capable of surfacing—the best way she could describe it—to direct thoughts and actions. This was different than before, when she'd been in Carrington's head. There, she'd felt more like an observer, while here she was herself and Annie at the same time.

I'll never be able to explain this to Andrew.

"Young lady. I don't know what's gotten into you. Such language! Your mother nearly swooned with her distress."

Genuine shame from Annie overwhelmed Cassie's senses when she saw the mother's shocked expression. The woman was as tall as Annie but still shorter than her father. The girth of her middle pressed tight against the blue of her calico dress.

"I'm sorry, Momma. Something startled me, and it just slipped out." Realizing Annie might never have sworn before, Cassie blurted the excuse. She hung her head for dramatic effect, if not for Annie's genuine feelings of guilt. Her mother continued to frown, still in disbelief at her daughter's wayward behavior.

"You're not too old for me to give a whippin' to, young lady. Don't go thinking you are." The patriarch wagged a stiff, bony finger at her. "Now, get on with you. We're going to continue enjoying this exciting celebration."

Three women eavesdropping nearby overheard Annie being admonished by her father. They whispered among themselves and ogled her like she was a bug they couldn't swat away. With the dramatic moment over, they turned their backs and strolled off, far away from where Annie stood.

Cassie needed a moment to assess her situation. Seeking an escape from the crowd, she backed away until she was butted up against a row of lilac bushes. The heady, sweet scent from the purple flowers washed over her, effectively soothing her frazzled nerves.

If what she believed was true, she'd landed in the year eighteen ninety. She also assumed she was in Caldwell. It made the most sense, if any of this made sense.

From her vantage point at the end of a street—the one she'd glimpsed before when Carrington stumbled past it—she saw buildings, both brick and wood, lining the unpaved roadway. Far down at the other end of the business district stood the large water tower she'd also observed that other time. On the corner building closest to her, a banner tacked onto the façade read: Idaho – 43d State. Est. July 3, 1890.

So, she was at a fair of sorts after all. In eighteen ninety. And she was in Annie's psyche and body somehow—to the girl's potential detriment. Similar to before, when she'd been in that Carrington fellow's head, she knew Annie's thoughts. She shivered from head to toe because the journal indicated Annie met Carrington on this day. And at some point, she marries the man. Myriad images of her experience as Carrington flashed through Cassie's memory.

Panic threatened. She coached herself down with a reminder that as of yet, she was unharmed. This was only a dream. On steroids. She decided to let the scene play out and learn more about the past. Maybe she'd get to find out what became of Suzanne. What harm could it do? Clearly, she was meant to be here.

"That's it! I'm meant to help someone. A woman. That's what the voice has been telling me to do. But who? And how?" The past, the events she was experiencing right now had already happened. What could *she* possibly do to change any of it? And why her? She was nobody. Just someone who'd survived a brutal attack and lived to tell.

When the strains of a waltz rolled across the air, she tried to peer over the heads around her. Annie was enjoying the gaiety of the moment, so Cassie decided to absorb her host's happiness while she observed her surroundings.

She waved at Annie's parents who were eyeing her from the other side of the makeshift dance floor. They were engaged in conversation with a man clutching a Bible against his middle, presumably the local preacher. The mother offered a small wave back, but the father pursued his lively discussion with the holy man, periodically pointing her way.

The uncanny feeling that someone was watching her tickled at Cassie's senses. She scanned the crowd and beyond down the street where dozens of people milled about. Her heart lurched a few beats when she found a tall, dark-haired man staring back at her. Pressing her palm to her chest, she tried to remain calm as he weaved through the crowd, heading in her direction.

She was caught in a trance as much as Annie was. The stranger was now only four steps away.

A light tap at her shoulder made her jump. She turned to see who was behind her. All the air rushed from her lungs when she came face-to-face with the man whom Cassie knew without a doubt was Carrington. The one with the remarkable eyes. Annie was right.

"Would you care to dance, Miss?"

His voice sounded different from what Cassie remembered. It was like how hearing her own voice in a recording didn't sound the way she heard it in her own ears. Since she'd only heard his voice as if it was her own, the logic made sense.

His slight drawl added to his handsomeness. He was tall, too. Her eyes traveled the length of his body, from head to toe, before snapping back to his face.

One of his dark eyebrows lifted, and a corner of his mouth turned up.

"Uh, I—" Annie stuttered, embarrassed at being caught undressing him with her eyes. Before Cassie could think of something to say, the other man, presumably Blake, was at her side.

There was a notable difference between Cassie and Annie's heights—about three inches by Cassie's guess. She found the difference rather intimidating in her current predicament, book-ended by the pair of men as she was. Blake had lovely brown eyes, so dark they appeared black. He wore a black felt, open crown hat, a bit more worn than the fancier Stetson on Carrington's head. Cassie was from Colorado. Cowboy country. She'd seen her share of Stetsons and knew one when she saw it.

Sandwiched between the two strapping men, she couldn't help but compare them. Carrington had brown hair, rich and dark, with curls skimming against his collar. His fawn-colored hat fit his demeanor and appearance equally as well as the black hat and attire fit Blake.

"I'm Blake Hanson," Blake said. When he smiled, Cassie saw he had a small gap between his teeth. It gave him a rather boyish appearance. He looked past her, to a spot above Annie's head. "Boss," he said to Carrington before returning his attention back to Annie. "Dance with me, Miss?" His hand hovered in the air between them.

This was a tennis match of many a girl's dreams. Two attractive men vying for her attention. She considered her options, and then settled on the one that rose to the top of Annie's mind.

"I'm flattered, Mr. Hanson, but this gentleman has already asked me. Perhaps the next dance?" A ripple of excitement filled her when Carrington smiled. Not a full-blown, show-his-teeth sort of smile, but a sexy, heart-melting one, nonetheless.

His hand encompassed hers and he whisked her onto the dance floor, guiding her through the paces with strong, elegant grace. A short, awkward silence ensued as Cassie gathered her bearings, trying to figure out what she was supposed to do or say.

He spoke first. "I'm Carrington." The hand at her waist slid a fraction of space lower on her hip, causing her to melt and tense at the same time. He moved her around the floor with confidence. She had no choice but to follow. When she stumbled, he masked her blunder with ease.

"Hanson over there,"—he pointed with his chin at Blake where they'd left him—"he's my field hand. I own some land a few miles west of town, over near the river."

He stopped talking, but Cassie sensed he wanted to say more.

"I'll tell him to stay away from you. If you'd like."

Energy bubbled up around Cassie like charged air during a lightning storm. It raced up her spine. She thrilled at the delicious tingling sensation. Annie was thrilled, too. She was most definitely enamored with Carrington.

"I'm A-Annie. I've heard of you."

Carrington had quite the reputation in town; however, that didn't curb the girl's intrigue. She was a bit nervous, but he didn't frighten her. Cassie tore Annie's twitterpated gaze from Carrington's rather intense one.

There were at least ten other couples dancing close by. She smiled at some, noting how others refused to make eye contact. Beyond the dancers she saw Annie's parents. They both wore horrified expressions. The preacher beside them was blotchy red, his jowls jiggling as his head twitched with his dismay.

"I've seen you around town before," Carrington said, bringing Cassie back to their little circle of space. He smiled down at her.

She suspected he didn't smile much. His chin and jaw showed a hint of stubble. When she found the courage to look up into his eyes, she stepped on his toes.

He winked at her.

Cassie stumbled again as embarrassment warmed her skin. Carrington secured her by curving his arm all the way around her back. They were close now. She caught a hint of whiskey on his breath that was not unpleasant. Distracted, she stumbled yet again and yelped softly when his arm squeezed her until no gap remained between them. His palm pressed firmly against the small of her back, her hand encased securely in his. A quick glance at Annie's parents told her she was in for a tongue-lashing before the day was through.

"I'm sorry. I'm not the best dancer." It was true. Cassie was a terrible dancer. Apparently, so was Annie.

Carrington twirled her effortlessly about, making her appear much more graceful than she was. He didn't seem concerned that they were now the center of attention. Too soon, the dance ended. Before Annie's parents had the opportunity to rush the stage and whisk her away, for a Christian penance or a beating possibly, Carrington intervened.

"Come with me." With a palm splayed against her lower back, he guided her away from the crowd, away from where Annie's parents and Blake waited at the fringes, and away from the festivities.

It was Annie who giggled with mischievous delight as she jog-walked beside Carrington, his long stride twice the length of hers. The lively sound of the fair grew dim as they moved farther down the street perpendicular to the main drag. Cassie looked back over her shoulder, expecting God's wrath to be in pursuit, but surprisingly, nobody followed.

Annie's common sense began to war with her wayward actions. It finally dawned on her that she was practically running through town, away from the safety of the crowd and her family. And with a criminal no less. Thrilled at the idea of the scandalous behavior, the girl had enough sense to want to remain within respectable view of others.

Carrington must not have had ravishment on his mind, Cassie surmised, because he didn't try to duck into an alley for some privacy or anything of the sort. Instead, he stopped near an ice cream vendor and inquired if she would care for some of the cool treat, to which Cassie eagerly agreed. After paying and collecting their paper cups, they continued their walk, at a normal and unsuspecting pace, before coming to a park with a large elm tree in the middle.

The shade of the tree afforded them some privacy, while at the same time kept them in public view. Annie was still nervous, yet excited about being in such close quarters with the notorious Carrington Chambers. Cassie, however, worried about something more indecent. She was fully aware of what the man was capable of—she'd experienced it firsthand.

Taking a delicate spoonful of her creamy vanilla confection, she desperately searched for something to say to break the ice. Finally, she found the courage to ask if he was enjoying his ice cream.

"Mmm, this is delicious, wouldn't you say?" she whispered. When she looked up into his smoldering gaze, two descriptive words came to mind: Mercury and liquid heat.

He shifted and leaned against the tree, his arm braced above Annie's head. He was so close.

"Yes. It is." His lips were shiny from where his tongue licked across them. He dipped his head nearer to hers, like he was about to share a secret. "Here. Try some of mine." Scooping some of his ice cream onto his spoon, he raised it to her mouth. "Open."

Her lips parted, and he put the spoon against her tongue. She swirled the chocolate around. Annie's chest rose and fell heavily with each breath she struggled to take.

"You missed some." Carrington ran the pad of his thumb slowly over the corner of her mouth. Cassie felt his warm-cold breath on her cheek as his head lowered ever closer.

He was going to kiss her!

She searched for reasons why she shouldn't allow the kiss. To her joy and dismay, she found that Annie wanted him to. She braced an arm against the tree at her back, feeling the grooves of the bark. Her fingers anchored and clenched in anticipation. Resting the back of her head against the tree, her eyes fluttered shut—

"There you are!" A man's voice called out.

Cassie startled and stepped away from the tree and Carrington. Blake and—she choked on her own spit—Suzanne strolled up, arm-in-arm, neither seeming pleased at the scene before them.

"I was searching for this lady here." Blake nodded in Cassie's direction. "To collect on that dance. When I stumbled upon Suzanne, she said she'd been searching for you." The easy smile he gave Cassie shifted to a tight-lipped frown when he addressed Carrington.

"Uh, sure?" Cassie said, agreeing to the dance. She turned to Carrington. "Thank you for the ice cream. It was a pleasure meeting you."

Carrington's lips curved into what wasn't exactly a smile. "I'd like to continue our acquaintance. Walk with me?" Hooking her fingers into the crook of his elbow, they set off, away from the gawking pair. With barely a backward glance at Blake, he added, "I'll catch up with you at the farm. I think we have a fence down near the river."

Seeking sympathetic female support, Cassie glanced back at Suzanne and was caught off guard. Suzanne's lips curved up in a wry, crooked smile, as if she held a secret that Cassie wasn't privy to.

Cassie was still guessing at it when in a voice so low she shouldn't have been able to hear it, Suzanne said, "I knew you'd show up."

***

Cassie hurled back into her reality. She lay on the dusty wood floor of the attic, watching the rafters overhead fade from the fresh, golden hue of new wood to the gray brown of aged timber.

She was unnerved, but less frightened by the events she'd just experienced than she'd been the first time it happened. The unsettled feelings she had following Suzanne's strange words to her were overshadowed by the lingering anticipation from her near kiss with Carrington.

Overall, this dream was much more tolerable than the last one. Being in another person's body was challenging in its own right, but a woman's body—even if not her own—was at least familiar. Being in a man's body and mind was beyond weird, and she hoped never to experience it again. It was raw and aggressively male. Carrington's thoughts were black and white, hard and direct. In the heat of passion, his mind was like a raging storm, turbulent and wild. Until he found his release.

Cassie trembled with the buildup of sensations aroused in her from having been so close to Carrington. Licking her lips, she was surprised to discover the distinct taste of chocolate ice cream. Whatever was happening, it carried through from the past with her. She held her hands above her. Pressed into the soft pads of her fingers and edges of her palms were the jagged creases from where Annie had clenched the tree bark.

"Oh, you've lost it now, McAllister."

Unsure how or when she'd wound up sprawled on her back, she sat up to clear the haze from her head. The book lay face up beside her on the floor. Her head cocked to the side with her confusion.

"Wait a minute." Grabbing the journal, she flipped to the entry she'd just read. "He was with Suzanne a few months before this dance!" She thumped the page with an index finger while processing through the timeline.

"It's no wonder Suzanne seemed jealous. Carrington was a womanizing bastard! I sure hope Annie got smart and left his sorry ass once she figured out what a creep he was." Perhaps Annie hadn't really married Carrington, and had only childishly written the name Chambers after her own? Like young women often did.

There was a sudden, noticeable shift in the air, something Cassie had experienced once before. Slowly, she circled about to face the far wall. A sliver of light again revealed the half-sized door that had previously been hidden in darkness. From the attic's shadows, a tall, solid shape shifted forward. It crossed the room, into the light, and stopped at her feet.

To take in the entire height of the person standing before her, Cassie had to tilt her head back to nearly a ninety-degree angle.

She felt all the blood drain from her face when the man before her spoke.

"My wife didn't leave me. She's dead."

SIX

Adrenaline coursed through Cassie's veins, triggering her body's fight or flight response. She screamed with all the effort she could muster while scrambling backward and away from the stranger.

"Help! You—get away!"

He advanced another step. Cassie scuttled back until she met the wall. She was trapped.

"No!" she demanded. "Get away!"

Crouched in the corner, she shrank into herself. Her body trembled, and she was breathing too fast. When her vision began to narrow, she knew she was about to pass out. Escape was her only option. The window. She mentally judged the distance to the ground from the third floor.

Springing to her feet, she made it across the room and dove at the opening. With arms and legs through, she wriggled to get the lower half of her body over the ledge. When fingers squeezed tight into the flesh near her hipbones, she shrieked.

"Help!" she cried out as she was tugged backward. It was unlikely there was anyone nearby to hear her scream, but she screamed anyway.

Fully inside the attic again, the hands at her hips released their grip and she crumpled to the floor, her hope of escape fading. Pulling her knees to her chest, she curled into a protective ball, fingers interlaced tight atop her head.

And waited.

In her huddled space, she mentally went through what her best line of defense would be against an attack. Kneeing him in the balls was an option, but that wouldn't work if he didn't make her stand up. When he bent over to grab her, she'd have to gouge his eyes. Or bite off his ear. Both options were horrifying, but she'd do it.

Her body began to shake from head to toe. She couldn't control it. The adrenaline rush was passing, which meant shock could set in soon. She knew how it happened, because she'd experienced it before.

Silence descended over the room. There was not a creak of wood or the sound of breathing, besides her own.

"Are you finished?" The man's voice wormed its way past her palms where they pressed tight against her ears.

"Don't hurt me," she beseeched.

Flashbacks to another day, another man towering over her, and another moment of helplessness clawed at her insides. She'd survived Jimmy's attack only to succumb to a similar fate? After she'd finally taken drastic measures to get her life back? Tears squeezed past her scrunched-tight eyelids.

Her anxiety skyrocketed when she heard movement, fabric shifting against skin. Lungs deprived of air burned in her chest as fear immobilized her. The man was so close now, she smelled him. Sniffing, she tried to pinpoint what it was that seemed vaguely familiar. It was distinct, not pine, but something close, something that made her think of fresh air, wood, and the outdoors. She'd report these details to the police, in the event there might be a connection to other assault victims.

A few more silent seconds passed. Something had to give.

Cassie peeked up. The man was kneeling in front of her, a foot away, one knee on the floor, the other bent before him with his elbow resting over his thigh. Clutched in his hands were the newspapers and journal.

"I'm not going to hurt you."

She'd heard that voice before but couldn't, and wouldn't, admit the possibility of how she was hearing it now, in her attic. In the twenty-first century. Tendrils of air once again carried that vaguely familiar scent of him to her.

Impossible.

She did not care to evaluate how she knew there were tiny creases, barely visible, that fanned out near his temples. Or how the groove between his brows deepened when he pondered something intently, or was irritated, like was happening now. And how shallow lines bracketed his mouth on the rare occasion he smiled.

"Wh-Who are you?" She waited for his response, processing the fact that she hadn't been killed, raped, or tossed out the window.

She'd already memorized every detail of his face, and some of his body that she should have no way of knowing. His clothing was a bit more casual than what she'd last seen on him; a button-up, long-sleeved brown shirt adorned his torso. His pants were blue denim, but not the same as how Levi's looked today. Then there was the hat. The hat was the exact same fawn-colored Stetson that hid wavy brown locks of hair from her view.

A gravelly chuckle resonated from deep in his throat. "I think you know who I am." His smile broadened and his eyes darted to the objects in his hand before returning to Cassie.

She mimicked the action, pursed her lips, and tilted her head. Dawning realization niggled at her memory and she shook her head, slowly at first, then faster.

"Uh-uh. Nope. It's not possible."

The man whom she'd presumably dreamt about on two different occasions now, whose warm, solid muscles had flexed beneath her hands—well, technically, beneath his own hand and Annie's—could *not* be kneeling in front of her.

She continued her animated denial. Likewise, he nodded in equal time.

Rising to his feet, he towered above her, all six feet three inches of handsome, strong, muscled man. Removing his hat to reveal that full head of soft hair, with the ends curling a bit at the collar, he dipped his chin at her.

"I am Carrington Chambers. And this is my home." His slight drawl was smooth enough to curl Cassie's toes. She'd heard it before, just as he'd been about to kiss her near a tree in a place far from where she was now.

That's when she knew she'd lost it. With some hysteria, she began to laugh. What she assumed were dreams had just become hallucinations. Next stop: The looney bin.

In those darkest times, those years when fear of life itself held her in an iron fist, she'd joked with Andrew about the unlikelihood of coming through her past unscathed. She'd never really meant it, of course. It was just her way of healing. But nothing like that had happened because Cassie believed that mind over matter would allow anyone to overcome anything. It seemed very logical that if she didn't buy into the crap her fears had generated here—Carrington-the-hallucination—then he'd disappear.

Long ago, she swore never again to be a victim, but fear and stress caused different reactions in people. Cassie's response resulted in a hysterical outburst of laughter.

***

Carrington's sudden appearance had been a shock to the woman, understandably so, but he'd soon explain everything. That is, if she wasn't unhinged.

When she pressed a hand against the wall and pushed into a standing position, he took a precautionary step back. She continued to laugh, though it was no silly laughter to be certain. He'd once heard a prison mate do something similar, following a stint when he'd been celled alone for nearly a month; the man was never the same afterwards. Carrington needed to tread lightly and ease her into acceptance. So, he waited quietly.

After some moments, it appeared his tactic was working. She mumbled something he couldn't make out and cursed softly. Following a few hearty, deep breaths she looked up at him.

She had lovely eyes—a unique, dark purplish-blue. And she was tall for a woman, much taller than his Annie. The top of her head reached his shoulders. Her mouth curved like the shape of a bow, especially when she smiled. He knew because he'd been watching her from the moment she set foot in his house.

A thick lock of her hair bound into a tail of sorts was perched high atop the back of her head. The shade of it was a strange mix of blond and red-brown. When freed, the tresses reached far enough to brush against the curve of her back.

"I won't harm you." He inched closer, extending a hand in a peace-making gesture.

She side-stepped along the wall, creeping toward the attic's entrance. About every third step, her eyes darted from him, to the open trunk, then to the ladder.

In a sing-songy voice, she muttered, "Andrew is gonna have you locked away, McAllister."

Carrington monitored her progress around the room. By nature of his presence in the house, he'd been eavesdropping on her and had heard her say the name Andrew on several occasions. She also used that name in those one-sided conversations she had while talking into the rectangular box she put to her ear.

Long ago, here in this house, there'd been others who'd talked into something similar, only then it was a handle of sorts. He'd heard it referenced as a telephone. This Andrew person must have been talking to her somehow.

"Who is Andrew?" he asked.

Cassie halted a few feet from the opening in the floor.

"Andrew?" She eyed him suspiciously. "He *used* to be my psychologist. I'm sure once I tell him about this"—she pointed at the trunk and at him— "and how I'm having sexy dreams about someone I don't know *as that someone*, I'm sure he'll want to get me back on his client list." She inched sideways, getting too close to the ladder for his comfort. He followed her movements until they stood in a face-off, a mere foot from the room's exit point.

"Sexy dreams, you say?" Maybe teasing was the way to calm her.

She made a sound through her nose and shifted uncomfortably on her feet. A scowl knit her brows so tightly they nearly blended into one.

"Mind over matter, McAllister. Mind over matter," she crooned reassuringly. "I'm going to count to three. When I finish, you will be gone from my house." She pressed the heels of her hands against her eyes while her lips moved in a silent count, as promised.

Her hands lowered, and her eyes popped open.

"Still here." He lifted his arms out in a large shrug. "Technically, this is my house. I, however, can't leave. Lucky for me that you came along."

She remained quiet and still a long moment. He was optimistic that she was coming to terms with his sudden presence, until she tightened an arm about her waist and covered her neck with one hand. That's when he realized her distress. After watching her for two days, he knew that was a reactionary response to fears chasing her. He'd heard her mention someone named Jimmy during her conversations with Andrew, and with herself—she talked to herself a lot. It had to be Jimmy who'd hurt her.

So caught up in his observations and revelations about Cassie, he missed the subtle change in her body language. She nearly escaped his reach when she rocketed toward the hole in the floor and the ladder. He did manage, however, to grab her around the waist and set her on her feet before him.

Understanding finally dawned on him. She'd been attacked by a man before, brutally attacked. Yet here Carrington was, appearing out of nowhere, in a place where she'd assumed she was alone and safe. He'd literally but unintentionally cornered her in the attic. Of course, she was terrified.

Raising palms in supplication, he lowered his voice and spoke to her as he might a horse when it was agitated. "I don't mean to frighten you. I know this is hard to understand, but you're safe with me."

A shadow of some new emotion darkened Cassie's eyes. Anger. This was a good sign. If she was angry, that meant she was getting past being shocked and frightened. He smiled encouragingly.

"Did Jimmy send you?" Her hand trembled where it curved against the front of her neck.

"No. I know you don't believe me, but I am the man you read about." He held up the journal.

Cassie flinched. "Come on, McAllister. Please wake up." She pinched the soft underside of her arm.

Carrington scraped a hand over his face to mask his grin. "You're not asleep. And I'm not a dream," he offered reassuringly. "What happened to you was real. And . . ." He wavered a moment, certain she wouldn't react well to his next request. "I need you to finish reading the journal, so I can find out—"

Her lips parted on a quick indrawn breath and she shook her head. "I don't know you. You're an intruder in my home. You need to leave. Now."

He blew out an exasperated sigh. "Hear me out. I told you that you're safe with me, but you *will* help me. You're the only one who can."

Her eyes widened in surprise. Before Carrington could blink, she lunged again for the ladder. He caught her in one stride, hands locking about her arms. Lifting her easily, he planted her on her feet directly in front of him.

"Damn it, woman. Stop!" He gave her a firm shake, then felt terrible when she drew back from him and lowered her head. Striving for calm and compassion, he softened his tone. "Jimmy didn't send me. I don't know who Jimmy is, but I'm guessing he's who did that to you."

When Cassie looked up at him, his gaze flicked down to her throat. The jagged white line across her neck, left behind after having the skin torn wide was now fully on display.

"I am not Jimmy." His hands still cupped her shoulders, and he gave her a tiny shake. "I am not here to hurt you. I need your help." His grip on her body eased, but he didn't step away—he'd learned his lesson.

Indecision flitted across her face. Carrington waited patiently, allowing her time to come to her own conclusion.

A shock of uneasiness raced through him when he recalled where he'd seen hair the color of hers. It had been only a split-second vision, but he remembered it now. He'd seen that hair, unbound and lifting about her shoulders on a breeze the moment his world went dark long, long ago.

"If you're not going to hurt me, as you say, then let me go downstairs. I really need to call someone," she said in a low voice.

There was a moment's hesitation before he granted her request. It was a peace treaty of sorts, yet he was wise enough to follow closely behind as she disappeared through the attic's opening.

SEVEN

"Andrew?" Cassie's voice wobbled and she had to clear her throat.

One of the side effects of having her vocal cords damaged was that when she was stressed or scared, they tightened up, which made her sound like she was on the verge of tears. In this instance, the frail quality of her voice might have been equally as much the latter as the former.

"Hello, Cassie. How's my favorite ex-patient on her second night in the house?" At the comforting, familiar lilt of her friend's voice, Cassie sagged with some relief.

"Hey, Andrew. I'm not so sure."

Carrington was nearby, one hip hitched up on the kitchen table, half standing, half sitting.

"What is it?" Andrew asked, instantly alert and concerned. Sometimes it seemed he knew her better than Cassie knew herself. "Are the dreams back?"

Were the dreams back? she silently scoffed. The question was one Andrew had asked her a million times. Before, it was always a straight-up response—yes or no. Now, she didn't know what to say.

She needed a drink. Skirting wide around the kitchen to the refrigerator in the corner, she pulled out a bottle of white wine.

"I think I may have had an out-of-body experience," she blurted. There, it was out. Let Andrew work with that.

Through the phone, she heard him shift in his leather chair. "What do you mean, Chassandra?"

Cassie cringed at hearing her name. She knew Andrew was really concerned now. Not only had he switched to his official doctor voice, he'd also used her proper name, with its unusual spelling and pronunciation. Which she hated, and he knew it.

When she was a kid, some of the older boys in her school had teased her, calling her Chassis, like the frame on a car. They'd joked about how good a ride she'd be, if she'd let them take a test drive. It wasn't until she reached the eighth grade that she learned from some of the older girls in her school what those boys meant. It was then that she began writing her name as Cassie. The tactic worked, and over time, the boys found other targets to pick on and forgot, for the most part, about her.

Still, it didn't take away the fact that Chassandra was her name. Apparently, the "ch" spelling was some sort of family tradition on her mother's side, or something along those lines. Since Cassie disliked her name so much, she never took an interest in researching the history behind it. Her mother hadn't pressed the matter either.

With the phone wedged against her shoulder, she retrieved a glass from one of the kitchen cabinets, then found a corkscrew and began opening the bottle. The cork pulled free with a satisfying pop. She poured a shallow amount of the bubbly white into her glass, turned her back on her unwanted guest and drank. The cool liquid warmed her insides.

How did she summarize *this* story for Andrew? He would listen professionally, of course, but there was no way he'd believe her. And, if he of all people didn't, who would? She envisioned padded white walls in her future.

Boot heels scraped over the floor behind her. She turned to find Carrington repeating her action of collecting a wine glass from the cupboard. He held it out toward her, eyes alight with intrigue. Cassie hesitated before filling his glass.

He swirled the liquid around and sniffed the contents, pulling back, his brows jamming together. Drawing a large swig of the fruity beverage, he sloshed it around inside his mouth a few times.

Cassie watched in awed silence, trying not to focus on the sheen of moisture on his lips or his strong jaw as it moved the liquid back and forth from cheek to cheek. The wine he was sampling was one of the more expensive brands she'd splurged on—she paid twenty-two dollars for that bottle. So, she was rather surprised when his face twisted into something resembling an old man without his dentures. Then, to add insult to injury, he rushed to the sink and spat out the contents.

"That's horrible!" he exclaimed. "Whatever happened to plain old good whiskey?" His tongue raked across his teeth. He set the glass with the remainder of its contents on the counter, pushing it as far as his arm would reach. Cassie spun back around to face the window and resumed her phone therapy session.

"It felt so real, Andrew." She pulled at her ponytail, twirling the end around her fingers. "Tell me I'm not crazy." If she could survive a violent attack and not lose her mind, she certainly could survive a few slightly erotic dreams.

She hoped.

Andrew sighed. "You say the experiences were good ones? Pleasurable?"

Cupping a hand over the end of the phone, Cassie lowered her voice. "They were quite romantic in nature, yes." She felt her skin heat up and stiffened irritably when she heard a throaty chuckle behind her.

"In my professional opinion," Andrew offered, "I think the dreams were your subconscious opening up to the possibility of a relationship. Finally. What was it about them that was so appealing?"

With certainty born from years spent sitting in front of Andrew spilling her guts to him, she knew he was grinning.

"Well," she lowered her voice to a mere whisper, "the first was gross. Like I was in some guy's body and could feel everything he felt." An image of Andrew experiencing what she had in that moment of Carrington's release tried to form, but Cassie shoved it back into the darkest recesses of her mind.

She peeked over her shoulder. Carrington was leaning on the counter again, concentrating on the greenish-white liquid in his discarded glass. He picked it up and sniffed at it, his nostrils pinching tight. When he caught Cassie watching him, his revulsion gave way to a quick, easy grin.

"The second dream was pure, old-fashioned romance. The guy was polite and had manners." Andrew couldn't hear her and asked her to repeat what she'd said.

"I said, he *was* polite and *had* manners." She emphasized the past tense, refusing to give her houseguest any praise, since he was an intruder and had just offended her sensibilities. "He was also a little overbearing. The way he touched me, er, the person I was in the dream. It was nice, but if he were real, I'd avoid him like the plague." Her body hummed with remembered pleasure, even as the lie slipped over her lips. She'd *totally* give in to him . . . in her dreams.

Once again, she ignored the throaty rumble behind her.

As embarrassing as her confession was, she knew Andrew would not mock her. She'd always been able to say anything to him without fear of being judged. Considering her current state of mind and circumstances, she appreciated that more than ever.

"You've spent the last seven years of your life healing from trauma. Your experience with Jimmy didn't exactly inspire romance. As a result, in your head, you've lumped all men into the same category as your abusive ex." He paused, allowing her to digest his words.

"I think what's happened is that you fantasized about the past, a time when stories tell us men were men. Kind, well-mannered, and respectful of women. Your subconscious is trying to let go of what you've grown to believe and is seeking happiness. Deep down you know not all men are bad, Cassie."

She made a non-committal sound in her throat. "I suppose. But it was more than a dream. It was *very* real." A flush of red heat traveled up her neck and over her cheeks again. In the window's reflection, she watched a gloating smile appear on Carrington's face.

Andrew's voice carried a smile, too. "Everyone has wet dreams, Cassie. Even me. I think you're finally on the verge of healing and your body is letting you know you're ready to love again."

"Ick. Andrew. I did not need to know that about you. You're wrong, too. I don't want a relationship. You may very well be the only man I ever trust again." She sniffled and smoothed a hand across her forehead. "I'll be fine. I just needed to talk through it." Turning to face Carrington, a new determination settled about her. "There's a lot I want to get done here tonight." The first of which would be exorcising the ghost, as she'd come to believe he was, but who certainly didn't look or act like any ghost she'd ever imagined.

"Andrew? Promise you won't share any details of your sex life ever again." She ended the call to the sound of his laughter ringing in her ears.

The excitement of finding an old trunk and its hidden mysteries disappeared like a puff of smoke.

"Oh, for shit's sake." She pressed her hands flat on the counter and gathered her wits before meeting Carrington's probing stare.

"You have ten minutes."

EIGHT

Carrington was delighted by Cassie's willingness to hear him out, regardless that her participation was mildly coerced. With only ten minutes given him, he needed to share the most pertinent information first. The rest would reveal itself in due time, as she helped him fill in the blanks.

"Nine minutes," she said, her voice steely, cold. The careful, warm tone she used with Andrew had disappeared. She had her back against the counter near the sink, her elbow resting on the arm crossed at her waist. Her fingers weren't covering her neck in the usual manner. However, the wineglass she held close to her chin effectively accomplished the same objective.

He began a slow walk around the kitchen, remembering it as it had been back when he was alive. Happy memories of Annie surfaced, as this was her room, her space. He stopped before the rusted iron stove.

"I bought this for her. For Annie," he said, recalling the joy on her face when she'd cooked her first successful meal for him, though he'd savored all the unsuccessful ones, too. His finger scratched over the surface. "It needs some work, but it's salvageable."

Resuming his stroll about the kitchen, reminiscing over his past in a way he hadn't done in decades, he eventually came to a halt beside Cassie. She didn't move away when he braced his palms against the edge of the sink before the window. His hand was so close to her hip, he could feel warmth radiating off her body. It was no wonder, as her long, slender thighs were exposed nearly to her womanhood. He'd had two days to adjust to her meager apparel. It distracted him, but he wouldn't allow it to hinder his seeking her assistance.

"As I tried to explain upstairs, before you interrupted me, I need your help to find out what happened to my wife. At first, I thought she'd run off, that she left me for someone else . . . someone better, perhaps."

"But you said she's de—"

He held up a finger, silencing her interruption. "But it didn't make sense. We squabbled some, true, but nothing so bad that suggested she'd want to leave."

Annie's disappearance from his life crushed every ounce of joy and love he'd been capable of feeling. It wasn't until much, much later—decades perhaps—that his anger at the devastation left in her wake abated.

He'd never learned the details of how or why she died, only that she had. The wait had been long, but fate had finally intervened, and Cassie was here. All the answers were imminent. Why she, but none of the others who'd lived within these walls, could see into the past, Carrington didn't know. Nor did he care. She was the one.

Cassie lowered her glass. "She must have had her reasons for leaving," she said brusquely, the same assumptions in her voice as he'd heard from those back in his time—those who judged him unworthy of Annie.

He ignored the old feelings that threatened to resurface and instead opted to relieve Cassie of her ignorance.

"It wasn't until Annie turned up dead that I knew she hadn't run away. She'd been murdered." In his peripheral vision, he saw her fingers clutch the counter, her face going paper white. It didn't take a genius to guess her thoughts; the hand that crept around her marred throat did the job.

"I did *not* hurt my wife. I know all this seems impossible, but I assure you it's real and you're the only person who can help me get the answers I seek."

Despair mingled with hope as he waited for her to respond. He stepped away from her, putting the space of an arm's length between them. A wide range of emotions flitted across her face as endless questions raced around inside her head. The grandfather clock gonged in the living room, each second between the hour's call seeming as long as the decades he'd waited for this opportunity.

She rolled her eyes, mumbled something Carrington didn't quite catch and snagged the bottle of wine off the counter.

"I need to sit, and I need to drink," she said as she stalked from the room. "I'm not really sure why I'm believing all this, but I suppose I don't have much of a say in the matter."

Carrington collected the newspapers and journal off the counter where he'd set them earlier and followed at her heels.

Cassie deposited the bottle and her glass on the coffee table in the living room, and then went around turning on nearby lamps. It was getting late, and though it wasn't yet dark, twilight was approaching. She appeared to be preparing for a long night. That was a promising start.

Once she was seated, he sank down opposite her on the oversized sofa that smelled strongly of tanned animal hide. He angled toward her, one arm draped over the back of the seat and waited as she fidgeted as far into the seat's corner as possible. Unwilling to risk her changing her mind, he jumped right in with his story.

"As I said before, that day she disappeared, we fought, and I'd left to cool down. When I returned, my house was on fire, and she was gone." He rolled his shoulders back, easing the tension that pinched deep into his muscles as he retrieved the haunting memories.

"For a long time, I could only assume that it was she who lit up the house before taking off for parts unknown. It devastated me to think she hated me that much, and that I'd been oblivious to her unhappiness. Then they found her body, and I knew she hadn't left of her own accord." The years of waiting was suddenly overwhelming, and his head drooped forward with his despair.

From the moment he'd met Annie, it seemed their lives had been set on a path of destruction. "I have to know what went wrong, what I missed that could have changed the outcome." He didn't add that he wished he could change both their outcomes because he wasn't ready to share that part of his story yet. If Cassie knew everything, she'd run. He needed to tread carefully, earn her trust and confidence. Only then would he tell her the circumstances surrounding his own death.

"That's why I need your help."

Cassie pulled the tail of her hair over one shoulder and played with it. "How can *I* help? I can't believe I think I'm sitting here talking to a real person. You certainly seem real enough. No different in fact than how you looked, oh, I don't know, before indoor plumbing was a thing."

Prior to his demise, he'd read about the concept of indoor plumbing and was considering the possibility during the rebuilding of his house. He'd not managed to get it added before his world, and quite literally his life, ended.

"It's Annie's journal. I think if you keep reading, you'll find out what happened to her. I only know what took place in her life when I was with her. Like at the dance."

Cassie had shifted forward and sat with elbows balanced on top of her knees. She rubbed at her temples and forehead, but at his words, she spread her fingers and peeked over at him. The dance had been the beginning of it all, and she'd gotten to feel what Annie felt that day.

"Why don't you read it yourself?" she questioned.

He shook his head. "It doesn't work for me. You're the first person it's ever called to."

She leaned back into the seat, her arms curled across her waist. Her knuckles turned white when she squeezed her elbows. "I've heard the excuses before. Men swear they didn't do anything wrong. Men who swear they'll never hurt their women again. But they lie. And they do hurt them. Sometimes worse. Why should I believe *you* didn't kill her?"

Without directly saying as much, he knew she was speaking of her own circumstances. She wasn't hiding her scar from him, either. She sat open and exposed, allowing him the chance to witness the damage that had been inflicted upon her.

With genuine empathy, he simply replied, "You'll have to trust that I'm not a bad man and that I didn't harm her."

She made a frustrated sound in her throat. "When did you die? How did you die? You're a ghost, right? I'm really not totally making this all up in my head. Am I?"

Had the table been turned, he'd have never believed the possibility, either. It truly was a strange phenomenon to experience death and the afterlife. Smiling, and relaxing in a way he hadn't in years—he hoped not prematurely—he attempted to put Cassie's mind at ease.

"I died long ago. I promise to tell you everything, in due time. And yes, I suppose 'ghost' is what I am."

She considered him, processing the limited information he divulged. Fortunately, she didn't press for the specifics surrounding his death, as he anticipated. Instead, she asked, "How does it work? Was it like the movie *Ghost* where white shadows come for you if you're good and black ones if you're bad?"

Carrington cocked his head. "I beg your pardon?"

Her head tilted likewise, but she waved a dismissive hand at him. "Never mind. Just, how are you a ghost?"

The answer to that question escaped him. He didn't know exactly how it happened. That explanation wouldn't appease Cassie, of that much he was certain. Yet he didn't want to say anything that might scare her off, either. He couldn't risk that, so he chose his words carefully.

"I'm not completely sure that I understand what happened. The term 'passed away' is as close to a fit as possible, I suppose. As I was transitioning from life to death, I was sort of pushed toward something I could anchor to."

She was paying close attention. She'd lifted her head and was watching him, less wary and more confused, but interest lit across her face, too.

"Anchor to what?"

He shrugged. "It's almost as if I had help. Like something or someone, I don't know, formed a path that I was able to follow. It led me here."

"Like the yellow brick road," she mumbled.

"What was that?"

Cassie huffed, causing strands of hair across her forehead to lift with the burst of air. "Nothing. What exactly do you think my reading her journal will do?"

Carrington held the diary up between them. "Go back. Find out what she did each day. Who she talked to or where she went. I need to know. Only then can I be free." He turned his head and gazed out the window. The rush of a small flock of birds settling down for the night in nearby trees outside punctuated the silence around him. When he felt the book ease from his grasp, he flinched.

"When I woke up before, after reading about you and then Annie . . ." Cassie traced the pad of an index finger over her lips. "When I returned, I don't even know if that's what to call it. Return? Wake up? Whatever. When I came back to being me, I tasted chocolate from the ice cream we had. And my fingers had marks from where Annie had gripped the tree trunk."

Strained seconds passed as she pieced together what Carrington worried about most: All the unknowns.

"The things that happen when I do that, go back I mean, are coming through to me here somehow, aren't they?"

He didn't want to acknowledge that. Not because he was trying to be evasive but because he truly didn't know the full extent of the risks Cassie faced in this endeavor. He saw what happened to her when she read from the newspaper and then the journal, or rather what happened through her. Following that logic, should Cassie find Annie's killer, she'd risk facing the same peril as his wife. His murdered wife.

With that grim potential in mind, he replied as honestly as possible, "I don't know for certain. But it does seem that you are affected somehow by what happens when you're there."

"How is any of this possible? I mean the papers and the diary. Why me?" Lines appeared across her forehead as her face tightened into a frown of confusion.

"I don't know," he said, somewhat apologetically.

"So, you're a ghost who once lived over a hundred years ago, who is now in my living room, whom I'm having a conversation with, while"—she sucked in a large breath—"not enjoying the nice wine I offered, I might add, and sitting on my couch with me in the year twenty-twenty." She tipped her wineglass back and drained it. Her cheeks bulged as she filled the cavern of her mouth with as much of the liquid as possible before gulping it down.

"I hear a lot of 'I don't knows' from you, which does not instill confidence, especially since what you're asking me to do is search for a murderer. And to really make things more fun, I'll be searching for that person while that person is likely stalking Annie." She pressed her fingers to her temples again and rubbed small circles there. "What's Andrew going to say about this?"

Carrington took one of Cassie's hands in his and squeezed. The last time he'd felt this hopeful and optimistic of what the future held was the day he'd wed Annie.

"I don't know what Andrew will say," he said with barely suppressed excitement. "But I can't tell you enough how much it means to me. I'll be forever in your debt."

NINE

"All right, I'll just go to the last entry she wrote and see who Annie had contact with before she disappeared." Cassie clutched the edges of the diary. She told herself if she went along with this fantasy, it would play out and Carrington would just disappear. He wasn't real. But it certainly felt real when his knee bumped against her thigh as he scooted closer.

She flipped to the last page that had writing on it and sagged with disappointment. The entry dated August 18, 1890, had been torn through and only a few words of each sentence were visible. She turned back one page and read an entry there instead.

"It's not working. Nothing's happening."

She flinched when Carrington covered her hands with his and pushed the pages open to the front of the book. He pointed at the second entry.

"Then we must have to start at the beginning, from where you left off earlier."

His skin was warm, solid. Not cold and ethereal. She didn't want to contemplate why or how that was possible but did so anyway. In all ways that were obvious, he was a flesh-and-blood man, except for the one: He was a ghost. She'd seen him alive—had *been* him alive, even—in a different century. Being a ghost was the only explanation for his presence that seemed plausible. But how could a ghost feel warm and appear so alive?

"I'm not going to stumble upon anymore scenes with you and Suzanne, or anyone else for that matter, am I?"

A slow grin spread across his face. "You won't find me with anyone but Annie. However," he added, the color of his irises shifting to a dark gray, "as you've already experienced, what's written in the book and what you live through are different. I can't promise that what happens won't include things my wife *didn't* write down, things we did together when we were alone." Both his eyebrows flicked up.

Cassie smiled sarcastically. "A witty ghost. That's what I need in my life right now." She should be terrified, yet for reasons she couldn't identify, she wasn't. Maybe it was because he'd had ample opportunity to inflict harm but hadn't done anything suspect, yet. Except, of course, be his ghostly self.

"I'll be right here beside you the whole time." The smooth tenor of his voice rattled her senses.

"That's what I'm afraid of," she admitted. Lifting the journal, she read out loud, for Carrington's sake.

"'August third, eighteen ninety. I was in town today and stumbled across Mr. Hanson. He asked if he could call on me. I'm certain he's not who I favor, so I suggested instead we walk at the park.'"

Cassie paused to verify something. "Blake was your field hand, right?"

Carrington shifted in his seat, pushing one leg out, giving off an air of casual calm; however, his angry scowl contradicted his body language. "Yes. He was a bit of a lazy cuss. I spent more time telling him to get back to work than he spent working."

"Why didn't you just fire him?" At the tight look of perplexity across his face, she restated her question. "Why didn't you let him go?"

His lips pursed in silent consideration. "He was the only person around town willing to work for me. As bad as he was, at least he was some help."

A flush of excitement warmed Cassie's middle when Carrington tapped his heel, which resulted in his leg brushing up and down against hers. It was unpresumptuous, but electrifying, nonetheless. She was beginning to understand Annie's difficulty in choosing which man to pursue, Blake or Carrington, if pursue was the right term. Carrington exuded strength and sex appeal, while Blake was somewhat shy and sweet.

Cassie knew girls didn't date back then, certainly not more than one man at a time. They courted. They entered semi-relationships, something close to a marriage without the vows. Or the sex. She highly doubted it would be considered acceptable to meet Blake for a walk outside the confines of parental acceptance or courtship. Annie was clearly a bit more progressive than her time permitted it seemed.

"You go, girl." Cassie raised her glass in a silent praise before taking a restorative swig of wine.

"I believe it may have been Blake or Suzanne who killed Annie."

Liquid spewed from Cassie's mouth. She coughed several seconds to clear the bit that crept down her throat wrong. Once recovered, she turned to Carrington. The muscle at his jaw twitched. The intensity of his demeanor unnerved her. She swiped across her lips with her forearm.

"Blake invited Annie for a walk in the park. And you want *me* to go back and spend time with him after saying that?"

"It's clear that Annie remained alive during and after that little visit with Hanson." He nodded at the journal, implying the future entries Cassie had yet to get through. "Read," he commanded, in a tone suggesting he was used to people doing whatever he said.

With exaggerated slowness, Cassie swiped at some invisible crumb and pressed a corner of the book's already flat page even more flat. If she was going to agree to this, she'd do it on her own terms.

When she did finally begin to read again, she was better prepared for that feeling of all gravity leaving the room as she slipped into the different world of the past.

***

Annie and Blake were rounding the corner near the bank, headed down Seventh Avenue toward the park. It was the same path she and Carrington had taken after he'd whisked Annie away from the dance. She wasn't holding onto Blake's arm or doing anything that might be deemed inappropriate, at least Cassie didn't think so. Still, many of the men and women they passed stopped to stare or turned and spoke in hushed whispers once they believed they were out of ear shot.

She knew Annie was equally exhilarated and nervous about her uncharacteristic break from the conforming little lady that she'd been brought up to be. She also knew Annie wasn't feeling any sense of regret about it.

It was mid-afternoon and the day was very warm. She scratched at her forehead where the hat perched atop Annie's head rested against her scalp. Cassie hated hats.

A lone gentleman with a large paunch straining against the fabric of a shirt stretched to its limit walked past. He had a fat cigar pressed between his lips. Cassie walked straight through a billowy puff of white smoke escaping from the man's mouth. She coughed and fanned the disgusting carcinogen-laden cloud away. At least they were outdoors. She held her tongue, not blurting out that cigars were cancer sticks. She'd need to be careful not to extend her twenty-first century dictates on the less civilized nineteenth.

Except for this stupid hat. She scrubbed at her forehead again. The object of her disdain didn't budge when she ran a finger beneath it, which meant there was a hatpin somewhere. As casually as possible, she poked about the hat's surface, searching for the spherical end.

"You look pretty today," Blake said as they neared the park.

They were walking at a slow stroll, a respectful distance between them. Cassie tried to assess her companion out of the corner of one eye.

"Thank you," she replied, demurely.

Annie was a proper young lady. But beneath the exterior, there was a girl desperate for something exciting. She was brimming with restless energy, wanting more than church on Sunday or the ladies' prayer group on Wednesday.

She was titillated by all the events happening in the country. At the forefront of her daydreams was the women's suffrage movement. Annie desperately wanted to take part in something so bold and thrilling. But she feared her father's response as well as those of the eligible bachelors in town who were her only prospects for marriage. Suffragette or not, she didn't want to end up a spinster.

It was becoming clear to Cassie why Annie had been willing to buck society not once—the dance and Carrington—but here again with Blake. The girl had grit!

But, grit or no, she would soon die. And Cassie had become party to determining why.

"So, tell me a little about you, Mr. Hanson. What brought you to Caldwell?" That seemed like something Annie would inquire about, and relevant to Cassie's research.

There was a reflective pause, as if he didn't want to talk about himself. "Not much to tell about me. I'm a bit of a loner, came over from California. After mother died, I landed here. Had nothing really, and this place was booming, so I decided to put roots down and see what happened."

He'd removed his hat, and it dangled from his hand. His hair, a bit unruly, looked like the wind had grabbed it and tousled it about. He ran his fingers across his head, isolating the cause of the disarray.

She noticed an interesting quirk about him—he kept his head down almost boyishly, rarely making eye contact with her. All that was needed to complete the image of youth was for him to force his hands into his pockets and scuff the toe of his boot in the dirt. But he was no juvenile. He and Carrington couldn't have been more than a year apart in age.

"I'm sorry," she said kindly after catching the hint of sadness in his voice. "What about your father?"

"My father died before I got to meet him. I have no family left." He lifted his head and smiled.

In contradiction to his darker persona, Blake's gap-toothed grin made him appear easygoing, mischievous. Fortunately, he grinned often, too. He certainly smiled more than his boss, she thought.

Recalling Carrington's opinion of Blake and his wont for not being at work when he was supposed to be brought Cassie to a halt.

"What day is it?" She finally located the nub of the hatpin and released the slim weapon. Annie's hair was rolled into a bun against the back of her head. Releasing the pin had caused a few strands to pull free and they lifted out and around her face when she removed the hat.

Blake, curiously observing her liberation, shook his head at Cassie's sigh of delight. "It's Sunday. Did you forget that you went to church today?"

Covering up her blunder, she laughed. "Of course not. I, uh, just wondered why you weren't out working."

A look of apprehension crossed his face, causing tiny lines to form around his mouth and the corners of his eyes.

The hum of voices from a small group of women out for a stroll in the park filtered through the air. A few feet behind the women were an equal number of men, most had their jackets flung over their shoulders.

Parallel to the park was the street where horses and riders clopped past. Various buggies glided by while the larger wagons and buckboards rattled off to whatever their intended destination was. Birds twittered away in nearby trees and the sun beat down, warming Cassie's skin. All the elements combined were relaxing and peaceful in a way that someone from the future could, or should, appreciate. Considering her predicament, it helped her to remain calm. Even though the circumstances were wildly strange, she realized she was enjoying the past.

"I get Sundays off to observe the Sabbath, like most folks," Blake said as he settled his hat back on his head.

"Of course. I didn't mean to imply you shouldn't get the time off." She bit one corner of her lip. Carrington had put it in her head that Blake was some sort of slacker. She'd have to be careful and take his remarks with a grain of salt, and learn things as they were on her own.

"How long have you worked for Mr. Chambers?" It was time to get to the heart of why she was there.

"Chambers? A bit shy of a year, I reckon. It's a decent job. He's fair, and we get along well enough, I suppose." His fingers drummed against the side of his thigh in an unsteady rhythm. Cassie wondered if it was a nervous habit or if the thought of Carrington caused some unease.

"What's his deal anyway? Why aren't folks here nice to him? I mean, he did the crime and served his time. Shouldn't he be given a second chance?"

The article she'd read indicated that he killed a man and served seven years in prison. She admitted that in her own time, even she would have a hard time giving him a second chance. There had to be extenuating circumstances. They wouldn't set a murderer free. Would they? Considering that she was there to find a murderer, the questions she neglected to ask about Carrington seemed very relevant all of a sudden. Questions she probably should have gotten answers to prior to agreeing to her current endeavors.

Blake slowed his walk and peered down at her with a bewildered look in his eyes. "People here don't trust a man who'd shoot someone in the back. I know you're too young to know much of what happened, but the town's leaders are working hard to be rid of the reputation so typical in these railroad communities. You should be cautious around him. Most folks steer clear of him with good reason."

Was that genuine concern in his voice or was he intentionally trying to redirect her focus away from Carrington?

"Except for you," he went on. His hands thrust down into his pockets and he lowered his head before continuing his previous pace. "Why are you so intrigued by him?"

Cassie wondered the same. The answers were there, in Annie's memories. She was able to discern that the girl was only twenty-three, brimming with a desire to escape the dull, conforming life her parents steered her into. She was bored. So, when Carrington asked her to dance that day, she threw caution to the wind. The rumors tagged him as a monster, but Annie found him charming, polite, and civilized, apart from the near kiss beneath the tree.

But she'd wanted that kiss, too.

A warm, fuzzy feeling slithered up Cassie's spine at the memory of Carrington: all long legs, tough body, biceps she couldn't wrap her hands around, and his lips . . .

A heated blush rose up Annie's chest. She pressed her hand against her throat, hoping it blocked the embarrassing hue of her skin.

"Well?" Blake urged.

"Mr. Chambers has already been punished." Cassie offered him a sad smile and shrugged. "We shouldn't cast judgment." Her voice lowered to a dreamy whisper as she stared off at the passersby along the street. "He deserves a chance, I think." For reasons unknown, she believed what she just said. But she would most certainly press Carrington for the details of what landed him in prison, once she returned to her time.

Blake reached down and clasped her hand in his, giving it a squeeze. "Most people 'round here do judge. Ever since the sheriff decided the town needed to be civilized, that is. Sheriff Anders has made it his personal mission to cast out everyone who doesn't fit. Especially Chambers." He inched closer and pressed their joined hands to his chest. "You and I are much better suited."

So focused was she on the forlorn and sympathetic feelings she held for Carrington, Cassie didn't immediately notice that the man of her current dreams—or nightmares—was standing at the street's edge about fifteen feet away.

And he was staring directly at her. More specifically, at Annie, but for Cassie, there was no distinction between them.

"Shit!" Her reflexive expletive had come out a little too loud.

Blake's shocked expression disappeared as his attention followed hers. Upon seeing Carrington, he waved with his free hand.

Cassie could tell Carrington was pissed. She had to force her rapidly beating heart to slow down. Distressed at finding him there watching her, she didn't notice the other person standing behind him, snuggled tight against his back.

Suzanne.

Guiltily, Cassie tugged her hand from Blake's grasp. The action didn't go unnoticed by Carrington. He tensed, and his eyes shrank to slits.

Suzanne beamed and wiggled her fingers at Annie in a triumphant wave. She then splayed her palm over Carrington's abdomen, as if to prove their intimate relationship, which Cassie unfortunately couldn't burn from her mind. Before she could say something, which both she and Annie wanted to do, Carrington turned away and staggered off.

"Oh, for shit's sake," Cassie whispered.

Blake laughed, low. For all his darkness, he had a light, playful temperament that helped dispel some of her nervousness. At least for the moment. And he'd just suggested that he'd like to be more than a friend to Annie.

"Chambers would do himself a lot of favors if he wouldn't drown his sorrows in the bottle and wind up in a jail cell on a regular basis. He should steer clear of Miss Thomas, too. She's got some strange ways about her," he added.

Cassie shook off the rush of excitement at mention of the time Carrington had left the local jailhouse, and the scene that followed. Nervous habit had her reaching for her ponytail, but all she found was the bun Annie sported. So, instead, she captured a wisp of hair that had broken free of its constraints and twirled it nervously around a finger.

"Yes. If he wouldn't do that."

The rest of her time with Blake was unremarkable, with him doing his best to entertain Annie. The distraction helped ease Cassie's turbulent thoughts.

So far, she found Blake a perfect gentleman. There was nothing in his behavior or story that would give her cause to suspect him as a possible murderer. His declared romantic interest was mostly innocent, too, as he didn't mention or press the matter again. She wondered if jealousy would come into play later.

At the end of their walk, Blake escorted her almost all the way home, but Annie made him stop short, so her parents didn't catch them.

"Thank you for a wonderful visit, Miss Annie." Blake leaned in and brushed a light kiss across her cheek, setting Annie's heart to flutter. With nothing left to say, he bid her farewell and strolled off, whistling a happy tune.

But Annie had other plans that didn't include going home.

***

Carrington eased Cassie down onto the couch after she'd slumped against him. His lap was her pillow. A lock of hair tumbled over her forehead. He pushed it aside. The skin beneath his fingertips was soft and warm. It had been a long time since he'd touched another person or had one touch him. Now here he was with a lovely woman, albeit one with the darndest inclination to curse, slumbering peacefully against him. Helping him.

He knew she was scared—scared of that which she couldn't explain. He could appreciate that. If the same had happened to him when he'd been alive, his response to seeing a ghost might have been similar. But her fears extended beyond just him. She was haunted by someone far worse than him, someone who lived in her nightmares. The one who had hurt her.

Carrington knew that time would help him prove that *he* posed no threat to her. As for the other threat? Jimmy. That he couldn't change. If what happened to Cassie had happened in his lifetime, he'd have killed him for her.

Still, fears notwithstanding, she was allowing herself to be vulnerable in order to help him. He'd never had anyone sacrifice themselves like that before, not for him. Suzanne helped him some in his darkest hours, but only when it benefited her. Cassie's willingness was humbling and a bit overwhelming. His instinct to protect her was blurring his desire for redemption. Which couldn't happen. He'd waited too long for answers.

So angry was he about Annie's death, and his own, he'd refused his soul to depart this world, allowing whatever guided him to this place to do so. Over the years he'd given some consideration to giving up and crossing over to wherever it was that people went after they died. However, those plans were short lived. Not only because of Annie, but also because he'd never been able to figure out how to leave. It seemed he was destined to spend eternity waiting for answers that would never come.

Until Cassie arrived.

Somehow, he knew that his wait was over, and his ghostly life would cease once she unearthed the truths hidden in the past. But if what he believed might be true, her life could be the price for his eternity. Could he exist afterward knowing that?

He lightly traced a finger along the path of the jagged scar over her throat. The skin was puffy and soft, rising a hair's breadth higher than the surrounding tissue. His fingers splayed wide, fully covering the front of her neck like a shield. Beneath his fingertips, he felt her strong, steady pulse where her blood—her life—raced through her veins.

She'd experienced a terrible trauma. Had nobody been there to help her, afterward? Unbridled disgust at those who'd failed to protect her—like he'd failed to protect his own wife—consumed him.

Cassie was doing her best to put up a brave front, out here alone, until he'd made his presence known. His eyes roamed every soft feature of her face. She didn't resemble Annie at all, except maybe the freckles on her nose. She certainly didn't act or talk like his wife, yet there was something about her that drew his interest, something reminiscent of his past.

Suddenly Cassie gasped, and her pulse began to race beneath his fingertips. When she uttered the words "Oh, shit," his mood darkened.

He remembered the day Annie had written about. The day she'd met Blake at the park.

Suzanne had found him stumbling along the boardwalk and latched onto him. As they passed near the park, he'd seen them—Blake and Annie. When he lurched to a halt, Suzanne had admonished him for being drunk. He hadn't been that drunk.

Annie was beside Blake, her hand in his, tucked close against his chest. It appeared Carrington had interrupted a tender moment between them.

He knew he hadn't had the right to be angry. He was, nonetheless. Suzanne tried to veer him in the other direction, but he'd shrugged her off as his anger festered.

She'd slipped her hand around his torso at the same moment that Annie looked their way. Annie hadn't cursed like Cassie had just done, but the tight knot of worry on her face had relayed her hurt all the same.

He'd felt so conflicted, as that day beneath the tree, the day of the dance, he was certain he hadn't misunderstood her desire for him. Seeing her with Blake made him question if it had only been his imagination that she wanted him to kiss her.

Hurt and angry, he'd turned away, unwilling to watch his only real prospect for a wife—Suzanne didn't count—choose another man.

He shifted his leg, as it had begun to fall asleep. Cassie stirred. Gently, he stroked her forehead until the crease that appeared there smoothed away. The journal lay open on her lap and he read the next entry, smiling smugly as the words on the page brought forth another memory. One that had apparently been as memorable for Annie as it had been for him. Enough that she'd written about it, at least.

Cassie made a small sound before her eyelids fluttered open. They widened in mild alarm, before she jerked upright.

Carrington watched the past she'd been enmeshed in fade as her mind caught up to her body in the present.

"Well," she started in immediately, ticking off on her fingers her observations. "The only things I garnered from that encounter are that Annie liked Blake. She also liked you. You were drunk—again," she berated him. "And, Suzanne has apparently laid claim to you."

Exhaustion suddenly had her wilting like a flower. She yawned and stretched her arms high overhead. "This is all very tiring. I don't think I can take anymore tonight. Can we continue tomorrow?"

He nodded as she got to her feet. Retrieving a flashlight that had been left on the end table, she headed up the stairs. Halfway up she stopped, her hand gripping the railing.

"You were here watching me that first night, weren't you? There, in the corner." She pointed toward the spot near the fireplace.

He smiled a little sadly. "I was. I haven't left the property in a *very* long time."

Confusion flashed behind her eyes, then she bobbed her head firmly, once, before trudging the rest of the way up and off to her room.

TEN

The following morning when Cassie woke, she recalled with great clarity the feel of Blake's hand in Annie's and the smell of the man's cigar. There was no distinction in her mind between those memories and her own.

"This is just crazy." She tossed the quilted bedspread aside, drew her knees up and laced her fingers over her belly.

She was in the master bedroom of the house. This part of the structure hadn't existed in Carrington's days. Considering the layout of the original design, it stood to reason that what was now the den off the living room below had been Carrington's bedroom. It was small and probably wouldn't have fit anything larger than a double-sized bed and maybe a nightstand, possibly an armoire or vanity.

But the house Carrington had shared with Annie had burned down. What Cassie owned now was the rebuild, with remodel and upgrades. The room below her was the living room. The chimney running up the outer wall of the house connected to the fireplaces in both the rooms, above and below. Whoever did the redesign, made the master bedroom impressively large, big enough to accommodate Cassie's king-sized bed, a nightstand, a tall dresser, and an armoire. The space was additionally cluttered with a ladder, tarp, and various other supplies. When the movers unpacked the truck, she had them deliver those items straight to her room, knowing it would be the first place she'd paint.

This bedroom would have fit Carrington, both his size and personality, much better than the original master.

In the bathroom down the hall, there was a claw-foot tub, which she couldn't wait to try out. Carrington likely hadn't had indoor plumbing back in his day. The main floor had a small half-bathroom off the living room now, but she'd wager it was added when the second floor was built. She'd have to ask him about it.

She imagined him leaning against the fireplace mantel downstairs, his foot propped on the raised hearth as he contemplated his day or mourned a wife he no longer had. Had he been the one to rebuild the original part of the house after the fire, in hopes that Annie would return? Did he dream of the two of them basking in the glow of a fire as they lounged on a bear skin rug after some passionate lovemaking session?

Cassie knifed up into a sitting position. "You have *got* to get your act together, McAllister. I mean really, who has a bear skin rug?"

Sliding her legs over the edge of the bed she stood and stretched from head to toe. Mid-stretch, she froze. It was a new day. Was it possible everything she'd experienced, the reading, the drifting through time, and Carrington, had only been a dream? Aside from distinctly recalling the feel of Blake's hand in hers and knowing that up close he had a dark mole along his hairline near his temple, it could have all been something she'd made up.

"Oh, wait," she chided herself. "Let's not forget that you don't even know anyone with the names of those people you keep encountering in dreams or . . . or . . . whatever it is that's happening."

She stomped across the room and rummaged through one of the boxes arranged in the corner in search of clothes and toiletries. Without electricity to the bathroom yet, she was unable to do little more than run a comb through her hair and put on fresh clothes. But that was good enough for now, considering she hoped to spend most of the day unpacking.

Ten minutes later, she was dressed and had her hair pulled up high in a ponytail. The yellow and white print sundress she wore was bright and summery. It reflected exactly the way she wanted her mood to remain all day. Needing a much-deserved break from her own crazy thoughts, she decided to run to town for a few things.

First, she needed coffee.

She fairly skipped down the stairs and into the kitchen . . . before coming to a screeching halt in the doorway.

Kneeling, with his back to her, a shirtless Carrington was vigorously scrubbing the black stove with a wire brush. Cassie's breath caught in her throat as she saw his muscles flex and bunch with every movement of his hand. She followed the curve of each muscle from his shoulders, down over his triceps, to the center of his back. In a strictly platonic way, of course, she admired his extraordinarily fit torso, glistening with sweat, and his tight oblique muscles that trimmed down to his waistline.

The breath she'd been holding exploded in a loud rush of air.

Carrington twisted about on his knees. "Good morning, darlin'."

He couldn't help his sexiness, the way his smooth words rolled off his tongue. Calling her darling was just a bonus. Cassie swallowed a fast rush of saliva that filled her mouth. She hurried to the counter and got a pot of coffee on to brew, desperate for the caffeine.

"Good morning," she said. No "darlin'" from her. "Did you sleep well?" She watched the first few drops of coffee trickle into the pot, while at the same time chiding herself for wondering if ghosts slept.

Carrington set aside the wire brush and stood. Facing her, he stretched, flexing the muscles of his chest. Cassie ogled him in the window's reflection.

"I rested," he replied.

"What's going on here?" She turned and pointed with her chin to the stove, ignoring his rippling pectoral muscles as he wiped his hands on one of her small kitchen towels. She tried hard not to imagine her fingers stroking over his chest and smoothing the hair down to—

"It needed some cleaning first, before I could polish it. I've never had the supplies, or the desire really, to clean it up. Until now." He flashed a smile, which caused butterflies to lift and flutter about in Cassie's chest. "Are you going out today?" His eyes roved over her body from head to toe and back up.

Cassie shivered at the arc of electricity that shot up her spine. To disguise her involuntary response to his attention, she retrieved two cups from the cupboard.

"Yes, I need to get a few things. Is there anything you want?"

"There is. I need some polish to finish the stove. While you're at the livery or mercantile, I could also use some nails and a saw." The coffee pot gurgled, and the smell of the rich brew filled the air. Cassie poured out two cups.

He accepted the one she handed him and sniffed its contents before taking his first sip. His face broke into a mask of sheer delight. "At least this hasn't changed much."

Cassie was ignorant as to what a ghost might not get to experience, but so far, the list included whiskey and coffee.

It also occurred to her that he'd not eaten anything. Of course, she hadn't stopped to eat much since his appearance in her life, so it was possible she was the cause for his fast. That had to be it. She didn't want to speculate on how long it had been since he'd eaten.

"When was the last time you had coffee? Or food?" She shook her head at her mouth's unwillingness to comply with her brain.

Carrington moved closer. Close enough that she had to tilt her head back. The color of his eyes had changed to a dark gray, which she'd already learned meant he was angry or feeling some other intense emotion—neither boded well for her. One of his hands came to rest on her shoulder, his thumb making small circles above her collarbone.

"It's been a very long time," he said, hypnotizing her with the soothing movement.

"Have you ever heard of the Beatles? Elvis?"

He smiled and nodded. "I have, actually. Though not how you'd understand, I imagine." The circular motion of his thumb stopped.

"When did you die?" She'd asked before, but he'd evaded answering. For all she knew, his death might have occurred as late as the nineteen-sixties. It was possible he'd known of the legendary entertainers through radio or television. Every muscle in her body went rigid, tense and alert.

His fingers squeezed lightly on the top of her shoulder. He nudged her chin up with a thumb and forefinger. "I died long ago."

Her mouth opened but no words came out. She clamped her lips together. Before she could formulate a response, he inched even closer, into her personal space.

"I'd go with you if I could."

Cassie's legs wobbled like Jell-O in a mold, and she would have slid to the floor were it not for the counter at her back. She finally blinked, breaking the spell he'd woven around her.

"What?" she asked, trying to recall what he'd said, after intentionally not answering her question.

"To town. I'd go if I could. Are you going to put on the rest of your clothes first?" His palm slipped down to cover her bare shoulder cap, his fingers squeezing against her scapula while his thumb massaged the upper pectoral muscle.

It was another few seconds before she comprehended that he was criticizing her attire. "What's wrong with my dress?"

"It's barely more than a shift," he admonished lightly.

"What?" she asked again. The dress she'd selected offered relatively modest coverage. Then it dawned on her that the level of modesty between his time and hers had drastically changed.

She held her arms out. "This is definitely appropriate in today's society." Cassie forced her hands onto her hips and told him she could wear anything she wanted. She wasn't Annie nor was she living in the nineteenth century; therefore, he couldn't boss her around.

He *harrumphed* but acquiesced. "If you say so. Maybe I could persuade you to read the next entry in Annie's little book before you go?"

It appeared that he was bargaining acceptance of her attire for a trip back in time. She wasn't certain there was a bargain to be had. When he smiled, the resulting effect transformed his typical stern, hard features into an image that could land him on the cover of GQ.

Cassie scrubbed one hand over her face, trying to dispel the tingly feeling that ignited deep inside her. He seemed eager for her to read. She checked the time. It was still early, so she agreed, but only after she finished her first cup of coffee.

They say if it's too good to be true, it probably is.

That was her new motto when it came to Carrington. He was everything Jimmy and most men of her time were not, especially the ghost part. That alone threw him out of the market, if she were interested in shopping.

She'd tried to go on dates with a few guys, after Jimmy. But she'd lost her ability to trust men. Trust was something that required being earned, and she'd not been able to give anyone the time to earn it. As a result, she gave up on men and escaped into her own small world, protected by her status of being alone. Single. Forever.

She eyeballed Carrington suspiciously as she sat cross-legged on the couch, dress tucked between her legs. Her inner voice screamed that she wouldn't like what she was about to read. Still, she reached for Annie's journal and returned to the page where she'd left off and continued with the next entry, which happened to be the same date as the last.

"'August third, again. I know I shouldn't have done it, but I snuck away from the house after my walk with Mr. Hanson. I needed to think and couldn't stand the idea of being cooped up inside on such a lovely evening. While strolling along the boardwalk I stumbled upon Mr. Chambers. Quite literally. He was outside the saloon, leaning against the wall.'"

Cassie paused in her reading and fixed Carrington with a derisive glare. "Really? You had your fun with Suzanne, then immediately went after the innocent one?"

Carrington's irises darkened, and he smiled mischievously. "Think what you will. Keep reading."

"You're sure a bossy figment of my imagination." She ignored the throaty sound he elicited and continued to read, until her present surroundings faded away into the darkness.

***

Annie had chosen to go for a stroll through town after her visit with Blake. Cassie sensed her worry that her father would severely reprimand her for wandering about alone—but only if she got caught.

She was slinking around the area of Seventh Avenue and Front Street, keeping within a respectable distance of the Pacific Hotel. However, whenever someone approached, she ducked behind nearby beams, barrels, and any other sort of obstacle she could find.

Cassie wondered what Annie was up to . . . and then she heard it. The lively tinkling of a piano and twang of a banjo chased up the street. There was also the sound of raised voices of several men. Mixed in with the raucous chatter was an assortment of women's laughter and squeals of rowdy delight. Annie's skin heated at the thought of *those* women. The town whores. She'd heard of them and had even seen one or two in the mercantile on occasion, but never had she witnessed them during their . . . whoring.

What on earth is this girl doing? Cassie wondered. No respectable young lady would be out and about at this hour, at least not without an escort. Annie's father would indeed tan her hide if he ever found out. What was of such interest that she'd do something this risky?

Was she searching for Carrington? Is that why she was in this area of town? A second later, she stumbled upon her answer. The words "quite literally" written in the diary were spot on.

"Hullo, sweetheart," Carrington slurred as Annie inched past the doorway where all the loud noises came from. He was perched against the wall of the wood building, one booted foot propped against the structure. As she walked past, he reached for her, gripping her arm tightly but not in a hurtful way.

Cassie let her arms hang at her sides. Carrington's eyes were a little bloodshot. He didn't appear to be as drunk as she first imagined, when she'd seen him with Suzanne earlier.

A curious foreboding settled over Cassie. What had ghost Carrington gotten her into? Why was he so eager for her to read this scene before she left for her errands?

The bawdy words of at least two men inside the establishment reached Cassie's ears. When a woman squealed in laughter and replied with an equally vulgar phrase, Annie's face bloomed hot and she took a hesitant step back.

"Come on, sweetheart. Don't run away."

He tried to pull her against him, but Cassie held him at arm's length. He may not be stumbling drunk, but he'd certainly had his fair share of spirits. The smell of whiskey washed over her, sharp and a little overbearing. That flicker of suspicion nagged at her again, whether it was fear or anticipation she wasn't certain.

"Let's walk." He snatched at her hand and tucked it in the crook of his arm, firmly holding it in place before shuffling them down the street. Their destination appeared to be a large cluster of trees just ahead.

It was late summer in Idaho, which meant long days, late sunsets. As such, it was still light out as the sun reached for the western horizon. Entering the copse of trees, Cassie's eyes didn't immediately adjust from the bright light to the darkness of their shelter. Her hand flexed on Carrington's arm as they headed along a small path to the far side of the circle. They stopped near a large tree growing in the center of the cluster of smaller ones. It didn't take much to understand the situation and Carrington's intent. Annie chewed at the corner of her lip, excited and nervous.

Carrington maneuvered them around an impressively large cottonwood and pressed her back against the tree. A flock of chirping black birds lit off from a nearby bush, the racket soon fading to a warm silence. In the distance, the sharp blurt of a train's whistle called out twice.

"Let's end this day right." Carrington's hands sank into her hair and he forced her head back as his lips lowered to hers.

Cassie's response was automatic. Her lips parted when his mouth moved against hers, warming her insides as pleasure rolled through her. The muscles beneath her palms were like coiled steel. They perfectly matched the vision she'd had of him in her kitchen only minutes ago—well, technically more than a century from now, but she wasn't going to think about that just then.

She opened her eyes and found him staring down into hers. The fire burning in their depths seared its way into her being. A warm, tingling sensation radiated upward from somewhere low in her belly. She squirmed against it, the movement bringing her body into contact with his.

He pressed closer, his leg wedging between hers. His hips nudged against her pelvis. Annie's sensibilities were becoming overwhelmed by all the sensations firing to life inside her. Carrington was relentless, fervently kissing her, not giving her time to draw breath. Her arms stole around his waist. She was lost on a tide of intense emotions and heat, drowning in it.

He was her life preserver.

His hand slid down the column of her neck and over one shoulder, then lower, his touch feather light as it brushed against the outer edge of her breast. He moaned when his palm cupped around the soft curve. Cassie felt him squeeze so gently she might have imagined it. All too soon, his hand fell away.

It was scandalous, yet exciting as hell. Annie was absolutely, one hundred percent turned on. Cassie disliked admitting that she was, too. But her mind struggled to wrap around the idea that the lithe, sweaty, muscled body she'd seen in her kitchen was as real as the man he was here.

She pressed both palms against his chest, believing she had the will to push him away. "We shouldn't be doing this here. For that matter, we shouldn't be doing this at all."

She turned her head, but all that did was give him access to another sensitive area of skin to kiss. His lips pecked along her jaw, across her ear, and lower, until they stopped to nuzzle a spot that made goosebumps prick up on her skin.

A glimpse of movement behind shrubbery ten feet away made Cassie still. She pushed harder, with real intent this time, against Carrington's chest. He pulled away, and she immediately missed the heat of his mouth against her skin.

"Shit," she hissed.

"You cuss like a sailor," he said against her lips before crushing her to him again. Then, like a light switch had been flipped, he stopped and rested his forehead against hers. They stood that way for countless seconds.

"I knew it would be like this between us." His voice was deep with emotion.

Cassie didn't know how Carrington knew, but whatever made him think it, he'd been right. Annie had just been swept away by a simple kiss.

She didn't stand a chance against him.

ELEVEN

When Cassie returned to the present, Carrington was sitting on the chair opposite from where she lay on the couch. She sprang to her feet and rounded on him.

"You seduced her? In a public setting no less!" she spat, while pointing an accusing finger at him. "Wouldn't that have ruined her reputation?"

A devilish smile lit across his face. "That was my intent." There wasn't the hint of regret or shame in his voice.

"What? I can't believe you'd—"

"You cuss like a sailor," he said, interrupting her tirade.

"You said the same thing in the trees a minute ago. When you were *seducing* the poor girl!"

"Annie didn't use language like that. *Ever.*"

Cassie lifted her chin and shrugged. "She does now."

"You're changing things."

"I'm sure it's fine. I didn't change anything other than a few little words. I don't think." It hadn't occurred to her that her actions might alter Annie's life. She'd have to be more careful as she traversed the past.

"How, uh, far did the two of you go, in the trees?" She sank back down onto the couch and began to fidget with the hem of her dress. "I mean, I pushed you away when I remembered I had a job to do. But did Annie stop you, or did I do something different there, too?"

Carrington barked out a laugh. "Well, I didn't do what I think you're getting at." He feigned offense, but the lively sparkle in his eyes said otherwise. "Did you want me to go further?" He winked at her.

Cassie sputtered with indignation, yet it was more likely her own guilt that caused her to act offended. She genuinely liked Annie. The girl was an innocent, someone who just wanted to explore life and be loved by somebody. That somebody was Carrington.

Being stuck in Annie's mind had Cassie feeling a bit like the other woman. That, of course, didn't make any sense. Carrington-of-the-past only saw his wife. She couldn't help what the couple did together. She also couldn't help the residual effects their actions were having on her.

"I think someone saw us, er, you and Annie that is. That poor, unsuspecting girl." She stood again and paced the room, one hand on her head, pulling her hair into a fist. "Why would you do that?"

One of Carrington's brows quirked up along with the side of his mouth. "Annie wasn't an unwilling participant, you might have noticed."

No, neither she nor Annie were, but she wouldn't admit that to him. "And you were drunk. Again!"

His smile disappeared. "You don't know anything about my life. There are things I'm not proud of, I admit, but sometimes . . ." He bowed his head in shame or despair, Cassie wasn't certain. "Sometimes the liquor was the only thing making life tolerable."

Her face tightened with her confusion. "Why did they hate you so much?" She scrambled to find anything that was *that* bad that a town full of derelicts, railroad men, miners, and the likes couldn't forgive.

A full range of emotions crossed over Carrington's face. He riffled through the old newspapers. Tucked between the pages of one, he located a small square section and pulled it out.

"Here." He thrust out his hand. Pinched between his fingers was a single page from one of the old newspapers, its fragile thinness revealing its age. It was more yellowed than the others, the ink faded almost to the color of pale pencil lead.

"Read this."

She eyed him skeptically then squared her shoulders, spine ramrod straight.

"Uh-uh." Her head moved side to side. "The last time I read one of those"—she pointed at the stack of newspapers in his lap— "I landed in *your* body doing unspeakable things to Suzanne." She wrinkled her nose in revulsion. "*With* Suzanne." A shudder raced through her at the erotic memory. It was one thing to be seduced by a man, as had happened while she was Annie, but to *be* the man and experience things from that perspective? That was something she hoped never to try again.

Carrington laughed, a rich, warm sound that she hadn't heard from him before. "Come now. It couldn't have been all that bad." His laughter died down and he added in a husky drawl, "And what we"—he pointed at her, then touched his finger to his own chest—"were doing, you seemed to have enjoyed some."

She scrunched her face tight again. "I found none of it pleasant."

She lied, and his wolfish grin told her he knew.

"Darlin', I was on this side, watching. From my viewpoint, I'd say you found it to your liking."

"What-why, how—" She snatched the paper from his fingers, mortified at the possibility of what he might have seen, considering the outcome of her first newspaper reading. She dipped her head down and skimmed over the words on the page without actually reading them.

"You're very beautiful when you blush."

"Ugh." She groaned with embarrassment. "Stop. I'm obviously willing to help you, which my therapist would have a heyday with, but that doesn't mean I'm going to be engaging in . . . in anymore sex," she said in a forced whisper, "every time I read something. And," she held up her index finger, "I'm especially not going to do it *as* you."

"Read it," he directed. "I was four years old in the article. I can assure you I was a bit young for any of that."

Unconvinced, and more than a little untrusting, she braced herself before skimming the words of the first sentence of the article Carrington pointed out to her. Nothing happened, so she cautiously read the next sentence of the article from *The Idaho World*, dated August 9, 1864.

She shifted the paper closer to the window to take advantage of the morning light.

Local Man Strikes Gold at Grimes Creek

Based on her knowledge of Carrington so far, at least the version of him from the past, there was no way an article dated in eighteen sixty-four could have been about him. Reassured, she continued.

John Chambers of Mountain Home found what some say is the last bit of gold in Grimes Creek. Most men left the area in 'sixty-three, but

Chambers stayed behind, determined to find something in the muddy waters. Rumor has it he did indeed find his weight in gold, which may be just a tale as nobody saw any of it. Chambers, along with his young son, left the mountain soon after to homestead out west.

Cassie contemplated the significance of the article and came up with nothing. Shrugging, she handed it back to Carrington.

"What's that got to do with any of this?"

"Everything," he said with a shake of his head. "My father did find gold. We moved here, settled on this land. My land," he added pointedly. "Things were good for the next seventeen or so years. Until a man showed up on our property."

Carrington got up, walked to the front door and went outside. Cassie followed, stopping beside him near the top of the steps.

"I had just returned from checking the crops and heard yelling as I settled my horse in the barn." His gaze shifted to the antiquated, dull wood building across the drive.

"I ran out in time to find some man had shot my Pa." The past replayed behind Carrington's eyes, raw and painful still. "I raced out, pistol drawn, and confronted the stranger. He claimed to be after the gold. Said Pa stole it from him and that if he didn't give it to him, he'd make sure Pa didn't get to enjoy it, either."

"What did you do?" Cassie asked softly, intruding on his anguished memories.

"I rushed to Pa, praying he was alive, but the blood . . . There was so much. I knew he wouldn't make it."

Cassie placed her hand on Carrington's arm and squeezed. The pain of losing a parent was hard under normal

115

circumstances. But to witness their murder? That alone would have required therapy, which likely didn't even exist in his time.

"I'm so sorry," she whispered. "But—"

"The bastard walked away! Like he'd done what he set out to do and was about to go on with his day." A darkness descended over him. His muscles beneath her hand grew taut with his suppressed anger. "I didn't think. I raised my gun and shot the stranger—in the back." Heaving a deep sigh, he finally looked down at Cassie, his hand coming to rest over hers on his arm.

"I turned myself in. Claimed self-defense. As I'd shot him in the back, they couldn't find the logic in it being self-defense. It didn't matter that I was a witness to my Pa's murder." A contemplative silence followed, punctuated by the rumble of a tractor somewhere beyond their line of sight and the plaintive, trilling call of a killdeer.

"I was sentenced to fifteen years in prison. Served seven, then was let out early."

Cassie was beginning to understand what life might have been like for a young man of, she quickly did the math, twenty-eight or so, to be released back into what had become a relatively civilized society. Even though he'd spent most of his life in this vast, untamed area, the folks who'd moved to town following the railroad all arrived during his time in prison. With his dad gone, there was nobody there to support him. She was surprised that he stayed around, or that he hadn't turned to a life of crime.

"The townspeople turned their backs on you." She'd seen the way folks there treated him. It all started to make sense. She had a newfound respect for Annie, for ignoring society's expectations of her and giving him a chance.

Carrington's thumb smoothed back and forth over her hand where it still rested on his arm.

"Not a soul would talk to me beyond the basic business dealings. The only conversation I got was when I went to town to drink and was drunk enough not to care who I picked a fight with. Suzanne was the one person willing to be around me, even in public and," he paused, choosing his next words carefully, "and offer a bit of what you saw already."

Like a priest had just absolved him of his sins, Carrington drew in a deep, cleansing breath of fresh air and smiled down at her.

"And that's why I drank."

"Oh," Cassie said on a sigh, unaware she'd been holding her breath. "I'm so sorry." Unexpected tears pooled in her eyes. She blinked them away and went back into the house to retrieve her purse.

TWELVE

Three hours later than originally planned, Cassie had completed her errands at the hardware and grocery stores, buying things she needed as well as those items Carrington requested. Considering her ghostly friend drank beverages, she assumed he'd want food, too, and so she bought some of that as well. Her drive to town had been fraught with nightmares, daydreams, visions of Carrington half naked in her kitchen, and a charming Blake.

Her thoughts were also filled with concern for Annie. The victim of someone's rage, jealousy, or hatred, Cassie didn't know which. Now, whether she liked it or not, she had to find out what happened, because the alternative was to go live in a psych ward and move out of *her* new house. She needed to get a grasp on her ghost problem and get him back to where he belonged.

"Getting a grasp" on Carrington had new meaning, after *being* him for that brief time. She recalled in vivid detail what it felt like, what Carrington felt when Suzanne wrapped her fingers around *that* part of his body. Cassie held her hand up, resting her wrist on the steering wheel. Her fingers formed a C as she guessed how far they'd circle his—

"Oh, for shit's sake!" She snatched her phone up from the passenger seat and dialed Andrew. Pressing the speaker button, she set the cellular device on her thigh.

"Hello?" Andrew came on the line.

Usually, hearing him was like a balm to whatever Cassie's state of mind was. Now however, her frustration was beyond the usual and his voice didn't have the desired effect.

"Hello, Doc. Thought I'd check in," she said, trying, but failing, to sound happy. Normal.

"How are you doing?"

Cassie wondered the same.

She was in her car, parked near the corner of Seventh Avenue and Main Street, which was Front Street when she'd seen it last—circa eighteen ninety. Visions of past and present superimposed on each other in her mind, much like the pictures of a children's book she'd once read with images printed on transparent pages. As each page turned, the overlap formed a different picture, a new part of the story.

She saw the Short Line Railroad's water tower overlooking the tracks. Turn the page and there was the addition of a monstrous, coal-powered train engine, complete with black smoke pluming from its stack. On the next turn of a page, those things disappeared. In their place was the building before her.

It was a train station—a very old one, but not the one she'd seen in her travels through time. This one was constructed of a red-brown stone and capped with red shingles. The façade bore rusticated detailing along the edges of all corners and around the main entry. There was an oversized, arched doorway with a Palladian window above it, fanning out like the sun's rays. The building had three dormers and a heavy roof overhang high above and along both sides of the entryway. This solemn edifice stood majestically, as though holding myriad secrets and stories within its walls.

Along Main Street, gone were the many wood-fronts interspersed between the newer brick buildings she'd seen in the past. Now, every structure lining both sides of Main was constructed of brick or stone, some single story, others multi-level. The hotel Cassie had hurried past at this very corner in another time, that day Annie stumbled into Carrington outside the Sagebrush Saloon, was gone. In its place was a much newer two-story building.

According to the Caldwell Historical District placard hanging on the façade, it was built in the early nineteen hundreds to house the Commercial Bank. Albert Steunenberg had worked there as the cashier. The Bank Building, as it later became, connected to another. On the face of that one, in large three-dimensional block letters displayed across the top, were the words Steunenberg Block.

Cassie recalled that Carrington had briefly mentioned the Steunenbergs, brothers who'd run the local paper, *The Caldwell Tribune*. They'd been the ones to employ Suzanne, giving her the freedom to print every sideways step Carrington made for the world to judge. One brother, Frank, would go on to become the governor of Idaho. Cassie's previous internet search about him found that a few years after his second term ended, he'd been assassinated outside his home.

Was it possible this building was named after those same Steunenbergs?

"Chassandra," Andrew said, startling her.

Cassie's knuckles were white from the death grip she had on the steering wheel. "Sorry. Got distracted. So," she said, dragging out the single syllable while formulating the next few words, "if I were going batshit crazy, you'd tell me, right?"

A curious laugh filtered out from her cell phone. She imagined Andrew shaking his head.

"If I thought you were, then yes, I'd tell you. I don't think you are. Do you think you are?"

Leaning an elbow along the car door window ledge, she let her head fall against her open palm. "I don't know," she groaned. "I mean I've spent two nights without a security system and I'm still alive. So that's a positive." Andrew made enough of an affirmative noise from his throat that gave her the encouragement needed to continue.

"I'm not as terrified as I was when I first started out. And," she rushed on, "I've not had any nightmares in two days." This was quite true, unless she considered ghost Carrington a nightmare.

Aside from her initial fright upon meeting him, she hadn't experienced that deep, gut-wrenching fear she'd lived with these last few years. In fact, she'd even begun to feel safe in Carrington's presence.

"Well, then. You're already doing better." Andrew's style was to allow Cassie to babble on about whatever issue weighed on her. This typically resulted in her coming to her own conclusions. "Here's what I think we should do. You specifically moved to BFE," he endearingly tagged Idaho as bum-fuck-Egypt, eventually shortening it to the acronym, "to regain your self-confidence. I think you and I should cut down on calls to, let's say, once every two weeks."

"But I—"

"That way," he continued, talking over her, "you learn to be less reliant on me and more on yourself. Of course, in a true crisis," which she knew meant if she had thoughts of harming herself, which she'd never considered, ever, "you can call. What do you say?"

Her immediate response wanted to be that she didn't like the idea at all, but she knew he was right. She'd have to get the ghost and the other demons that haunted her out of her life on her own if she was ever going to be normal again.

Begrudgingly, she agreed. "Fine. But if I call, you'd better answer." She knew he would, anytime, day or night. She just wanted to make sure he knew she was still counting on him. It was a good thing they'd become friends, otherwise these little chats would cost her a fortune.

"You'll be fine. Call me in two weeks." The call was disconnected before she had time to change her mind.

Two weeks wasn't all that long. Right?

Giving the historic train depot a parting glance, she started the car and drove off in search of the public library. Once there, she sought out the librarian, and asked where she could find archived newspaper articles. After a few short minutes, Cassie was seated in a room off the main library area before an ancient microfiche machine. The librarian helped her locate the film file that contained news articles from *The Caldwell Tribune* between April and November 1890. That was the timeframe of the papers at the house, and included the date of the fire, according to Carrington.

The images on the screen before her whizzed by as she turned the control knob. Her eyes skimmed over each black-and-white page, in search of the name Chambers.

"'You're fine,'" she mimicked Andrew's slightly effeminate voice, when she imagined what he'd have to say about her current actions.

The screen slid too far past a page and she pulled her hand back before placing it on the dial again and reversing.

Leaning in close, she scanned the document present on the screen before settling on a name that was familiar.

"November fifteen, eighteen ninety," she read in a library-appropriate voice, even though she was alone in the room.

The home of Carrington Chambers mysteriously took fire last Tuesday at about half-past five o'clock, raising quite a breeze of concern for the town's residents who saw the smoke from miles away. The house located a few miles from town burned nearly to the ground. Nothing was saved. Not even his bedding or personal belongings. Chambers had been returning from town when he glanced up and saw a column of smoke coming from the direction of his home. Fearing for his wife, who had been in residence when he departed earlier that day, said he tried entering the house, but the flames were beyond control.

So, ghost Carrington had told her the truth. Cassie scrolled ahead, curious about what, if anything, was determined as the cause of the fire. Had there been some sort of struggle? Did Annie maybe tip over an oil lamp? That certainly seemed possible.

A month of issues later, she found another article.

A most heartrending calamity has overtaken the town. It seems that the fire that consumed the Chambers place last month may have taken a victim. Mr. Chambers reported that his wife has not been seen or heard from since the night of the blaze. When asked where she may have gone, Chambers confessed to not knowing. It has since been discovered that on the day of the fire, he'd been at the Sagebrush Saloon in town.

"Of course, you were," Cassie mumbled.

As of today, Mrs. Chambers has not yet been located. Witnesses in town claim they'd seen the Chambers couple argue on several occasions. The young lady's parents are worried about her whereabouts. Sheriff Anders has stated Mr. Chambers is most definitely a person of interest in this disturbing matter.

Cassie surged up out of her chair as if it had suddenly been electrified. She backed away from the dinosaur microfiche machine. Her hands and legs began to tremble. The hazy, yellow screen taunted her with its truths. Fears of her own past with a violent man resurfaced. She rubbed her neck, the tingle of dark memories making the scar there burn with a phantom pain.

"What did he do?"

Carrington had suggested that Annie may have started the fire. But he also said he suspected someone murdered her. Which was true? What he didn't tell her was that *he* had been under suspicion of foul play in her death. Was all this reading and her going back in time, nothing more than a way for him to hurt his wife again? Or someone else perhaps?

"What do I do now?" It occurred to her that she'd read one of the news articles, yet she'd not traveled back. Why? The only difference was that she wasn't physically holding the paper. Well, that and she wasn't at the house, and Carrington wasn't present. Which object held the power to pull her through time?

Retrieving her purse from the back of the chair, she rushed through the library, calling out a quick thank you to the librarian who'd assisted her. Once outside, she jogged to her car and fell into the driver's seat. Thrusting the key into the ignition, she cranked the engine and rolled down all the windows. Her fingers worked over her throat, massaging at the tension built up there.

"Okay. You're going to go home, march into the house, and demand that Carrington leave. Next, you're going to take the old trunk from the attic, return its former contents, and toss the whole thing in the trash." A firm nod of her head solidified her plan. She yanked the car into gear and roared off toward her home, her sanctuary.

Carrington was standing in the doorway near the barn when she drove up to the house. He waved at her as she rolled slowly past. Her hand lifted automatically in reply, but then she remembered her resolve to evict him from the premises. She parked the car and waited for the cloud of dust around her to settle. Collecting her purse and keys, she was about to exit the vehicle when a sweaty, shirtless Carrington strode through the billow of dust, the wind ruffling his hair. He was Adonis in the flesh, ghostly flesh, but flesh, nonetheless.

Stopping beside her car, he pulled the latch to open the door. Like a true gentleman, he offered his hand to help her out. Cassie's curiosity had her placing her hand in his, allowing him to pull her up and out of her seat. Caught up in her own fears and concerns about his real-ness, she'd neglected to ask all those burning questions she should have asked about the man he'd been.

"I thought you said you couldn't leave the house?" she challenged. All her suspicions and doubts, those that had surprisingly simmered down only recently, rose quickly to the forefront of her mind.

He smiled down at her, the usual hard lines around his mouth softening, easing into subtle brackets. "I said I couldn't leave my property."

True. That *is* what he'd said. "When did you say you, um, died? What year again?" She knew darn good and well he hadn't said when. But Cassie could be very persistent.

Carrington didn't rise to the bait. She sensed the wheels turning in his mind as he pondered some memory, and she wondered at it. Why the hesitation? Clearly, he'd died, hence the ghostly status. Every nerve ending in her body prickled with apprehension. She forced herself to remain calm, as he'd not yet done anything untoward.

He boxed her in the triangular space between the car door and his body. "I haven't said when I died. But if you must know, it was the year eighteen ninety-four."

His confession stole her breath. "What? Only four years after Annie disappeared? Why? How?" The list of questions she had for him grew another page length. She needed to stop guessing at the answers, because no matter what she imagined, it would never be right. She understood that now.

He pressed closer, into her small space. "Yes, only four years. I promise you'll know everything soon. Now is not the time for that. Trust me. Once I find what I need, the rest will be revealed."

She considered him a moment. Measuring him. He wanted her trust. The one thing she struggled with the most. A quick glance at the house unleashed numerous more questions in her head but they'd all have to wait.

"Okay. Tell me this, then. Why is it you weren't curious about my car? How did you even know how the door opened?"

Carrington's laugh washed over her, warm, hearty, almost comforting.

"I've not been able to leave the property; however, others came and went, people who lived here. I've learned a lot through observation. Cars, for one. That thing called television was fascinating, too." His eyes dueled with hers. "I learned a lot of modern things watching those people. What they did, how they did it."

He had the audacity to wink at her. Cassie twitched at the unbidden images his insinuation brought about.

"At least until they stopped coming," he added.

It took her a moment to fully comprehend what all he'd have seen. The changing eras, the people, clothing, sex, drugs, rock-'n'-roll.

"Oh," was all she could muster. She needed to break the awkwardness caused by his nearness. "I got your stuff." She shoved the bag she'd been holding into his torso and ducked past him.

He made that two-beat throaty humming sound as he collected the item from her hands. "Thank you. By the way, the electrician stopped by while you were gone. He said to tell you he finished up and that he'll let the security company know they can come back now."

"Okay, good. Thanks." Soon she'd have her security system in place. She just hoped the greater danger wasn't about to be locked inside the house with her.

They carried the groceries inside. As they moved around the kitchen unpacking in a strange sort of domestic silence, Cassie struggled through a few revelations. First, there really had been a man in eighteen ninety named Carrington Chambers whose wife had disappeared under suspicious circumstances. The newspaper she'd read in the safe, controlled, and official library environment confirmed it.

Second, she had survived an attack by a man she thought loved her. And, until she set foot in her supposed sanctuary, had been damaged, but still sane, up to that point. Which brought her to the third revelation.

The third revelation, the most disturbing of all, was that all things being possible, Carrington Chambers was indeed a ghost, residing in her new house which was his old house. A house he had apparently rebuilt after the fire which she had just read about in the official archive setting. And she was now, in the strangest way, cohabitating with him. Drawing in a long, deep breath through her nose, she turned to him.

"I stopped at the library on my way home." One of Carrington's brows lifted. "I searched for articles about you. About the fire. You didn't tell me that you were a suspect in Annie's disappearance that night."

He tensed, and at the same time suddenly appeared immensely tired. "She disappeared and there was a fire. It made sense they had to lay blame or at least suspect someone of foul play." The hard lines around his mouth returned and the muscle at his jaw twitched.

"I was the criminal nobody liked already, so it was easy for them to suspect me of doing something terrible to my wife. I was an ex-convict after all, the worst of the worst. At least that's what Anders wanted everyone to believe."

The similarities between Cassie's life and Annie's were numerous. Instinct had her touching her throat. Was it possible she was dealing with another abuser? She shuddered at the idea.

"I'm not the sort of man to hurt a woman," he said, as if reading her mind. "I've had ample opportunity already, here, alone with you. Yet here you still are, hale and hearty." He smiled reassuringly. "If you read more, you'll learn everything."

Time travel. Ghosts. Maybe it was her revelations and willingness to accept the unbelievable, or maybe it was the sincerity she heard in his voice. Either way, she was suddenly ready to take this adventure to its conclusion.

"Okay, then. I'll keep reading. But let's make some lunch first." Quickly assembling peanut butter and jelly sandwiches, she grabbed a bag of chips from the counter and adjourned to the porch swing. Carrington followed, but at her request, he went out to the barn, and retrieved his discarded shirt. A shirtless Carrington was a bit more than she could handle, up close and personal. As he strolled back across the yard, she saw the diary tucked beneath his arm.

"So, you're a ghost but not the see-through type that can move through walls," she said before sinking her teeth into her sandwich. They were seated-side-by side, with only the bag of chips separating them. All the questions she should have been asking all along trickled out, now that she felt less worried over her safety.

"Why is it I can touch you?" To test this, she poked a finger into his bicep. "And you eat and drink. What did you do all these years you've been"—she swallowed hard, choking down her food—"dead?"

He marveled at a can of Pepsi before figuring out the snap top and handing it to her. "I am a ghost," he began, answering her questions in the order they were asked.

"I can move through walls, in a way. It's how you couldn't see me at first, but I was there. I don't understand any of it, really. I'm just here. But I am most definitely a real man."

The color of his eyes shifted to liquefied pools of pewter. She'd watched that happen on a few occasions in her travels to his past and knew enough of the promise it held. She licked her lips before biting into her sandwich.

"I eat and drink with you because I can, but I don't need to." The unsaid phrase "because I'm dead" hung in the air.

"Why did you do it?" She needed something to distract her from Carrington's overall sexy demeanor.

"Do what?"

She popped a potato chip in her mouth, enjoying the salty crunchiness of it. "You said you intended to accost Annie at the park. If you knew it would ruin her, why do it?"

He stretched his long denim-clad legs out, crossing one booted ankle over the other. His relaxed pose did funny things to Cassie. She hooked one sandaled foot over the other and pushed the swing minutely forward and back.

"As you've learned, Annie liked Blake. I needed to do something to ensure she didn't end up with him." His expression grew thoughtful. "I knew there was someone in the park who'd be watching us that day."

"What?" Cassie exclaimed. "Who was it?" She scrambled through her memory, skimming past the heated intensity of their shared kiss and his touch on her body. She remembered there had been someone behind the bushes but hadn't seen who.

"The local preacher was there. It was a regular habit of his to sit on a bench on the other side of that shrubbery, doing whatever preachers do in their spare time. I wasn't positive, but guessed he, or someone, anyone, might see us."

Cassie stopped rocking while Carrington continued his explanation. "Annie told me later, that the preacher and sheriff showed up at her house that same evening to tell her Pa."

"Oh, that poor girl." Cassie imagined Annie's shock at strangers telling her father the inappropriate things she'd been caught doing, and with the criminal in town no less.

He nodded, following her thoughts. "The next day all four of them rode out to my place. They told me I would marry Annie that afternoon." Carrington grinned devilishly.

"I did ask her if she was willing to be my wife. I'm not a cad," he said with a wink.

At first, Cassie was appalled at the underhanded way he'd gone about forcing Annie's hand in marriage. When he winked at her, a warm tingle came to life in her belly, working its way lower. She shifted in her seat, angling her body toward his.

"I daresay you're not." She masked all emotion and cocked her head at him. "So, she was forced to marry you. That day? Times have sure changed, thank goodness. In today's world, you could do what you did and much more without anyone ever giving you a second glance."

A mysterious smile spread across his face. He picked up the journal from where he'd set it on the porch beside him. The swing creaked loudly with the movement.

"From what I observed of those people who'd been in the house years back, it most certainly has changed." He stretched his hand toward Cassie, offering her the book in answer to her building curiosity. "Here, find out for yourself how Annie felt. I at least got her father to wait two days, so she wouldn't feel like she was being forced into it."

Cassie considered herself an intelligent woman, never mind that she conversed with a ghost and was secretly growing attracted to him. So, when she opened the journal to the next unread entry, she shouldn't have been surprised by the events that followed. Her lack of foresight would soon offer a very rude awakening.

With the latest revelations and determination to get the answers to solve this mystery, she obligingly read the entry dated August 5, 1890.

"'Today I become Mrs. Carrington Chambers. I'm thrilled and terrified at the same time.'"

Cassie inserted a soft *harrumph* at the disclosure before drifting into the grayness that pulled her once again into the past.

THIRTEEN

"Do you, Carrington Edward Chambers, take Elizabeth Anne McDonald as your lawfully wedded wife, to have and to hold, to love and to cherish, until death do you part?"

There was no slow lead up. No moment alone in a back room fussing with her dress. When Cassie came into Annie's life, she was front and center before a preacher. It was Reverend Boone of the First Presbyterian Church. Annie's church.

Annie's nerves were on high alert, and Cassie felt every bit of the girl's exhilarated distress. Instinctively, she moved to cover her throat, a nervous habit, but when she went to raise her hand she couldn't. She looked down and found the cause. One large, very masculine hand encompassed Annie's smaller, more delicate one. She unclasped her fingers and tugged, but the manly paw gripped tighter.

Slowly, she tilted her head up and found Carrington, the non-ghost version—not that there was much of a difference between versions—gazing down at her with an intensity that verged on indecent. She was happy to note that he appeared sober for his own wedding. For good measure, she sniffed the air between them and was delighted to find no hint of whiskey on his breath.

Annie's excitement about the nuptials was evident. Her palms were sweaty, and she was breathing much too fast. When she heard Carrington's affirmative reply to the preacher, she melted a little with relief. Apparently, she'd been having misgivings about him following through with the marriage.

Reverend Boone's voice buzzed in her ears. The sounds of the small crowd assembled behind her faded away as Cassie tried to read Carrington's mind by way of his facial expressions. His lips moved but she didn't hear his words. His clean-shaven jaw would wreak havoc on Annie's skin everywhere it touched—

"Annie." His fingers squeezed around hers, forcing Cassie's attention back to the moment. "Say your words."

She felt a flush creep up Annie's neck and over her face. Apparently, the preacher had already asked if she'd take Carrington as her husband.

"I-I do," Annie whispered.

"I now pronounce you man and wife." Reverend Boone's strong voice boomed the announcement.

The small group of people in attendance clapped hesitantly and not boisterously, as was typical at joyful occasions such as a wedding. Annie's parents in the front row smiled dutifully, but their uncertainty about the rushed nuptials showed. Her mother's lips pursed tight like a prune and her father's two brows became one above his spectacles as his frown deepened. Cassie offered a reassuring smile, hoping they'd understand that their daughter was truly very happy.

"You may kiss your bride."

Carrington's strong arms wrapped about her waist, pulling her snug into his embrace. His head bowed, and his lips touched hers, claiming her. Cassie had no choice in her response, as it wasn't hers to make. She admitted to enjoying the kiss, here in this secret place where she lurked unnoticed. Her lips parted to the pressure of his tongue. She let him in, feeling the soft heat as it scraped past her teeth to caress the inside of her mouth. When the kiss ended, Annie blushed furiously, realizing everyone had witnessed their intimate moment.

As they left the church, she felt like a queen, waving regally to the small gathering of well-wishers who cheered somewhat heartily—finally. The newlyweds rushed toward the buggy waiting out front, Annie taking two steps to Carrington's one as he pulled her along beside him. She smiled to those milling about in front of the church as they set off.

Cassie glanced back over her shoulder. She hadn't deemed it noteworthy at the time, but now she recalled the smell of fresh lumber and varnish inside the church. It was brand new. Bright white, unfaded paint stood out against the brown landscape around it. The unblemished shingles atop the spire would protect the building for many years to come. From Annie's memories, she knew that Reverend Boone issued his first sermon in the church just that year.

Cassie added a field trip into town to her list of to-dos to check whether the structure was still there in her own century.

By the time they rolled into the yard at Carrington's place a half hour later, Annie was shaking like a leaf. The reality of her new status finally hit. She was a wife now. She'd soon be sharing intimacies with her husband. Cassie quietly chuckled at Annie's worry over waking up in the morning beside him, wondering if her hair would be messy and how she'd need to rise early and freshen up before Carrington woke. Then she worried at her role as a homemaker. Would her husband hate her cooking? Would she be enough to keep him home at night?

The buggy drew to a stop. The house before her, slightly different from the one Cassie owned in the future, was but a single-story structure, rectangular in shape. However, the covered porch that ran from one end to the other was nearly identical in both past and present abodes.

The fire hadn't happened yet, so the house before Cassie now had to be the original. The main floor of her home in the future was the rebuilt version. It was similar in size and shape to this one. The upstairs would be added later, along with electricity and plumbing. The front door, painted a dark green in contrast to the white exterior, guarded the new life the couple was about to embark upon.

Cassie whooped in surprise when Carrington whisked her into his arms and carried her up the steps.

"Welcome home, wife." He kissed her tenderly before stepping over the threshold with her in his arms, then carried her through the living room to a small bedroom at the back of the house. It was exactly where Cassie imagined it would be.

What felt like an interminable number of moments later, Annie stood frozen in place beside a small four-poster bed. Fear welled up within her as her groom moved purposefully about the room. Cassie was doing her best to force Annie's nerves to thaw, rather unsuccessfully, while she peered around, uncertainty and shyness holding her body in its icy claws.

With his back to her, she watched him remove his jacket and toss it over a wicker chair near one corner of the room. When he turned around, shyness had her looking away. To distract herself, she traced the detailed scrollwork of the bedpost, looking anywhere except at the mattress. Or at Carrington.

Despite being an intelligent woman, Cassie, caught up in the intensity of Annie's nerves and emotions, had overlooked one tiny, yet monumental, detail about weddings.

"Come here."

She jumped when large, warm hands slid over her hips. Carrington reached up and twined his fingers with hers on the bedpost as his lips nuzzled against the side of her neck. He peeled her fingers away from the post, releasing their vise-like grip. Leading her across the small room, they stopped before a large mirror perched in the corner.

In the reflection of the glass she saw a dark, burning hunger in Carrington's eyes. Cassie had fantasized about that look on more than one occasion. Desire unfurled in Annie's body—and Cassie's mind—like an orchid reaching for sunlight.

Carrington's hands crept over her ribcage, his touch light as a feather, burning a path along her body beneath the dress. Annie's breath caught when his fingers worked the buttons at the neckline. The white lace and cotton material dramatically contrasted with the golden brown of his skin. Heat traveled over her body as she awaited that moment when he'd ease the garment off her shoulders and push it lower, until it slipped from her body to land in a puddle at her feet.

Okay, McAllister, now's the time to wake up. Do not go down this road any further.

Oh, but for the life of her she didn't want to stop. She had the unique opportunity to explore this passionate Carrington, so different from the other one who only demanded her help. No one would be the wiser.

Cassie knew she wouldn't be sharing this part with Andrew—it would be one secret she kept to herself.

With shyness befitting a new bride, Annie eased her hands back, pressing them firmly against Carrington's thighs. Squeezing gently, she gripped the hard muscles hidden beneath his dark trousers. Her head tipped back to rest against the cushion of his chest, the position exposing the column of her neck.

One strong, work-roughened hand spread over the pale skin of Annie's throat, like marble against satin. The fingers of his other hand hooked the edge of her dress. His thumb moved in circular patterns against her skin, massaging each area made visible as he pushed the fabric lower. Eventually, the dress floated to the floor in a hushed crumple of air. Next, the spines of the corset ceased their tight grip on her ribs as Carrington untied the contraption and let it, too, fall to the floor. He nudged it aside with his booted foot.

They made eye contact in the reflection of the mirror. One corner of Annie's lip, tucked beneath her teeth, was set free on a hiss as his hands skimmed across the tips of her breasts before cupping around their fullness. Carrington's head dipped down again, hot lips tracing a fiery path over the top of her shoulder.

"Carrington." Annie's voice shook, and she gripped his legs tighter, feeling the hardness of his erection push against her backside.

"We were meant to be like this," he whispered near her ear.

With agonizing slowness, he fingered the lacy edge of her camisole, slipping the thin straps down slowly. The dark circles of her areola edged into view, followed by the peaks of her nipples. Audible, panting gasps escaped Annie's lips.

138

Carrington stood more than a half foot taller than Annie. His expression reflected in the mirror was dark and fierce. He must have seen the intensity on his face, because his mouth softened into a smile.

Cassie liked it when he smiled.

She watched Annie in the mirror. Plain little Annie, skin so fair she obviously never basked in the warmth of the sun. In contrast to Cassie's own violet eyes, Annie's were hazel, and dewy with suppressed emotion. She had a pert nose with a light smattering of freckles. What was missing in the reflection that stared back through the shared vision of Annie and Cassie was the puffy, white parchment-paper scar across her throat. She touched Annie's neck with tentative fingers, feeling it without the jagged keepsake from the attack. Carrington's hand followed hers.

Cassie dispelled her own bad memories, allowing herself to feel what Annie was feeling. Nervousness. Fear. Embarrassment. And above all that . . . love.

Okay, she thought, chalk one up for Carrington for somehow knowing that Annie loved him.

There was a sudden rising urgency in him as his hands worked at freeing her from the combined camisole and bloomers, pushing them expertly down over the curve of her hips. Before Cassie could comprehend her situation, she stood fully exposed to him, the first time a man had ever looked upon Annie's naked body.

She shifted uncomfortably and attempted to cover herself. Carrington placed one large hand over both her dainty hands, holding them firmly against her belly.

"No. Let me see you."

Her body flushed a rosy pink at the new and visual intimacy. Cassie couldn't help but agree with the girl's response; she'd most definitely be blushing too. Heat and sensation exploded inside Annie as she watched his hand slip between her legs. She choked back a cry of wonder when he began to work in a slow, circular pattern over a particularly sensitive area before dipping lower still.

"You are mine." His warm lips pressed tight against a spot near her ear just as the pressure of his finger eased inside her slick, heated core. She gasped at the intrusion and at the bolt of electricity that zinged through her body.

As a delicious tension began to build within her, Carrington stopped. Annie nearly toppled over when his body and roaming hands were suddenly no longer supporting her. He moved away to divest himself of his clothing, tossing each garment aside in haste before reaching for her again and drawing her toward the bed.

There was a notable difference between Cassie's experience as Carrington when he'd been with Suzanne and her current one as Annie. With the former, she'd experienced his feelings, lusty and in charge of his manly cock. Whereas Annie, who'd learned about what happens between a man and woman in more demure terms, had been imagining Carrington's body in the more clinical sense.

Cassie laughed nervously, envisioning the penis as Annie was doing now: the male genital organ, flaccid and uninspiring in its natural state. She was inclined to agree with Carrington's more flattering perception of his anatomy, large and imposing, designed perfectly to give a woman pleasure.

"What is it, darlin'?" He rested his forehead against hers.

"Uh, n-nothing." Cassie quivered, and squelched her wandering imaginings, hoping he would assume Annie was nervous, which, not surprisingly, she most definitely was.

With a tenderness unexpected in a man so bold and domineering, Carrington eased her onto her back, kissing his way up the length of her body until he covered her with his solidness. Every inch of her skin tingled where his body touched hers. She reveled in the sensations that overwhelmed all her senses.

A slight nudge against the insides of her thighs forced her legs to spread apart. Annie lay uncertainly beneath his large presence. Cassie felt the pressure of her body stretching to accommodate him as he began to enter her. It was tight and uncomfortable, but she forced that part of Annie to relax as much as she could.

"This will hurt, but only once." His voice was sharp, tense.

What?

Warning lights of alarm flashed inside Cassie's brain as reality finally caught up to her and she realized what was about to happen. She tried to scoot up on the bed, away from the urgent pushing and stretching happening between her thighs. She managed to shift back a little, but not far enough to prevent Carrington from slipping inside her body.

The pressure suddenly stopped, and Cassie breathed a sigh of relief. That wasn't as bad as she remembered from her first time. Before she could extract herself from the situation and the past altogether, Carrington surged his hips forward, tearing through the thin barrier of Annie's innocence.

"Fuck!" Cassie cried out as pain ripped through her core. She squirmed beneath Carrington's now still body, trying to dispel the weight of him and the width of him from within.

He pushed his palms against the mattress and braced himself above her. Cassie saw the strain of desire, restraint, and shock etched in the hard set of his jaw.

"Darlin'. Never say that word outside this bedroom," he warned. Then he eased nearly all the way out of her body before sliding slowly back in, until his solidness was seated deep inside her. The friction warmed her from her toes to the top of her head.

Pulling her legs up, he instructed her to wrap them about his waist, as he lay atop her, then reached down to curl his hands around the backs of her thighs. Trapped beneath his solid weight, Annie tossed her head side to side in growing frustration as she began to tingle everywhere with each thrust of his hips.

"Holy fu—" Cassie stifled the expletive as she veered up toward what she was willing to bet would be the best orgasm of her entire life. Dream or not, this was going to be amazing.

Carrington made a throaty hum-growl sound near her ear which she presumed was his acceptance of her naughty language. It also appeared to be a turn-on, because he leaned up on his elbows and pressed his hands on either side of her head, clenching her hair into his fists. He drove into her, wild with passion and need.

The ache between her legs was now nearly unbearable in the most amazing way. Cassie gripped her fingers into the hot, sweaty skin on his back. "Oh, my god! Yes!" she cried out. A second later, her world exploded. She was held suspended on a tide of pulsing sensation, floating on air, before falling gently back to earth.

FOURTEEN

Cassie tossed about until she was sprawled indelicately across the swing, one ankle draped over the armrest, her other foot pressed to the wood floor. Her head settled against Carrington's shoulder. The hem of her skirt had inched up. He attempted to adjust it back down, but the fabric only went so far and didn't hide enough skin to his liking. He ceased trying but averted his gaze.

He'd enjoyed watching her relive his wedding day, and her reactions to the things that Annie felt. When he married Annie, he'd known she'd been nervous. God, he'd wanted her. It had taken all his resolve not to toss up her skirts the moment they were alone. Fortunately, he'd taken his time. Seeing Cassie writhe about, hearing her cries of pleasure, knowing it was Annie's feelings coming through was both heartwarming and bittersweet.

Annie had been so innocent, yet willful, and daring enough to chase after the likes of him. Unfortunately, her obstinate nature had backfired when she'd agreed to marry him. He'd hoped in time she'd forgive him for manipulating the situation leading up to their hurried nuptials. They'd laugh about it all later, he'd thought.

He was wrong. Everything went wrong.

Now, here was Cassie. Even scared as she was of him and the other monsters in her past life, she continued to fight for her place in her world. He didn't want to be another of the demons that haunted her. He should leave now, figure out a way to cross over into whatever was waiting beyond, before it was too late for her. Like it had been for Annie.

He'd tried to leave many times over the years. But strangely, each failed attempt resulted in an overwhelming sense of peace washing over him. The calm feeling came with an unusually peculiar inner knowledge that his wait was almost over. In the afterlife, however, "almost" was a relative term that could mean days or centuries. Fortunately for him he'd only had to wait a little more than one century.

Cassie's hand shot out and Carrington jerked his head back to avoid impact with it. When she lowered her arm, her fingers clamped across the back of his neck. Her other hand sought purchase in the air in front of him. He weaved his fingers with hers. She squeezed them so tight her knuckles turned white.

He never imagined being with anyone besides Annie, after they'd wed. Without a doubt, he'd intended to spend his remaining days with her and the family they'd create. Instead, he'd existed in eternity feeling nothing, biding his time, waiting for the promised end to happen—and then Cassie arrived. Carrington found her irresistible.

Time heals all wounds, it had been said, and he'd had a long time for his heartache to mend, even if his anger still raged. The intensity of his desire for Annie that short time they'd shared so long ago was his best memory. Yet, unexpectedly, new feelings began to stir within him.

Cassie clung to him as she relived Annie's awakening to love, when he'd taken her virginity on their wedding day. There were times, before wedding Annie, he thought he'd perish for wanting carnal knowledge of her, but the wait had been worth it.

It would be worth it again with Cassie.

When she cried out, Carrington experienced two feelings: The first was shock at her vocabulary. Never had he met a woman who cursed so much. The second feeling brought about a slow satisfied smile. His dignity as a man had been restored, knowing, by way of Cassie's responses, that he'd given his wife as much pleasure as she'd given him.

Her hand at his neck released its hold and lowered back to her chest. Cassie stirred but remained locked in the other world, in the languorous aftermath of lovemaking. All the tension she'd been harboring since the day he met her, vanished as she reached that pinnacle of pleasure.

Her eyes fluttered open, and she blinked several times, slowly returning to her reality.

"Welcome back," he said. She didn't immediately release her grip on his fingers, and he savored the moment, knowing this peaceful interlude would turn about-face soon.

"I am so confused." Her voice was husky, sultry. "Why Annie? I don't get why you picked her." She searched his face for answers. "Don't get me wrong, she's lovely, but so innocent and . . . and plain." Her head moved side to side in wonder. "I'll give you some credit. She genuinely loved you. Apparently, you weren't a shallow asshole after all."

His grin broadened, and he laughed a deep, hearty laugh. "Oh, darlin', you have the most shocking mouth I've ever heard on a woman. But I think that was a compliment, so I'll thank you. Has it not occurred to you that my attraction to Annie went beyond physical appearance?" He paused long enough for Cassie to reflect on Annie's other attributes.

He gave her hand a small squeeze. "She was kind and had a good sense of humor. She smiled easily and she was very intelligent. I knew a life with her would never be dull."

As Cassie contemplated his description of Annie, an air of intimacy settled about them. She seemed content to stay close to him. He was grateful for the quiet moment they shared now.

The scar across her throat was on display for his inspection. He'd not questioned her overmuch about it yet, but since they were in a rather companionable state, he felt it was the right time.

"Tell me what happened." He trailed his finger over the misshapen line of skin then stopped at a point beneath her ear. His finger swiped across a small red mark before sliding back down the other direction.

She blanched, as if all the blood in her veins froze solid. Then she exhaled long and slow between pursed lips, forcing the thaw throughout her body.

"I wondered when you'd ask." A flicker of something, relief possibly, skittered across her face. "It's not a pretty tale." She stared off out at the blue sky. "I'll give you the highlights." A bitter laugh followed. "When I was twenty-one, I met a guy. There's always a guy, right? Anyway, we dated. By the way, dating in my time is very different from yours. Within a year, I moved in with him."

"You were unwed when you moved in with a man?" He didn't mask the censure in his voice. Those couples who'd resided in the house over the years he assumed had been wed. He questioned his assumptions now. His observation of the world from within the boundaries of his property was limited. Much had changed since he'd lived in it and he had little choice but to be open-minded.

Her chuckle was a sad-sounding attempt at a laugh. "Yes. Although, we did marry soon after. I'd like to say things were fine at first but to be honest, I knew from day one there was something not right about him. Andrew had quite a time with that, by the way."

Carrington hadn't a clue what she meant by that, but nodded his head anyway, unwilling to interrupt.

"One day we had a terrible fight over something stupid and one thing led to another and he attacked me." Her brow furrowed.

"I found out later he'd used some meth. Methamphetamine," she added, gazing questioningly at him. When he shrugged, she offered the explanation. "It's a drug, a substance that he smoked that basically made him go berserk."

Her hand involuntarily shifted to span over her throat, protecting it or trying to heal it Carrington wasn't sure. He placed his palm over the back of her hand, offering support. After a moment, she calmed.

"Anyway, he attacked me one day, out in the yard, the front yard even, and . . . and did this. And more."

Tiny drops of perspiration appeared on her forehead, she swiped her forearm across it, removing the outward sign of her distress. She hadn't given details, which he was glad of, but at the same time he wanted her to share everything, so he could help erase the pain. Betrayal and fear could be as damaging as the physical scar on her neck, he knew all too well.

"Jimmy's in jail. I heard you say it the first night you were here."

"Yes. Because the meth made him crazy, he claimed temporary insanity and got charged with felony aggravated battery and sentenced to, get this"—she quirked a brow at him and he smiled at her assumption that he had some understanding of what she was talking about—"five to ten years in prison with the possibility for parole after six years." She shook her head.

A muscle in his jaw twitched as he remembered his time behind bars. He was almost afraid to ask but did anyway. "How long has it been?"

Haunted, violet eyes met his. "Six years last month."

The crunching sound of gravel preceded the vehicle rolling up the driveway, interrupting their conversation. Cassie bolted upright as a white van drew to a stop beside her car. The bright letters of Phelps Security identified who it was before Brian got out and waved.

"Afternoon, folks. I'm here to activate your alarm system."

Cassie turned to Carrington, her head cocked to the side. "Other people can see you? How is that possible? Why?"

Carrington laughed and shook his head at her. He smiled in humorous delight as they both walked the half dozen steps toward the stairs.

"There's not a person alive who'd recognize me. So, why not? Brian here will likely be expecting a man around the house. I doubt he'd think anything out of the ordinary."

Clasping Brian's hand in a firm shake, he greeted the younger man. "Good afternoon." Glancing down at Cassie, Carrington gave her a knowing wink. Her gaze darted back to his and Brian's joined hands, then abruptly, she spun about on her heels and led Brian into the house. Carrington followed, chuckling as he went.

It was at least an hour later when Brian finished up the last touches to the security system, explained how each door and window were wired, and what happened on the other end should a break-in occur when the alarm was activated.

"This is top quality stuff here." Brian nodded at the wall panel located near the door. "Anything slides past one of the sensors, this alarm goes off, and the local authorities are called immediately. Either of you have any questions?"

His gaze dipped to Cassie's neck, and he stared boldly for one uncomfortable second too long. Carrington's heart squeezed when she raised her hand up in that protective gesture so common to her.

"Um, I don't think so." She turned to Carrington.

Never having seen a security system or half the modern gadgets that had been installed in the house since she moved in, Carrington shook his head. "No. I think we're fine."

"Thank you for getting out here so quickly after the electrician finished up," Cassie added.

"Well, I could tell you were in a hurry to get it going. So, I rearranged my schedule and moved you to the top of the list." He smiled proudly. When neither Cassie nor Carrington responded to his personal accolade, he added, "Okay, then. If you do think of something, feel free to call me." Brian handed Cassie a business card, casting one parting glance at her neck. With a cheeky grin directed at Carrington, he bobbed his head and turned to leave through the front door.

"He seems different from the last time. Must be that you're here," she said with a dismissive shrug.

"He appears to be a competent young man," Carrington added as they watched Brian's departing form.

"I suddenly feel like soaking in a warm bath. Would you care if I slipped off for a bit?" She clapped a palm lightly against her forehead. "So now you're seeking approval from a ghost. Nice, McAllister," she mumbled as she turned toward the stairs.

Carrington heartily encouraged her to take some time for herself. Perhaps too heartily. Cassie slanted him a peculiar glance before he managed to duck off into the kitchen. "I'll just finish up the stove," he muttered.

It was precisely seven minutes later, when he was kneeling over the black iron stove spreading a sealant on its surface, that he heard a blood-curdling scream. A second ear-piercing shriek followed before the rapid thump of bare feet tromping down the stairs sounded.

Cassie barreled around the corner and into the kitchen.

"What. The. Hell. Is this?" she shrieked from a point somewhere close behind him.

He squared his shoulders and rose slowly from his kneeling position. Spine straight, he pivoted around to greet a very irate Cassie. She was wrapped in a fluffy, purple robe that was belted at the waist. The fingers of one hand clenched tight around the front of the robe at chest level. Her other hand hovered in the air, index finger stiff and pointing hard at her neck.

"What is this?" she repeated, chest heaving, hand quivering noticeably. Her eyes narrowed to slits.

He stalked toward her, wiping a dark, oily substance from his hands onto an old, stained towel he'd retrieved from a drawer. She took a hesitant step backward when he crowded into her space.

"Is something amiss, darlin'?" he asked calmly.

"Amiss?" she squeaked. "Explain this!"

He bent forward to inspect her neck. Below the left ear, right at the top of where the scar ended, was a purple-pink mark, circular in form.

"It appears to be," he said contemplatively, giving the mark careful consideration, "a love bite."

"A love bite? You mean a *hickey*?" Her skin flushed a lovely shade of red, her brows slamming together. "I can't have a hickey! I don't get hickeys!" Her hands fell to her sides and clenched into fists. "Explain to me how it is that I have a hickey!"

She paced around the kitchen counter. "*That's* why Brian was gawking at me so strangely." She stopped on the other side and whirled around to face him. "He-He—" she stuttered. "Thought we—" Her hand moved back and forth between herself and him. "Were—"

Her rising mortification had her skin turning splotchy red, like what it had done while she'd been in Annie's life only a short time ago, when she'd climaxed right along with Annie. Carrington didn't dare share *that* piece of information with her, but he couldn't help his warm grumble of appreciation at the vision she was now.

"Calm down, darlin'. He probably assumed we'd been engaged in nothing more than a lover's tryst."

The range of color her skin exhibited impressed Carrington. It was now so dark, it verged on a purple that closely matched her robe.

"But we didn't! We couldn't!" she choked out.

With a playful quirk of his brows, he replied, "No. We did not. However, we most *certainly* could." He winked affectionately at her, which he instantly learned was the wrong thing to do.

"Aargh!" She marched toward the arch leading out of the kitchen. "I am going to go take a long, hot bath," she said through gritted teeth. "And when I'm done, I really need you to not be around for a bit. I need some time alone." She heaved an exasperated sigh and turned away from him.

"Please," she added, before storming out and tromping back up the stairs.

FIFTEEN

Cassie had a hickey—a *hickey!* Actually, she had more than one; a pale pink one over her trapezius muscle in the crook of her neck and another darker purple one on the outer edge of one breast. She leaned sideways to see it better in the full-length mirror.

When she'd confronted Carrington, she knew right away that he'd already seen the one high up on her neck, near her ear. He couldn't have known about the others. Could he?

Hickeys! At her age! She wasn't ancient by any means, only thirty-one, but still, she wasn't some silly teenager. In contradiction, she huffed and stomped one foot.

It was Carrington-from-the-past who'd marked Annie during the consummation of their marriage. Cassie didn't recall him suckling or kissing Annie's skin in such a way that would leave behind not one but three hickeys. In her defense, she *had* been overwhelmed by the heady, sensational feel of him touching her body. Everywhere. So caught up in the things he'd been doing to her, a train might have run through the room and she wouldn't have noticed. It was possible, she supposed, that he'd left the marks. She hated hickeys.

She knew, or had a general understanding, that what happened to Annie while she was possessing her life would or could happen to her. Still, the reality of it on her person was alarming and caused icy claws of foreboding to take hold.

The idea of a bath no longer sounded appealing. What she needed was some physical exertion. Slipping on an old pair of shorts and a tank top, she went downstairs and grabbed an opened bottle of wine from the kitchen— completely ignoring the room's other occupant. For good measure, she stomped back up the stairs to the master bedroom.

Armed with a paintbrush and a gallon of paint the color of revere pewter, she set about the job of bringing the walls back to life. The irony of her choice in paint color, one that was a shade off from that of Carrington's eyes, didn't go unnoticed. Had she not already paid for twenty-five gallons of the stuff, she might have returned it all, but she'd paid, so it stayed.

Two hours passed where she managed to block most thoughts of her current circumstances from entering her mind. ABBA's *Super Trooper* blared from her cell phone where it sat atop a dresser clustered in the center of the room, along with most all her other furniture. But, like sunlight dappling through the leaves of a tree, tiny flickering images of *him* snuck into her mind. He was like a drug injected into her veins. One taste and the cravings for him threatened to turn her inside out. Where was he now?

"Are you watching me?" she called out, only half expecting a reply. No quiet cough or shifting among the shadows followed. Nothing. Where does he go when he's not visible?

"Where the undead go of course, McAllister," she chided, in response to her own question.

Realizing she'd painted over the same spot four times, she physically drooped, shoulders hunched, arms lifeless at her sides. It appeared her reprieve from thoughts of Carrington were over.

Closing the can of paint, she wrapped the brushes in a plastic bag before heading off to the bathroom to wash up. Back in the bedroom, she flounced onto her bed, desperate for a good night's sleep. She lay there, staring at the ceiling as her mind traveled to places she really wished it wouldn't. To him. To the past.

A treacherous, yet pleasant, tingle danced across her skin. She lurched up and off the bed, tiptoed downstairs to collect the journal from where Carrington had left it on the coffee table earlier and then crept back up to her room.

"You leave me be while I find out what went on next," she called out to the walls. He wasn't around that she could tell, but she was certain he heard her.

Opening the diary, she found where she'd left off and skimmed the next entry, then the next, and again the next. Wherever she read *his* name she intentionally moved past it until she landed on one three pages later that didn't mention Carrington. Having already tried to skip to the end, which didn't work, she hoped that by at least glancing at each entry it would count in this game of time travel she was playing. It was cheating, but she seriously didn't think she could handle all those exchanges with him just now.

"It's about time you wrote something else that didn't revolve around him." She grew irritated as she considered all the entries with his name, but there was no venom behind her words. Annie was a newlywed after all. It made sense she'd write of her husband.

August 10, 1890. I went into town today and bought a couple new things to wear. I bumped into Blake outside the dress shop.

The point of Cassie's travels to the past was to find out more about Annie's interactions with Blake and others who might have wanted to hurt her. Satisfied there was no mention of Carrington, she leaned back into a comfortable position against the headboard and continued reading.

At the mercantile, Miss Jane was cool to me.

She felt a moment of dizziness, like a head rush, as the words on the page swirled and then vanished altogether.

***

Cassie was alerted to her new surroundings by the sound of a tiny bell tinkling above her head. Annie had pushed open a door with *Caldwell Mercantile* painted in gold across the glass. She cast a brief glance around, observing the long room filled with dry goods in various-sized burlap bags stacked in piles along one wall. Beside those were shelves brimming with canned items. There were jarred pickles, beets, and peaches; boxes of oats and flour as well as tins of coffee, tobacco, and sardines. She moved past a glass case filled with pipes, reading glasses, and various knives.

Annie's purpose in the mercantile became clear as she headed straight to the back of the store. There she found bolts of cloth, spools of thread, strands of edging, and even a real Singer sewing machine and cabinet, complete with the iron foot pedal. Cassie was not a seamstress, and she hoped Annie didn't have plans to waste away the day in front of a sewing machine—a talent and hobby Cassie had never found appealing.

Along the back wall, adjacent to the sewing supplies, was a headless mannequin covered in a huge monstrosity of gray silk with a high collar and what resembled miniature drapes hanging from each shoulder.

A small bell sat on a counter that ran along the wall near the mannequin. Cassie picked it up and shook it. From somewhere beyond a doorway that led to a room in the back of the building, a woman's voice rang out, "I'll be right there."

Cassie's attention returned to the gray outfit. "Yuck." She wrinkled her nose in distaste. She couldn't imagine Annie's wispy figure being swallowed up by such a thing. There was only one other dress on display in this pseudo-clothing store. She nodded her approval at the A-shape design, belted at the waist with a simple button-up blouse beneath a crisp jacket. The poufy sleeves at the shoulders didn't impress her, but at least the rest of the outfit was decent.

"Sorry to have kept you waiting."

Cassie turned to find a large woman, presumably Miss Jane, lumbering around the counter much like a pregnant bear might move through a forest. The dress she wore easily contained more fabric than the gray one on the mannequin.

"How may I help—" Miss Jane's jowls fell slack and the welcoming smile that had been present vanished. Her eyes shifted past Cassie to the front of the store, then over to the headless mannequins around her—anywhere but at Annie. The pile of hair atop her head leaned haphazardly to the side, tiny strands poking up. Her throat convulsed as she swallowed nervously, and she brushed away specks of lint from the front of her dress. Still, she hadn't greeted Annie properly.

Cassie shifted the reticule hanging from her wrist to the other arm. In a pretense of interest in one of the dresses, she circled the mannequin with the A-line skirt. Miss Jane approached. The swish of fabric filled the silence as her thick legs moved her about the room.

"I'm in need of a few articles of clothing, ma'am," Cassie said respectfully, thinking maybe the woman's initial coolness toward her was merely her misunderstanding.

Miss Jane cleared her throat, the sound loud in the space between them. "What exactly do you need?" Her tone of voice was matter of fact and not welcoming like it had been when she'd first called out from the back room.

Cassie considered her current attire as she wondered about her needs. She had on a drab, brown cotton dress, long-sleeved, as was typical for the time, even in the unbearable heat. Rubbing her thighs together, she felt the shift of a thinner, smoother fabric against her skin. Delicate fabric to cover the more delicate parts of a woman's anatomy. It was a combination camisole attached to bloomers. In place of a bra, which she wasn't certain had been introduced yet, was the tight, rib-squeezing contraption of a whale-bone corset. Cassie enjoyed the freedom of not wearing a bra; however, the corset she could, and would very soon, do without.

Good grief, she bemoaned silently, lifting, and then dropping the weight of fabric that was her dress. It was no wonder she felt like a turkey roasting in an oven every time she landed in Annie's body. She shook her head, determined to ignore the volumes of fabric that threatened to suffocate her.

Standing before Miss Jane, she shifted from one foot to the other, still uncertain what articles of clothing the store would have on hand, or those she'd be expected to make herself. She didn't want to make anything, so she asserted her own requests, certain Annie would approve.

"My husband said I should get about everything I think I'd need, so I suppose, everything."

The shopkeeper's interest was piqued at the potential of a large sale, but the disdain in her demeanor didn't lessen.

It occurred to Cassie that everyone in town already knew that Carrington Chambers had wed, and they knew whom he had wed. By the way Miss Jane so coldly greeted her, it seemed poor Annie might be taking on some of the hate that had been doled out to Carrington alone up to this point. Cassie couldn't change Annie's personality, but she couldn't sit back and allow others to be mean to her, either. It couldn't hurt to speak up for her now. Could it?

"Look," she said, annoyed by the woman's haughty attitude. "I understand you may dislike me, or more specifically my husband, but do you want this sale or not? I'd prefer not to, but I'm sure Mr. Chambers would take me to Boise to find what I need."

Was that true? Would Carrington take her to the bigger city for a shopping spree? Did they do that in the nineteenth century? In a buggy, the journey would be a long arduous trip, so different from Cassie's time when she could hop in her car and make the trip in less than an hour.

She tried, but found it challenging to appreciate her current circumstances, such as the antiques that were everywhere, the old buildings, and living out real history. Instead, she longingly recalled the luxuries she lacked, like a shopping mall, or for that matter, just one other clothing store where she could take her business. She knew for certain she'd be a laughingstock if she had to wear clothing that she'd sewn herself. That just wasn't going to happen.

Miss Jane's eyes bulged like a squeezed toad as she realized her error in judgment. Before Cassie could say more, the woman's attitude softened, and she jumped into action. They sifted through several patterns displaying images of women's apparel, from day dresses to riding dresses to a variety of underwear. Seeing that Miss Jane intended for Cassie to purchase the patterns and the fabric to make on her own, she rushed to explain her circumstances.

"I'm sorry, but I'm going to need someone to make all these things for me. You see, I only recently got married and haven't yet purchased a sewing machine of my own." The large woman gasped—like not having a sewing machine was the crime of the century—but covered up her dismay with a knowing, sympathetic nod.

"Of course. I'm happy to put these together for you." If ever there was the inaudible sound of a cash register *chinging*, that time was now.

"It'll cost some, you understand," Miss Jane said.

"Oh, I understand. I do appreciate it." Cassie smiled pleasantly. She was holding the pattern of a woman's undergarment similar to what she currently had on beneath her dress.

"I'm wondering," she added as an afterthought while Miss Jane directed her to a pedestal where she could take Annie's measurements, "could you alter this here pattern so that it's two pieces instead of one?" She lifted the paper envelope up and pointed at the image on the front. "Separate it here," she drew her finger across the area of the bodice at the midriff. "And the bottoms, if you could shorten them up to about here." She pointed to a spot that drew another shocked gasp from the shopkeeper. Essentially, Cassie had just asked for a pair of shorts with a crop top.

Miss Jane's eyes suddenly twinkled with something akin to admiration, even if two bright spots of red appeared on her cheeks. Leaning closer, and lowering her voice, she whispered, "I've seen something like that in the Montgomery Ward catalog. It's called long-jer-ay." She pronounced the word in three hard syllables, no French softening of the g.

For whatever reason, Cassie's request for the intimate underwear brought down the barrier the woman had raised the moment they'd met. By that simple, silly request, did she cast a shadow of doubt on Miss Jane's perception of Carrington, different from the one she'd up to that moment assumed? Like everyone else's assumptions.

Whatever it was, Cassie was glad of it. "Thank you kindly," she said. "When should I expect to return?"

Miss Jane assured her she'd have the underthings ready in a couple days and the dress finished by the following Tuesday. Cassie gave her nod of approval and sauntered back through the mercantile toward the front door. Behind her, she heard a whispered sigh of relief.

Feeling triumphant, she exited the building a bit too enthusiastically. As she stepped out onto the wood-planked walkway, she stumbled and was about to fall to the ground when strong arms caught her and enfolded her in a saving embrace.

"What the he—" A startled Blake grabbed at Annie's shoulders, balancing both himself and her while she danced about to keep from landing face down on the boardwalk. Once securely back on her feet, flushed and feeling a moment of comic relief, Cassie raised her smiling face to his.

"Blake! Thank you."

Blake stepped back a respectable distance, releasing his grip on her. "Ma'am." He tipped his hat. "How are you faring, Mrs. Chambers?" The smile he gave her reflected kindness, but Cassie saw a flicker of something else in his expression too. Anger? Irritation?

How was she faring? The greeting was stiff and formal, something Cassie was not. However, Annie probably was, so she needed to strive for something in between. "I'm doing well. Thank you."

Blake began walking in the direction he'd apparently been headed when Cassie slammed into him. She followed, forcing a leisurely pace. When they reached the end of the boardwalk, he held her elbow as she stepped down into the dirt alleyway between buildings. Once back on the wood planking on the other side, he immediately released his grip on her.

At the corner, she peered up at the two-story building beside her. This one would eventually be replaced by another, according to the placard on the Bank Building she'd seen in her time.

"Amazing," she whispered in awe, rubbing a palm against the freshly painted wood. Blake touched her elbow again, concern etching lines across his forehead.

Cassie laughed. "Pardon my daydreaming. I've been meaning to search you out to say . . . to say . . . Well"—she lifted her hands, palms up, at the same time her shoulders lifted then lowered— "to say I really hope we can remain friends, now that I'm married to your boss."

It may be a different, less advanced time in history, but women were certainly able to have male friends. Weren't they? It was silly to think a husband could direct who she could or couldn't associate with. That only happened way back in really old times.

"I'm certain your husband won't take kindly to us being friends, ma'am. We'll just be fine acquaintances," he said through a tight smile. "Can I assist you with anything while I'm here? I should be getting back to the farm soon."

As Cassie was about to respond and ask that he stroll along Front Street with her—so she could see history happening—a familiar high-pitched voice called out from somewhere nearby.

"You hoo! Blake? Is that you?"

A dark feeling of jealousy within Annie pulled Cassie around at the sound. She felt the blood rush from Annie's face. Coming up the walk was Suzanne. Cassie, less shocked now about her circumstances than the last two times she'd seen the woman, silently measured up Annie's competition.

Suzanne's bosom was protruding absurdly high above the precariously low-cut bodice of her emerald green gown. Annie was embarrassed for her, while Cassie grudgingly admitted that the green was a spectacular color for Suzanne's complexion. The color of the fabric offset her luxuriant auburn hair, which today she wore draped rather elegantly over her shoulders. Her skin was fair and flawless, her eyes as green as the turbulent ocean waters Cassie had seen off the California coast that one time she went.

Suzanne smiled at Annie, but her eyes flashed darkly. Instead of giving Cassie the warm feeling of the makings of a new friendship, the woman's demeanor made her skin crawl. Cassie pulled her shoulders back, shrugging off the dark shroud of whatever it was she saw in that gaze.

"Miss Suzanne." Blake smiled warmly at her, warmer than Cassie certainly expected. "You remember Mrs. Chambers?" The introduction was followed by a slight shake of his head, silently communicating with her.

Cassie's brows pinched together. What was he up to? The pair held each other's gaze for a long second before turning their attention back to Annie. She forced a polite smile. "It's nice to see you again, Suzanne."

The lushly curved woman squared up to her. "And how is Carrington these days?" she inquired, her tone oozing familiarity. It irritated Cassie to no end how Carrington's name rolled off the woman's tongue like a sweet wine. She even had the audacity to lick her lips, as if she were tasting a memory.

Oh, for shit's sake. Cassie plastered on a fake smile. Were Suzanne and Carrington still involved? The idea irked her. She began to wonder if Carrington was right, that Suzanne had some hand in Annie's death.

The way Blake was acting seemed suspicious too. Were the two of them conspiring together? Crimes of passion happened all the time, so it was certainly a possibility that jealousy was a factor in Annie's demise. But whose jealousy?

She'd have to tread lightly around these two yet remain close enough to gather information. And ghost Carrington would soon get a severe lecture about his involvement with the likes of Suzanne. Cassie truly hoped he'd told her the truth about their affair ending after he'd married Annie.

"Why, my husband is just wonderful. Thanks for asking." Cassie kicked herself for her inability to control the lash of jealousy that weaved its way into her host's voice. She was only protecting what was rightfully Annie's, she thought, rationalizing away the unbidden emotion.

Derogatory terms began tumbling about in Annie's brain. Slut. Whore. Annie didn't like Suzanne either. With good reason.

Cassie needed to derail this situation as quickly as possible and get Annie far away from Suzanne. "Is your . . . chaperone or daddy about?" She peered around, searching for the absent male escort.

Suzanne's head cocked slightly, a slow grin climbing across her face. "I'm a widow. I no longer need a chaperone. I get by on my own, doing whatever I want. And right now, I think you and I should go talk. Alone."

Cassie pulled back, rattled at the way Suzanne seemed to have read her mind. Impossible, of course, but the way she said it was really creepy. No way was she going anywhere alone with her.

She was contemplating another tactic for her escape when the clinking of chains paired with the rumble of horses' hooves sounded nearby. In unison, all three of them turned to watch as Carrington rode up atop his horse-drawn wagon. His hat shadowed his face, but Cassie could still see the hint of a beard on his cheeks and chin.

"Annie. Did you get your things?" Carrington's gaze shifted to Blake, his expression turning hard. "You're supposed to be out on the east property."

Blake smiled and addressed Annie and Suzanne. "Ladies. I have work to get to." With a tip of his hat, he added, "Good day," and strolled off in the opposite direction from where Carrington had just arrived.

"Hello, Carrington," Suzanne purred. Cassie watched her sashay over to the side of the wagon. "You seem a bit out of sorts. Is marriage not treating you well?" She glanced over her shoulder at Annie and smiled wickedly.

Carrington's lip curled into a grin of veiled politeness. "Suzanne." He nodded once before returning his attention to Annie. "Are you ready?" His voice softened a mere fraction, but Cassie heard it, nonetheless.

She immediately went to the wagon, reached a hand up to Carrington's extended arm, and allowed him to pull her onto the seat. After scooting in close to his side, she gushed like a newlywed when he dipped his head and placed a gentle kiss at her temple. Annie felt a sense of possessiveness and excitement over being kissed by Carrington, while Cassie derived more pleasure from that exchange than she should have. It felt good knowing Annie had won the man over someone as striking, and experienced, as Suzanne.

She waved sweetly to the auburn beauty when Carrington clicked his tongue and set the horses in motion. Something flashed in Suzanne's eyes that caused slivers of ice to stick in Cassie's veins.

"You can't escape fate," Suzanne said, her voice so low Cassie wondered how she managed to hear, "unless you save her."

What on earth was that about? Cassie was about to ask what Suzanne meant, but the woman turned her back and walked away. When Annie glanced up at Carrington, he merely smiled at her, like he'd not heard Suzanne speaking to his wife.

Cassie was still pondering the strange encounter when Carrington called the horses to a halt. They'd made it only as far as Third Avenue when Sheriff Anders walked out into the middle of the dirt-packed street, blocking their path.

He stood, feet spread wide, one wrist resting over the revolver at his hip. "Afternoon, Mrs. Chambers." Annie huddled closer to Carrington as traffic around them continued past. "I was wantin' to ask how you was doing. Make sure you're gettin' along all right in your new situation." Anders spit a thick stream of brown saliva to the ground and licked his fleshy lips.

Carrington's jaw clenched, the muscle flexing with his effort to suppress his ire.

Annie cringed, and pressed her thigh against Carrington's. Cassie noticed for the first time the pistol seated inside the holster attached to his belt. "I'm fine, Sheriff, thank you for asking," she replied.

In a gesture of support, or for show, Carrington reached over and clasped her hand in his, lacing their fingers together. The pad of his thumb made slow circles around the base of hers.

The sheriff didn't miss the intimate display between Carrington and Annie. "Well, I hope things stay that way," he sneered, and spit again before turning on a heel to clear out of their way.

Passersby and people on the boardwalk stopped to gawk, the old-fashioned version of rubbernecking. The street had gone eerily quiet. To punctuate the awkward silence, a hawk flew overhead, its screech echoing through the still air. Cassie peered around and saw dozens of townsfolk out and about on their various tasks, paused as if frozen in time, watching the scene play out.

For some reason, this display in the street was a straw that broke the proverbial camel's back. She had a feeling the sheriff did this sort of thing every time Carrington came into town.

Cassie, who couldn't keep her mouth shut when she should, called out, "Excuse me, Sheriff. Has my husband done something wrong here? Is there any specific reason why you continue to harass him?"

An even heavier silence descended over the town. Nobody moved. Even a baby who'd started to squawk was hushed.

Sheriff Anders' chin quivered, and his face reddened. He looked like a balloon about to pop. When he spoke, he choked on his own spit before pushing a big glop of tobacco to the ground, then turned malevolent eyes on Annie.

"Your husband here is a criminal. In my town." He thumped his chest, speaking more to the crowd that had formed than to her. "I aim to keep it peaceful and that means keeping a close eye on the likes of him." A fat finger pointed toward Carrington, who remained silent.

Cassie took his silence as consent for her defense of him, so she squared her shoulders and continued. "Last I heard, he went to prison and served his time." Each word struck the air like the bong of a clock. "So, what you're doing now is nothing more than harassment, which we could sue you for." She had no idea if that were true or not. In her time, it might be, but where she was now, she didn't know if that was the case. She didn't care. Her rant sounded believable and she smiled smugly.

"Believe me," she continued, her confidence growing, "we have enough money to keep a fight like that tied up in the court system for as long as necessary."

A palpable wave of warning emanated from Carrington. He squeezed her fingers. "That's enough, wife." His voice held an edge so sharp it could slice the air. His lips tightened and the creases around his eyes deepened when he turned his dark gaze on her. "You've said enough." He pulled his hand from hers and urged the horses forward again, clearly intending to run over the sheriff if he didn't slither out of the way first.

Cassie's confidence left her, like a bird flying a coop. Carrington's behavior was unpredictable. He'd even pulled away from her, so their thighs were no longer touching. Fear inched into her chest, squeezing it like a vise. She couldn't read his face to determine if he was angry or pleased.

Fearing imminent bodily contact, whether from a lusty Carrington or an angry one needing to blow off some steam, she pinched the underside of her arm hard enough to make her gasp . . .

***

. . . And wake up.

The idea of an angry Carrington made her laugh a bit tremulously. She admonished herself for fearing something that happened long, long ago, something that hadn't even happened to *her*.

The book lay across her lap. The sooner she got through this the sooner ghost Carrington would be gone. She needed to read on.

With a sinking feeling in the pit of her stomach, she turned the page and scanned the next entry.

Carrington made me dinner.

Nope.

She quickly flipped past that one, tossing around thoughts of Suzanne, her words, and the threat she posed to Annie and Carrington's wedded life.

SIXTEEN

It was nearing midnight by the time Cassie turned the page to the entry dated August 12, 1890. She'd like to say her motivation was strictly the desire to end all this craziness and get the dreams to stop. The truth was, she wanted to know more of what Carrington was like. Alive. She yawned as she began to read.

I spoke to Blake today.

The eerie pull grabbed at Cassie, and she willingly gave in to it and entered the past again.

***

Annie had plans to cook her husband some breakfast. It appeared that she wasn't overly adept at starting a fire in the black wood-burning stove. The kitchen appliance was practically new, not the rusted version it would become—the one that ghost Carrington was restoring now.

Unfortunately, Cassie wouldn't be able to offer Annie much help with the current situation, as her fire-starting skills were also lacking. But she'd give it a try. It wasn't like she had to rub sticks together or anything so extreme.

Bending down, she reached in and moved some of the wood around in the cavern of the stove. Next, she struck a match she'd located on the nearby shelf and held it to the kindling piled beneath a teepee of wood.

"Come on, you stupid thing." She blew furiously on the smoldering pile of tinder. When a thin wisp of smoke appeared, she blew harder. An encouraging haze of white billowed around the inside of the stove's cavern, some escaping into the air around her. Thrilled at the prospect of getting a fire going much faster than she expected, she kept blowing, waving a hand at the plume drifting up into her face.

"Fuck!" she exclaimed, when she accidentally touched her finger against a glowing twig while adjusting the pile of wood with a short stick. Instinctively, she sucked on the tip of her finger, running her tongue over the pea-sized blister that had formed there. With hand on hip, she scowled at the stove before seeking out something to use as a salve.

When she turned around, she stuttered to a halt. Carrington stood in the doorway, wearing a white cotton nightshirt that reached past his knees. His fists were clenched at his sides, and he was breathing hard, like he'd run a race.

"What in damnation are you doing?" He marched to the stove, turned a spoke on the chimney pipe to open the damper. Next, he added and adjusted the wood inside into another teepee . . . just like Cassie had done. Striking another match—ditto for Cassie—he held it beneath the kindling. After a few gentle puffs of air—hers might not have been so gentle—a flame kicked up. Finally, he added a larger chunk of wood before closing the iron door with a clang.

Cassie hovered a foot away, fingers clutching the apron at her waist. When Carrington looked her way, she licked her lips nervously. His gaze lowered to her mouth, and his pupils dilated, the color around them a thin ring of gray. The heat in the room suddenly had nothing to do with the fire in the stove.

"I distinctly recall telling you there was only one place that word you said was permitted." His brows inched upward and there was an unmistakable lilt to his voice when he added, "Unless you feel this is that place." Both his hands lifted away from his sides, indicating the kitchen at-large. His words, his eyes, and his body, so minimally covered, triggered an illicit tremor through to Cassie's core.

She knew that her vocabulary verged on unacceptable at times, even in the twenty-first century. She wasn't about to have that discussion with Carrington now, though, because that would require remaining in close proximity to him.

This scene was supposed to be about Blake. Where was Blake?

Her voice was unsteady when she said, "Sorry. I'll try to—" To what? To only use the word exactly as it was meant to be used, in the prime moment of passion when the act and the word became one? She fought against the flush of red she knew was mottling Annie's cheeks.

As the fire in the stove crackled softly behind the iron door, Carrington advanced toward her, stopping three feet away. His nightshirt exposed his legs from his knees down, showing off the dark press of fine hair over muscular shins and calves. She squelched a groan when her gaze wandered higher—he did indeed have something more specific on his mind.

Circling around to the other side of the counter, Cassie shied away from him. "I wanted to make you something to eat this morning."

A low hum emanated from his throat. "Good. I'm starved." His drawl got heavier, and his eyelids lowered.

The temperature in the room was stifling. She ran a finger beneath the high-necked, tightly buttoned collar of her simple lavender cotton dress. Good grief, she'd be sweating buckets by noon. Her hair wasn't pinned up yet, either. It hung in long locks that reached nearly to her waist. She flipped the ends over her shoulders, clearing it away from the sides of her face and her neck.

In Carrington's presence, the way his hungry gaze was devouring her, it was no wonder Annie never felt plain. Not that she was ugly, but as overdressed as she was, Cassie certainly didn't find anything sexy about her. Carrington, however, was noticeably attracted and interested in her just as she was.

"I, uh, think I'll head on out to gather some eggs." She skirted around him and bolted for the front door. "Be right back," she hollered over her shoulder before escaping outside. "So help me, Annie, your journal entries should warn people when you encounter your husband. Give a girl like me a heads up about a wild kitchen tryst."

Of course, Annie wouldn't dare to write about such intimacies. Cassie's mind was still scrambling over the possibilities surrounding that idea as she fast-walked all the way through the barn and out the back door.

Hens squawked and scurried out of the way at the intrusion as she approached the chicken coop. She leaned heavily against the doorframe, grateful for its sturdy construction, and waited for her wildly beating heart to calm down. Inhaling deeply several times, she savored the warm smell of straw, hay, and the briny scent of horse sweat and manure.

Recovered somewhat from her near miss at sex in the kitchen, she stepped inside the coop and retrieved a basket hanging from a nail along the wall. From one of many equally sized cubbies that covered the length of one wall, she collected an egg from a nest. As she placed it carefully in the wicker basket, she saw Blake exiting the barn.

"Blake," she called out.

Blake glanced up and offered a small wave. "Hello, Annie," he said, less formally than he'd been on other occasions. Cassie wondered at it but concluded that he knew Carrington wasn't nearby. The little gap between Blake's teeth showed when he smiled at her. She encouraged him to join her in egg collecting, which is how they came to be standing shoulder-to-shoulder in the small enclosure of the chicken coop.

Cassie wasn't exactly sure where to start the conversation. Asking, *So, are you planning to kill me?* didn't seem right. She sensed that he genuinely cared about Annie, as a friend, and she couldn't fathom him being a monster. Instead, she chose to let the conversation lead itself. "I feel we've hardly had the chance to talk. How have you been?"

"I'm real good. Spend my days workin' and my nights, well," he faltered, staring abashedly into the egg basket, "well, I spend my nights with friends mostly."

This, she assumed, meant he spent his nights at the Sagebrush Saloon. He'd also probably found a woman who frequented that type of place. Someone like Suzanne? Cassie's fingers curled around the egg in her hand almost too tight. She placed it gently in the basket.

Suzanne *had* appeared rather friendly toward Blake the other day. Could it be they had something going on? A tiny spark of concern snuck into Cassie's brain. She understood she had no right to be bothered by anything Blake did. If he liked Suzanne, and what she offered him, at least it would keep the woman that much farther away from Carrington. Annie was thinking similarly.

"So," Cassie teased, "are you and Suzanne courting?" She nudged her shoulder against his arm.

Blake lowered his head and shifted on his feet. "Oh, I wouldn't go so far as to say we're courting. We get along fine enough."

And just like that, all his uneasiness disappeared, and he began chatting up a storm. He shared with her his desire to buy one of the adjoining properties. Someday, he hoped to have his own farm, raise his own crops, start a family, and all the things a young man his age might dream of.

Cassie was laughing at something Blake said when Carrington rounded the corner of the barn. The laugh caught in her throat as their gazes collided.

"I wondered what was taking you so long, wife," he said in a low, menacing voice.

She could tell by his rigid stance and his overall demeanor that he was not happy.

Blake ducked out of the enclosed structure. "It was nice to see you, Mrs. Chambers. I got work to do. You have a nice day." He dipped his chin at her before exiting. "Mornin' boss," he said as he strolled past Carrington.

Before Cassie could follow suit and escape the chicken coop, Carrington's glowering presence filled the space where Blake had been a moment before.

"I'm curious," he said, his tone so gentle it was all the more intimidating. "There's not a woman around for a hundred miles who would purposely marry me, considering my past." He retrieved an egg from a nest and set it in the basket Cassie held tight against her waist. The feigned air of calm was contradicted by the hard set of his jaw. "Yet, here you are, my bride, who I keep finding in company with my field hand." Another egg bumped against the others.

"There's nothing for me to be concerned about, is there, Annie?"

The hard soles of Annie's shoes scuffed against the straw-covered wood floorboards when Cassie took a nervous step back—away from his intimidating presence. She had to tilt her head back as he drew nearer. He was standing so close. Too close.

"Of course not." Her words came out breathy. She was beginning to feel like a trapped animal. She didn't miss the flinty expression in his eyes as the tension in his face changed.

"Is this"—he nodded in the direction of where Blake had disappeared into the barn— "what I can expect every time I turn around?" He pried the egg basket from her fingers and set it on the ground. Taking another step closer, he forced her to move back, deeper into the corner of the shed.

"You're my wife," he said darkly. "Don't put me in a position to have to call him out." Jealousy rolled off him like steam from a boiling cauldron. He advanced another small step toward her.

"I-I don't know what you're talking about." He was so close now that Cassie could feel his warm breath on her cheek. "We're just friends." She wondered if by calling out Blake that meant he would duel in her honor. Did that still happen? Her head thumped against the wall at her back.

Resting his hands on either side of her shoulders, he leaned in close enough that she could smell the fresh scent of the musky soap or shaving lotion or whatever it was he used. It made Cassie's mouth water and did funny things to her insides. She drew in a slow, deep breath to capture it. His hand came up, and he pushed her hair off her face, tucking the strands behind her ear.

"Why did you marry me?"

"C-Carrington," Annie's voice quivered. Cassie pressed her palms to his chest. His skin was warm beneath his shirt as she pushed firmly against him, trying to create distance between them. She didn't dare say, "I married you because I had to," which was the truth. She knew that she, Annie that is, had no regrets from the outcome.

"I-I married you because I wanted to." She pushed against his chest again before giving up, realizing he wasn't budging.

His fingers curled around Annie's more delicate ones where they fluttered against his shirt. He bent forward, pressing his forehead against hers. There was a palpable silence between them, broken only by the quiet, pleasurable trill of a dozen contented chickens.

"I admit to being a jealous man and will try my best to harness those feelings," he whispered. "But do not test me, Annie."

Cassie smiled at the quiet confession made by a man clearly in love with his wife. She reached up and curved her hand against the back of his neck, her thumb touching on the pulse pounding rapidly beneath his skin.

"I will give you no cause to be jealous," she promised.

His head dipped lower, his lips touching against her ear. "Let's go back into the house."

There was not one moment of doubt as to his intentions. Cassie's heart skipped a beat. She braced her legs and pulled her hand back against his, but he didn't release his grip.

"That is, unless you would prefer to stay right here." He pressed closer and she tilted her head to the side, exposing her neck to his eager lips. "I am not opposed to either," he stated as he pecked small kisses against her neck.

"Carrington." Annie's chest rose and fell with her increasing excitement. Cassie imagined in fine detail the wild tryst they could have there, with her pressed to the wall. "Blake's nearby," she whispered. A second later, her ability to speak evaporated as Carrington's thumb brushed against her jaw, tilting her head the other direction so he could lavish attention on the opposite side of her throat.

"Then let's go back inside," he murmured, his voice husky with his desire.

Cassie lost all ability to think coherently as he straightened and pulled her along with him out of the chicken coop. Delicious vibrations of electric heat triggered every nerve in her body. As curious as she was to experience more of what he offered, she knew she shouldn't. She hated to do it, but bit down on her tongue, hard enough to force herself to return to her reality.

***

"Is that all you two did?" Cassie growled, flopping onto her side, on her warm bed in her new house, arms curled tight around her pillow. Tiny flickers of emotional intensity raced along her nerve endings. Unbidden desire left her tense and wanting, and she doubted she'd be able to fall asleep.

SEVENTEEN

Carrington waited near the riverbank's edge, mesmerized by the black creature that was the Snake River. It slithered past in silent search of some unidentifiable prey. He flicked a rock across the water. The moonlight shined so bright he was able to follow the path of the rippling circles of the rock's journey over the dark glass.

He was at the western edge of his property, or what was left of his property. The river marked the boundary. At Cassie's request, he'd wiled away a few hours distanced from the house. He was unaffected by the cool night air and gentle breeze that drifted up from the murky water gliding past.

It was well after midnight. There was still a light on in the upstairs window of the house, off in the distance. However, he was uncertain if that meant Cassie was awake, as she always slept with at least one light on. He'd stifled the urge to check on her a dozen times. Assuming she was asleep now, he decided it was safe to peek in. He'd done what she asked and had given her time alone. Hopefully, it was enough for her to have calmed down.

When he entered her bedroom, he found her asleep, safely ensconced in the warm glow of a nearby lamp. He eased down onto the bed. Cassie's bare legs shifted, her knees coming to rest against Carrington's thigh. His wandering gaze took in the shimmering pink color on her toenails and her exposed, shapely calves and thighs. He shook his head. She had yet to wear appropriate attire for a woman. The closest had been the yellow shift, which she called a dress, but even that only scantily covered parts of her body she should keep guarded.

Cassie shifted one leg, bending it so her knee hovered above her hips.

"Jimmy. Stop." Her hushed murmur drove through Carrington like an arrow.

Deep lines formed between her brows as her expression twisted into a grimace. He wanted to awaken her but chose instead to allow her mind to process whatever it was that held her locked in its clutches. One clenched fist slid down her thigh. She whimpered again, "No, Jimmy."

Her eyes opened, but Carrington could tell she wasn't awake. She saw only the nightmarish theatrics happening behind her eyelids. Her head thrashed against the pillow.

"Stop, Jimmy!" Her voice broke on a choked cry and she pushed furiously at the hem of her clothing. Suddenly, she rolled across the bed, away from Carrington and jumped to her feet, hands in the air in a defensive pose. Her sightless eyes stared right through him.

"Please, no." Fat tears rolled down her cheeks.

She whirled around, her back to him. Carrington got up and slowly moved to stand in front of her. Both her hands gripped at some imaginary force against her neck. She shot an elbow backward, then shrieked before falling to the ground. Curled up into a ball, she clutched at her throat.

"Help." The word was but a choked whisper.

Carrington knelt beside her, one hand balanced on his knee, the other he placed on the least threatening spot he could think of—the top of her head. The pad of his thumb made light, comforting strokes in the deep V between her eyebrows. After a few seconds, her face relaxed, and her breathing settled into a natural cadence.

"Rest easy now. I'm here."

Her hands eased their hold on her neck. Carrington retrieved a blanket and pillow from the bed, draping them carefully under and on her without waking her. Then he sat back, propped against the bed, and let his hands hang limp across his raised knees. And he watched her.

She'd survived a horrific act of violence, yet still had the ability to feel and show compassion for others. Even him. Her sense of humor and sharp tongue were positive traits in his opinion. They showed her true character beneath the façade of fear fabricated into a shield.

A life with her would be interesting, if not a bit challenging. She'd argue with him on everything and curse when she didn't get her way. He'd reprimand her for her excessive use of foul language, even if he found the trait both entertaining and shocking. Never would he break the spirit that was so much a part of her—like Jimmy tried to do.

Anger coursed through Carrington's veins, so intense he felt he might burst into flames. If he could, he'd kill Jimmy. Unfortunately, that possibility only existed if the man made an appearance while Carrington was still here. But time was growing short for him with each passing entry Cassie read. He doubted he'd be able to help her like she was helping him, no matter how desperately he wanted to.

The sun was past seven o'clock when she began to stir. Should he stay or go before she woke? He opted to stay. She had to keep reading. The sooner they reached the end, the sooner he'd be able to depart this world. Feelings were awakening within him that would do neither of them any favors, should he give in to them.

Cassie stretched her arms high above her head and groaned as all her muscles pulled. Rolling onto her side, she plumped the pillow beneath her head.

The hours Carrington had spent highlighting her qualities were speckled with other, more sordid, imaginings. He tried blocking them out, but some made it through—like what it would be like to make love to her. She was reckless and unconventional, qualities he surprisingly found irresistible. He masked those unbidden emotions when she opened her eyes.

Upon finding him beside her, she stiffened anyway. "What are you doing here?" Her voice was a sleepy rasp. The chaos of reliving the past was displayed in the tightness of her features and in the stiffness of her shoulders as she pushed up on one elbow. Slowly, she climbed to her feet and tossed the blanket and pillow back on the bed.

"I had a nightmare," she said, matter-of-factly. "The first since I got here."

Sliding up to sit on the edge of the mattress, he confirmed her statement. "You did. I'm sorry."

Her face blanched. "What did I say? Never mind. I don't want to know." Skirting around the end of the bed, she pulled the blankets back into place. Carrington helped from his side.

"It's your fault." Her voice was incredibly even in her accusation.

Carrington drew back, affronted. "I beg your pardon. *My* fault? How could you blame such an awful act of savagery and cowardice on me?"

A small laugh bubbled up from Cassie's chest. "Because, I read a couple of Annie's entries last night and learned that you were a fiercely jealous man." A telling flush of red told him more than her words that she'd experienced something else, something she liked, in her recent journey to the past. She turned and bustled off toward the closet.

"You cannot put me in the same category as that bastard." He stalked after her. The sharp challenge in his voice brought her head up. She spun around, the ready retort frozen in her throat when she saw him coming at her.

"Carrington." She held a hand up in a small effort to halt his progress as he bore down on her.

"I had every right to be jealous." His words were clipped, brusque. He stopped before her, forcing her head up by pressing his thumb beneath her chin. His bare toes touched hers. "I'm certain what you're referencing had to do with Blake. You saw the way he was with her. The way he was always around."

She shook her head, her hair scratching softly against the wall. "It wasn't like that." Her tongue peeked out to lick her lips, leaving behind a shiny gloss. "They were friends."

"Tell me what you read." He leaned close enough to see the little dark flecks in the irises of her eyes when she raised them to meet his. She blinked, and he forced a smile at the nearly indiscernible tremor that raced through her.

"I went to get eggs. Blake came out to the chicken coop and we talked. Then you—" She cleared her throat.

Carrington issued a questioning grunt. "I don't recall an altercation in the chicken coop." He lowered his head half an inch. His lips stilled near the spot on her throat where she was most vulnerable. The place where he wanted more than anything to kiss. She fidgeted against the wall, like she wanted to disappear through it.

"Well, um, it started in the house. Annie was trying to make a fire in the stove." She raised her finger to display an angry, bubbled blister. "You, uh, came rushing in."

He nodded as the memory tickled at his brain. "I thought she was burning the house down."

"Yes. Well, you got the fire started, which Annie would have been able to manage, had you not taken over, by the way." His brow quirked up and she went on.

"You tried to, you know, had intentions of—"

He made a purring sound so close to her skin he could almost feel the repercussion.

"Mm. I recall now. We nearly christened the kitchen that morning." He drew in her scent, the one he'd grown accustomed to that was specifically Cassie. It was an enticing blend of rose and musk. His tongue flicked out against her throat, at the top of her scar, near the purple mark of the hickey. Her breath hitched in her chest and she turned her face away.

"Do I frighten you? Still?" he asked.

Instead of answering him, she inched sideways along the wall. He planted his palm against it, arm straight, effectively blocking her escape.

"Yes." She was alert, poised to run if the opportunity arose.

"Why? I've been a perfect gentleman. Practically." A grin tugged at his mouth. Her breathing grew shallow and her pupils dilated.

"You're close to a gentleman *now*," she bit out, "but back then, I saw you angry and I don't know what you're capable of. Like, like," she bit her lip, "Jimmy."

"Tell me more about what happened that day," he coaxed, leaning close enough that their chests touched when they both drew a deep breath.

***

It was such a simple request on the surface, but one that brought with it fear and uncertainty. Especially coming from the man before her who defied odds and existed in a world where he shouldn't. A man who had the potential to hurt her. Even still, her growing attraction to him was as unearthly as he was, and it had her quaking in her skin.

She gathered herself before saying, "I don't want to have this conversation with you." Aiming for stern, her words came out sounding weary, defeated. Her head drooped forward and she looked down to his feet. They were bare, toes touching hers. So intimate.

Carrington was unrelenting. "Tell me."

Tell him?

Tell him how in the early years when she first met Jimmy, he'd been a rebel bad boy who targeted her because she was young and innocent? Tell him that she'd learned quickly that he was a narcissist who expected everything his way, or no way? How she, being a young woman, was strong-willed and not weak like he'd assumed, and wouldn't comply with his demands?

After schmoozing her with the love and affection she craved, like any young girl does, he found other ways to bend her to his will. Still, she resisted. The three short years they were together had taken its toll on her. After the first beating, instead of leaving, she grew too terrified to even try.

Would Carrington think that normal, considering the time he existed, where women were property that men controlled? Yet he'd been so kind and gentle with Annie at every turn. Except for that admission of jealousy in the chicken coop, there'd been no indication that he was a brute. Insecurity, doubt, and fear washed through Cassie.

"Obviously, he hurt me," she finally said. "I was just a stupid girl." Shame leaped on the tails of those other emotions and she tried to pull away.

"Did you fight him?" His tone had softened, but that didn't make him any less frightening. Not frightening but intimidating. She quickly concluded that she wasn't truly afraid of him. He was nothing like Jimmy. What she feared most, she realized, was the ache in her heart that Carrington's departure would leave behind.

She pushed her head back into the immovable wall, her chest thrust out. Anger and frustration spilled from her mouth. "Of course, I fought him!" She wanted to shrink into her cocoon of protection, where pain couldn't reach her. "He'd beat me down so much by the time of the last attack, I was no longer whole."

Wherever Carrington's body touched hers, searing heat followed. "What did he do to you that makes you not whole?"

"What? I don't want to go into all the gory details." This was her dark past and it was none of his business.

The steel set of his jaw told her more than his words that he wouldn't back down. "I want you to tell me." His other palm pressed against the wall beside her head. "Go on. Tell me."

Maybe it was the feeling of being trapped or maybe it was all her past and current fears colliding, either way, something dark and volatile brewed inside her. Like a pressure cooker at its peak, she vented all the emotions boiling within.

"Is this—" She turned her head and pointed a finger at her throat. "Is this what you want to see? You want to know how big the knife was that sliced open my throat?"

He surveyed her with a cool, level gaze. "No. I can guess that. I want you to tell me how you fought him."

She brought her hands up to his chest and attempted to shove him away. He was a solid wall, insurmountable, unable to be breached.

"Tell me how you could have escaped him. Show me." There was an air of intimidation about him as he grabbed her wrists and locked them in one hand above her head.

A gut-wrenching fear tore through her. Here she was, in a house with a man who had been a convicted killer and whose wife disappeared under questionable circumstances. An image of Jimmy immobilized her. Jimmy had locked his hands around her wrists once, like Carrington was doing now. She yanked hard, but he didn't release her. Panic threatened to drown her.

Once a victim, always a victim?

Never again. All the anger and fear she'd felt during and after Jimmy bubbled to the surface. She fought for the life she'd lost once, so long ago.

"He did terrible things to me," she yelled while trying to yank her arms down. Carrington still didn't ease his grip on her wrists.

"I fought as hard as I could." She choked back a sob. "I even got away from him." Her head moved side-to-side as she recalled the pain from the memories that swamped her. "I thought I was safe, you know, out of his grasp."

She tugged her arms again. This time he released her. She stilled, free but unwilling to lower her arms.

"Running was the wrong thing to do," she added, gravely.

Carrington's hands slid slowly back up Cassie's arms until his fingers clasped with hers. He lowered them along the wall, releasing them at her sides. Then he touched both his palms on either side of her jaw. His thumbs smoothed away the tears that had spilled over her lashes.

"I'd have killed him, even if it meant going back to prison," he said matter-of-factly, a steely edge to his voice.

She believed without a doubt that he meant it and at the same time feared the truth that he was capable of that act. He'd done it once, killed a man in cold blood, even though that man had killed his father. Had he been capable of doing the same thing to Annie?

"It was a long time ago," she whispered. No matter how hard she tried, she couldn't escape the vivid clarity of that sharp blade tearing open her throat. She recalled the sound of her blood gushing from the wound with each beat of her racing heart. It made her a victim every day of her life.

It seemed she was destined to fall for bad men. The latest happened to be a ghost capable of murder. He'd put her in an impossible situation of finding the truth of his past, a past she would never really be part of. He was a man she could never have a future with. She knew that for the fact that it was.

She flinched when his thumb slid down and touched her neck, across where her jugular vein hid, and along the length of the jagged scar.

"This," he emphasized by applying pressure at the thickest edge, near her ear, "does not make you a victim. It makes you a survivor. You didn't die."

"Why are you doing this to me?" The gut-wrenching cry, born of years spent fighting demons that, in her mind, represented all men, tore past her damaged throat. She fought back against the remembered pain.

Leaning in, his lips brushed against her ear as he whispered, "Just because men have the physical strength, doesn't mean they should ever use it against a woman. We're not all like that."

Cassie raised a hand up to swipe at her nose. "I'll never be free of what he's done to me. I don't think I'll ever be able to get close to a man or trust one again. Except Andrew." She hiccupped back a cry, determined to be done with this pathetic demonstration of weakness.

Carrington's laugh startled her. Not because she hadn't heard the sound before, though it was rare. What surprised her was the quick transition from his intensity to the light-hearted warmth she saw in his eyes. He pulled her the scant few inches into the wall of his body.

"I'll take *that* as a challenge. Now, would you mind very much if I kissed you?"

She barely had time to give consent before his lips met hers in an age-old dance. Her hands, hanging lifeless at her sides, stole up around his waist, then higher up, until her palms were pressed tight against the hard muscles of his back. A cry, or moan, she wasn't sure, sounded in her throat as she relished the sweep of his tongue over her lips. She met the thrust of it with her own and anchored her body to his with a tight grip.

His palms slid over her arms and settled about her hips, his fingers taking a firm hold on her backside. She groaned and pulled tighter to him, then stilled when she brushed against the hardness pushing against her pelvic bone.

She jerked away. "Oh. I didn't mean . . ."

Carrington demurred and stepped back, too.

"What would your therapist say, McAllister?"

She began to laugh when a monotonous buzzing interrupted the moment. It stopped a few seconds later, then repeated.

"It's my phone." She ran a shaky hand over the top of her head.

"It did that several times while you slept."

Like a rag doll, Cassie leaned forward and pressed her forehead into his chest. "I should check it." His warm, solid hand on her back held her to him for a few more seconds. Then their shared moment was over.

Stepping around him, she weaved her way across the room on unsteady legs to retrieve her phone. Pressing a finger to the screen, she frowned. "It's Andrew. I wonder if this qualifies as an emergency that warrants a conversation with my shrink," she muttered, as she stared at the display.

Before the phone stopped buzzing, she set it back on the dresser. Andrew said she needed to work through her issues alone as best she could. If she answered his call, she'd be relying on him to calm her, as always, instead of relying on herself, which she knew she had to do.

Wrestling with some decision, she steeled her resolve. She had just shared her story with a man she barely knew, yet somehow, she knew him more intimately than she'd known her own husband. And that reflection led her right back to not trusting her own instincts when it came to men.

Something happened in the past that wasn't adding up. Annie of all people was the only innocent one of the bunch. And she'd loved Carrington, lusted after him at a minimum, and with good cause. But was he completely in the clear yet? With each passing scene in the past, he grew darker and stewed more with jealousy. She hoped beyond all else that Annie didn't lie when she said nothing was going on between her and Blake. Cassie was determined to find out what happened. She'd just have to be very careful and not let herself get hurt in the process—her heart, if not her person.

"I have to use the bathroom. When I come back, we're going to . . . well, I'm going to keep reading." She heaved a sigh as she stepped from the room into the hall. "I really need to finish this so I, and you, can move on with our lives."

She disappeared down the hall, missing the streak of hurt and sadness that flashed across Carrington's face.

EIGHTEEN

Cassie peered into the mirror. Her lips were slightly puffy from the kiss, her neck pink from where the stubble on Carrington's chin had brushed over it. Not only had he *not* been put off by the ugly scar, he'd devoted special attention to it. It was like each kiss was an undo button that had the power to make the damage disappear, one gentle touch of his lips at a time. For the first time in a very long time, she didn't feel like a hideous monster.

"If only he were real," she whispered. If ever magic existed, she fervently wished it would grant her request. But wishes only came true in fairy tales. The fact was Carrington was a ghost. She rolled her eyes at her reflection. The fact? Like it was any other ordinary day when she encountered a ghost? There were people who made their living hunting ghosts. It was that knowledge that gave credence to her acceptance of Carrington.

She angled her head. The hickey came from the past. Her thumb slipped back and forth over the tender blister on her finger; another thing that happened while she'd been Annie.

The movie *Fight Club* came to mind where the main character got involved in a secret club where men could beat the crap out of each other. The physical impacts of those fights increased as the movie progressed. The viewer saw the character riddled with bandages, blood, black eyes, cuts, and bruises. The story unfolded to reveal that the whole thing had happened in his mind—he had an alternate personality—and all along he'd been inflicting the physical damage on himself.

Cassie was certain—or at least very hopeful—that wasn't the case here. These things were really happening to her, and ghost Carrington was really a presence in her house. With a resigned sigh, she exited the bathroom and returned to the bedroom where she found her ghost near the dark fireplace, lost in his own memories.

She scrambled for something to chat about, something to distract her from the strange feelings awakening inside her heart. It was like being a teenager again, on the precipice of new love. She felt awkward, shy, and aroused.

Peering around the room, she noticed that one of the walls was freshly painted. Not one that she'd done, either. "When did you do that?"

He gave her a rueful smile. "While you were sleeping." A gentle crease appeared between his brows and his mouth opened as if he were going to speak. The words didn't form, and he turned his head.

Cassie's chest constricted at the thought of his many losses and having to spend all those years alone, not knowing what happened to his wife. It saddened her and renewed her hope that what she was doing would help. If she were truthful, not all of it was as dreadful as she'd been making it out to be.

"Come here." She moved to the bed and sat down. With a soft *harrumph*, she added, "I'm starting to sound like the bossy you." Patting the bed beside her, she grabbed the journal, intent upon finishing this task she'd been given. The mattress dipped when he sat, causing her to lean into him.

"Let's get through this so . . ." she began, hesitantly, "so you can do whatever it is you need to do. After." Clearing her throat, she flipped open the book.

"Hmmm. 'August thirteen, Carrington was at'—Nope." She traced her finger quickly to the next entry.

That two-beat throaty sound he made sent a jolt of electricity straight through her.

"'August fourteen. The sheriff was out at the house today.'"

The sound that reverberated near her this time was more of a growl, not the warm chuckle she enjoyed so much.

Carrington nestled closer to her, but before she slipped into the past, he said, "I want you to know that there are things that happened in my life with Annie that I'll not say I'm proud of." His words sounded ominous and Cassie's nerves tightened. "I just want you to know that before you experience them firsthand." His arm slid behind her, a palm resting against her hip on the bed, bracing her as she drifted away.

***

The day was sweltering. It had to be nearly ninety degrees in the house. The main source of the unbearable warmth came from the stove beside her. She made choking sounds as she attacked the top four buttons of her dress, opening the front down far enough to where she could see the lacy edge of her camisole. Next, she unbuttoned the sleeves and rolled them as high as they'd go on her forearms. There really was no notable difference, but at least she felt less constrained.

"Who in their right mind starts a fire in this heat?"

She flung open the door of the cook stove. Inside was a cast-iron Dutch oven. Bubbling away in a meaty brown broth was a beef roast complete with potatoes and carrots. It appeared Carrington was an old-fashioned meat and potatoes kind of guy, but then again everyone in this time probably was. She doubted there were many vegetarians running about in this era.

There was a flash of movement outside the window. She leaned over a small table with a metal bucket sitting on top to peer out the window to the yard beyond. It occurred to her that the bucket before her was most likely the equivalent of a sink, which meant hand-washing dishes. She instantly missed her luxuries.

Whatever she might have seen outside had disappeared. Curiosity got the better of her. After a quick test of the potatoes with a fork to determine how much time they had left to cook, she rushed from the room. Her sturdy heeled boots clacked on the wood floor as she headed out the front door.

There was nobody in sight as she advanced across the yard. Inside the barn, she slowed, taking a moment to adjust to the darker space.

"Hellooo," she called out. "Is anyone there?" Walking along the row of stalls, she saw that both Blake's and Carrington's horses were absent. Two other mares bobbed their heads over the railing, their dark, soulful eyes blinking at Cassie's intrusion upon their domain. She rubbed a hand across each horse's neck as she passed.

A tinny, crunching, scraping sound drew her attention. She followed it out beyond the back door of the barn. The sound came again. *Crunch. Scrape.* Turning the corner, she drew up short.

"Sheriff? What are you doing here?"

Startled, Sheriff Anders stilled, one foot on the edge of a spade. He quickly covered his unease by relaxing his tight grip on the handle and leaned heavily against it, feigning an air of nonchalance.

"Miss Annie." He nodded at her, but his eyes darted this way and that before he responded. "I was just doing a favor for Blake." The star-shaped badge affixed to the lapel of his wool vest glinted dully in the shade of the barn. Similarly, so did the top of the Colt revolver set in the holster low on his hip.

Cassie knew right away that he was lying. She saw the wheels turning in his mind as he searched for words to string together. Did he think she was stupid enough to believe he'd do anything kind to help Blake or anyone else associated with Carrington?

At his feet was a mound of dirt that had been turned up. Two other similar piles ran along the building's edge.

"Interesting," she said. "What is it Mr. Hanson needed?"

His eyes darted about again before coming back to Cassie. "Dead cat."

Her eyebrows shot up and she crossed her arms over her chest. "Blake asked you to bury a dead cat?"

It didn't take long for the sheriff to catch on that Annie wasn't buying his ridiculous tale. Perching the shovel against the barn, he straightened, spat a glob of brown spittle to the ground, and approached her. He bristled with irritation at her interruption.

"Well, I understand if you might not want me to do this. I'll take the critter on outta here and dump it someplace else."

"That's so kind of you," Cassie said sarcastically. "I'll let Blake know you were here, when he returns. Which should be any minute now." Out of habit, she turned her wrist to look at the watch she typically sported, in her own life. She had no idea if it was true that Blake would show up soon. She just assumed she'd been cooking for someone besides Carrington, considering the amount of food in the oven. It could very well have been for both men, she reasoned.

"I hope you're doing fine out here with Chambers. I was right sorry that you had to marry him," the sheriff added.

Cassie imagined there might have been a flash of kindness in his expression. But, just as quickly as it appeared, it vanished.

"You shouldn't be sorry. I'm exactly where I want to be." Initiating the movement that would encourage him to leave, she headed back through the barn. The sheriff followed, veering off to the other side of the building as they exited. He'd left his horse tethered to the wheel of a wagon, out of sight of the house.

"Have a good day, Miss, er, Mrs. Chambers." He spurred his mount and bolted off. The dust left behind hung like a heavy drape in the hot, still air.

"Ugh." Cassie swiped her palms over the back of her neck to remove the sweat dripping beneath her collar. She contemplated digging up one of the holes to see what the sheriff had really been burying but remembered the food cooking on the stove. Later would be soon enough to investigate, she thought, as she scurried back into the house, cursing the blasted heat. She swore the first thing she'd have her general contractor take care of in *her* time, when he finally showed up for work, was to arrange to have central air installed.

A quarter hour later, she heard the clopping sound of horse hooves. It was Blake riding into the yard. Near the barn, he dismounted and removed the saddle off his black

196

stallion. What was it with that man and black anyway? It so contradicted his boyish appearance.

All the bad people in movies wore black. Cassie worried at her lower lip wondering if that was only Hollywood theatrics. She'd soon find out. Racing back outside, she called out from the top of the porch.

"Blake. I have some dinner ready, if you're hungry." She waved, bidding him to come over. It was lunchtime, so she assumed that was the reason he had come in from the fields. Which also meant Carrington would be arriving shortly for the midday meal.

Cassie scrambled through Annie's thoughts to determine if she was supposed to feed Blake. It seemed rude not to. She found that Annie didn't have any qualms about the invitation made. Cassie would have done so regardless, as she needed to utilize every opportunity that arose to ask questions about Annie's life.

Blake gave her a smile. From this distance, she couldn't quite see the small gap between his teeth, the one thing that detracted from his darker countenance.

"Be right over," he called out.

Cassie was near the stove when he strode into the kitchen several minutes later. He'd removed his hat. Droplets of water fell from the ends of his dark hair, his neck and collar absorbing much of it. She graced him with an encouraging smile before returning to her task.

"Roast beef, carrots, potatoes, and," she called out over her shoulder as she stirred the contents in the pot warming on the stove top, "I'm finishing up some gravy. Have a seat. It'll be ready in a minute."

A chair scraped the floor at the table, and she heard him ease himself down with a tired sigh. When she placed his meal before him and sank down in the chair opposite, he balked.

"I'll take this back to my bunk in the barn. Thank you kindly." He made to get up, but Cassie halted him.

"Stay. Please. I want to talk some." Blips of warning started going off in Annie's mind, like the strobe of a fire alarm. Cassie considered it but couldn't find anything in her behavior that was out of place. She and Blake were separated by a table and eating a meal. There was nothing suspect in her actions.

Blake's attempt at a smile failed. "I don't imagine your husband will be too pleased that I'm supping in the house, alone with you here."

She waved a dismissive hand through the air. "Oh, don't you worry about him. I'll handle it." She followed that with a willful laugh, imagining how unlikely it would be that the sweet and submissive little Annie could keep Carrington in line.

Cassie was here now and would be the one encountering Annie's bear of a husband. Steering the conversation away from the often-grouchy spouse, she asked Blake about his day and more about his plans to start his own farm. She soon learned that he'd set his hopes on a property that adjoined Carrington's vast lands. It had rich soil, perfect for growing crops. This subject brought to mind her encounter with the sheriff.

"Sheriff Anders was here earlier."

The fork in Blake's hand hovered near his open mouth.

"He said he had a dead cat to bury, at your request."

The fork continued its journey as he scooped a mouthful past his lips. He chewed thoughtfully a moment before swallowing. "He said I told him to?"

She nodded. "I know. It seemed strange. He was burying something, he said. Or was he digging something up?" That hadn't occurred to her. Cassie knew there could be only one thing he'd be searching for, but that was ridiculous. Even Carrington didn't know where his father hid the gold—gold she was beginning to think didn't exist. Digging random holes about the yard would be like searching for a speck of lint on a lamb.

"Well, that is strange," Blake said before attacking his meal with gusto, and showing no obvious concern over his name being used in the sheriff's duplicitous act.

Before Cassie could inquire if Blake had any recent conversations with the sheriff, ones that mentioned gold perhaps, the sound of voices outside interrupted her. She went to the window to see what the commotion was.

Carrington had returned . . . with Suzanne in tow. The pair strolled up the drive, side-by-side, their horses trailing along behind them. Suzanne was doing all the talking. Cassie couldn't hear what she said, but Carrington lifted his head and smiled at whatever it was. Then the blasted woman placed her hand around his bicep and threw her head back and laughed much too boisterously.

The scrape of a chair behind Cassie made her whirl around.

"Well, I'd best be gettin' on outta here. Thanks for the meal." Blake was already on his feet. He wiped his mouth with his napkin and dropped it on the table beside his half-emptied plate.

"No. You don't have to go anywhere. Finish eating." She pointed a finger, directing him to sit as she would a dog. She could feel Annie's uncertainty about Blake's presence, and her hurt at Suzanne's interference, both of which angered Cassie.

Footsteps sounded in the entryway. Two sets of footsteps. Cassie planted her fists on her hips, while Blake lowered his head and began chewing his food. Carrington strode into the kitchen, Suzanne still at his side, but at least she wasn't clutching his arm or any other part of his body now.

"Hello, husband." Annie's confusion showed in the tilt of her head, but it was Cassie who made her voice sound sickeningly sweet. Carrington's eyes darted from Blake to her before raking over the buttons opened at her throat and at her rolled-up sleeves.

"Wife," he said in a way that caused a ripple of heat to move through Cassie's body—and wonder if she'd just made a colossal mistake challenging him. "Is *my* dinner ready?"

Suzanne's hand inched around Carrington's bicep again. A tight frown pinched his face, and he shrugged her off before stepping deeper into the room

"Of course, your meal is ready, sweetheart." Cassie began preparing his plate. "I made just enough for the three of us."

She didn't know if Suzanne seriously considered staying for a meal, or what her intent was, but Cassie intended to make it clear that she wasn't welcome in Annie's home.

Carrington came up behind her and dropped a kiss along Annie's cheek, startling Cassie and warming Annie's heart.

Blake's chair scraped the floor again. "I should be heading out. Thank you, Mrs. Chambers." He wrapped his arm about Suzanne's shoulders and turned her around to lead her out of the kitchen.

"Suzanne, I'm glad you came out to visit *me*," he said, emphasizing the real reason, presumably, for the woman's visit.

Cassie stilled with her surprise. Why would Blake think she was there for him when she clearly had her sights set on Carrington?

Suzanne flashed a fake smile at Annie. "Well, I'd hoped to visit a bit with Mrs. Chambers, but I guess I got sidetracked." There was no mistaking her meaning as she caressed Carrington with her eyes. "I'll have to come back another time." It was a jab meant for Annie, and one that hit the mark, as Cassie sensed the hurt and jealousy the vile woman's words brought about.

"Come along, then." Blake physically pulled Suzanne out of the room. The front door shut an instant later.

Alone with Carrington, Cassie—and Annie—struggled to find conversation that would get him to relax the tight knit of his brows. Cassie was frustrated by these run-ins with him during her trips to the past because she'd intentionally been trying to avoid him. That was why she read entries that specifically didn't mention his name. It was also bothersome that at the end of each visit to the past, he was scowling at her. Couldn't she just once have a successful information-gathering visit with no sign of the husband?

"I think I should let Blake go."

Cassie choked on the bite of carrot she'd forked into her mouth, her eyes watering from the exertion. Coughing furiously, she finally managed to dislodge the particle of food that made its way down the wrong pipe. "What? Why would you do that?"

Carrington sopped up some gravy with a hunk of meat and plopped it into his mouth. "I'm tired of finding the two of you together," he said around his food. Then he leaned over his plate, planting both elbows on the table, and shut her out. Conversation over.

"Carrington!" Cassie had to bite the inside of her cheek to control her brewing anger. She knew from television shows she'd watched that the farmhands often ate with the farm owners. Annie had clearly made enough food for more than just him and her, so it couldn't have been a surprise to him that Blake was there eating. Perhaps she should have heeded those earlier warnings going off in Annie's brain.

"You can't mean what I think you mean. Just because we visit now and again doesn't imply there's anything between us."

He finished chewing, cleared his throat, and shrugged one shoulder. "I don't want to find the two of you together alone again. Do I make myself clear?" He didn't raise his head to acknowledge her.

A heavy silence descended on the room, punctuated, Cassie noticed, by the lack of modern sounds that she'd never paid attention to before, such as the quiet hum of a refrigerator. She absorbed the shock of hearing Carrington *tell* Annie what to do, like she was a child and not a grown woman. His wife. Pressing a hand to her neck, she shook her head in consternation.

"Why you over-bearing, arrogant . . ." Searching for the best word that fit her frustration, Cassie stomped one foot before adding, "ass!"

Of course, Annie would have never behaved the way she was behaving now or speak to him the way Cassie was speaking through her. It was just that Carrington's efforts to dictate whom Annie could or couldn't socialize with tripped Cassie's twenty-first century ideals button. He was just going to have to get used to this new version of Annie.

Cassie shoved her chair backward before stomping past a surprised Carrington. Her outburst had the intended effect. Leaving him to stew alone in the kitchen, she ran to the back of the house and slammed the bedroom door shut. There, she paced the room, fuming at how controlling he presumed he had the right to be.

Half expecting him to follow her, to remind her that he was in charge, she was relieved when she heard the front door slam. A few minutes later, the sound of a horse racing off at a fast pace drifted in through the room's open window.

As she stewed on her emotions, she looked about the minimally decorated room. A black-and-white photograph in a frame sat atop a nightstand. The picture held the image of a man whose expressionless eyes stared out; no smile graced his face, but the harsh creases of age, life, and weather showed everywhere on the visage. He had to be Carrington's father. The likeness was undeniable.

Her fingers brushed over a worn book, a comb, and a pitcher and basin situated on a vanity beside the mirror located in the corner. They were personal things, Carrington's things.

Her ire having ebbed some, she changed direction and began scrounging through drawers, in search of the modified underwear Miss Jane was to have made for Annie. The shopkeeper had promised they'd be ready in a couple days, which had already happened. In a drawer assigned to women's delicate things, she rifled through it until she found what she was searching for—tucked at the very bottom, far into the back corner.

Stripping off her clothes, she slipped on the underwear. The length of the bloomers stopped three inches above her knees, very modest for sure. The camisole's shoulder straps were two inches wide and the hem now boasted a yellow satin ribbon that Cassie pulled, tightening the garment around the curve of her rib cage. She tied the ribbon into a tidy little bow that nestled square against her diaphragm.

Perfect. All her lady parts were adequately covered, and air could now reach her skin. She heaved a blissful sigh.

As appropriately covered as she was by her modern-day standards, the thin cotton fabric gave Cassie pause. Through it, she could see the dark outline of the area near Annie's crotch as well as the shape of her breasts and the buds of her nipples pointing out. Seconds ticked by as she considered this little dilemma.

She discerned from Annie's thoughts that Carrington wouldn't return until supper time. Trotting through the small living room, she peered out the window that overlooked the yard toward the barn. There was no sign of Blake or Suzanne or Carrington. She was alone and could snoop around while at the same time get some of Annie's chores finished up without basting in her own sweat. She'd change back into regular clothes when the time neared for Carrington's return home, assuming she'd still be there in the past.

NINETEEN

"Damnation, wife! What are you doing out here in your underclothes?"

Cassie bolted upright into a sitting position on the porch swing. After hours of working inside the house, she'd grown sleepy and decided to take a break. With hopes of catching a faint breeze to cool her down, she sought refuge on the front porch. Apparently, she'd dozed off. Startled back into consciousness, she found hard, gray, and somewhat bloodshot eyes glaring down at her.

Seeing that it was only Carrington, she quickly settled. Sitting tall, she stretched her arms high overhead, groaning with pleasure. There was nothing quite like napping in the quiet country air, especially in the past, where no sounds of airplanes, trains, or automobiles broke the serenity.

She froze mid-stretch when she found Carrington's unblinking gaze roaming over her somewhat visible curves. Her arms lowered to her waist, hugging it like a shield. But not before he had time to see her exposed midriff and the hint of varied tones of color beneath the fabric sparsely covering her body.

"I must have fallen asleep," she admitted. Neither Cassie nor Annie were immune to the hunger burning in Carrington's eyes.

It had grown late while she slept. The night was far from cool, but at least the blazing sun had dipped nearly to the horizon, offering some relief. It was also way past suppertime. Carrington weaved a few steps toward her, faltered, and reached out his hand. Cassie jumped up and grabbed him about the shoulders before he toppled over.

"You're drunk!"

His bleary gaze didn't travel up to meet her angered one. Instead, they burned through the fabric of her meager apparel. She immediately questioned her impromptu decision to wear the modified underwear.

"I'm up here," she snapped.

He listed forward and back. Fearing he'd topple over she planted her hands against his chest to brace him. He lowered his head and touched his lips to hers. Cassie stood rigid beneath the pressure of his mouth. She fought against it at first but couldn't deny the pleasure roiling through her. Was her natural response duplicitous? She was helping Annie, and Annie wanted this. Who was she to keep a husband from his wife?

Feeling bold here in Annie's world, she embraced him. Carrington's roughened palms touched wherever they found exposed and not-so-exposed skin. When he pulled her tight against him, she tucked her head into the crook of his neck, basking in the warm scent of him. The hint of something sweet flickered about her senses, but she couldn't put a name to it. She kissed the stubbled skin at his jaw and ran her tongue along the cords of his throat, enjoying the light saltiness on his skin. He tipped back unsteadily, nearly taking her to the ground with him.

"Let's go inside," she suggested as she helped him remain steady on his feet. She felt victorious, for Annie and for herself, and oh so ready for what was to come, even if it was third party. The lust-fueled air between Annie and Carrington was exhilarating.

Once in the bedroom, Cassie turned him, so his back was to the bed. She kissed him, hard, while his hands touched her wherever they could reach until they settled about her breasts. Desire rushed through her and she tingled with anticipation. With a gentle push from her, he toppled backward and lay flat across the bed.

It had been a long time since Cassie had been with a man, in her own body that was. Longer than she cared to admit. If she was going to allow this to happen again while she was playing Annie's role, she was going to do it right.

"Give me just a minute."

At the washstand, she hummed nervously as she made her ablutions. Feeling somewhat fresher—she doubted Summer's Eve had ever spent an August day in the arid Idaho environment—she returned to the bed. Now Cassie was ready to explore Carrington at length, so she could put to rest her growing curiosity for the ghost waiting on the other side.

"Carrington, I'm—" She was halfway over the top of him, one knee planted on the mattress, when a low, rumbling snore sounded. She stopped mid-straddle.

"Are you kidding me?"

Clearly, what she'd hoped would happen, wasn't going to. Flouncing down on the bed beside him, she pressed her face into a nearby pillow and screamed her frustration.

***

Cassie was not of a mind to be near Carrington upon her return to the present. However, even before she became fully alert, the warm, masculine scent of him reached her nostrils. There was something about that smell now, as compared to the past that niggled about in her brain. It was an unwelcome feeling, like she knew she was forgetting something but couldn't recall what.

She was still contemplating the lost memory when she turned to him. The heart-stopping grin he offered added to her irritation.

"What are you so happy about?" she grumbled, as she left the bed to go stand before the window.

Behind her, the bed frame creaked, and footsteps sounded. She flinched when his hands slid over her arms, moving from elbow to shoulder. When she turned around, his hands fell away, but where he'd touched a lingering heat remained. She countered his happy demeanor with her own indifferent one. The earth would have to swallow her up before she revealed to him the reason why she was so frustrated.

"You're welcome to finish what you started." He offered her a wicked grin and a wink.

Flickers of alarm blipped in Cassie's brain. "What do you mean by that?" *He couldn't possibly know what she'd been about to do, in her dream.*

"Well, you were doing your best to seduce me. And like that"—he snapped his fingers—"you stopped."

"Excuse me?" she squeaked. "I-I don't know what you mean?"

Oh, no, no, no. He can't be implying that he knows. She ducked past him and feigned interest in the brickwork of the fireplace. Did she talk in her sleep? Or worse?

"I did something to displease Annie, it would seem. I don't recall ever saying no to her."

Cassie whirled around, certain she was flushed red from the roots of her hair to the tips of her toes. "You were drunk and passed out! And I . . . I wanted to, I mean I, that is Annie was going to—" She pressed her lips tight together and folded her arms hard across her chest.

"My apologies, darlin'. I'm here now, happy to oblige." He followed the apology with a courtly bow.

"Ohhh!" She stomped her foot. Embarrassed beyond measure, she hurried over and grabbed the journal off the bed. Purposefully, she ignored the rush of desire flickering at more than a low flame for Carrington, present and past.

"I'm going out!" She rushed from the room with the sound of Carrington's laughter chasing her down the hallway.

***

Carrington was in over his head. His old life and his present were melding in ways he never expected. The burning need for truth that brought him to this unearthly space in time was shifting. He wanted to leave. No, he needed to leave. He couldn't remain in this limbo of eternity any longer, not with the desire he'd witnessed on Cassie's face. Desire for him, written there like words on a page.

But he couldn't just disappear. He'd tried. The only way out was to reveal the secrets buried more than a century ago. Whatever it was that controlled his destiny, something bigger than him awaited Cassie's revelations as well. He couldn't explain why he felt this, since he'd never encountered anyone like him during his long wait. He just knew, somehow, that Cassie's purpose here went beyond his own need for redemption.

Only recently, a stray idea began intruding on his thoughts, one that involved a future with her. Not that he hadn't loved Annie, but his life with her was so long ago. He couldn't undo that part of his past, and only recently had found a reason to let it go, let it rest cold in the dirt where it belonged.

What if he remained here? It would be as close to living again as he'd ever get. Cassie wouldn't notice anything different about him, compared to any other living person that is. At least not until she wanted him to go somewhere with her. Would she be satisfied with a life with him here on this property, and *only* on this property, with no chance to experience adventures together beyond its boundaries? He heaved an ancient sigh. If the story of the past were never to unfold, could he find joy knowing Cassie would never have a normal life?

No. He couldn't do that to her or to himself. Or to Annie.

Fortunately, for Carrington, Cassie was willing to help. She didn't realize it yet, but the more she focused on him and Annie, the less she guarded her neck. It was a sure sign of her diminishing fears. The quest she embarked upon, strangely enough, was bringing life back into her. There was a new strength about her that had most definitely not been there her first day in the house.

Her present state of frustration was something altogether different. It was a direct result of Annie's needs being unmet in the past. Cassie was experiencing all the young love and lust of his and Annie's romance. It was infectious, and Cassie was the victim of that ailment. She wanted their experiences, here, in her own life, not through Annie's. It was plain as day.

A grin spread over his face. He'd tried to tell her once that she acted out the scenes as they happened to her in the past, like a person sleepwalking—present but not fully alert to her surroundings. During this last trip to Annie's life, she was more assertive than usual. She'd pressed against him, kissing him in a way that left no doubt in his mind what was happening, or about to happen, with Annie.

All too soon, she huffed with disgust then woke up moments later, madder than a hornet, leaving him in a haze of lust-filled cravings for her. He badly wanted to rush after her, and continue what she started, what he knew she wanted. But he held back. Once he went down that path with her, he'd not be able to stop, and he couldn't risk frightening her with his intensity. So, he let her go off on her own, giving them both time to cool down.

More than an hour passed before he sought her out.

She'd wandered out to the river's edge. It gurgled quietly, an ominous backdrop to where she sat facing away from him. The water reflected the bright sunlight shining overhead. The muffled sound of dirt beneath his feet, dirt that should be thriving with the green life of a crop this late in the year, was lost in the quiet gurgle of the water's movement.

"Cassie." He was uncertain he'd spoken loud enough for her to hear, but the sudden tension in her spine told him she had. She scooted over on the log, inviting him to join her. He squatted beside her, drawing his knees up, arms draped over them, fingers clasped against his shins.

"Hey," she said.

"Tell me what you learned when you went back." He spoke softly, as he would to a skittish mare. Tension vibrated through her where their legs touched.

Drawing circles in the dirt at her feet with a stick, she didn't immediately rush into the tale. Minutes ticked by.

"It's all so confusing and frustrating. Sheriff Anders is up to no good. He was lurking around the place. I think he forgot that Annie was there. I caught him behind the barn burying or digging up something." Either Cassie didn't notice, or she disregarded how she was blending her life with Annie's in the past.

"Interesting. I think he secretly cared for Annie."

"Ha!" she scoffed and shook her head. "No. I don't think Anders is capable of that kind of caring. I think he's just waiting for you to screw up." She slapped the stick hard against the ground. "What a pathetic ass."

"What else happened?" He didn't need to be told that the sheriff was an ass. His knowledge of that was firsthand. It was the others, the ones he assumed had his back, his so-called friends, who were in question.

"Annie invited Blake to the house for lunch. You showed up and sent him away, and then threatened to fire him if you saw the two of them alone together again."

"He was always around. Too much."

Cassie made an exasperated sound. "Well, he is your field hand. They're just friends, from what I've seen so far. He and Suzanne have been acting a bit suspicious, but I haven't found anything specific yet that implicates them." Her tone sharpened as she continued, the subject matter bringing out the change.

"Suzanne, I don't trust. That witch has the audacity to show up on *my* property, well, Annie's, I suppose, and insinuate she has a claim on you." She flicked her wrist, whipping the stick at the ground.

"She meant nothing to me. You have to know that," he countered, uncertain as to why he felt compelled to justify himself. He'd never done anything untoward with Suzanne, at least not after he got married.

"I don't know that! And I don't think Annie knew that." Cassie jumped to her feet and turned on him. "You came home drunk. Annie kissed you." She tried to hide the flush of red creeping over her cheeks by searching the ground for a rock. Finding one to her liking, she picked it up. "You looked and smelled so good." She slanted him a perplexed glance. "But there was something wrong. I couldn't figure out at first what it was."

She chucked the rock into the river. It made the sunlight on the water sparkle like diamonds before it disappeared into the murky depths.

"And then it hit me. When I read that first article, about you getting out of the drunk tank, you went to Suzanne immediately afterward. I smelled what you smelled. I smelled her." She shook her finger at him accusingly. "And then in that last scene with you, on your skin I smelled her again. You'd been with Suzanne." The harsh accusation hung in the air, heavy and unsettling.

Carrington rose to his feet, standing as tall as his six-foot three-inch frame would stretch. He pulled Cassie around to face him, his hands squeezing tight around her upper arms. "I swear, on all that is holy to me, I *never* touched her while we were married."

"Did Annie believe that?"

A ribbon of Canadian geese flew by, their formation swaying in the sky like the tail of a kite. They honked as they passed, apologizing for the intrusion. Cassie watched their progress against the blue background, waiting for Carrington's response.

"Yes, I think she did. If you'll continue reading, you'll find out." He quirked one brow, aiming to lighten the heavy mood. "I can't say for sure what all happens beyond the words she wrote. I will admit that we fought later that evening, after I woke up. But we made up eventually."

"Wait. If you passed out that night and missed what Annie was trying to do, how is it that you know what scene or where I was in her journey? I mean, like you said, what's written down certainly isn't all of what I've been experiencing."

She folded her arms across her chest and eyed him suspiciously, chewing her lip nervously.

"I've told you before. When you're in Annie's life, you rather animatedly live out the scene here. This last time you did so with more . . . purpose." When Cassie's mouth shaped into an O, Carrington nudged her chin with a finger. Her teeth clacked together audibly as her jaws clamped shut.

"You don't take your clothes off or move entirely like you would in certain situations." He stepped back when her eyes shrank to thin violet slivers. "But you do move some and you do make a lot of interesting sounds and say a lot of colorful words."

Her mouth fell open again, this time to heave air in and out of her lungs while her face drew tight with suppressed embarrassment.

"You mean to tell me—" She poked a finger hard against his chest for emphasis, "that you"—she poked again—"see me"—poke, poke—"doing . . .?" At his nod of acknowledgment, she stopped. Her lips moved as she counted silently to three, then she whirled away from him and stormed off in the direction of the house. He was growing accustomed to her abrupt departures when she was frustrated.

"So help me, Carrington Chambers, if I find out you're lying about Suzanne, I'll-I'll find a way to haunt *you!* And don't come and watch me!" she called over her shoulder.

Carrington controlled his urge to laugh as he watched Cassie storm off, arms swinging, knees high, and hair swishing across her back. He fervently hoped Annie had written about the following day, their day to make up. He also hoped that Cassie would finally lower the wall she'd constructed around herself and give in to what he knew she wanted as much as he did.

TWENTY

Cassie roamed the property for a long while before skirting around the back of the barn by the old horse paddock. The remains of a split-rail fence circled an area half the size of a football field. She climbed through the rotted wood planks and then veered off toward the chicken coop. It wasn't the first time she'd noticed that the small building had weathered the years well, much better than the barn had fared. Stepping inside the coop, she tested the strength of the floorboards with a light hop. It was solid.

She leaned against the far wall. Memories assailed her of Carrington and Annie squeezed into the small enclosure, with him pressing his body against hers. Her heart fluttered wildly in her chest. She rushed out of the building, running away from the unbidden images of the things he'd suggested he and Annie had done that day when they'd gone back to the house.

Inside the barn, Cassie took mental notes of the areas that showed more decay and did a rough calculation in her head as to the cost of repairs. She found where someone, presumably Carrington, had added a few newer, sturdier boards to reinforce some of the worst spots. Since he obviously couldn't run to the lumber yard whenever he wanted, she assumed he'd located the extra wood somewhere on the property.

Exiting the barn, she wandered over to the porch. It was a warm day and the shade was welcoming. She plopped down on the swing and eased it back and forth with a toe. The journal, which she'd been lugging about on her stroll after having collected it from the house, now sat heavy on her lap—like an anchor threatening to pull her under.

August 16, 1890.

That bitch Suzanne showed up again today.

"Uh-oh. It appears I might be rubbing off a bit onto Annie." Cassie smirked, thinking of Carrington's reaction to that tidbit of knowledge as she allowed the past to play out in its own unexplainable way.

***

Cassie re-entered the nineteenth century out on the front porch where Annie was sweeping and humming merrily. She wondered at the young bride's apparent state of happiness, so she worked through her memories to find the source. Just as she isolated the cause, she heard Carrington's voice coming from somewhere off in the direction of the barn. Searching for him, Annie's happy mood darkened when she found Suzanne with her husband. The woman had her arm curled about his waist as they hobbled from the dark interior of the barn.

Suzanne looked Annie's way and then stumbled, her fingers gripping at Carrington's shirtfront. "Clumsy me," she cried out in her ridiculous-sounding voice. "I'm so glad you were here when I needed you, Carrington."

Carrington cast a careful glance at Annie before leading Suzanne toward the side of the barn. He mumbled something, but Cassie couldn't make out the words. Before the pair turned the corner, Suzanne swiveled her head back around toward Annie, her lips curling up in a haughty smirk.

"That bitch!" Cassie seethed. Annie's expletive in her journal entry was spot on.

"Well, I don't have to sit here and watch him fawn all over her, that's for sure." Fuming, she decided to show Carrington that Annie was no simpering wife to be mocked by him or his mistress. She'd finally caught him in the lie she'd threatened to haunt him for.

Dropping the broom, she marched across the yard, the exaggerated stride of her legs causing the teepee of her A-line cut skirt to swish out forcefully with each step. She came to a halt near the stall where Carrington's mare stood lazily chomping on some hay.

Cassie had never ridden a horse, so didn't know how to saddle one. To be honest, she wasn't in the mood to take the time to see if Annie knew how, either. Slipping into the next stall over, she approached a smaller, less intimidating-sized mare. Armed with only basic knowledge of how to bridle the horse, she somehow managed that task, while determinedly ignoring Annie's worry about riding bareback. Her intent was to get away, not run a race.

She located a log on its end that would suffice as a mounting block and led the horse over. With one hand looped tight through the reins, she grabbed the mare's mane with the other, then steadied herself before launching up and onto the horse's back. With a light tap of her heels, Cassie nudged against the mare's belly to set them in motion, her legs gripping the rounded sides beneath her like a vise.

"Come on, girl. We can do this." She steered the horse toward the fence line, hoping that would keep her close enough to home, yet far enough away from Carrington and the meddling Suzanne. Fortunately, the horse was gentle and easy to control, allowing Cassie to settle into a somewhat comfortable light trot.

Carrington's property stretched far and wide. From the paperwork she'd skimmed through during the transfer of it into her name, she'd read that it had once been an estate boasting one-hundred sixty acres. Through the years, presumably following Carrington's death, the holding company had sold half of it. What remained, and what Cassie now owned, was eighty acres. Still not a bad chunk of land. It was quiet and private. Riding through this much larger parcel was a bit overwhelming as she realized there wasn't a single neighbor or building in any direction.

Still feeling distinctly out of her comfort zone, Cassie's mood was at least improving, due, most likely, to the increasing distance between her and whatever was happening back at the barn. She clicked her tongue, urging the mare into a slow lope. Reflexively, her knees squeezed tightly against the mare's sides, which inadvertently caused the horse to speed up. Cassie dug her heels into the horse's sides to secure her seating. The mare, however, took the motion as a signal to go faster. She fell forward against the horse's neck, the sudden jarring canter nearly spilling her from its back.

She'd barely righted herself, when something startled her mount. Before she could fully comprehend what was happening, the beast turned in the opposite direction and broke into a full gallop. Cassie's panic quickly escalated to terror when she saw that the horse, having heard the whinny of Carrington's horse approaching, had spun about so it could barrel across the ground toward the oncoming rider.

"Whoa!" she cried out, pulling back hard on the reins without the desired outcome. "Whoa!" Her voice hummed brokenly, as it would if she were driving over a washboard road. She screeched again at the top of her lungs for the mare to stop.

In the closing distance, she saw shock register on Carrington's face as he kicked his mount into a gallop. There wasn't time to be concerned or pleased at his presence as she bounced like a rag doll on the mare's back. Bending forward, she wrapped her arms around its tawny neck as it continued its headlong charge. Ahead, the raised stretch of a ditch bank appeared between her and Carrington. Tearing over the lush green of potato plants growing in furrowed rows, Cassie's dread began to build when the horse didn't slow.

"Oh, no!" she cried out as the mare leaped the ditch. Her arms sought purchase around its muscled neck as it landed hard on the other side, causing Cassie to lose her grip entirely.

The series of events that followed happened in slow motion in her mind. She flew through the air, arms and legs flailing wide, before landing with a muffled *whumpf* in the mounded hill of a potato plant.

All the air escaped her lungs and she fought to draw a breath. She stared up at the bright sun beating down, gulping in precious bites of oxygen as she wiggled her toes and fingers, assessing for any potential injuries. When everything moved as it was supposed to, she sagged with relief. Pulling one knee up, then the other, she rocked her legs side-to-side, checking for a broken hip or torn anything.

In her peripheral vision, she saw Carrington leap from his horse and race toward her, stumbling once in the dirt. Before she could sit up, or say something, she was staring up into smoky eyes, wide with worry and flickering with some other emotion.

"Annie! Are you hurt?" He searched her body from head to toe, checking for visible damage.

She blinked against the sun as his head moved, first blocking the rays, and then not blocking them. Lifting an arm to cast a shadow over her eyes, thankful the appendage worked properly, she tried to put his mind at ease. "I-I'm fine, I think."

Strong hands slid behind her neck, helping her into a sitting position. Her skirts lay in wild disarray, one side hiked up over a hip. She hurried to push it down and winced in the process.

"What on God's green earth were you doing, woman?" he asked harshly, his worry and gentle assessment quickly giving way to frustration. The deepening lines across his forehead and the dip in his brows were a sure sign of his irritation. The muscles at his jaw twitched, too. A lot.

Reflecting on the reason she was in such a predicament, Cassie's anger returned, right along with the pain in her backside where she'd landed. "Nothing. I just wanted to go for a ride."

His eyes narrowed. "Can you stand?"

"Yes. I think so." With his assistance, she got up. Her pride had taken a beating, as had her backside. She rubbed it shamelessly. "Oh, that's gonna leave a mark."

One corner of Carrington's lip twitched before he managed to tighten his expression back into a dark scowl. Cassie knew he was furious.

"I'm sure it will. Now, explain to me what the hell you were doing." His voice held a warning, even if his touch was gentle. He swiped his thumb over her cheek, removing dirt stuck to her face.

"I told you. I was just out for a ride." *A barrel race, more like.* She hobbled with his forced assistance back toward her horse. Off in the distance was the house. She contemplated the time it would take her to walk back, uncertain she wanted to try riding again anytime soon.

"You're lying." He steered her progress with a hand pressed to the small of her back. "I know why you ran off."

"I didn't run off." She didn't mean to sound pouty, but that was the resulting effect.

He pulled her around to face him. "Suzanne twisted her ankle, so I helped her to a place to sit where she could wait for Blake."

"Well, it seemed like she was after more than that." She made no effort to hide her jealousy.

Since they were discussing Suzanne, it seemed a good time to talk about the blasted woman, but the idea didn't appeal at all to Cassie. But the dreadful broad and her possible role in Annie's death was part of the reason why she was here, so discuss her she would. What little she did know was only of their sexual affair, not about the person Suzanne was. Was she a jealous lover who went so far as to kill her competition? Cassie had to unearth the truth, regardless of how unpleasant the conversation might be.

They crested a small hill. Below them was a large pond surrounded by trees.

"This is lovely." She wondered if this part of the property was still within her eighty-acre plot in the future, or if it had been part of the other half.

"I come here often. To bathe. To relax, when time allows." He guided her to a spot in the shade and helped her sit before easing down close beside her, arms wrapped about his knees. After plucking a blade of grass, he popped it between his teeth, gnawing on the sweet end.

Cassie winced as her bruised hip settled against the ground. A soft breeze kicked up and caught her hair, gently blowing it around her face and shoulders. Grabbing the mass in a fist, she pulled it forward, marshalling her courage to begin the interrogation about Annie's nemesis.

"How long were you and Suzanne, er, lovers?" It bothered Cassie that she feared the emotions Carrington might exhibit when speaking of another woman.

He looked aghast at her. "I beg your pardon! That is not a discussion I feel is necessary. You're my wife. What happened in the past has nothing to do with you and me."

She'd overlooked the fact that Annie asking about her husband's past lovers would seem odd. Still, they were questions lurking in Annie's mind, so Cassie asked them on the girl's behalf. "I know it's strange, but in order for me to let that part of your past not worry me, I need to know."

He ground his teeth determinedly on the grass for a minute as her words rumbled about in his brain. "We were . . . friends . . . for several months before I met you."

"How well do you *know* her?"

Something akin to panic flitted across his face. The muscle at his jaw flexed again. Cassie wanted to brush her lips against the spot but didn't act on that feeling. The last thing she needed was to bring about another scene in which she had to deal with Annie's raging desire for Carrington—and her own burgeoning one.

"I would say I know her . . . intimately."

"Aaargh." She shook her head. "I know you are, or were, intimate with her." She glared at him, daring him to clarify which tense was the truth. "Everyone knows that," she said a bit lower. "I mean, who does she spend time with, now that you're not with her?"

Kicking out his legs, he pushed back onto one elbow, his free hand twirling the grass between his teeth. "I don't really know. I didn't socialize with her, you understand. It appears she and Blake are getting along well enough."

Carrington only corroborated what Cassie had begun to suspect. If Blake and Suzanne were a couple, why would they need to get rid of Annie? Was their plan to go after Carrington next? If he were out of the picture, his property would probably be auctioned off. And, she already knew Blake wanted land and a home, just like Carrington's; that might be incentive enough.

"Carrington, may I ask a question?" Cassie dipped her head down, avoiding his prying eyes.

He bent over and peeked up at her. "Isn't that what you've been doing?"

She laughed awkwardly. "Yes, I suppose it is. I want to ask about what happened. After your father died."

The flash of pain that lanced across his face was impossible to hide.

"I already told you what happened. What else do you want to know? Did I have to kill the man? Or," he paused, "am I lying about the gold?"

When she didn't immediately respond, he shot her a questioning glance. She shook her head. "Neither. You were just a young man. I wanted to ask why you stayed here, in this town, when everyone is so . . ." She searched for the right word.

"So unforgiving? So quick to judge?" he finished for her. At her nod, he half-smiled. "I had nowhere to go. This is my home. Pa built this place with his own hands. From the time I could ride a horse we worked the land together. It was everything to us. I couldn't just leave it behind, not to mention there *is* gold hidden somewhere on the property."

She was beginning to better understand his loneliness and his need to find some form of companionship. This was where he belonged, where he'd planned to spend the rest of his days. Even Suzanne, being the only person who'd associate with him, began to fit into the puzzle.

"You must have been terribly lonely." She reached out to squeeze his hand where it rested palm down on the ground beside her.

His fingers curled into hers. "I was. Until you accepted that dance." He leaned close. "We're going to have it all, Annie. I promise."

Cassie nearly drowned in his intensity. His hand wrapped around the back of her neck and pulled her to him. Unable to resist the love and passion she saw in his eyes she freed her own desires and met his kiss with equal enthusiasm.

TWENTY-ONE

Okay. Maybe Cassie was wrong to think there was still something between Carrington and Suzanne. The way he kissed Annie just then was one hundred percent the way a man in love should kiss his wife.

Their passion was escalating to a fevered pitch, with no sign of ceasing. Annie's body and Cassie's mind were in conflict. What one desired the other warned against. Cassie knew without a doubt that she'd enjoy this tryst, but it would only leave her aching for more of something she could never truly have. With a strength of will she didn't think she had, she forced herself to return to the present.

The man she'd begun fantasizing about in two different centuries crossed into her line of sight. He was shirtless, again—oh, have mercy—his chest and shoulders glistening with sweat in the afternoon sunlight. With a hammer in one hand and a board in the other, he strode with purpose past the far end of the house, disappearing from her view. A moment later, the familiar sound of a hammer hitting wood echoed across the dry air.

Good, keep busy so I can concentrate.

She turned the page and began to read an entry about Blake, written two days after the scene at the pond.

***

Annie was walking along one of the hundreds of rows of potato plants in a field near the house. Cassie filtered Annie's memories and found that her intent was to dip her toes in the cool water at the pond. As proof of the reason why, a trickle of sweat crept beneath her collar and slid down between Annie's breasts.

Apparently, she'd learned her lesson about wandering about in her recently modified underwear, since she was fully dressed now. Cassie briefly contemplated returning to the house to put on those thinner garments but quickly squashed that idea. It had taken her awhile, but she was finally catching on to the fact that Carrington somehow always happened to turn up when she least expected him to.

Annie wasn't inclined to wear the skimpier clothing, nor to skinny dip, which Cassie would respect. She would, however, hike up her skirt to get air and sun on her skin. There was a light blanket draped over Annie's arm, which meant she had plans to spend a bit of time outside. Cresting a berm, she found herself gazing upon the same pond as before, the place where Carrington had taken her after the horse debacle.

According to the journal entry, he was working out in the far reaches of the property and wouldn't be home until late. Blake had gone with him. Their absence gave Annie a chance to enjoy the day, away from the house.

Cassie had the place all to herself.

Spreading the blanket over the ground, half in the shade of a tall tree and half in the sun, she sank down onto it with a blissful sigh. Rays of heat beat down on the earth around her, bringing to life the smell of rich soil, algae forming around the edge of the pond, and that warm, heady aroma of summer.

Casting a quick glance around to be certain there was no one about, she hiked up the hem of her dress and shoved the wad of fabric between her legs. Lifting her hips, she tucked the sides beneath her, keeping all the essential areas decently covered.

Leaning back on her elbows, her face protected by the shade, she released all her pent-up energy in one slow, meditative exhalation. Annie's memories danced about in her head. The one foremost in her mind was what had happened after the kiss by the pond. As she suspected would happen, Carrington made love to Annie right there beneath the clear, blue sky. Cassie's eyes glazed over as she fantasized about the scene as it replayed through Annie's mind.

"Keep focused, McAllister." Reining in her daydreams, she contemplated Suzanne. She'd set her hooks into Carrington before Annie had met him. And, even if Carrington was unwilling to believe it, Cassie knew women like Suzanne didn't stop until they got what they wanted.

Would she go to the extent of killing Annie? That seemed farfetched; however, jealousy could make men and women do any number of horrific things. Cassie knew firsthand what a person could do to someone they claimed to love.

She shook away feelings of her own dark past and lay back, hands cupped behind her head. Big, puffy white clouds floated lazily past. A fly buzzed around her. She yawned wide. The leaves on the trees above her rustled on a breeze as the clouds strolled by, soothing her turbulent mind. She yawned again and drifted off into a peaceful slumber.

The sound of a horse's snort startled Cassie awake. Struggling to shake off the drowsy feeling that follows a satisfying mid-day nap, she sat up and stretched. When she leaned too far onto her bruised hip, she hissed her discomfort.

"What the hell is this?" Carrington barked behind her.

Annie's heart lurched wildly. She was fully awake now. Twisting about at the waist, she came face-to-face with a very angry Carrington. His chest rose and fell with his heavy breathing as he glared down at her from beneath the shadow of his hat.

Cassie turned back forward when he moved to stand in front of her. She felt strangely immobile and unable to leap up and greet him—his countenance was that menacing. Dawning struck when she remembered her skirt was still wedged around her hips. That would explain his unrealistic flash of anger. *It's a bit over the top, don't you think?* She flipped the fabric down to cover her legs—legs that were now beyond their normal shade of pale pink.

She couldn't halt the stray fantasy of Carrington dropping to his knees and repeating the scene in Annie's memory. Before she could further that imagining or encourage it along in any way, Carrington's gaze shifted to a spot past her. Curious, she twisted around, on her good hip, in the direction that drew his interest.

And froze.

Blake was there, lying on his back on the edge of her blanket, with his hat over his face, boots off and in his stocking feet. He was rousing from an apparent state of sleep. Her head swiveled back around to Carrington, then again to Blake.

Cassie felt Annie's adrenaline rush when her mind processed the gravity of the situation. Every emotion imaginable took a turn on Carrington's face. The one that emerged most notably: Fury.

Like a jack-in-the-box sprung from its hole, Cassie bolted to her feet. It felt like a vise had squeezed around Annie's chest, making it so she could only breathe in short, choppy gasps. She rounded on Blake.

"What are *you* doing here?" she demanded with a combination of bewilderment and fear.

Blake pulled on his boots with a considerable lack of concern over the damning situation. He even took a leisurely moment to stretch before crawling to his feet.

"Sorry, boss. I must have dozed off."

Cassie's jaw fell open and her eyes rounded to saucers. "That's all you have to say?" The pitch of her voice approached soprano level. She vigorously shook her head as she spun back to face Annie's angry husband.

"Carrington. This is not what you think."

His eyes shot daggers at both Annie and Blake. Cassie felt all the blood drain from Annie's face. Her legs began to quake when he glared at the space between where she and Blake stood on the blanket.

"I could kill you for this," he hissed.

Cassie froze, uncertain which of them he'd directed the threat. Blake opened his mouth to speak, but she spoke first.

"Oh, no, no." Like a robber held at gunpoint, she raised both hands up to chest level and stepped closer to Carrington, and off the impromptu bed. Even the birds in the nearby trees, which had been chirping so merrily moments ago, sensed the threat and shut up.

"Nothing happened. I swear!" The inside of Annie's mouth felt like she'd eaten a cotton ball. "I came out here alone and dozed off. I don't know when he showed up." She pointed an accusing finger at Blake.

"It's true. I stopped to water my horse then sat down and waited for her to wake up." Finally, Blake offered some explanation, but why he didn't just leave Annie be when he came upon her, Cassie couldn't fathom. "I must have dozed off." A small gap-toothed smile breached his face.

There was a heavy silence as Carrington considered the two of them. It was the most ridiculous situation Cassie had ever imagined. For a frightful second, she again wondered if Carrington *was* responsible for killing his own wife. The ludicrousness of it all hit her, and her irrational mind dealt with the situation the best way it knew how.

With fists clenched atop Annie's head, Cassie stood before the two imposing men and laughed wildly. Not a funny, bubbly laugh, but a hard, dark menacing sound, because she just didn't know what else to do. When she'd had enough of the ridiculous situation, she pivoted on bare feet, and marched off in the direction of the house.

"I will not stand here and be treated like chattel, with you both deciding my fate for something I didn't do!" Her hands moved through the air with her words.

Behind her, she heard Carrington call out, "I'll deal with you later."

***

Cassie returned to the present still roiling with the anger she'd brought from the past. She was furious at Carrington's refusal to listen to his wife, and even more furious at Blake's sabotage, intentional or not. He should have just left Annie alone out there by the pond. But he hadn't!

Every muscle in Cassie's body was taut like a bow. She needed a release and painting wouldn't cut it. Retreating to the barn, she grabbed a pitchfork and started cleaning one of the horse stalls. It was less of a cleaning and more of a scraping of old straw and debris that had collected over time, but it was physical labor, and the job needed done.

With a pang of longing, quickly quashed by the memory of Carrington's anger, she realized she was in the stall where his horse used to bed down. For the first time since meeting the ghost version of him, she wondered about the farm, his father's legacy that, to Carrington's peril, he had adamantly refused to leave behind. An icy sliver of trepidation tickled the back of her neck as she considered *how* he'd died. Why was it such a secret?

After breaching the first layer of her frustration, she reflected on the scene at the pond. It had revealed a lot that ghost Carrington neglected to mention—like the threat he'd directed at either Blake or Annie, she didn't know which. He *had* alluded to bad things he'd done, things she'd likely encounter during her time in the past. She assumed this was one of those things.

"Good. He shouldn't be proud of that," Cassie grumbled. "He had no right to assume the worst." She grunted with the effort of lifting a particularly large mound of muck before continuing her monologue—the voice of reason she relied on the most.

"Why would Blake do that? Was it on purpose, do you suppose?" She paused to wipe the sweat forming on her brow. "Or did he just stop and doze off like he said?"

She winced at the remembered image of Carrington, his eyes cutting through Annie like a blade through skin. Instinct had her rubbing at her neck.

So far, what she'd garnered during her excursions to the nineteenth century was a pissed-off husband, a raging sunburn, and a bruise on her hip the size of a watermelon. It seemed Cassie was getting more injuries than information out of this deal. Straw dust spun about in the air. She sneezed and wiped the back of her hand beneath her nose.

"Damn. It would help some if he wasn't so hunky, angry or otherwise." Her voice dropped to a mere whisper at the confession. "As fine as any Chippendale dancer I've ever seen, all muscle and male pride." She stopped and fanned her face with one hand before leaning on the pitchfork handle and shifting sideways, stretching one hip, then the other, sighing with pleasure as her muscles loosened.

"My therapist would say—"

"What *would* your therapist say?" Carrington's voice echoed like a gunshot through the empty barn.

Cassie spun around, pitchfork raised. "Fuck!"

He was standing just beyond the stall, his back against the wall, one booted foot propped at an angle, and his Stetson tilted forward over his brow. It occurred to Cassie that his attire never changed, not that he had anywhere to go. He was a ghost after all.

"Carrington! You scared the crap out of me."

"What are you doing?" He pulled away from the wall and stalked toward her.

"Uh, just thinking." Why was he there? He should be off doing whatever it was that ghosts did, not lurking about in dark barns, and appearing out of nowhere.

"Who were you talking to?" His lips teased up in a slow smile.

"Nobody. Well, nobody." She shrugged. Getting caught talking to herself was a common enough occurrence throughout her life. For some reason, his catching her made her uncomfortable, probably because of what she was thinking or saying about him.

When he took another step closer, she took one back. They played this game until she bumped against the wall. "How long were you there eavesdropping?" Her voice was calm, collected, yet a slow burn sparked to life in the region of her pelvis.

His hand came to rest over the top of the stall wall. He contemplated the same empty space she had, the one where his horse would have been, a long time ago. "Hmm, not long."

She knew he wasn't telling the truth. What had she said? About Carrington? About Blake?

"What is a Chippendale?"

A choked sound that might have been a laugh escaped her throat at the same time a hot blush raced up her neck. She flicked her hand in the air. "Oh, just some male exotic dancers who take off their clothes before an audience. Strippers."

A look of appalled shock forced his jaw and eyes wide open. "You saw men disrobe?" His voice had risen to an abnormally high pitch, unlike anything she'd heard from him before. "What kind of world has this become?"

Cassie used his moment of disbelief to skirt around him, but his arm shot out, blocking her. Forced to stand close, she tried to hide her visibly shaking hands by tightening her grip on the pitchfork.

"What did you read that has you so agitated?"

In the tight proximity of the stall, it didn't seem that he towered over her as much as she'd expected him to. She'd become accustomed to being this close to him as Annie.

"I'm not agitated."

"You were a bit riled up when I arrived."

She put her hand against his chest and shoved, but he didn't budge. His fingers clamped around her wrist before she could retract her arm.

"I was not riled up, as you put it." She gawked at him, tugging hard at her arm again, to no avail. He laughed, low in his throat. He knew she lied.

"It was you," she finally admitted, "and your righteous, overbearing attitude that has me riled."

"Why? Or let me guess, Blake had something to do with it?" The soft tissue around his eyes tightened and his lips compressed into a sneer.

Refusing to admit that Blake was at the center of the scene, she tried to redirect the blame. "What if I said it was only you in the scene and I'm mad at something you did. I mean, that Annie was mad at you for something you did." Cassie set her expression in a display of haughty resolve. The response she got, which she assumed would be an argument, was not what she had hoped for.

Instead of releasing her hand with indignation and moving away, he crowded as close to her as physically possible. This was not going as planned.

"What was the entry about, Cassie?" he asked, too calmly.

Cassie couldn't recall him ever saying her name. The sound of it now, in his deep, sexy voice, caused her heart to trip inside her chest.

She forced her thoughts back to the events of her most recent travels into the past, and its potential ramifications. He was capable of hurting people when he'd been alive. That she knew. He'd made a threat moments ago, in the past—a past where Cassie could be hurt. But here, in the present, he was a ghost. Certainly, he didn't have the ability to hurt *her* here. Did he?

She pulled at her wrist, feeling the solidity of his firm grip. If he squeezed hard enough, it would hurt. His fingers tightened with a fraction of pressure, which she felt.

She swallowed hard. "It was at the pond. Annie was relaxing and dozed off." His thumb began a steady slide over the bottom side of her wrist. Cassie frowned.

"And that bastard just happened to doze off, too, right beside her." The same angry darkness she'd seen on his face while at the pond returned. "She claimed nothing happened. I have to admit, I never believed it."

Carrington forced her fingers to open and flattened her palm against his chest. She felt the steady pounding of his heart beneath the fabric of his shirt. *How is that possible?*

"It's the truth." Her voice shook, as did her entire body. "Did you threaten Blake or Annie that day?" She held her ground, certain she'd burst into flames at the intensity of the emotions shifting across his face. The grip at her wrist finally eased. His head lowered close to hers.

"I don't know," he whispered. The confession wrenched from some deep part of him, guttural and raw with emotion. "I wanted to hurt them both at that moment, I think."

She swallowed what bit of moisture there was left in her mouth. "I'm not sure what happened next. I got mad. At you, for accusing Annie, and so I stormed off." She didn't understand why she felt sympathy for him. He did after all admit to wanting to kill either or both Annie and Blake. Yet beneath all the anger and the harsh words, she sensed hurt and pain.

And how many times in her life did she wish for someone to take away her pain? She fought against the voice in her mind telling her to retreat. It was the opposite of what her body wanted, and the opposite of what she did next.

A shudder moved through Carrington when her free hand slid across the back of his neck.

"We argued," he confessed. "Blake wandered off, wisely enough." The growl in his voice was barely suppressed. "And eventually I left her there, afraid of what I might do."

"Where did you go?" She bristled, assuming she knew the answer, and didn't try to hide the acid behind her next words. "Did you run to Suzanne?"

He pressed his palm against the side of her face before tangling his fingers in her hair. Tugging gently, he forced her head back. Cassie made a mousy squeak when he touched the tip of her nose with his lips. A flicker of some internal struggle drew a crease between his brows.

"I got fiercely drunk and landed myself in a jail cell." His lips pressed down over hers. She grabbed at the front of his shirt and held him to her.

So, he hadn't gone straight to Suzanne after all. He'd been hurt, angry, and jealous and had gone off to a place where he could find a fight. His assault was merciless, leaving her breathless until he finally moved away to trace light kisses across her collarbone.

"How old are you?" she asked, angling her head so he could access the column of her neck.

"Thirty-four."

Thirty-four. Only three years older than she was, give or take a hundred or so years.

She was lost and relished his affections. He bent slightly and ran his hands up her legs, tantalizing her as they traveled higher, across her bare thighs, up and over her denim shorts. His thumbs pressed against her hipbones as they passed.

She turned to jelly, quivering with anticipation. When her legs buckled, she clamped her hands over his shoulders while his hands curved around her ribcage. The heat of his fingertips passed through the fabric of the white, eyelet blouse she wore, searing her skin beneath.

She wondered if he'd been this loving and thorough with Annie when they were together. Then she remembered in full, colorful detail their wedding day.

They'd been so happy; he an attentive lover, she an adoring wife. Cassie's heart ached over their loss, so soon after they were married, when he'd had their whole life planned out. The sadness of their tragic end tore through her. Unlike Cassie's monster of a husband who got off on inflicting pain and controlling what he claimed belonged to him, Carrington had cherished Annie.

A heart-wrenching cry stole up her center. She wrapped her arms around him, trying to give him comfort—comfort that Annie might have given in his darkest times, if she'd been alive.

"I need you, Cassie."

The words tore at her being like the claws of a lion tearing at the flesh of its kill. All the years of pent-up emotion poured from a place deep in his soul. He needed his wife. He needed his past. But at this moment, in this weird thing, whatever it was, he needed her.

There was only one problem: Carrington was a ghost. It wasn't possible. Was it? Somehow, somewhere in her mind she was dreaming this or fantasizing it. She wanted this fantasy over her more painful memories more than she could say.

"How?" Her lips were tingling from the onslaught of his against hers.

"Let me show you." He began to nibble her ear, the sensation causing goosebumps to form on every inch of her body.

"We can't." Her voice trembled with her growing desire. He straightened, and she whimpered at the distance his movement created.

"We can." He forced her chin up with his thumb and forefinger. She denied his words with a small movement of her head. He merely smiled. She gulped another dry swallow. His fingers squeezed lightly against her scalp.

"Yes," she finally agreed, the word rushing out on a hiss of air.

Seconds ticked by as he gauged the seriousness of her response. With a gentle urging, he pulled her tight against his tense body.

Cassie's hands stole up over his back again, seeking purchase.

"To the house," she said between kisses.

They rushed from the stall, neither willing to break physical contact. Side-by-side they walked, each with an arm around the other's waist.

A muffled buzzing, combined with a vibration at her back pocket, interrupted their focus on each other. Carrington's hand reached Cassie's cell phone first. He withdrew it and read the digital display.

"Larimer County DA. Who is that?"

TWENTY-TWO

There were only three instances in Carrington's life that had made him feel as helpless as he did while listening to Cassie talk to the Larimer County District Attorney. The first was when he watched his father die. The second, when Sheriff Anders informed him that they'd found Annie's body. And the third was at the gallows, when the floor beneath his feet fell away.

He stood near Cassie now, listening in quiet bewilderment, once again experiencing that feeling of helplessness. She had her back to him, the cell phone pressed tight to her ear. In a hushed voice, she asked a series of questions: Why? How? When? What if he shows up? By the time the call ended, the flush that had been high on her cheeks minutes earlier had faded, leaving her skin ashen.

When she set the phone on the counter, her hands trembled like the leaves on the maple tree out in the backyard. Mumbling something about needing to be alone, she turned and rushed from the room, leaving him there to ponder what the DA might have said. He'd learned over his short time together with Cassie that when she was frustrated or scared, she sought physical labor or time alone. This situation apparently called for the latter.

It was late now. He lay on the bed in the spare room, ankles crossed, hands tucked behind his head. He'd been contemplating the day's events, and worried that Cassie's recent conversation with the DA would interrupt her willingness to help him. She'd garnered a lot of information so far in her journeys to the past, but he didn't know enough yet to make any determinations. It was a selfish request, he knew, but he needed her to continue reading so he could move on.

Whoever had framed him for Annie's murder did it so perfectly he'd paid the ultimate price. At the gallows. Many times, he'd considered giving up and searching for a way to cross the astral plane. Doing so meant allowing the Chambers name to remain tarnished, his heritage forever lost. He thought he could accept that. But then he'd think of all that Annie had missed out on in her life, and his need for vengeance and redemption was renewed. So, he bided his time until that one person came along who could help him.

Now, here she was, struggling with her worldly problems, while he greedily held out hope that she'd keep helping him with his other-worldly ones. The fact that she could potentially be harmed, fatally even, ate at his conscience. Did she fully understand the ramifications were she to confront Annie's foe? Was he willing to let her face that?

When she'd spoken to the DA, Carrington heard a different level of fear in her voice from what she'd expressed when she'd encountered him, a ghost. The sound struck a bad chord within his conscience. He wanted to help her conquer that fear, one borne from something so terrible most would have succumbed to it.

He blew out a century-old sigh. Over one hundred years had passed waiting for Cassie. She was the one. Now that he'd spent time with her, he was no longer certain he wanted to pursue truths long dead. The risk to Cassie's wellbeing suddenly far outweighed his need for answers.

He should leave. The mystical urge to cross over and be done with this world and his haunting pulled at him in a way it hadn't before.

The feelings and urges she'd awakened in him, dormant for so long, would only lead to pain. She'd be stuck with him in a life that wasn't really a life and she'd grow old before his eyes. Then, she'd die and leave him to exist alone for eternity.

As had happened on thousands of endless nights, Carrington's memories turned to his brief time with Annie. He smiled a sad smile. Assailed by regrets, he imagined that if he'd spent less time being jealous of Blake, things might have turned out differently for them. He and Annie should have been happy, but in the end his actions destroyed what could have been.

Even Cassie was enamored with Blake. Granted, she was living through Annie's memories, but still, she seemed to have her own presence of mind while in the past. The chicken coop encounter was one example, and her leaving during the pond confrontation another. An image of Annie, no, Cassie lying beneath Blake in a lover's embrace entered his mind. He forced it away and flopped over onto his side.

"Damn it all to hell!" Carrington knifed upright and off the bed. He paced across the dark room. It was larger than his old room on the main floor, yet smaller than the one where Cassie was now. This was her home now, not his, and she occupied the largest bedroom.

Should he go to her? No. The last thing she needed was him, a ghost, interfering with her inner turmoil. He'd be gone soon. She needed to find her inner strength on her own.

Lying back down on the soft mattress, he tried to sleep, something he'd not done in a very long time.

He was angry with himself. Cassie didn't know the end to the story, what was to come, because he hadn't told her. She'd blindly given him her trust. He'd even taken the remaining newspapers back to the trunk, so she couldn't read them on her own. If they were out of sight, she wouldn't have the opportunity to learn his worst secret. She wouldn't turn fearful eyes on him, allowing him to see the naked terror lurking there, like he'd seen at the mention of Jimmy.

Carrington clenched his fists tight against his chest. His desire to enact revenge on Cassie's behalf was overwhelming. He'd do it without a second's thought, if only he could leave his property to find Jimmy.

Restlessness had him up and standing before the window to stare out into the night as it settled around his land—what was left of it, anyway. He missed his old life. When he went to prison, he'd arranged to have Blake move into the house and take over running the farm. It rankled to do it, as it contradicted all his opinions about the man. But there'd been nobody else to bestow his property to in order to safeguard it for him. So, Blake got it by default. Carrington never expected to be executed for a crime he didn't commit, and had no idea, at first, if Blake stayed on the property or not. After.

Even though he'd been provided a pathway of sorts back to this place, the haunting business wasn't as easy as people imagined. He spent nearly a year figuring out how to return from that space in between this world and the next. When he finally managed to anchor himself to the house, he'd found Blake still in residence, and doing a fine job farming the land.

It had shocked him to see Suzanne residing there with him. Carrington knew they'd shared carnal knowledge of each other, beginning sometime after he and Annie had married, but he'd assumed it was only a dalliance for them both. It seemed Suzanne's constant appearance on the property had been about Blake, not about vexing Annie, which is what her presence did, rather successfully. He never believed Suzanne and Blake would remain together as a couple.

Another year later, Suzanne had a baby. A little girl. The child and parents appeared to be a very happy family. That gave Carrington some peace, knowing the home he'd built with plans for his own family had one living there.

One day, Blake and Suzanne left the house with their child and never returned. All their belongings remained behind. Even the laundry had been left out on the clothesline, flapping in the wind.

Soon after, Sheriff Anders showed up. Carrington followed him silently about the house as he roamed through it. He rummaged through closets and drawers, then stared a bit forlornly out the window. When he went outside, Carrington was at his heels. Anders wandered around the yard and the outbuildings before climbing into his buggy and departing the premises. It was the last time he saw the man.

A gentleman in a suit and several other men dressed in coveralls were the next visitors to the house. The workers emptied the place of all Blake and his family's belongings. Then the suited man closed the front door and left. He returned for a short visit once each year, quickly assessing the property before leaving again. Carrington watched from the shadows as he returned year after year, his hair grayer at each visit.

Workers eventually came to add indoor plumbing, electricity, and the second floor of the house. After that, tenants started moving in. A different gentleman in a suit wandered through the home with them, going over conditions of their renting the property. Tenants came and went, with new couples taking their place every few years until sometime into the nineteen-seventies. Then it sat vacant until Cassie showed up.

Carrington had no idea why the place hadn't been demolished in all that time. He knew only that his land had been parceled off. The boundaries within which he was able to travel shrinking significantly to its current eighty-acre plot. He could no longer roam one hundred sixty acres. His limits were very small, indeed.

From the moment Cassie arrived, he'd watched her every move. He quickly learned that she was on a mission of sorts. Searching for peace? Herself? What she found was him. He smiled with pride at how much she'd changed already. Even she wasn't aware of it yet.

Until that phone call, she'd begun to worry less about the scar on her neck, no longer covering it out of nervous habit. Whether from his influence now or what she was encountering during her visits to Annie's past, there was a new sauce and grit to her. She was fiery and feisty, and he liked that side of her.

Until the call.

When he first met her, he assumed she was timid and shy, like Annie. It didn't take long to figure out that she wasn't shy, she was afraid; terrified of the monsters that lurked about in real life. Rather than succumb to that fear, she'd moved into the house alone, intent upon fighting her demons.

Each time she read the journal, she returned to the present more outspoken and more frustrated at her interactions with him in the past as well as their encounters in the present. They'd been a heartbeat away from satisfying their pent-up needs before that damned cell phone buzzed.

From across the room, Carrington heard a sound. The bedroom door eased open. Long, slender fingers gripped the edge before Cassie's silhouette darkened the doorway.

His heart stilled in his chest as he watched in wide-eyed fascination as she glided toward him. She stopped near the edge of the bed, her eyes glimmering in the moonlight shining in through the window. Her hair was down and hanging in a glorious curtain over her shoulder. He loved long, silky hair on a woman.

He whispered her name. "Cassie."

She wore a light-colored dressing gown that hung to a spot just above her knees. The moonlight highlighted the peaks of her nipples where they pushed against the delicate fabric at the front of the gown. Carrington tore his gaze away.

She knelt on the edge of the mattress. Was she uncertain, or waiting for acknowledgment? He leaned toward the latter and shifted to the center of the bed before turning on his side and patting the spot he'd vacated. She eased down beside him, facing him. Curling her knees up so they bumped against his, she settled into the pillow, hand flat beneath her cheek.

"Are you all right?" he asked.

Clearly, she was not. She'd been fighting with him and avoiding contact with him here and, from what she'd indicated, in the past, too, for the last few days. Yet here she was in his bed in the middle of the night, touching knees with him.

No. She was not all right.

A tremor rippled through her body. If it were Annie hurting or afraid, when he wasn't in a jealous rage, he'd have curled his arms around her and comforted her. But this was Cassie, the woman with a naughty mouth and a sharp tongue. The woman who needed to find her own strength. The woman who was broken and wanted to be whole again.

"No." She sucked in a deep, shuddering sob. "But I'm going to be. I just need to get through tonight." She brought her hand up and let it come to rest on his waist. The warmth of it radiated deep beneath his skin.

Carrington wrapped his arm around her and pulled her close. Rolling to his back, he brought her with him until she lay snug against his side with her head on his shoulder. He pressed his palm firmly against the middle of her back. They lay that way for a very long time, with him stroking her arm, her hair, her hip, while her body trembled with fear. He kissed the top of her head. The smell of tart green apples tickled his senses. She made little sound as she lay against his chest. Gradually, her shuddering eased and eventually stopped as she slipped into an exhausted sleep.

If Jimmy showed his face at his doorstep, Carrington swore he'd do what needed to be done to end Cassie's torment. He was a ghost, after all, and had nothing to lose by committing the act for which he'd once been executed already.

TWENTY-THREE

James Lancaster was released two days ago.

The DA claimed that she'd attempted to contact Cassie in advance of Jimmy's release, but the number on file for her had been disconnected. Sadly, this was true. Prior to the move to Idaho, she'd changed her number, fearing Jimmy would attempt to communicate with her from prison, regardless that it wasn't permitted. She hadn't gotten around to updating anyone besides Andrew of the change.

To Andrew's credit, he had tried to contact her, too. But Cassie intentionally ignored him. She wanted to prove she could survive on her own. Between that and her distraction over reading Annie's diary, she'd not bothered to check her phone for texts or messages. When she did finally look, she'd found many frantic messages from Andrew in voicemail and text.

The DA's words were an oppressive weight Cassie couldn't escape. Suffocating. She kicked at the sheet covering her feet, desperate to be free of all constraints. The freedom to move without constriction was a balm to her troubled mind. Still, she refused to rouse fully and begin the day.

Jimmy was free.

How long would it take him to show up on her doorstep? There was no question in her mind that he'd find her. What would happen next? Would he succeed where he'd failed before?

She pressed her fingers against her scar, hard enough to feel the pulse in the jugular vein beneath. Jimmy had had every intention of killing her that day. But miraculously she'd survived. That meant something.

She moved to Idaho to make the most of the second chance at life she'd been given. Her hope was that she'd get past the trauma and eventually meet someone to share her life with, someone good who loved her and wouldn't hurt her.

A man like Carrington?

The name came to her, unbidden. She rolled over and stilled when she found him beside her. He was lying flat on his back, hands crossed over his bare chest.

Easing up on her elbow, she propped her head in her hand, and stared down at him. His hair was spiky, disheveled. A curl formed just below his ear. She reached for it, but stopped mid-air, imagining how it would wind around her finger.

Long eyelashes swept against his cheeks. His lips were . . . magical. Hidden behind them she knew were straight, healthy teeth, with only a slight overlap of two on the bottom. Considering the time that he'd lived, having good teeth was a rather remarkable feat. His smile was nearly perfect, unlike her own—she had one lateral incisor missing—the tooth directly next to her front tooth. A hereditary trait, her dentist had said.

Her finger air-traced over Carrington's bristly jaw to his throat where the small curve of his Adam's apple bobbed when he swallowed. A mat of black hair covered his chest.

It looked like it had been combed flat over the solid wall of muscle beneath. Even in repose, his abs were solid, not soft. Hair tapered to a line that disappeared at the edge of the sheet across his hips.

When she had climbed into bed with him the night before, she'd been seeking the comfort she knew he would offer. She wanted to absorb some of his strength—strength she'd need for the coming days. As expected, he'd welcomed her without any demands and made her feel safe, if only for that moment.

It was morning now and she still felt safe, even with a half-naked ghost in her bed. She wanted him, plain and simple. He wanted her, too, and probably needed her more than she needed him.

"Get a grip, McAllister." She whispered the words so low even she could barely hear them. Fantasizing about a ghost couldn't be healthy. Being left all alone, after she'd found the answers to set Carrington free, would be even more unhealthy for her.

"Good morning."

The sound of his voice startled her.

Like a dam that had too much water to hold, she forced back sudden tears, her lips pouting in the struggle. Try as she might, she couldn't stop one fat drop from slipping over her eyelash to roll down her cheek. She choked on a sob as the bed rocked beneath her and strong arms enveloped her. Before she could comprehend her situation, she was wedged tight against Carrington's body from chin to toes.

"Wh-what am I going to do?" she cried against his throat.

"Shhhh. It's going to be all right," he promised, soothing her with his words and the comforting support of his body.

She relished the warmth and solidness of him. He was a shield. Feeling helpless, she whimpered, then in a voice drenched in fear uttered, "You don't know him. He swore he'd succeed . . . the next time." Her body trembled with the force of shock and fear.

Carrington's muscles flexed around her and his leg slid over hers as he tucked her tighter to him. "Listen to me." His words rumbled in her ear where it pressed against his chest. "He will never hurt you. Not as long as I'm here." One free hand stroked the side of her face. He forced her head up. "I won't let him hurt you ever again."

The kiss that followed was gentle yet demanding, kind yet fierce in its intensity. He stole her breath. His tongue grazed her lips, demanding entry. She opened to him. He took from her exactly what even she didn't know she had to give.

She was in bed with a man who wanted her, who had brought her pleasure more than once without ever having touched her. He was here now, greedily stealing kisses that caused a rush of warmth between her thighs. A tingling need shimmered up her spine, like a low electric current that was seeking a ground. She wanted him to be that ground.

Determined to show him without words what she wanted, she pressed her hands along his jaw and kissed him like she'd never kissed anyone before. Her leg straddled his thigh as she tried to get even closer to him, her desire turning to desperate need.

"Make love to me," she urged, nipping at his earlobe. She grinned at the tremor that went through him. If the air around them were any more charged, it would ignite.

Reaching for the buttons at his waistband, her hand skimmed over the straining bulge beneath the denim. She'd dreamt of this moment, even if she'd sort of done it once already. But *she* hadn't touched him with her own hands or tasted him with her own tongue. Only through Annie was she aware of what he could do to her body.

Before she could make any progress, Carrington sat up and pulled her up from the bed. His hands slid over her arms and up the column of her neck. She pushed up on her toes and wrapped her arms around his shoulders, pulling him down to her.

He bent lower, reaching for the hem of her nightgown. Easing it up her body, neither broke eye contact until the garment slipped over her head. It fell from his fingers to the floor.

He stepped back and lifted one of her arms, staring curiously at her bare armpit. Cassie's body grew hot under his perusal, but she remained still. He trailed a fingertip over her scar lovingly as his eyes lowered to her breasts.

The skin over her ribcage pulled in and out around the bones beneath as she breathed. Carrington's hands roamed over her body, past the softness of her belly to the juncture between her thighs. His knees buckled, and he sat back on the bed, pulling her closer. His face was at eye level with her crotch.

Laughing nervously, Cassie tried to move away from his intense survey of her personal geography. His fingers squeezed into her hips, halting her progress. When he blew a soft puff of air on her, there, she nearly melted into a puddle at his feet. She was mesmerized by the sight of him as he traced his finger from hip bone to hip bone.

He swiped a hand across his brow. The intensity of his restraint showed in the set of his jaw. Cassie's skin prickled, like she was chilled. But this wasn't a cool chill. It was a hot and vibrant charge of energy pouring through her veins.

When her legs threatened imminent collapse, he pivoted her about and pushed her backward onto the bed.

She scooted back, bringing her knees up and together, shielding herself from his brazen view while he undressed. He made fast work of the buttons of his trousers. Cassie couldn't contain her gasp when his erection sprang free from its confinement. He was the most spectacular specimen of man she'd ever seen, at least this intimately. Chippendales didn't count.

Carrington stood before her, legs slightly parted, arms hanging at his sides. She studied him at leisure. When his hand shifted to grip the object of her current curiosity, Cassie's eyes widened, and she swallowed nervously. Determined to know if her imagined measurement had been accurate, she clamped her fingers around him. She'd guessed correctly.

He twitched at her touch and made some guttural sound as his jaw clenched tight. His head dropped back on his neck and a groove formed in the space between his brows. She rubbed her thumb over the drop of moisture on his tip. He lurched away, releasing her hold on him.

"Stop." As he climbed onto the bed, he pushed her legs apart and nudged her thighs with his knees, spreading her wider. Hovering above her, he braced one hand beside her head.

"Wait!" she cried out, leaning up onto both elbows. "What about a condom?"

Carrington glanced at her sideways, like she'd just asked him to hand her the moon. It made Cassie wonder if condoms had even been around back in his day. She quickly considered her options. He was a ghost who hadn't had sex in over a hundred years. The chances of him having any sort of disease were virtually zero, and she couldn't get pregnant by a ghost. Could she? Myriad questions rambled around her brain.

"What would your therapist say, McAllister?" His voice was strained, like it took everything he had to speak.

She snorted a laugh. "He'd tell me I've finally gone over the deep end."

He nudged against her core.

"Since I'm already headed over . . ." They were both shaking with restrained need. "Yes! I want you."

She fell to her back as he eased into her, stretching her wide until he was in as far as was possible. Then he stopped and pressed his forehead against hers. His hips didn't move, but Cassie felt the muscles in his back and shoulders tense from the strain of holding himself rigid.

"Carrington?" She bucked her hips. Maybe he was having regrets. She wasn't Annie after all, and Cassie *had* only known him for a week. He came from an era of old-fashioned men. Was he concerned about her reputation? Was he regretting his actions? Or worse, did he think she was some loose woman? He'd shared a bed with Suzanne out of wedlock. He'd better not dare cast judgement on her.

"What's wrong? What are you thinking?"

He let go the breath he'd been holding. "I'm thinking of the field I should plant potatoes in next year." His jaw was clenched as he spoke.

"What?" she said, rocking against him, encouraging movement. And then understanding dawned and she began to laugh. Carrington opened his eyes and she saw the sparkle of humor in their depths, but the tension hadn't left his face. He wasn't having regrets.

She wrapped her legs around the backs of his thighs. "I suppose I need to work a little harder at distracting you, then." She rotated her hips and he groaned.

"If this is going to last for any amount of time, you might let me tend crops in my head for a minute."

She reached up and kissed him. "We'll just have to try again later, won't we? Once you've recovered, that is." She nibbled at his shoulder, leaving a pink mark there.

He reared up, beautifully and powerfully above her. "Don't say I didn't warn you, then."

With unleashed and long-buried need, he took from her what he'd missed out on for an eternity.

She held tight to him, meeting him with her own thrusts. She was getting close but didn't want it to end without him coming with her.

His teeth nipped at the tip of one jutting nipple, and the shock of it rocked her body. "Oh, my god!" She thrashed her head side to side.

With a satisfied grunt, he angled his hips, striking against a spot that brought her to the brink. She made humming noises in her throat that grew louder with each stroke. When his teeth nipped at her again, it triggered her exploding ascent. She cried out his name as she fell. Writhing beneath him, she tried to prolong the sensations roiling through her as his release collided with hers.

TWENTY-FOUR

Blissfully content. Every fiber and every muscle in Cassie's body was as pliable as warm wax. She couldn't recall ever having experienced anything so perfect, so natural.

"Why did I wait so long for that?" She sprawled languorously beside Carrington, half on, half off him, his pectoral muscle her pillow. She traced her finger along the trail of fine hair that ran down his torso. His hand stilled hers when it dipped beneath the cotton sheet.

"Oh, I know why," she added, before Carrington could respond. "Could it be because you're a ghost and none of this is real?"

Her blissful sigh was cut short when Carrington moved, quick as a cat, flipping her onto her back. Her head sank into the fluffy pillow, and she squealed in stunned delight when his hand slipped between her legs.

"Are you implying this isn't real?" His voice was deep and lazy but held an edge of challenge. She bucked forward when his fingers dipped inside her still-slick body.

Cassie arched her back and pushed against his hand. She wanted him again, wanted to feel the press of his naked body against hers, surrounding her with his essence as he settled deep inside her. She wanted to forget the world and never have to think about anything outside this room, especially Jimmy. Under Carrington's expert tutelage, she believed she'd succeed, at least for the next few hours.

He was proving a point, rather effectively, and she willingly gave in to his ministrations. All her nerve endings were still on high alert from their previous round of play, so it didn't take her long to peak. She cried out before falling back into a sated repose.

"I suppose *that* didn't really happen, either?" He crawled back up the bed and flopped down beside her with a satisfied grunt.

"Alright, alright. I believe, but I still don't understand it." She snuggled back into place at his side. "How can any of this be happening?"

His finger twirled around a lock of hair that fell against her shoulder. It was an intimate gesture. Something Jimmy had never done. The man she'd married, whom she thought would take care of her forever, never touched her like this. What he got pleasure from was hurting her. Cassie had been too young, or too naïve, to fully comprehend the monster he was until it was too late.

However, she'd survived him, survived his attempt to take her from this world. What she had now, with Carrington, made her feel a sort of vindication. She'd rid her life of Jimmy, who'd forever be a bad person. He'd always struggle and would never know what love was or what it was like to be loved. He'd never feel what she was feeling at this very moment.

Carrington was a lover, not a fighter, Cassie was positively certain of that. What he'd had with his wife started out pure and sweet, but it had been jaded by unwarranted jealousies, on both sides, his and hers.

He was a good man who'd witnessed his own father's murder who was then shunned by his peers after committing the crime any number of them might have committed, under similar circumstances. To twist the proverbial dagger deeper into his back, his wife had been taken from him before they ever had a chance to nurture their love. And there'd been nobody there to help him pick up the pieces.

Cassie at least had had people—Andrew and her parents—supporting her when she'd needed them most. Granted, Andrew was a paid therapist, but from day one, he hadn't shied away from the damage displayed on her neck. He saw past the scar, just like Carrington had done.

Unfortunately, there were a few she'd presumed were friends who turned their backs on her. The scar was too violent, too much for them to deal with, especially early on when it was fresh, angry, and raw. She was surprised to learn later that it was the fear of being associated with her that kept those former friends at arm's length. They were terrified that Jimmy would return one day to try again, so they retreated far from her circle. They hadn't wanted to be anywhere nearby if, or when, he struck again. Cassie couldn't fault them for their concerns over their own safety.

Tears threatened at how happy she suddenly felt, and she sniffled.

"What's the matter, darlin'?" Carrington pressed his lips to her forehead. Nobody had been there to help him or Annie. If they had, Annie might not have died, and he might not have had to spend an eternity alone waiting for answers. It tore at Cassie's heart.

Her feelings were conflicted. If Carrington weren't a ghost, Cassie would never have met him. But he was a ghost; and helping him would result in her losing him. The thought wrenched her heart. She dared to imagine what a life with him would be like, knowing that possibility was but a fairytale—once upon a time. She leaned over and pressed her lips against his belly while resuming the lazy exploration south that she'd embarked on earlier, before he stayed her hand.

A warm, satisfied smile crossed her face. "I'm just happy. For the first time since . . . well, since forever. I suppose I should go back and bail your drunk ass out of jail."

A grunt of agreement, or denial, issued from his throat, whether about her going back, or her physical exploration of his body, she wasn't sure. He didn't halt her progress down the length of his body, so she continued her efforts.

His expression quickly shifted from relaxed and satiated to playful and hungry. The corners of his lips turned up in a slow smile. "Or you could let the past be and show me again how much you're enjoying this particular ghost." He winked, the gesture causing butterflies to lift off inside Cassie's belly.

She wasn't going to let the past be, but she would postpone it long enough to satisfy her current curiosity, and to satisfy Carrington. His guttural sounds of ecstasy made Cassie feel like the most powerful woman on earth. He relinquished that power to her. She felt revered, beautiful, and if she dared, loved. Jimmy only ever demanded and took, degrading her, making her feel worthless. Carrington restored her sense of self by giving over to her all control, which in no way unmanned him. It was the most extraordinary feeling ever.

A short while later, their passion spent, they were propped back against the headboard contemplating the next step in their search for answers to the past. In a half attempt to prevent further distraction, Cassie pulled the sheet up and over her chest, tucking it against her sides.

"We're so close to the end. I want to go back and find out what happened." She gave him a wan smile. Once she found out all there was to know, he'd be free to go. It was all so unfair.

"We don't have to." He shifted away from her and stretched out on his back, one arm propped behind his head. "I don't need to know anymore. Not like I did." His tone was melancholy, but not the same level of devastatingly sad as before, and he no longer seemed angry.

"Why? You have to know what happened to her." She gawked at him. "*I* have to know. If we find the truth, I don't know, maybe we can change the past." She placed her hand on his arm where it draped over his chest.

"What do you mean?"

The idea wasn't one she'd pondered for very long. During the hours following the call from the District Attorney, she'd considered Annie and her death. When Cassie had gone back in time, she'd known Annie's thoughts, but she'd also had free will to think and do what she wanted. What if she could find out what was going to happen and then alter the past? The voice had been saying, *"Save her."* That had to mean it was possible. She said as much to Carrington.

"Something has to happen with someone before she disappears on the night of the fire. What if I can find out who or what it was and stop it? Or, at least change . . ." she sought the right word, "the outcome."

"You can't change what's already happened."

Cassie wasn't sure that was true. "You said what went on in the chicken coop didn't." A rush of pink covered her face and she shrugged it away. She was naked in bed beside him, after having done some of the most intimate things two people could do together. There was no longer any room for blushing.

"I changed something there. What if I can change something else?"

Carrington's fingers drummed against his belly as his mind played through the possibilities. "It might be worth a try," he agreed hesitantly. "But if I sense anything is going wrong, I'm waking you up. And I won't allow you to return there again," he warned.

She started to scoot off the bed the minute he'd agreed. Her stomach grumbled loud enough to be heard over the shifting of the mattress. She pressed a hand to her belly. "I guess we should eat something first. I get so caught up in reading, I forget about food."

He climbed off the bed and met her halfway across the room. "Good idea. You make us something to eat." She giggled like a teenager when he swatted her on her bare bottom as she turned to leave the bedroom. "But you probably shouldn't try to cook anything. Your fire-making skills need a bit more work, I think." He passed her in the doorway and hopped a few steps beyond her reach when she swatted back at him, missing her target.

"Bossy won't win you any favors," she huffed, yet the smile never left her face. She bustled into the hallway and down the stairs, naked as the day she was born, humming a tune she'd heard Annie hum once.

Several minutes later, Cassie was back in the room carrying a tray arranged with coffee, yogurt, toast with peanut butter, and a banana. She felt lighter in spirit than she'd felt in years. "I hope you're hungry."

Sitting on the edge of the bed, still marvelously naked, Carrington patted the mattress. She placed the tray beside him on the nightstand and jumped away from his reaching hands.

"Food first." She reclined against the headboard. After handing her the food items in the order requested, she spooned in a few bites of the yogurt before flipping open the journal to where she'd left off.

"What about Jimmy?" Carrington asked.

She pondered the question a moment before saying, "I don't know. He's taken so much of my life already. I'm not going to give him anymore. I hope he's smart enough to not show up here. If he does," she stretched her neck, easing the tension that threatened at the memory of her ex, "I'll figure out how to deal with him." Too bad she couldn't go back and change her own past.

She had the security system, which would alert her of an intruder, but if Jimmy arrived while she was unconscious, she would be at his mercy. Unless Carrington was there, of course. She'd had an idea she wanted to explore at the first opportunity she got while back in his world. If it worked, she might never have to worry about Jimmy ever again.

"Okay, let's read." She'd taken only two bites of a banana when something occurred to her. "By the way, *did* Annie bail you out of jail the day after you argued at the pond?"

"No," he bit out. "The sheriff released me before noon as I recall." A flicker of hurt flashed in his eyes. Was he hurt that they fought, or hurt that Annie hadn't come for him?

"Well, she's going to now." She winked at him, and he smiled.

"'August nineteen, eighteen ninety. Carrington didn't come home again last night.'" The word again had two underline marks beneath it. Cassie gave him a sideways glance. "Again, huh?"

Carrington looked away in a presumption of shame. "As I've already mentioned, before Annie I frequented the bars. Following our marriage, I didn't go a lot. Just when I got angry."

The sheet draped over his hips had shifted down, falling well below his waist, barely covering his lower body. She forced her attention back to the pages, ignoring the distraction. "You seemed angry a lot in what I've experienced so far."

He shook his head. "I wasn't angry all the time. Just jealous. The pond that day?" His voice lowered to a steely edge. "That day I was angry."

Cassie reached around to grab her hair and pulled it over one shoulder. "You're much calmer, less intense now than you were back then."

He touched a finger against the honey-gold lock, his hand brushing softly against the side of her breast. "I've had a long time to grow calm."

She couldn't let him distract her, not yet. Clearing her throat, she followed the words on the page with her finger as she continued to read.

"'I didn't want to be alone at the house today, so I went into town.'"

Without resistance, she slumped against Carrington's warm, protective body and let the past come into view.

***

Annie was walking along the boardwalk. There were no boxes in her hands, so it appeared she was at the start of her outing. That was good. Cassie didn't want to deal with anything other than retrieving Carrington and beating some sense into his head. If he'd stop being jealous long enough to realize Annie loved him, maybe he'd be in a place to prevent whatever would happen soon.

Up ahead, a flash of a woman's auburn hair drew Cassie's attention. A second later, she saw the sheriff. Cassie set her expression into one of hard determination. She'd plead Carrington's case and get him released right away. Picking up her pace, she hurried along to catch up to Sheriff Anders, her heels clunking against the boards beneath her feet.

The sheriff ducked down a nearby alley, the same space where she'd seen Suzanne go. Cassie scurried after him, not caring if it wasn't ladylike that she was practically jogging. Once in the alley, she took a moment to catch her breath. There was no sign of the sheriff or Suzanne.

When she heard voices nearby, her ears perked. Taking another few steps deeper into the alley, she stopped to listen. From the vestibule of a doorway about twenty feet away, there was a glimpse of teal, followed by Suzanne's muffled voice.

Cassie drew in a sharp breath when she saw the edge of a dusty brown hat in the same doorway. It was the sheriff's hat! A teal-sleeved arm came into view as it rose up and rested over the sheriff's shoulder. Cassie pressed tight against the building at her back, hoping to blend into the wall.

"What the hell?" she muttered before gulping her shock when Suzanne's voluminous skirt, now only half hidden by the doorframe, fluffed upward. To Cassie's utter disbelief, a bare leg rose up and hooked around the denim-clad hip of the sheriff.

She pressed tighter against the wall, unable to move, for fear she'd be noticed. Her heart hammered against her chest when the sheriff braced his arm against the doorway above Suzanne's head. When a distinctive feminine moan reached her, Cassie's jaw fell open and her brows lifted high on her forehead. The telltale movement of Suzanne's bared thigh and the view of her creamy white skin was visible in the doorway. Her muscles contracted and released around the sheriff's hip.

Their muffled grunts and moans grew more intense. When Anders' arm lowered to cup Suzanne's buttocks, Cassie jerked and bumped her head against the brick wall. Rubbing at the tender spot, she was about to interrupt the disgusting rendezvous when male and female cries of ecstasy interrupted her shock.

Then all was quiet. There were fleeting glimpses of clothing and body parts shifting about as the two participants hurriedly put themselves back together.

Cassie rushed back out onto the sidewalk and stood against the wall fuming, waiting for the sheriff to come out. Was Carrington aware Suzanne and the sheriff had been lovers? When Cassie had been in Carrington's body, when he'd sought the blasted woman out, she heard Suzanne exclaim concern over her reputation had anyone caught him entering her apartment. From that, Cassie had assumed that Suzanne wasn't a prostitute. Now, she wondered if that assumption was false.

Sheriff Anders strolled out moments later, alone, heading off in the direction from which she'd seen him earlier. She peeked down the alley and saw Suzanne walking off toward the other end.

"Excuse me, Sheriff," Cassie called out.

Sheriff Anders turned, his sated smile dropping a notch when he saw Annie.

"Mrs. Chambers, how good to see you."

Cassie liked how that sounded. Mrs. Chambers. Her heart skipped a beat with the sad feeling that followed. She shook her head, dispelling the knowledge of the couple's fated outcome.

"Sheriff. I believe you have my husband in your jail. I'd like to take him home." Annie's hands were folded, prim and proper over her waist. Cassie forced her fingers to unlock and lowered her hands to her sides. For good measure, she straightened her spine and lifted her chin.

The sheriff advanced toward her, but stopped an arm's length away, just an inch too close for Cassie's comfort. She backed up and looked around, noting several unfriendly faces of passersby staring at her.

"Annie," Anders said, his voice oozing false concern. "He's no good for you. He's a drunk." He held his hands out to her, hands that had just touched Suzanne intimately. "You could do so much better."

Cassie curled her lip in disgust. "Sheriff. Let my husband out. Now." She braced her hands on her hips and tapped her toe. It was a ridiculous and completely useless gesture, but it was all she had in her arsenal.

The sheriff's gooey-eyed stare became a steely-edged one. "Suit yourself. One of these days he's going to do something he can't get himself out of. And I'll be right here waiting."

She wasn't certain if he meant waiting for Carrington to screw up or waiting for Annie to go running to Anders. Either option was a poor one.

They marched off in the direction of the jail without further conversation. Cassie collected Carrington, and quickly headed off in the direction of his and Annie's home. The whole way there, worry niggled at Cassie's brain that Suzanne and Anders were working together to rid Carrington of his home. She was certain it had to do with the gold. But if that were true, poor Blake was being duped by Suzanne, too.

Of all the information she'd collected so far here in the past, one common denominator rose to the surface: Suzanne.

TWENTY-FIVE

Carrington watched tiny goosebumps prickle across Cassie's body when he nuzzled her neck. It happened every time he touched a certain spot below her ear. Her body responded easily to his ministrations, even while she was off in another world.

Her hand moved, coming to rest on his bicep. "You're distracting me." She stifled a laugh, even as she tilted her head to give him better access.

"You distracted me. You began breathing hard and made some very interesting sounds." His tongue stroked along her throat as his hand squeezed her breast. "I was just watching these"—he pinched her nipple lightly and stared with hungry interest as it tightened into a hard peak—"do that when I touched this one little spot beneath your ear." His tongue passed over the area referenced to identify its precise location.

She hummed with pleasure. "I saw the sheriff and Suzanne . . . doing things. In the alley!"

"So that's what had you all excited? Interesting. I didn't take you for someone who liked watching others. Then again, you did say you've seen men disrobe." He tried again to suckle her, but she thwarted his efforts.

"What? No! It wasn't like that." She smacked his shoulder. "They were in an alley. I didn't want them to notice me. The longer I stood there trying to remain unseen, the angrier I got. I mean, *in an alley!*" She hit him again softly. "That's why I was breathing heavy. I was appalled."

She narrowed her eyes at him, but Carrington knew she wasn't mad. He lunged forward and she squealed with delight as he latched his mouth around one beckoning peak. A sudden vision of someone else coming into her life and seeing her like this cut through him like a sharp knife.

"Did you know? About them?" she asked.

"No." His reply vibrated against the hollow below her ribcage. "What I did find out later, after—" He stopped, not wanting to draw attention to anything pertaining to his death. Not yet. "I learned that she and Blake were a couple. They lived here and even had a child together." He shifted lower. "A little girl."

The response Cassie was about to make was momentarily lost when Carrington dragged his tongue across her belly button. Her head fell back against the headboard, as her hands pressed against the top of his scalp.

"Was Suzanne a prostitute?" she finally asked.

He paused in his quest. "Not in the sense that she got paid for her affections. She liked the independence gained from working at the newspaper office. A husband might not have found that respectable behavior for a wife, so she chose not to rush into another marriage." He traced a finger from Cassie's waist up to beneath her arm. She shuddered at the soft touch, her fingers clenching fists of his hair. "But she did like men. And men liked her."

"I can't picture Suzanne as the mothering type. What was the baby's na—?" Cassie's words caught in her throat when he placed both his hands on the inside of her thighs and pushed her legs apart. When his lips touched her center, a strangled sound issued from her throat.

Carrington didn't like to give Suzanne credit for many things, but there was one thing she'd been adamant that he learned and mastered. This was that thing. She said a man should know more than one way to pleasure a woman, because there might come a day when that was the only thing that worked. He'd, of course, adamantly refused to consider that notion. She was a crass young woman indeed, but he was never more grateful than now that he'd heeded her advice.

After a few minutes of driving Cassie deliriously mad, he answered the partially asked question.

"Charity was the name. Or something like that."

Like a marionette whose strings had been clipped, all tension left Cassie's body. A dreamy smile spread over her face. He loved seeing her like this.

"You didn't think it was relevant to tell me Blake and Suzanne had a child together?" she asked between breaths.

"No. I don't see how it mattered. The kid didn't kill Annie." The conversation continued despite his having just made her body sing. "One day, when the baby was about six years old, I suppose, they didn't return home." He lifted a shoulder. "I never found out what happened to them."

Carrington was obsessed with Cassie, couldn't get enough of her touch, her laugh, or the sweet taste of her that lingered on his tongue. She tasted like roses and something spicier, something exotic and musky. Hunger and desire had him reaching for her again.

"Carrington. Stop. We need to stay focused and read some more. I did manage to get you released from jail, but I didn't find out anything new after that." She held a pillow up as a shield, blocking his progress. He backed down, suppressing this wild craving he had for her. He even stayed his hands when she leaned past him to retrieve the journal that had fallen to the floor.

She halted mid-reach.

"Where did those come from?" She pointed at the newspapers he'd set on the nightstand. Her arm retracted and she eased back into her position against the headboard.

With a resigned sigh, Carrington gave up trying to seduce her and settled in beside her. He did, however, close the gap between them, so their hips were touching again. "I went and got them." He handed her the diary. "After you finish reading this, I want you to read from those." He didn't intend his words to sound ominous, but the alarmed expression on her face told him of her concern.

There was a brief hesitation as unspoken words swirled in the depths of her irises. She didn't voice her worries but instead opened the journal, casting a dark glance at the papers just beyond her reach.

"Look here." She tilted the diary toward him. "We're at the part that was torn out." There were five lines visible on the damaged page. Each sentence showed fewer words than the previous one, and the last revealed only part of one word. Cassie thumbed through the remainder of the book.

"It's the last entry," she said.

Right then, he wanted nothing more than to return the materials to the trunk and pretend they didn't exist. He'd build a life together with Cassie and make it work, somehow. He'd bestow on her every promise he'd failed to provide Annie. It would be his second chance. Even if he only got half a century with Cassie, he'd take it.

"Is there another journal?"

"Not that I know of. Come to think of it, near the end, I don't recall her writing at all. She'd done so every evening no matter how good or bad her day was. I guess I didn't notice when she stopped." He felt sad with the sudden awareness that if he had been a better husband, he'd have noticed even the little things she did. And that might have been enough to save her.

"Well. Maybe it'll still work with what's here." She tugged the bed sheet up to her waist and cast a stern smirk his way, her meaning clear. Then she began to read.

"'August twenty, eighteen ninety. I was making jam when—'"

The line ended so she moved to the next.

"'How will I ever tell Ca—'"

Cassie's shoulders twitched subtly before her head listed to the side and she tipped against Carrington's shoulder. He eased her onto her back, head cushioned on the pillow, so peaceful and relaxed.

Collecting the diary from her hands, he wondered what had been so secret his wife felt the need to tear it out. It was possible, he supposed, that she'd written something of their bedroom life, and it had turned out to be more explicit than she'd intended. The second sentence indicated she agonized over telling him something. What could it have been?

Cassie stirred against him. All he could do now was wait.

***

Annie lifted a Mason jar from the black kettle of boiling water on top of the iron stove. Carefully, she set it on the counter beside her and repeated the process until six steaming jars stood in a row. Humming softly, she reached for a large bowl perched beside the kettle, then proceeded to pour thick, warm jam into the prepared jars.

Cassie dipped a finger in the gooey substance and touched it to her tongue. Apricot.

All three windows in the room were open. The yellow flower-patterned curtains covering them lifted on a breeze, yet it had no effect on the temperature in the close quarters of the kitchen. The heat that radiated from the stove kept the room hot and sticky.

Cassie already knew that Carrington had left the house early that morning, headed out to work, like any other typical day. It was the day after she'd retrieved him from the jail. Upon their arrival home the previous afternoon, he'd had the nerve to think his wife would slip off to the bedroom with him for a quick bit of loving. After catching a whiff of alcohol still on his breath, Annie had marched out of the bedroom, slamming the door in his face. Carrington passed out and didn't wake up until that morning.

Cassie fervently hoped he had a hangover from hell. It would serve him right.

She was sifting through more of Annie's memories, and learned that she'd been immersed in domestic chores all day. Mid-pour of jam into a jar, she startled when strong arms slid around her waist, pulling her back into the body pressed up behind her.

Annie shrieked, "Carrington! What are you doing back so soon?" She internally melted with joy, unable to stay angry at her husband. Cassie, however, was less quick to free him of his guilt. She tried to maintain her angry façade, until a stray daydream of makeup sex made her give a little.

After carefully returning the bowl to the stove, she turned in his arms, wanting to look into his eyes as he apologized for his bad behavior. Her smile vanished when she came face-to-face with Sheriff Anders.

"You!"

Panic threatened to overwhelm Annie when she saw the menacing darkness in the sheriff's eyes. Cassie had seen a similar expression on Jimmy's face, enough to know it was a viable threat. Instinctively, she pressed a hand over her throat and side-stepped a few feet away. Annie's heart raced like a jackhammer inside her chest.

"Get out of my house!"

Anders turned and swiped his finger through the warm jam in one of the jars. His fat, slobbery tongue poked out to lick away a sticky glob that didn't quite make it into the cavern of his mouth. He took up another finger full and sucked it clean.

"Why don't you come on over here and treat me nice?" His tongue swiped back and forth over his lips, his beady eyes raking down the length of Annie's body.

Cassie scurried around the corner of the table in the center of the room. She scanned its surface for a weapon, wishing she were nearer to the stove and the pot of boiling water. The best she could find in close proximity was a paring knife. Her fingers curled tight around the small handle.

"Get out of my house." Annie was too frightened to raise the knife at him, but Cassie had no such qualms. She'd find some vital area to plunge it to stop him in his tracks. A bead of sweat inched down over her temple and she swiped at it with her shoulder.

The sheriff ran his tongue noisily over his teeth, sucking something from between them. Cassie saw the brown stain of dried tobacco juice in the corners of his mouth. Her face pinched tight with disgust.

"Come on, now." His eyes danced again over her body. "I saw how you was watchin' me yesterday, when I was in the alley with Suzanne." His fat lower lip, shiny from where he licked it, had no curve to it when he forced a smile. "I know you're wanting a taste of what I gave her."

Cassie barked out a scoffing laugh. "Are you joking? You repulse me. I should tell Suzanne to stay away from you, and I don't even like her!" Her fingers gripped tighter around the knife, preparing for any slight, offending movement from Anders.

"Suzanne knew where her bread was buttered. Until you came along, she was on track for being the next Mrs. Chambers." His jowls quivered as he spoke. "I didn't care whether she married him or not, as long as I was able to get on the property."

"Is Suzanne in on this with you? What are you after?" Poor Carrington. He'd been right. The one woman he'd thought a friend had been duping him.

Anders' laugh was a raspy, watery sound. "Don't play dumb with me. You know about the gold and probably know where it's at." When he moved around the counter, he was a little quicker than Cassie expected and managed to reach out and grab her arm.

"The only thing Suzanne's in on is doing what I tell her, when I tell her. It seems like she wasn't giving Chambers what he wanted. Apparently, you do, so you're my new ticket to gettin' that gold."

She tried to pull away from him. He yanked her back against him, slipping his arm around her waist and holding tight.

"Let me go! There is no gold. It's just a rumor."

Anders squeezed her closer to him. Cassie felt a bulge near her backside. Her mouth filled with saliva and she suppressed the urge to vomit.

"I'll make this quick. You just bend over this counter and we'll have a little fun. You'll soon be begging me for more."

He reached his hand down to unbuckle his belt. Images of Jimmy flashed through Cassie's mind. Memories screamed at her of a time when he had her pressed to the ground with the same intent as the sheriff did now. She'd pushed Jimmy away, and her punishment for that offense had been a knife to the throat. The terror of reliving that moment boiled inside her.

Ghost Carrington's words to her when they'd been in her bedroom in the future, when he'd made her relive her efforts to fight off Jimmy, suddenly filled her head. She was a survivor. She beat Jimmy once. She could beat someone like him again.

"Get your hands off me," she growled low.

When Anders' hand pushed against a spot between her shoulder blades, forcing her down across the counter, Cassie twisted away and raised the paring knife. When his fingers snaked out to grab at her again, she brought the thin blade down, scoring a solid hit on his arm. He squealed like a boar as a four-inch gash opened across his skin, blood instantly spattering at his feet.

"You bitch!" His face contorted with pain and confusion as rivulets of red raced down his arm to drip from his fingertips. He grabbed the dish towel Annie had used to hold the hot jars and pressed it to the gaping wound.

"Get out of my fucking house!" Cassie yelled. The cut she'd left on the sheriff's arm had to hurt. His squawking confirmed it. He was all guts and bravado wielding his cock at what he assumed was some hapless, helpless woman. But the knife, in this instance, was mightier than the man.

The white kitchen towel was quickly turning a bright red. Anders spun about on his heel to leave. "You just made the biggest mistake of your life." He practically ran from the house as if the devil himself—or herself—was at his heels.

Cassie followed behind him and watched from the front porch to make sure he left the property. Her legs buckled, and she sank down onto the top step. Tiny black dots flitted through her vision. She lowered her head between her knees and waited until the dizziness passed. Thankfully, there was a microscopic breeze that cooled the moisture along her neck. It was another five minutes before the spots went away and she no longer felt like she would pass out.

On shaky legs, she raced back inside the house and marched straight to the bedroom. In a previous search through Carrington's home, she'd once seen a revolver tucked away inside his nightstand. The gun was different from the one he wore at his hip here in the past.

She retrieved the weapon from the drawer, cautiously turning it over in her hands. The only manufacturer of a gun she guessed might have come about in the early to mid-eighteen-hundreds was Colt. Presumably, this was a Colt revolver, which she knew next to nothing about. With little effort, she found where to release the gun's chamber. It fell open to reveal five bullets. She pulled one out; it was unfired and ready to go. Carefully, she returned it to its chamber and snapped the cylinder shut. She'd figure out how to use the gun, if, or when, the need arose.

Taking a gun back through time was impossible. But hiding one in a place that still stood in the twenty-first century might work—at least Cassie hoped it would. She ran through the house, bolted out the front door, and barreled her way through the barn to the chicken coop which Carrington said his father had built shortly before his death.

She searched the shed for a place where the weapon would remain protected all the way into the twenty-first century. Dropping to her knees, she scooted across the floor, testing floorboards for any that might be loose. The structure was as solid as a tree.

Beneath the panel of chicken cubbies, near the far corner of the floor something caught her eye. From where she was crouched it was noticeable, but in a standing position, it was hidden completely from view.

Reaching beneath, hoping she didn't find a nest of rats or spiders, her fingers touched on something that wasn't wood—a latch. She pulled at it, and then pushed. A piece of the floorboard flipped open on a hinge. Unable to angle her head beneath the boxes to view what she'd discovered, she instead held the revolver's barrel and eased the grip end down. About eight inches in, it hit bottom, scraping against gravel. She shifted closer, shoulder wedged against the wall of cubbies, and lay the gun flat inside the hiding space before closing the small hatch. Fluffing some straw over her tracks, she stood with a satisfied huff.

It was time to wake up.

***

Cassie shot upright on the bed. Carrington hovered nearby.

"Anders!" she exclaimed, out of breath. "He attacked Annie and tried to rape her."

Her face had a green hue to it.

Carrington tensed and his blood boiled to the surface, heating his skin. "When?" The single word ripped past his vocal cords, deep and full of suppressed rage. "Why didn't she tell me? What did he do to her?" Too many questions jumped around inside his brain, he didn't know what to ask first.

Cassie shook her head, dazed and confused. "He wants the gold. He's been using Suzanne to get to you. She was supposed to marry you, so he could gain access to the farm through her. Then you married Annie. He tried to force her to have sex with him, so he could blackmail her with it. Like he was doing to Suzanne."

Carrington sagged onto the bed. He needed to retain his composure, for Cassie, who was clearly upset. He had to be calm for her but inside he was anything but calm.

"I heard you tell him to get out. I take it that worked?" His fingers clenched the bedding beneath him.

"No. It didn't."

He lurched back to his feet. His skin twitched from the tension he was trying hard to suppress. "She didn't . . . with Anders . . .?" The words struggled to breach his lips. He was terrified to learn that that disgusting human being befouled his Annie, and she'd been too afraid, or ashamed, to tell him.

Cassie made a dark, resonating sound deep in her throat. "I don't know. I think I interrupted the scene and changed whatever might have happened. I didn't just allow things to progress as they may have before." Her expression was serious but quickly gave way to one of hopeful excitement.

"I stabbed him with a knife after he threatened me. Carrington, I'm certain he killed Annie. He was so angry." Her hands trembled and he clasped them in his. "What happened to the gold? Was all this just a senseless tragedy that resulted from rumor?"

He snorted, both in acknowledgment and disgust. The infamous gold. Something men, and possibly his wife, died for. He squeezed Cassie's fingers.

"Oh, it exists. I just haven't been able to find it. Pa spent some whenever it was necessary, but he never wanted me to think we were better than anyone else. We probably could've had as nice a place as Strahorn's over on Filmore Street. Pa wouldn't allow that. He'd be right shocked at what the house looks like now." Carrington's eyes traveled around the expanse of the bedroom, taking in the grandeur of it, comparing it to the plain, basic design of the floor below— the part of the house he'd built with his own two hands.

"Pa never got the chance to tell me where he hid it before he died. After Annie disappeared, I spent all the next year rebuilding the place. I didn't find any sign of the treasure in the rubble. If it was there, it's gone now. After a time, I forgot all about it, and then, well, then it no longer mattered." His shoulders drooped forward like he was weary of some burden he carried across his back.

Suddenly, Cassie smiled wide. "Carrington," she whispered excitedly. "I think I know where it is!"

She told him about how she'd taken the old revolver from his room in the past and where she'd hid it in the chicken coop. "Why else would your Pa build that hidden cubby?"

When he asked why she'd done that, she said she wanted to be prepared for when Jimmy showed up, because she knew he would. Her face drew down into a frown.

"You'll never get to do anything with it. The gold, I mean." Her sad whisper made him smile.

"Oh, darlin'. *I* won't. But you will. Take it, and never worry about anything for the rest of your life. Pa told me once it was a fortune's worth." Who knew what a fortune was, though? Life should be the fortune, but money was mightier. There was nothing he could do about the past and the greed that had struck him and his family down.

"If Anders was working with Suzanne, she could have had some part in Annie's death, too," he said. Unexpected pain lanced through him at the thought that Suzanne had betrayed him. He'd never had real affection for her beyond an occasional dalliance, but he'd believed they'd had a mutual understanding. She'd been a friend to some degree.

Now, he questioned every memory he had of her, and everyone else in his life.

Cassie shook her head. "No. Suzanne was a puppet. It was Anders. And I think I know a way to stop him."

TWENTY-SIX

Carrington wanted to slow down, consider all his options and the possibilities of what his future with Cassie might be like. He tried to distract her with ideas of making love for hours on end, telling her he had years of lost time to make up for. Unwilling to divert from the mission she'd set herself on, she shunned his advances, but promised to make it up to him later. This appeased him, but barely, as he didn't know if there'd be a later.

Cassie skimmed back through several pages of Annie's journal, searching for something—Carrington wasn't sure what—without reading enough to pull her back into the past. What strange destiny, or perhaps what cruel fate, brought her to him?

"I have to go back to the day of the fire," she blurted, as she scrambled off the bed.

"No," he replied, without hesitation. He'd always assumed Annie had died during the fire. Instead, they'd found her buried in a shallow grave. Besides the obvious cause of her death, which he prayed had happened after she'd passed, he was never given details about her tragic circumstances. It was for this reason he couldn't allow Cassie to go back. He had no advance knowledge to arm her with, no warning of what to watch for—a gun, a knife, an axe. Reliving that day, he was certain would bring about Cassie's demise. No matter the cost, he was determined to keep her safe from Annie's fate and even from Jimmy if the bastard showed up.

"It's the only way, Carrington."

She was bent over a box with CLOTHES written on the side in bold black letters. "Do you realize I've been here a week and have yet to unpack half my stuff?" When she turned around, she was holding a small piece of fabric, not much bigger than his hand. He wouldn't even begin to guess what article of clothing it was supposed to be. She rummaged more, grumbling about spending too much time fantasizing about ghosts, and then triumphantly came up holding a pale green gown.

"You're wearing a nightdress today?" In all her naked splendor, she approached the bed, stopping just beyond his reach. When she lifted one side of the mass of hair hanging down her back, the bright light streaming in from the window lit on the darker underside. There, he glimpsed a hint of red in the mane. It was a bold, red brown that contrasted with the honey color on the outer layer.

She planted a fist on her hip and gave him an exaggerated smile. Transfixed, he tried to pinpoint what it was about her smile. It was slightly imperfect, and vaguely familiar. He sat up on the edge of the bed and peered closer.

"This isn't a nightdress," she intruded upon his speculating. "It's a sundress and perfectly acceptable for daily wear. In public even." She turned her nose up in defiance, daring him to question her, then held up three other articles of clothing. "This is a bra." With both hands she raised it to her chest. "Were bras around yet? In your time?"

"I don't believe so. At least I never saw anything of the like on Annie. Or Suzanne. I did see somewhere a new bodice of sorts that had the corset built into the fabric, not a separate contraption."

Cassie worried a corner of her mouth with her teeth and tapped her lip with one finger. "I think I saw that, too. In a *Ladies' Home Journal*. That first day, when I was . . . I was you." Her arms lowered to her sides. "You flipped through her magazine. There was an ad, but you were distracted, waiting for—" She stayed her tongue, shrugged, and spun away. "I have to bathe. I'll be just a few minutes. We'll continue the discussion of my going back when I return."

"You go ahead," he said as she reached the doorway. "And no, we won't discuss it. I'll meet you downstairs." He ignored her flash of frustration as he got up from the bed and followed her out into the hall.

A half hour later, Carrington was out on the porch waiting. It was a warm day. Soon enough, the weather would begin to turn as fall neared.

Fall and spring were his favorite seasons. He missed the smell of hay and manure after a cool rain. It was a deterrent to many, but to him, the earthy smell was the cleanest one imaginable. He missed the life. Missed the feel of dirt running through his fingers during planting season. He missed everything he'd never gotten to experience during his time on earth in general.

Cassie could have it all someday. There was plenty of land left to work. She could have a few barn animals, a couple of horses, and a dog. If she married, she'd have beautiful babies that would fill the house with happy noises. He leaned heavily against the pillar, one foot propped over the other. Eventually, some other man would come into her life and take his place.

The door screeched behind him. He turned on his heel and was grateful for the solid pillar at his back. The green dress she wore accented her coloring and outlined the curve of her hips as it floated against her thighs. He stepped toward her. Later, if there was a later, he'd cherish those curves, again.

Today was the day he'd have her read the news articles. His gut clenched into a knot. Cassie knew Annie had died under mysterious circumstances, but she didn't know everything. He'd been weak and too afraid to tell her his story. The reaction he expected from her when she learned what had happened to him and to Annie lay heavy on his mind. Ignorance was bliss, and after more than a century to ponder what he'd lost in his life, for the first time, he was beginning to prefer this bliss.

"You are the most beautiful woman I've ever known." He enjoyed that she blushed. After all they'd done together, she still had a certain innocence about her.

"Thank you." She glided up to him and wrapped her arms around his waist. His arms mimicked the gesture. After a moment enjoying her closeness, he straightened his spine, and pulled her with him toward the porch swing. The fragile newspapers he'd retrieved from the bedroom crackled as he gathered them off the wooden seat. Her face tightened into a dark frown when she glanced at them.

"What is it?" she whispered. "Why are those here?"

"It's time that you read these."

Shadows of alarm darkened her eyes. She ran a hand over her hair. Pulling her knees up to brace her feet on the bench, she leaned into him. He let her curl against his side as he draped his arm over her shoulder. It felt so natural to be with her like this.

"I'm only reading the one about the fire. So, we can find the truth. Right now. Today!"

He shook his head and released a long, slow breath. "Not yet. First, I want you to read something else. You deserve to know everything. It's time."

"Why do I have a bad feeling about this?" She fidgeted with her hair and her eyes glazed over in an unfocused stare as she considered his request. A minute passed, then finally, she heaved a weary sigh. "Okay. Fine. I'll do it. I'm ready." She tilted her head and cast him a hesitant glance. "I think."

"Start with this one." He handed her the paper dated October 15, 1891. Moving his finger down a column on the page, he pointed to where she needed to begin reading.

Bones Found in Shallow Grave on Chambers' Property

Carrington winced at her shocked gasp, but he urged her with a nod of his head to go on. She eased her feet to the floor and leaned forward, bracing both elbows on her knees. Her hands trembled as they clutched the pages, but she continued to read.

The remains of a woman's body were found near the river's edge on Carrington Chambers' property.

Cassie drooped to the side. He caught her before she toppled over, and pulled her back, squeezing his arm tight about her shoulder. He held her as if it would be the last time. The past would soon reveal the truth and set him free . . . or condemn him to an unimaginable eternity alone.

***

Carrington slumped over his saddle, barely able to hold his head up as he crested the hill that overlooked his property. He'd been out plowing fields since dawn and could hardly keep his eyes open. The evening sun beat down on the house now, casting a gold glow on the white façade. In his mind's eye he could still see the angry orange-red flames as they'd whipped from the windows and roof of his house, like fiery tentacles of a demon octopus in the wind.

He'd rebuilt the house. Gone was the ominous skull-like structure, with black holes where windows used to be. Once again, it was white, bright, and fresh with green contrasting doors and shutters. Yet still, there was nothing within that made it a home. It was dark and cold since Annie left. He wished he was anywhere but here.

He entered the barn exhausted, dirty, and hungry enough to eat one of the mule deer that roamed about the desert terrain. After settling his horse in its stall, he made off toward the house. About halfway across the yard he came to a stop, tense and alert. And downright angry to his core.

Sheriff Anders was on the front porch waiting for him, three deputies at his side. Blake was there too, his hip propped against the rail post, casual as could be.

Carrington's mood, already dark, blackened further at the sheriff's harassment, a common occurrence ever since Annie went missing. He pulled up short of the porch steps. Lifting his hat slightly, he ran a hand through his hair, sweaty and grimy after the day's work.

"You've crossed the line this time, Sheriff, coming onto my property to harass me." He propped his foot on the lowest rung of the steps. "Get off my porch and off my land." He eyed the motley crew of deputies before settling his gaze on Blake.

Sheriff Anders' tongue swiped across his lips with a wet smack. He flicked his fingers and the deputies instantly moved down the steps at the silent command. They circled around Carrington. Blake moved to the edge of the stairs, hands shoved into his pockets, his head down.

"You're finally at the end of your rope, Chambers," the sheriff said calmly. Too calmly.

"What the hell are you talking about?" Carrington's eyes darted to Blake. "What's going on here?"

Blake pushed his hands deeper into his front pockets. Tight lines creased his forehead. He scuffed his boots against the wood as he shuffled on his feet. Finally, he met Carrington's confused stare.

"I found some bones. Down by the river when I was checking fences." Both his shoulders lifted then fell. "Decided it best to get the sheriff out here."

The muscles in Carrington's neck formed a knot. The leg supporting his stance threatened to buckle. He pulled his shoulders back and planted both feet firmly beneath him. "What does that have to do with me?"

The deputies inched closer, the circle tightening around him.

"What are you implying? That it's Annie?" He scoffed at the absurdity.

One of the deputies put a hand on his shoulder. Another grabbed his elbow.

The sheriff shifted his ample body the remainder of the way down the steps and stopped in front of him. He spat a thick stream of tobacco juice into the dirt. "That's exactly what I'm saying." His jowls jiggled with the vehemence behind the statement. "We're here to take you in for the murder of your wife."

Three sets of hands now clutched at Carrington as he tried to break away. He cast a pleading glance up at the porch.

"Blake! You know this isn't true!" He fought against the deputies, but there were too many and they easily forced him into submission.

"Ain't no mistake. It's her body. Her clothes." Sheriff Anders said as he walked past him, toward the horses tethered off to the side of the house. The deputies dragged Carrington along behind. He wrenched his head around.

"Blake! You know I didn't do this. Tell them!"

Blake shook his head before stepping down one step, thumbs hooked in his pockets. "Boss!" he called out.

The posse halted near the horses. Carrington was forced up onto the back of a black gelding. At Blake's call he swiveled around in his saddle to look at him.

"Her head was missing."

TWENTY-SEVEN

Cassie lunged back into the present gasping for air, like she'd been submerged under water too long.

"Oh my god, oh my god, oh my god." She rocked back and forth, arms wrapped about her waist, tears rushing down her cheeks.

"It's not true!" she exclaimed, fighting to keep the images alive in her mind. She wanted to go back into the dream and finish it through. Find out where someone said it was all some cruel joke.

That they hadn't found Annie's body.

Carrington released his grip on her as she whirled away from him and ran to the other side of the porch. "They found her body. Here?"

Her eyes shifted past Carrington to the line of trees in the background along the river's edge. Her arms wrapped tight across her waist again and she began to shake violently.

"Cassie. I didn't kill her," Carrington said, almost pleadingly. He remained like a statue in front of the swing, not advancing toward her.

She lifted both arms and gripped the sides of her head, her fingers clenching wads of hair. *They'd found Annie's body. Without a head!* Her stomach roiled with a sickening churning. She raced to the end of the porch, leaned over the rail and heaved the contents of her stomach over the side.

Without a head.

A dry heave squeezed her gut. She swallowed it back. Just because they'd taken Carrington in didn't mean he'd killed his wife. Right? Innocent until proven guilty. That was the system's motto. She shouldn't be so quick to judge.

She stared at the spot near the bottom of the steps where Carrington had been apprehended. Tension didn't release its ugly grip on her body. Stiff and shaking with nerves, she turned to him as a terrifying thought weaved its way into her mind.

"How did you die?"

He didn't respond for a quarter minute. Instead, he turned his back to her and leaned against the porch railing.

"Read the last article, Cassie." His shoulders, normally strong and wide, caved forward.

A foreboding unlike any she'd ever experienced gripped her. She shook her head. Part of her wanted to rush to him and ease the pain she knew he must be experiencing. The other part of her feared what he might be or had been capable of. A ghost couldn't hurt the living. She ignored the fact that if a ghost could make love to her, it most likely could hurt her, too, in the physical sense as much as the emotional one.

She crept over to the bench and retrieved the other paper, scanning the contents for his name. When she found it, she sat down on the porch's top step while Carrington remained locked in his own torment off to her side. Her hands shook, and the words blurred behind the tears welling in her eyes. She needed a moment to collect herself and stopped trying to read. She cocked her head, her hopes suddenly lifting.

"You had to get off! Otherwise this place wouldn't have landed in a trust, and I wouldn't be here in this house."

With renewed hope that overshadowed the trepidation threatening to swallow her, she placed her finger below the text and prepared to read. She just knew the first few words would include "exonerated." It was the only logical answer to all of this. Why couldn't the bones be someone else's?

Then she read:

Carrington Chambers
Convicted of Murder
Executed by Hanging

Black dots floated in her vision. She tried to force them away but couldn't prevent the world from fading to gray as she slipped into the past.

***

Something pulled tight around Cassie's neck. Instinctively, she moved to press a protective hand over her throat. A panic much like the one she'd experienced the day Jimmy attacked her crawled over her skin. Her hands were shackled together, stifling her freedom to move. She clawed with all ten fingers at the abrasive rope around her neck.

"Stop!" She flailed about, trying to pull away from what bound her in place. *This can't be happening!* She immediately knew she was in Carrington's mind and body, but the outrageous truth as to what was really happening, she couldn't comprehend. A crowd formed around the wooden platform below her. She peered over all the bobbing heads, searching for something, anything or anyone, that would stop this madness.

Rambling fears rushed in and climbed over each other, stumbling, suffocating. *What happens to me here in the past, happens to me in my future.*

"Any last words?" Cassie recognized Sheriff Anders' voice beside her as he bellowed the request. Then, his mouth settled close to her ear. "That little wife of yours put up a good fight. I always did like a bit of spirit in my women." Drops of spit hit Carrington's face.

Cassie jerked her head to the side and felt a moment of satisfaction when she heard a crunching sound as Carrington's skull made contact with the sheriff's nose.

Anders howled and moved away, cursing loudly.

Desperately, she cried out on Carrington's behalf the words she heard raging inside his mind, "I am innocent! Anders killed my wife! He just confessed it!"

Below her, a man stepped forward. Cassie recognized him as Annie's father. Rage and pain etched deep grooves across his face. "No! You stole our Annie from us! May God *not* have mercy on your black soul."

A hissing pop and bright flash made Cassie look off to the side of the crowd at the man perched behind a camera. The photographer turned to the three women at his side, one of whom handed him a pencil and a small book. He jotted something on the paper, glanced up at Carrington, then jotted some more.

Cassie searched the crowd. Blake and Suzanne had to be there. They were Carrington's only friends. They were never his enemies, she now knew. It was Sheriff Anders all along. When she located the pair, Blake nodded, and Suzanne offered a one-sided smile. Then she took a step forward and said something from all the way at the back of the wall of people; something that was impossible, or should have been impossible, for Cassie to hear. But hear it, she did.

"You inherited this fate. Saving her is the only way to change it."

Cassie's eyes rounded and the air froze in her lungs. It was the voice. The woman's voice she'd been hearing in her head since the day her parents died. Why did Suzanne's voice sound like the woman's voice she'd been hearing telling her to "save her"? Why hadn't she recognized it before?

Before she had time to process the possibilities or call out to her, a shroud slipped over Carrington's head. The shuffle of men moving away alerted Cassie to the impending execution. The crowd hushed.

"For your crime, you are sentenced to death."

"Wait!" she cried out, as the crack of wood against wood shattered the silence—

***

Cassie writhed about on the deck, both hands clasped around her neck. A scream stuck in her throat, making the sound she emitted a choked bark.

When the world righted itself, and the dream faded into the past where it belonged, a sob of relief and despair tore through her. Tears of pain, anger, fear, and sadness bled from her eyes. She cried for Annie; a life ended too abruptly. Cassie's heart also wrenched at the pain and fear she'd felt in Carrington, when she'd *been* him during his arrest and subsequent execution. For good measure, she cried for herself, for being a victim as much as Annie and Carrington had both been.

A new panic tore through her and she shot up off the deck. She searched for him then. He was gone.

"Carrington!" She ran to either end of the porch and peered over, then scanned the yard and the surrounding area. There was no sign of him anywhere. With a frustrated cry, she raced into the house, the rusty spring on the screen door groaning as she flung it wide. It snapped shut with a loud *thwack* behind her as she ran about, calling Carrington's name.

He didn't leave. He *couldn't* leave. Not yet, not without telling her goodbye.

Sweat beaded across her forehead, and she was out of breath by the time she finished her search of the house. She plopped down on the edge of the bed in the master bedroom.

"Damn you, Carrington!" The agonized cry ripped past her lips. "We haven't finished yet." She pounded her fist against the mattress.

A few minutes ticked by before she regained her composure. Her neck ached. She rubbed a hand across her throat, wincing at the touch. Jumping from the bed, she rushed over to the dresser.

Her reflection in the mirror revealed an angry, red-purple abrasion that formed a half circle across her throat. Gently, she touched the raw skin, like she'd done so many times before where it followed a similar path as the scar. Moving her head side to side, she stared in disbelief and horror.

The impact of it hit her like a dump truck. While in Carrington's body, she'd been hanged. Had she not pulled out of the past when she did . . .

Facing the reality of the damage from the noose was mind-numbing. She would have died.

Carrington said that she was the only one who could find the truth. He said the contents in the trunk called to her. And Suzanne said she'd inherited this fate, but that she could change it. But why her? She'd already survived her own tragedy. Why was she meant to return and live through someone else's?

As if bidden from the past, she heard the voice—the one she now distinctly identified as Suzanne's.

"Save her."

"Okay! Clearly, I'm meant to save Annie. And risk dying in the process. Great," Cassie huffed to the empty room. "My life for hers. Is that what this is all about?"

The voice spoke again, only this time it was as clear as if she were standing right in front of her. Like when she'd heard Carrington the first time.

"Save her or fate will find you."

TWENTY-EIGHT

Time ticked slowly by. The grandfather clock in the lower part of the house chimed, indicating another hour gone. Carrington couldn't just disappear like that. She hadn't yet found the answers he needed to set him free. It wasn't fair!

"Oh, wait, McAllister. Risking your life for a ghost who broke your heart isn't fair. Get real."

She flopped backward on the bed, arms splayed wide. None of what she'd learned from the past made sense. Especially the fact that she was here, on Carrington's property which had strangely been left to her in a trust. She sat up and stared at the many boxes scattered around the room. Zeroing in on one, she went to it and rummaged through the contents. Finding what she was after, she lifted out a large expanding file organizer, nearly six inches thick.

Kneeling on the floor in the center of the bedroom, she dumped everything from the folder. Packets and various documents, some protected in clear plastic sleeves and some not, spilled out. On top of the pile was an introduction letter from the attorney who'd read her mother's will. He was also the one who'd informed her of the trust that named her the recipient of the property.

She rifled through more papers, locating her mother's Last Will and Testament. Her father had a will, too. In it, he'd left her the family home in Colorado, but nothing remarkable beyond that. The bulk of her inheritance was identified in her mother's will.

Cassie had refused to acknowledge the bequest until nearly a year after her parents' death. She opened the tri-fold document to read her mother's final wishes again. The pain of her loss was still as fresh and deep as it had been when she'd first read it.

LAST WILL AND TESTAMENT OF
CHANDRA LYNN MCALLISTER

"Oh, Mom. I'll never stop missing you." Tears welled in her eyes, and she blinked them back.

The first section of the will identified Chandra's family: Kevin Wayne McAllister, husband, and Chassandra "Cassie" Rose McAllister, Chandra's sole offspring.

There was a section that stated the resolution of debts her mom may have owed at the time of her demise. Another indicated her request to not be sustained on life support beyond thirty days, in the event such care was necessary. It hadn't been needed in either of her parents' cases.

The last section was the distribution of all her mother's assets. In the event of Chandra's demise prior to her husband's, all assets but one, as outlined in a separate clause, were to revert to Kevin McAllister. Should her death coincide with her husband's, all assets and possessions were to revert to Cassie. At the end of that section, there was an additional clause that read:

Upon my death, my firstborn daughter shall inherit the property located at 21 Pear Lane, Caldwell, Idaho, which will remain held in a trust, having already been established in her name, until the day she chooses to assume ownership and reside on said land. Conditions of the trust indicate that any firstborn female offspring born naturally to my daughter thereafter shall next inherit and so on and so forth, with the property remaining with the firstborn daughter of each firstborn daughter in the family line until such a time as no female offspring is issued.

There it was, bold as day, yet Cassie had never heard of or set eyes upon the property until after the lawyer had told her about it. The name of a trust agency and contact information was included. This was followed by several more sentences explaining how the transfer of the trust was the responsibility of the parties involved and should occur in a timely manner to ensure that it remained within the rightful family line.

The "timely manner" Cassie understood to mean, was that paperwork had to be processed to transfer the property to her before her mother's death, which had apparently happened. Something else Cassie hadn't been aware she'd done.

She set the will aside and reached for a packet of papers bound together with a large clip. Considering it was an inheritance, meaning she didn't have to purchase the property, the quantity of paperwork she'd had to sign to gain possession of the assets was still excessive, she thought. In total, the stack was nearly a third of the contents of the entire folder.

She licked the end of her index finger, and pushed at the corner of each page, flipping through them one at a time, scanning the words for what, she didn't exactly know.

Reading pages and papers from the past had a whole new meaning for her these days, and she was relieved to find that she didn't transport through time during her current task. Page after page outlined the details of the property she owned now. She wondered about the other half of it; the other eighty acres Carrington once owned. Half of that wide-open space she'd witnessed firsthand belonged to someone else now. Maybe, once her current task here was all said and done, she'd go check the state's archives to see who it belonged to.

The past was the past. It happened. Yet Cassie felt an unexplainable urgency to find something relevant that she might be able to change. It was as if each moment that lapsed without doing so was one minute closer to that floor dropping from beneath Carrington's feet. She scanned the papers as quickly as she could, searching for anything that explained . . . whatever it was that would explain all this.

She knew she had to go back to the night of the fire, but if she wasn't prepared it could mean she'd be going back to face her own death. If Annie died, the past wouldn't change. Carrington would still be executed. Their fates would be sealed.

Unless Cassie saved her—saved Annie.

Her eyes flitted across the disarray on the floor before her. Answers were there, she was certain. If she could just find a path to follow, she was confident she'd know it when she saw it. Digging through the property stuff gave her no leads, so she shifted her attention to another pile of documents.

She grabbed one closest to her. It had a faded, blue outer cover and was folded and stapled shut. She plucked the staple out and opened it. It was her Granny's will: Charla Louise Thompson. She remembered very little about her

Granny. Like Cassie's mother, she'd died much too young, following a freak accident at some factory where she'd worked. Cassie's mom had taken it about as well as Cassie had taken the loss of Chandra.

She'd just picked up one of the plastic-sleeved documents, with multiple pages held together by a gold brad, when the door behind her creaked softly on its hinges. Whirling around, the pages slipped from her fingers when she saw Carrington standing motionless in the doorway. The anguish in his expression tore at her heart.

"Carrington." It was meant to be a greeting, but the word flowed from her mouth as a plea. She needed him. Her heart ached for him and she wanted to fix everything. Rising from her seated position on the floor, she went to him.

He didn't move as she rushed up and pressed her body to his, her arms wrapping about his torso. Like an ice cube that had hot water poured over it, he slowly thawed against her. His arms slipped around her until he was squeezing so tight, she began to squirm.

"I'm sorry I didn't tell you." His jaw moved against the top of her scalp. "I just couldn't stand the idea of you fearing or hating me." His throat convulsed against the side of Cassie's head.

She leaned back. "Why would I think that?"

"You saw that I was executed for murdering Annie?" She frowned and shook her head, so he offered more of an explanation. "They don't execute innocent people, Cassie. It would only be natural for you to believe I did it."

Cassie pressed her head against his chest. His heart pounded beneath her ear. "That's not true. People are wrongfully accused all the time. I can't imagine you're the only person ever killed for a crime you didn't commit."

She slipped out of his embrace and swept an arm out toward the pile of papers on the floor. "Somewhere in here are answers."

The pages she'd dropped upon Carrington's arrival lay in the shape of a fan across the wood floor. A stray scrap of yellowed paper sat off to the side. It was a news clipping. She bent to retrieve it.

"What's this?" Carrington moved up behind her. Both his hands rested over her hips, warm and comforting. "It's another news clipping."

Local Couple Meets Tragic End

This past Friday, on June 6, 1902, Blake Hanson and Suzanne Thomas Hanson died in a boating accident near Caldwell. It seems they were caught in a swirl and their boat overturned.

At the time of the tragedy, the couple's young daughter was being cared for by a family friend. All efforts will be made to contact next of kin of Hanson and Thomas Hanson. If none are located, the child will be placed in the orphanage in Boise.

"Oh, Carrington." Cassie turned into his arms and pressed her face to his chest as sadness wrenched through her. The pain she felt at Blake's loss was as real as if she'd known him in person.

Carrington held her tight to him. "That had to be when they didn't return to the house. That was why."

She felt him shudder beneath her. In a strange way Blake had been his friend, too, beyond all the jealousy. Suzanne's loss also had to hurt some. She understood why, yet she struggled to feel much sympathy for the woman. She stroked his back, offering comfort.

"I'm sorry. I know they both meant something to you."

"Do you think Anders had some hand in it?" he asked. Cassie drew in a sharp breath and pulled away from him. She scrambled to her knees and began searching through the papers strewn about the floor. "He admitted it, Carrington," she said in a hushed voice. He tensed and cocked his head in confusion.

"At the gallows. Just before—" She closed her eyes. "He said that Annie had fought him and that . . . and that he liked that she put up a fight."

The torment on Carrington's face was almost more than Cassie could bear. She reached for his hand. "There's something else." Squeezing his fingers, she added, "When I was there, as you, Suzanne spoke to me. It was her voice that I've been hearing all along telling me to 'save her.' She's the one who's called me back to save Annie."

Lines of doubt and concern etched around Carrington's eyes and across his forehead. The look he gave her was skeptical, like he doubted what she said she'd heard was true. But she wasn't crazy. It had all really happened. Carrington. The past. The voice. Suzanne.

Suzanne had found Cassie through some bizarre telepathic means on the day of her parents' death. Had her grief been so great the barriers of her mind lowered, allowing Suzanne the way in? But how could she have known Cassie would come to live in this house? Because clearly, the house was the key to the past. Carrington was here, and only here, as were the diary and the newspapers.

"Why would Suzanne seek you out?" He asked aloud the same question Cassie had in her head.

"I don't know. But I'm not crazy. It really is her who's beckoned me." Her gaze traveled around the room, then to the papers, and finally back to Carrington. "There has to be answers here somewhere. Help me search."

She handed him the huge stack of paperwork from the trust company while she whittled away at the other documents. They mumbled back and forth the different dates and names of people who'd come in to rent or do upgrades on the house.

When Carrington reached the last two pages in his stack, he stilled. Cassie turned to him. A stricken expression appeared on his face.

"What is it?" she asked, shifting up to sit beside him on the bed, scooting in until her thigh pressed against his.

"It's a deed to my property." His hand trembled as he held the page out. The shocked look of a moment ago vanished as Carrington's face reddened with anger.

The document indicated that in the state of Idaho, Canyon County, a deed had been filed for record on June 6, 1902. Cassie frowned.

"Carrington. This date." She pointed at the faded ink of the official record date. "It's the same as the other article, the one that told of the boating accident."

Carrington gripped the edge of the deed, his eyes scanning its contents, the furrow between his brows deepening to a harsh V.

To the left of the signed recording statement it read:

Blake Matthew Hanson
TO
Dennis Lloyd Anders

Cassie took the deed from him. "Blake Hanson of Caldwell, Idaho, in consideration of a sum of five hundred dollars."

Visibly distressed, Carrington got up from the bed and walked to the fireplace. She watched his departing form a moment before reading on.

". . . acknowledged to hereby Grant, Bargain, Sell, and Convey to Dennis Lloyd Anders of Caldwell, Idaho . . ." she skimmed over much of the legal mumbo-jumbo, searching for specific details of what was conveyed.

"The 160-acre property in its entirety located at 21 Pear Lane, Caldwell, Idaho. . ."

She shot to her feet and approached Carrington. He had his elbow braced on the fireplace mantle, his forehead pressed into his palm.

"The son of a bitch sold my entire farm for five hundred dollars. It wasn't even his to sell!" He slammed his fist down. "I entrusted it to him temporarily." His breathing had become ragged.

Cassie held up the document and shook it. "Maybe Blake didn't have anything to do with it at all. What if Anders forged Blake's signature? It's too much of a coincidence this happened the same date as Blake and Suzanne's death, don't you think?"

It was then she noticed another page partially stuck to the back of the deed, like it had gotten wet before drying together. Carefully, she peeled apart the two pieces of delicate paper. Ink from the deed had bled through, superimposing a faded version onto the document behind.

"It's a letter from Idaho Trust. The date says it's from February 12, 1900." She tilted it in numerous angles until she found the one that provided the best in which to see the faded words behind the imprint.

"It says," she squinted and pulled it close to her face, then read in choppy sections what she could make out. "That a deed for this property," she pointed at the recognizable address of Pear Lane, "was filed with the state upon the date of this letter." There was a longer delay as she manipulated the angle of the paper.

"I think it reads the name Suzanne Thomas Hanson." Cassie's indrawn gasp drew Carrington's rapt attention. He pressed a hand against the small of her back. The rest of the page wasn't legible, so she gave up, lowering her hands to her sides.

"Suzanne?" She pursed her lips and squinted thoughtfully.

Carrington eyed the papers dangling from her fingers. "That's dated nearly two years before Anders filed the other deed."

Cassie shook her head in confusion. "If it was already in Suzanne's name, then that deed to Anders couldn't have been binding. It wasn't Blake's property to sell. It was Suzanne's." She looked down at the stack of papers scattered on the floor, then dropped the deed. With her toe, she nudged at the pile of documents.

Carrington's arm draped over Cassie's shoulder and he pulled her close to him. She nestled into his side, turning her head up to press her lips against the column of his throat.

"I have to go back to the day of the fire, Carrington. It's the only way to find out what all this means." Renewed determination coursed through her. "Wait here," she commanded before racing out of the room.

Her feet pounded loud on the stairs as she hurried down and out the front door. Grabbing the November 15, 1890, edition of *The Caldwell Tribune* from the swing—the last newspaper she had to read—she bolted back inside. The screen door twanged loudly behind her before it slammed shut. Seconds later she was back in the bedroom.

She skidded to a halt and drew in several heavy gulps of air before marching purposely to the bed. Carrington stood in the middle of the room, hovering near the pile of papers. Sinking down onto the edge of the mattress, Cassie scrolled the columns of the paper until she located the story about the fire.

When she tilted her head up, he was staring at her, his expression odd. His smoky eyes were drawn down into a half squint, assessing, or analyzing, her. There was a nearly indiscernible nod of his head, like he'd come to some unannounced conclusion. His gaze moved back to the news clipping in his hands and then to Cassie twice more.

"Come. Sit by me." She scooted over, though there was plenty of room on either side of her. He did as she requested and sat, causing her to tip into his side as the mattress dipped under his weight.

"Cassie."

"I know what I'm doing." She stopped him from arguing with her. "Just do me a favor." When she silently pleaded with him, he merely nodded. "If I cry out to you, be sure to wake me up. Before it's too late."

"Cassie. You don't have to do this." His voice was soft, filled with a strange emotion. He seemed slightly bewildered.

"Yes, I do. I have to try at least." Her voice broke as she rested her head on his shoulder and began to read.

A Fire Roared Through A Rural Caldwell Home
Last Tuesday Evening

Her vision blurred, and she shook her head. The dark, heavy fog she'd first experienced when she'd read while up in the attic rolled over her in a deep wave. She swallowed hard, uncertainty and anticipation leaving her mouth dry.

Her surroundings began to swirl as the present faded into the past.

TWENTY-NINE

Carrington was on his horse when Cassie entered his world. He was confident in the saddle, but she wasn't. Her fingers clutched the saddle horn and held it in a death grip while her legs instinctively cinched tight about the mare's sides. Recalling the last time she'd squeezed a horse's middle too hard, she forced her muscles to loosen and let Carrington take control. The mare snuffled, its abdomen heaving in and out as it took in air.

"Whoa, girl. Sorry." Rummaging through Carrington's memories, Cassie found that he'd barreled away from the house earlier that day after a bitter argument with Annie. On the ride, he'd replayed the scene over and over in his mind, and Cassie was not surprised to find that he was ashamed, once again, that his jealousy was the cause of their quarrel.

He'd been considering terminating Blake's employment, thus removing the problem at hand. Honest man that he was, he'd unwillingly admitted that Blake had never made any overtures toward Annie. He was no real threat.

"Son of a bitch," he barked out, before reining to a stop to appreciate the view of the high desert terrain.

The sun had lowered on the horizon casting a brilliant glow of orange and purple on the landscape. Under normal circumstances, Cassie might've taken a moment to appreciate the picture painted before her. It was a vision, she learned, that Carrington had dreamed of all the years he'd been locked behind bars.

But she couldn't allow him to sit there any longer. He needed to get to the house now, before it was too late. Cassie clucked to the horse, encouraging it to move. She hoped she'd make it in time.

Darkness had not yet fallen by the time she neared the last rise overlooking the house. There was an eerie orange glow in the distance, but it wasn't until the acrid smell of smoke reached her nostrils that Carrington's brain triggered an alarm.

Cassie forced down her panic. She knew part of what was about to happen but had no idea from which direction the threat came. Eyes wide open, she readied herself for whatever would soon take place.

She spurred the mare to a run. Wind pulled at Carrington's hat and he clapped it to his head as the horse raced to the top of the hill. Cresting the rim, his heart tripped several beats when he found his house engulfed in flames. Barreling down the slope, the horse skidded to a stop before the porch. It snorted with fright and backed away from the danger of the fire, wide-eyed and nostrils flaring.

"Annie!" Carrington cried out as he leaped from the saddle.

He raced up the porch steps two at a time. When he grabbed the knob to the front door, pain seared his skin and he jerked his hand away. Cassie hissed and clutched the blistered appendage to her chest. A loud cracking sound drew her head up in time to see the porch roof tilt forward on its columns. Carrington lunged off the steps and into the dirt as the structure crashed down onto the deck where he'd been standing. He watched in stunned silence as flames swallowed up his front door.

"Annie!" he cried out again, his voice laden with anguish and fear, unaware of the events that would transpire this night. Cassie, however, knew some of what was to come.

"Carrington!" Blake called out as he and Suzanne careened around the corner of the house. They were both winded, their eyes wide with worry. Black smudges marred Blake's face and hands. Suzanne's hair lifted around her head on the fire's tailwind.

"Where's Annie?" Carrington hollered above the crackling of the inferno.

Blake gulped in lungfuls of hot, smoke-laden air. A coughing fit set on him, and he hacked several times. He pressed a hand to his mouth and Cassie saw that the back of his hand was red and raw from where it had been scorched.

"Anders was here," Suzanne shouted.

Carrington turned his attention to her.

"I saw his horse earlier, when I arrived, but didn't think anything of it at first. We ran out when we smelled smoke. I think I saw him leave, heading that way." She pointed toward the river. Tears tracked down her cheeks, whether from fear or the irritating smoke, Cassie wasn't certain.

Three sets of terror-filled eyes watched the fire eat away the outline of the house. Smoke billowed like a fog around them, threatening to devour them, too. Cassie felt like she'd been caught in this nightmare for hours, yet the span of time that lapsed from when she rushed up the porch to now had been mere minutes. She knew where Anders was headed, maybe not precisely, but the general vicinity. And she knew he had Annie with him. Turning toward the river, she took off at a run.

"Follow me!"

She didn't look back, but Cassie knew Blake and Suzanne did as commanded. Carrington's long strides moved him quickly across the field that separated the house from the river. The trio raced toward the unknown.

"Where are we going?" Blake huffed from beside him.

Within Carrington's mind, Cassie discerned his confusion at what was driving him toward the river. Something told him that's where he'd find Annie. He offered up a silent prayer, begging for her safety as his feet sank deep into the soil of a turned field. The cold foreboding brought about by Cassie's knowledge of things to come weighed heavily on his mind.

They slowed as they approached the river. Cassie heard voices. She held a finger against Carrington's lips, suggesting silence as they crept along the bank. Beside them, the murky water glided past, like a giant serpent uncoiling and slithering off in search of its prey.

Blake halted him with a hand against his shoulder. Cassie turned and saw him motioning ahead. Suzanne was right behind him, gasping for air.

Stepping carefully in the fading sunlight, they crept in the direction of voices, one male, the other the choked sound of a woman crying. Rage boiled inside Carrington and he quickened his pace.

When they arrived at a spot not too far from where Cassie had once stood in the future contemplating events that had happened here, in this past, Carrington stilled. Sheriff Anders was there, maybe ten feet away. Annie was in a shallow pit, her face a picture of terror. Choking sobs racked her body as she pleaded with her captor.

"P-Please, Sheriff. Don't hurt me. Wh-whatever you want, Carrington will—" Her hands raised to cover her face. When she lowered them to her sides a second later there were tear tracks running through the dark smudges of dirt left behind.

Feelings that were part Carrington and part Cassie roared to the surface at seeing Annie begging for her life. Carrington stepped toward Anders, but his boot rolled across a rock. The sheriff whirled around, a pistol raised at chest level.

Carrington didn't think. He lunged through the air. The sound of gunshot reverberated across the water. The two men fell together and rolled toward the river's edge, Anders' gun escaping his clutches and landing against the hard bank with a muffled *thud*.

"I'll kill you!" Carrington promised as he positioned himself in a straddle over the sheriff's torso. Anders twisted and bucked him off. Carrington landed on his back in the recently shoveled soil surrounding the pit where Annie stood, frozen with shock. He rolled down the embankment landing beside her. Scrambling to his feet, he wrapped his arms about her waist and staggered.

"You'll never beat me," the sheriff sneered. He licked his lips as he reached for the shovel that lay nearby. "Give me the gold, or so help me God I'll kill her. You'll hang for the crime."

Cassie was struggling to stay alert but had the wherewithal to comprehend that Anders overlooked Blake and Suzanne who were there witnessing the events. Cassie struggled to keep on her feet. It was like a thousand-pound weight had been set on her chest. As weak as she was, she had no idea how Carrington was going to save Annie. Anders had the advantage.

It seemed not only would Annie soon die, but Carrington too, only not at the executioner's bidding. Subsequently, that meant Cassie would perish.

Carrington's legs gave out and he fell to his knees. With what strength he had left, he forced Annie behind him. "I'll tell you," he choked out, his arm hanging lifeless at his side.

Cassie knew what he said to be a lie. He didn't know where the gold was. But she did. She'd give it up to Anders, yet somehow, she suspected it wouldn't save either Carrington or Annie.

Anders held the shovel high over his head, ready to swing it down on one of them. "Where is it?" He leaned forward, his foot sinking into the displaced dirt.

The unmistakable sound of a revolver hammer locking into place drew all their attention. The sheriff turned, the shovel still raised overhead. Suzanne was behind him, legs apart in a shooter's stance, holding the sheriff's gun.

"It's over, Anders." She didn't give him the respect of calling him sheriff. Her gaze shifted past him to Carrington and Annie. "Are you hurt?"

Annie stifled a sob. "I'm not, but I don't know about Carrington. He's been shot." A bright red stain the size of a cantaloupe had formed over his left shoulder.

Ah, so that's why I feel so weak, Cassie thought.

Carrington had tipped over still farther and now lay sprawled on his back. Annie was on her knees beside him. "Carrington," she cried. "Don't leave me."

The sheriff stepped closer, murder on his mind. The bang of gunshot rang out. He fell to his knees, bellowing like a bull. "You can't shoot me, you bitch!" he snarled at Suzanne, before grasping his shin and cursing at the pain.

Annie shook Carrington and a hot fire seared through his arm, reaching Cassie as it went. Annie cupped her palms around her husband's face and turned his head toward her. "Don't you dare die on me!"

The world through Cassie's vision was growing dim. She tried to stay alert but struggled to hold at bay the darkness that beckoned. A loud, annoying buzzing began blaring in her ears, blocking out Annie's voice. Suzanne and Blake hovered close.

Suzanne scrambled down the embankment. "Did you ever wonder why you? Why you survived when the others didn't?"

"What?" Cassie asked weakly, struggling to comprehend what she meant. Carrington hadn't survived. What others? Was she talking to Carrington, or to Cassie?

In a much louder voice, Suzanne said, "All of this was for you." Her arm swung wide, encompassing the land around her and the house in the background. "You have to save her." She hurriedly lifted a chain from around her neck and pressed it into Carrington's hand. "Take this with you. It'll lead you back. Change your fate."

Cassie tried to sit up, but her strength was fading. "But, I . . . I saved Annie," she said weakly. And at what cost? Her own life? Her vision of Suzanne spun like a top, spiraling into a narrow funnel.

"Annie!" Carrington cried out just before his world went dark.

***

Cassie returned to the present to the sound of her alarm system's siren screaming through the house. She bolted upright on the bed and cried out as pain lanced through her arm. Her left shoulder had a small hole in it that was bleeding profusely. Her right hand, covered with several puffy blisters, ached terribly. Clutched in her palm was the object Suzanne had pressed there. She barely had time to register that it was a locket, before noticing the bright red pattern of blood covering her dress from shoulder to waist.

She let the necklace fall to the floor before staggering as fast as she could over to the clothes box. Grabbing the first piece of fabric her fingers latched onto, she pressed it against the wound. Gasping at the pain, she pushed hard against her shoulder to stanch the flow of blood.

From somewhere in the lower part of the house, Jimmy's voice rang out. "Cassie! Where you at, bitch?"

Panic clenched a fist around her chest. She spun around, searching for Carrington. He was gone. Had he left because she'd succeeded at saving Annie? Or, had he succumbed to the gunshot wound. No, that couldn't be. She would have died too, if Carrington had.

Jimmy called out again. Adrenaline raced through her veins, masking some of the pain and forcing her to action.

Provided the alarm system worked as it should, the police would arrive soon. She needed to avoid Jimmy until they did. A quick peek down the hall revealed it was empty. Inching her way to the stairs, she crept down the steps, not daring to breathe as she went.

The front door was open. Jimmy could be in the kitchen or in one of the back rooms. She didn't have time to wait for him to reveal himself. When she reached the final step, she bolted to the screen door and shoved it open. The springs screeched like a homing beacon.

Her left arm hung lifeless at her side as she ran awkwardly toward the barn. The screen door slammed loudly again behind her. When she dared a glance, she found Jimmy bounding down the steps two at a time. The loud crack of a gun being discharged coincided with the solid *whumpf* in the barn door as she barreled through its entrance, squelching an alarmed cry.

She made it to the chicken coop and fell to her knees, feeling skin scrape away as she crawled to the corner. Her hand shook so badly, it took two attempts to release the hidden clasp to the secret cubby. She flipped the lid open. Reaching deep inside, a cry tore from her chest when her fingers grasped air. Shoving her arm deeper into the hole, she found nothing but gravel at the bottom. Retracting her closed fist, she cried out in frustration when she revealed nothing but a cluster of misshapen, dull, Swiss cheese-like stones across her palm. She flung them aside and huddled in the corner, fighting to keep the panic at bay.

When Jimmy appeared at the barn's back door, Cassie stifled a gasp of fear. She was trapped. He had a straight-on view of the inside of the chicken coop and her where she sat.

"Well, look what we have here."

The sickening memory of his voice scraped over her nerves like fingernails on a chalkboard. He stalked to her, stopping at the opening near where she huddled. Disregarding the fact that she was bleeding, he stepped into the structure and towered over her.

"I told you I'd finish this. You just made it way too easy." He kicked her, contacting the side of her calf as she pulled her legs back.

Cassie recoiled but the torment of living with Jimmy, followed by the hell he'd put her through all the years since, festered inside her like magma beneath a volcano about to erupt. She'd been watching over her shoulder most of her adult life and she'd be damned if she was going to continue doing so. If he was going to kill her now, she'd at least go down fighting.

A vision of Carrington crossed her mind, giving her courage she'd never had before. He'd taught her to be strong, for Annie, for him, and for herself. His strength had become hers.

Pulling her feet beneath her, she used the wall as leverage to push herself up from the floor, not once breaking eye contact with Jimmy. Her shoulder felt like a hot fire poker was being held against it, but she ignored the pain.

Jimmy's mouth drooped open and his eyes widened. She'd surprised him by her uncharacteristic response to his abuse.

"That's right, you bastard. I'll never be your punching bag again." She took a step closer to him. "You want me? Well, here I am."

She lowered her good shoulder and plowed forward, catching him off guard, square in his chest. They spilled from the hen house onto the ground, leaving Cassie at a disadvantage. When she rolled to her back, Jimmy pounced, straddling her.

He laughed a dark, evil sound as he rose above her. She was once again at his mercy.

What was she thinking? He had a gun and he was stronger than she was. She knew fear was splashed across her face, but she didn't care anymore. Lifting her hips, she tried to buck him off and caught a hard blow to her cheek for her efforts.

"You, stupid bitch." His hand wrapped around her chin and he forced her head back. He whistled. "Look at that." The proud smirk on his face turned to a shrewd, angry glare. "Got yourself some pathetic man who doesn't care how hideous you are, I see." He poked the barrel of the gun against the spot where the faded hickey still showed.

"Hideous? Only one of us is hideous. And revolting. And pathetic!" she spat. How had she ever believed she loved him?

His face twisted into a sneer. "Who would ever want to get close to that?" His eyes flicked to her throat.

The subtlest shifting of air had Jimmy turning his head just as Carrington's voice broke the quiet.

"I happen to be rather fond of *that*."

Jimmy swung his leg over Cassie and ended up in a crouch facing Carrington.

Cassie scrambled backward away from her ex, holding tight to her shoulder. It throbbed, but the rest of her arm had gone numb.

"Carrington!" Tears of relief pooled in her eyes when she saw the revolver in his hand, his revolver from the past, the one she'd hidden . . . and it was aimed at Jimmy.

"Who the fuck are you?" Jimmy pointed his gun at Carrington.

"Are you hurt, darlin'?" Carrington inquired of Cassie, calm as could be on the outside, yet his presence was anything but calm.

She nodded, assuming—hoping—she wouldn't die anytime soon from a mere gunshot wound to the arm. "Yes, but I'll be fine."

There was something different about Carrington now. When he walked toward Jimmy, his feet didn't stir up any dust. Cassie's eyes darted to his chest. She saw a faded image of the crumbling split rail fence behind him.

Through him.

Their eyes met. She shook her head. "No. Carrington." A tear slipped over her lashes and trailed down her cheek.

"You think you're bad enough to stop me?" Jimmy intruded on Cassie's agonizing realization. He pointed his gun at Carrington's chest.

Carrington's translucent gray eyes shifted to Jimmy. "You have no idea how bad I am."

Jimmy fell back, sensing a new level of threat that he'd ignored up to that point. "Stop or I'll shoot."

"Go ahead. For what good it'll do. You see, you can't kill a man twice."

Jimmy's expression became one of alarm, genuine fear, and confusion.

"Carrington. Don't," Cassie said in a hushed plea even though she failed to understand why she didn't want him to kill Jimmy. Her heart seized in her chest at the love she saw blazing in Carrington's eyes. Love for her.

A shot rang out from the gun in Jimmy's hand.

"No!" She screamed as she lurched toward Carrington, pain halting her progress.

Jimmy balked in shocked amazement. Carrington hadn't fallen to the ground. A bloom of blood didn't show on his chest where the bullet had passed through. Instead, he continued his prowl toward Jimmy, a dark smirk on his face.

Jimmy shot again. A puff of dirt lifted on the ground about twenty feet behind Carrington.

"What the hell?"

"You've had your last go at Cassie. It'll be a long time before you get out of prison. *If* you ever get out." Carrington lifted the revolver in his hand.

Jimmy turned to Cassie, his eyes the size of half dollars. Before he could turn back around, Carrington had soundlessly moved up beside him. He brought the butt of the gun down against the side of Jimmy's head. It made a dull *thunking* sound that made Cassie wince. Jimmy grunted and crumpled to the ground.

The shrill cry of sirens reached Cassie's ears. She crawled to Carrington where he knelt beside Jimmy.

"I don't think he'll get out of prison again for a long time, Cassie. You're safe now, darlin'."

Uncontrollable tears fell down her cheeks. Carrington was leaving her. He was fading before her eyes.

"Please don't leave me." She cried harder and struggled to get the words out. He didn't envelop her in his strong embrace, like she desperately wanted. His transparency was becoming shockingly greater.

"You did it, Cassie. You saved Annie. I have new memories now of my life." The glorious smile he flashed at her melted her heart and made her cry that much harder.

In a way she'd never really be able to explain, he was evaporating before her eyes. The sirens screaming in the background were close now. She could hear the crunch of tires on the driveway.

"Do you have to go?" It was a silly question. He was a ghost, of course he couldn't stay. Even if he wasn't executed in the past, he still died at some point.

He became a blurry image on the landscape, like a heat wave rippling over hot pavement.

Before he disappeared altogether, he said, "I didn't notice it at first, but you look a lot like her."

She swiped her arm beneath her nose. "Who?"

There was no answer as the ripples of air that were Carrington settled before disappearing completely.

"Carrington!" Cassie dropped back to her knees just as two police officers crept around the corner of the barn, guns drawn.

"Hands in the air," one shouted.

Like air moving on a breeze, she felt as much as heard a whisper:

"We'll meet again. Someday."

THIRTY

Two weeks later.

"Andrew. This isn't necessary." Cassie tried to sound stern as Andrew's arm tightened around her waist while they stepped slowly up to the porch. He practically lifted her as he walked beside her.

"For once, McAllister, just do what your therapist says." They reached the front door and he grabbed the key from her hand before shoving it into the lock. Pushing the door wide, they stepped inside and stopped long enough for Cassie to enter the code to deactivate the alarm. The police had activated it for her after she'd been whisked away in an ambulance.

Entering the living room, she stopped and listened to the heavy silence. When she turned toward the stairs, Andrew turned with her.

"Help me to my room. I need to rest a bit."

"I can't believe you're actually going to do what the doctor told you to do," he mumbled as they made their way up to the second floor.

It had been two weeks since the police raced up and rescued her from Jimmy. Since then, she'd been stuck in the hospital fighting to save her arm after infection set in. It was likely more a result of the dirty chicken coop dust that caused the bacteria to eat at her flesh than the bullet that had passed through her shoulder. After hours of surgery and vats of antibiotics pumped into her veins through an IV, modern medicine prevailed.

The police had been in and out every day following the surgery, asking questions and taking her statement. Jimmy, who'd been released on parole, was found illegally in possession of a firearm—strike number one—after tracking her down—strike number two.

Violating the restraining order in place against him, he entered her property, shot her—so the reports indicated—physically assaulted her, and threatened her with intent to cause harm, otherwise known as attempted murder—strikes three through seven, or thereabouts.

His parole was immediately revoked, and he was headed back to prison soon, if not already there. The charges filed would result in a new round of hearings and court appearances, but Cassie finally truly felt free of him.

Andrew's appearance in the hospital was no surprise. His was the last phone number showing in her call history, aside from the Larimer County DA. When the police dialed his number, they inquired if he knew who her next of kin or emergency contact was. As it turned out, he was her emergency contact and arrived the following day. He'd mothered her ever since.

They entered her bedroom, and Cassie drew up short. All the materials she'd left scattered on the floor before Jimmy's arrival were neatly stacked on her bed.

"I'll run down and get my things. Will you be okay for a bit?" Andrew asked. She nodded, touching his arm affectionately before he pivoted on his heel and raced back down the stairs.

On her pillow sat Annie's diary. On top of it, like cherries on a dessert, were eight or so lumpy rocks. They varied in size and shape as well as color, ranging from a dull copper to a shiny, beautiful gold.

Her legs buckled, and she sank to the mattress. Picking up the journal, she thumbed through it. Page after page was filled with entries, all the way to the back of the book—she didn't dare attempt to read any of it. A warm, happy feeling settled in her chest as she set it aside. Next in the stack was a yellowed news article clipping from a long-distant past.

It was a lengthy news story about Sheriff Anders. It stated that he'd overstepped his reach as an authority figure in his dealings with Annie and Carrington. After being removed from his position as sheriff, he'd later crossed paths with Frank Steunenberg, before Frank became governor of the state of Idaho. Blackmail charges were filed against Anders, but before he could be prosecuted, he'd fled the area. As of the date of the news article he'd yet to be located.

Cassie felt a great sense of relief knowing Carrington didn't have to spend his life being hounded by that man. Anders was bad and would have stopped at nothing to hurt him.

There were other documents on her pillow, each tucked inside clear plastic sleeves. Cassie picked up the one on top. It was a court-filed deed similar to the one in which Blake sold the property to Anders. It was different now. The buyers' and seller's names read:

Carrington Edward Chambers, grantor,
TO
Blake Matthew Hanson and
Suzanne Marie Hanson, grantees.

The property description was different, too. The sale was for eighty acres. Carrington had sold his home and half his land to Blake and Suzanne.

"What on earth?" She set the deed down and picked up the next item. It was a property title listing an address of 25 Pear Lane with the sum of land totaling eighty acres, the other half of Carrington's property. The owners identified were Carrington Edward Chambers and his wife Elizabeth Anne Chambers.

Tears pooled in Cassie's eyes. "Get a grip, McAllister." She set aside the title paperwork and took a moment to collect herself.

Next, she lifted a document consisting of multiple plastic sleeves held together by a gold brad. The title immediately jumped out at her and she frowned as pieces of an unseen puzzle fell into place. She released a long, slow breath.

LAST WILL AND TESTAMENT OF
CHARITY ROSE HANSON

Flipping ahead a few pages, she found the same statement she'd read in her mother's will about the property, this property, being held in trust for the first-born daughter. She scrubbed a hand over her eyes and read it again before lowering it to her lap.

On display now atop her white pillowcase, there was a yellowed newspaper clipping that caused her breath to catch in her throat. It was a black-and-white image of Carrington wearing a dark vest over a white shirt. That same Stetson she'd seen on him dozens of times sat perched on his head. He was smiling. Beside him was Annie.

Cassie nearly cried with joy when she saw the pudgy face of a little boy in Annie's arms. He was a miniature of Carrington.

Beside Annie stood Suzanne. Her image was circled in pencil. Dark waves of hair hung nearly to her waist. Her head was slightly tipped back, and she wore a broad smile, like someone beside her had said something to make her laugh.

Cassie's gaze drifted over to Blake and his gap-toothed grin. His eyes were squinted with mischief beneath his familiar dark hat. In the crook of his arm he held a plump-cheeked little girl with wavy, dark hair. Cassie couldn't tell the color, but it might have been red, or a darker brown. The caption beneath the photo read:

> Carrington Chambers, his wife, Annie, and their son, Carrington, Jr., joined fellow neighbors and friends Blake Hanson, his wife, Suzanne, and their young daughter, Charity, at a benefit for local farmers last Saturday.

Her gaze flicked back to Suzanne. The black-and-white image was old, but well preserved. It was clear enough that she could see the slight flaw in Suzanne's smile.

Upon reflection, she knew from firsthand, up-close experience that Suzanne was missing a lateral incisor. And just like Cassie's, her other teeth had closed rank to fill the gap, so it wasn't glaringly noticeable. She'd even seen it that time she'd been in Carrington's body but hadn't given it much consideration. No wonder, too, considering the other more shocking events taking precedence at the time.

She picked up the will again. *Charity Rose.* Charity was the child Blake and Suzanne had after they'd moved into Carrington's house. That child was Cassie's great-grandmother. Cassie's given name, Chassandra Rose, was no coincidence.

She marked off the ancestry on her fingers. There was her mom, Chandra; grandmother Charla; great-grandmother Charity. Cassie couldn't recall her mother ever mentioning her own grandmother. Nor did she remember her granny sharing memories of *her* mother. Growing up, Cassie had been too wrapped up in her own life to find that odd. Now she did.

The still image of Suzanne felt alive in her hand. She struggled to suppress the jealousy and disgust she still held for the woman. But she was her kin, her great-great-grandmother. She needed to find it in her to forgive the past. It helped that she'd ensured that Cassie and all the first-born women in her lineage received their birthright. The house.

Blake and Suzanne had been Carrington's friends, the two people who didn't shun him or treat him like an outcast, and Carrington had unselfishly shared his property with them. More tears fell from Cassie's eyelashes. She hiccupped a cry-laugh before setting the pages aside.

Andrew came bustling in, dragging two large suitcases. "I'll just set these in the spare room across the hall, okay?" When he found her crying, he dropped the bags and rushed to her.

"What is it? Did you hurt yourself? Should I call the doctor?"

She laughed, a joyful, refreshing sound. Something she never thought she'd do again. "Oh, Andrew. What would I do without you?"

The sound of multiple car doors slamming came from out front. Andrew rushed across the hall, into the spare bedroom. "It's the contractor," he growled. "I told him you wouldn't be available until next week." Popping his head into the room, he said, "I'll tell him you're not up for visitors until Monday."

"Andrew," Cassie called out, easing up off the bed. "Don't. I've had to wait forever to get him to show up. The last thing I want is to send him away. It'd probably be weeks before he fit me into his schedule again. You go down and greet him. I'll be along as quickly as possible."

As she turned to leave, something caught her eye. There was a large manila envelope face down in the center of her nightstand. She lifted the package and opened the clasp. A musty odor wafted out, tickling at her nostrils. The smell reminded her of an antique store or a dank basement. Peeking inside, she saw the folded ends of a newspaper, possibly more than one.

Her previous experiences reading old newspaper articles nearly had her tossing the envelope aside and running from the room, but her curiosity won out over common sense. Carefully, she shook the contents free and let them fall to the bed. With the corner of the envelope, she gently separated the individual pages piled before her. In total, there were four, each folded and quartered.

The first and the second Cassie immediately recognized. One showed the image of a mangled vehicle mashed against a tree, ass-end up, down a steep, snowy embankment. The Colorado license plate of her parents' car was boldly centered in the shot. The second article, which Cassie recalled all too well, had Jimmy's mugshot plastered beside her own photo, one taken from her wedding day, with Jimmy's image cropped out.

Memories of both those events caused her chest to tighten, making it difficult to breathe. She quickly shifted her attention to the remaining papers.

The last two were older, Cassie could tell, based on the yellowed edges and the style of the print. One had a photo of a woman, stylishly dressed, standing beside a dapper looking man, boasting a dark suit and a bowler hat. The pair, Emily Black and Martin Abbott, meant nothing to Cassie, so she flipped the page over. Square in the center of the section on display now was a wedding announcement that made Cassie smile. Charla Louise Hanson to wed Gerald David Thompson. It was Cassie's granny and granddad. Turning back to look at the date, she found it was from 1945.

The last paper caused Cassie to frown again. Dated only a year earlier than granny's wedding announcement, it displayed an article about a missing woman, one Charity Rose Hanson. "What on earth?" Cassie desperately wanted to read the story about her great grandmother, but she feared the outcome of reading old papers. Later, she'd have Andrew read them to her, though he'd not understand why she wouldn't just do so herself. Someday, maybe she'd try and explain.

She gave a dismissive shrug and let the envelope slip from her hands. It landed on top of the other assorted materials on her bed. But before she could depart the room, Suzanne's shrill, pleading voice rang out in her ears.

"Save her."

Cassie's head jerked up. "What? No! I did what I was supposed to do!" Why was she still hearing Suzanne? She glanced again at the array of plastic and papers scattered atop her bed. "Who? Who am I supposed to save?" Dawning realization struck and she stepped back and away from the bed. Goosebumps danced to life on her arms and the back of her neck.

None of Cassie's ancestors mentioned in these articles or documents had even been born yet when Cassie met

329

Suzanne in the past, in Carrington and Annie's past. How would Suzanne have known about any of them, when she'd spoken to her back in eighteen ninety? For that matter, how did Suzanne know of Cassie's presence in the past at all?

As if she'd spoken the question aloud, the voice rang out in her ears again, louder than normal this time. *"You're the one who survived. Fix this or fate will find you."*

"I don't understand," Cassie said to the empty room. "You're telling me that I've got to chase after some fate monster, like it's a palpable thing, in order to save *her*?" She pointed to the bed. "Which her?" she asked. Fearing the possibility of another ghost or something worse sneaking in through her walls, she couldn't help but offer a quick glance around the room. But nobody appeared.

She heaved a very exhausted and frustrated sigh. "If I don't do this, whatever it is I'm supposed to do, you're saying my fate is to die? Is that it?" She didn't know for sure but assumed someone was "out there" listening.

Andrew's yelling up from below startled her, jolting her from her reverie. She cast a final glance at the papers on her bed and turned on her heel. Nothing would happen today, that she knew. But soon, she was certain she'd be researching her family's history to find out what happened to Charity. For one brief second, she wondered if this meant she could change the past, like she did for Annie, and bring her parents back.

Cassie did her best to walk straight-spined across the room, when her inclination was to curve her shoulder in protectively. To ease the pressure, she held her good hand beneath the sling supporting her bad arm.

As she neared the bottom of the stairs, she found Andrew at the front door talking with a young man, possibly in his early twenties, dressed in jeans and a white t-shirt.

She edged around her friend and started to push open the screen door. "Hi. Are you the general contractor? I'm sorry—"

The young man laughed, not impolitely, and interrupted her. "Me? The GC? Naw." He turned and called out, "Hey, GC! She's home."

"Andrew?" Cassie looked back over her shoulder. "Would you mind making us a sandwich or something? I'm starved."

The familiar *twang* of the screen door pulling wide drew her attention back forward. Another man filled the doorway. She tilted her head up to greet him. When she did, her legs threatened to buckle, and she had to grip the door for support.

"Carrington?"

GC. Ghost Carrington. But she knew somehow that this man was no ghost. He was vibrant and alive, hair clean-cut, but without the hat, and he wore Levi's, the modern 501 version.

He laughed, the sound impossibly familiar. "Yes, it's an old family name, so my parents say." When Cassie wobbled unsteadily on her feet, he stepped closer, into her space, and placed his hands on the caps of her shoulders.

They stared into each other's eyes the span of several rapid heartbeats.

"Sorry it took me so long to get here, darlin'" he said with a wink.

About the Author

Christine McFarland lives in Colorado with her husband and their old and cranky Chiweenie (Dachshund-Chihuahua mix); a very old black cat; and a much younger, spry little feline who refuses to allow a fence to hinder his desire to explore the neighborhood. She has two grown children, and two adorably perfect grandchildren. In her spare time, she likes to read, travel, golf, garden, and, of course, write. She is a member of Rocky Mountain Fiction Writers and the Historical Novel Society.

Check out Christine's website and join her mailing list to be the first to hear about new things on the horizon or follow her on Facebook:

www.christinemcfarland.com

fb.me/christinemcfarlandauthor

Acknowledgments

Writing a book takes a lot of time, dedication, patience, and the help of others. I'd like to praise Damonza for the incredible cover design for Inheriting Fate. It is beautifully done, and I absolutely love it! To Developmental Editor, Theodora Bryant, I can't thank you enough for helping me see the things that needed fixing to make this story right. Denitta Ward, I so appreciate all your support and guidance as I traversed this journey to publishing.

To my early readers, Kayla, Kim, Nicole, Michael, Laurel, Lisa G., Krissy, Diana, Monica, Sarah, Brittani, Christy, Janet, Carie, Lisa P., Mike, Mary, Dawn, Olga, Tatia, Irene, and Denise, I can't say enough how much I appreciate you volunteering your time to read the book and provide me invaluable feedback. Thank you so much!

To Gina Egusquiza and Debbie Sedelmeier, you both read each and every rendition of the manuscript that I asked you to read. I know I had to read it a thousand times, but your reading it more than twice (at least) went beyond the call of duty. You have been my cheerleaders and sounding boards from day one of this project and I couldn't have done it without you.

To my all-time number one fans: Duke, Eric, Kayla, and Chelsea. Thank you for encouraging me, humoring me, talking things through, and offering suggestions (whether I used them or not, Chelsea and Kayla). Whenever I wanted to talk writing, you let me, and that means so much.

Made in the USA
Columbia, SC
07 March 2020